A WORTHY CHAMPION

JODY SCHWENDIMAN

Paperback ISBN: 978-1-7378501-0-6
Ebook ISBN: 978-1-7378501-1-3

Cover photography by Katie Wells
Cover design by Shawnda Craig
Edited by Justin Greer
Typeset by Kaitlin Barwick

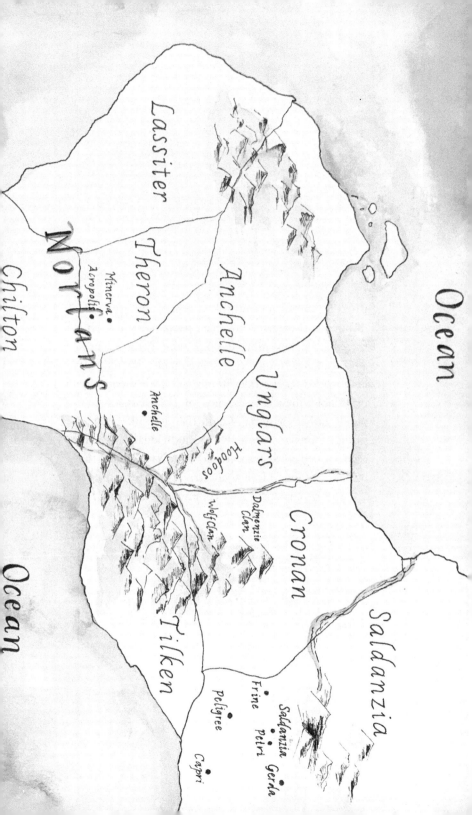

I find it fascinating to think of other habitable worlds in our vast universe. Are there people just like us? Is their history anything like our own? What scientific advancements might they have made? Would they have made bigger strides in medical fields sooner than us? Could they have learned of electricity or computers earlier than us? Would they talk like us, have similar foods and animals? Are individuals and races each treated with respect and equality? Would they believe in God? Have their struggles mirrored ours?

In my musings, I have conjured up this story.

PROLOGUE

Mason Kiefer, King of Chilton, had been impatient for the period of mourning to conclude following the richly deserved death of his sire—executed by Mason's own hand. The invitations that ensued from all of his neighboring kingdoms that covered the landmass known as the Norlans came days after the flag of mourning was removed. Chilton was his family's seat of power; the other sovereign nations included Theron, Lassiter, and Anchelle. Though Mason was interested in all the invitations, nothing held his interest more than that of Anchelle—the land of King Garrett and Queen Daniella. He was intrigued and anxious to meet the woman who had refused to accept a marriage proposal from his father. As he rode with his own royal entourage into Anchelle, Mason was met by Anchellian soldiers at the kingdom's border and was guided into Anchelle.

Where his land was dirt paths, unkempt homes, and hungry peasants abounding, Anchelle was the opposite. Cobbled lanes with manicured grass and tidy homes dotted his view. The majestic mountains as backdrops almost took his breath away. The citizens looked upon him, eyes never to the ground. They appeared robust, cheerful, and curious of the foreign dignitary without a hint of fear or concern.

Mason was directed to a well-maintained orchard that was a beehive of activity as old and young, male and female, worked with a tangible energy.

Mason had begun to think the escort was mistaken in his direction when a tall, regal man stepped away from a fruit-laden tree. The apples in his hands were set gently in a basket, and he'd wiped his hands on linen breeches before approaching Mason. Several other men gathered around him. The man was probably in his late forties, with a muscled, lean frame, a straight spine, dark graying hair, and a wide smile stretched across his sun-darkened skin.

"Welcome!" he called up to Mason, still on his horse. Mason was wondering who the man could possibly be. His sturdy yet fine clothing and bearing certainly bespoke nobility, but this meeting without ceremony—were they insulting him?

"I am King Garrett." The commanding voice rang out clearly despite the busy movement around him.

Dismounting from his horse, Mason met the man, surprised to find him only a couple inches shorter than his own imposing height. Rarely did he not tower over others. It was useful to be so tall, and effective for intimidation. He clasped the older man's callused hands into his own and greeted him. "Good day. I am King Mason Kiefer of Chilton."

"King Mason. I'm sorry for your recent loss," the Anchellian leader responded solemnly. Mason was sure this man did not miss his father, but he *was* a gentleman, after all. Royalty said things that should be said—but, in his own experience, not always truths. Though King Garrett's tone rang true in condolences, this greeting lacked all the anticipated courtly manners of receiving a monarch.

"Thank you," Mason said as the obligatory answer.

"Though your early arrival is happily received, I trust you understand the necessity of finishing the harvest. We yet have two more days. I cannot leave my duties to my family and people, so I must remain. But please take your respite at my home. I will guide you there presently. I'm in need of a walk to stretch my aching back and receive some refreshments. You are of course welcome to come observe or join once you've rested, if you desire."

Mason was incredulous. The man was working with his people! His father would never have deigned to lower himself to such a base activity.

Some of the people nearest them had stilled, observing the king, and seemed to be waiting for Mason's reply.

Mason indicated with his outstretched arm that the unusual monarch lead the way.

They walked further into the orchard, which appeared to lead to the castle. All were feeling the heat of the day. Both men were flanked by their own guards falling into a loose formation about the rulers. King Garrett asked after Mason's own harvest as they walked over the ample grass that had been trampled by many busy feet, forming a path.

"It has been a lean year," Mason admitted. Though he had been out surveying his own land's productivity in the days before his journey, he certainly had not considered participating in the annual harvest.

"'Tis most unfortunate," the senior king replied. Their path was carrying them toward a sizable group of people gathered around a tree. None noticed the royalty; their heads were craned, searching up into the tree's thick foliage.

"Luke?" the king questioned.

A young, muscled man with blond hair and a scanty beard was talking to someone up in the tree. He blanched with seeming guilt when he saw the approaching king before quickly turning his gaze back up the tree. Mason had to hold in the shock at the impertinence. The lad had barely given the king any sort of acknowledgment. A peasant woman also peered up into the tree, wringing her hands anxiously, while yet another man stood under some of the branches with his expression fixed firmly up. Others milled about, though not as close, their gazes riveted to something within the canopy of the large tree.

"Sorry, sir." Luke, the younger man, spoke softly and evenly, though his gaze remained fixed upward, not even turning to face his liege while speaking. "She insisted, saying she was lighter than any of us." His voice trailed into a whisper.

"Luke?" The king's voice held some urgency.

It was then that Mason caught sight of some blue fabric in the trees, following the floral pattern to note a young lady high above in the topmost branches, her position most precarious. She balanced on a tree limb, with the cloth of the dress pinned down the middle to be more like breeches, thus not revealing her undergarments, though that did little to hide shapely legs.

One of the guards closest to the king grabbed his shoulder, presumably to keep him from harm, but also motioning his silence. The king refused the help, pulled free, and moved directly underneath a branch below the girl, tilting his head to look up.

A loud sob surprised Mason, who belatedly realized that there was another person up there with the young woman, thus the reason for the quiet, distracted, and terse response to the king's queries. The daring girl didn't need distraction as she carefully shuffled her slippered feet along the same tree limb as a small whimpering child.

"There there," the young lady spoke soothingly to the child. "I'll get you."

A few more men rushed over to take up the position should the child fall. With so many branches below, it was not a direct drop to the earth.

The further the rescuer moved, the more the branch bowed down under the combined weight. A snapping sound elicited a collective gasp with those assembled; it looked like she could go no further or the branch would break.

How would she reach the hysterical child?

"Now there, you're so brave," she spoke carefully in cultured tones, easing down to straddle the branch, her movements slow and sure. "Scooch closer to me, and I will get you to your momma." The compelling voice sent a warm shiver down Mason's back.

The young child's dirty, tear-stained face searched down for mother and cried all the more, seeing the stricken face below.

Just then another young man with auburn hair came running with a blanket in his arms. "Here," he shouted to the men underneath the child. They all took a corner of the blanket and put it under where they thought the child would fall.

"You can let go, Joshua," exclaimed a man from underneath the child. "Papa will catch you."

The child looked down but was immobilized with fear. Both parents continued to coax the child to drop down. But the child stopped looking, his gaze riveted on the woman on the branch with him.

"It's okay, honey," she said, trying to talk the child into letting go of the branch. But there was no moving the child.

The girl continued to coax the child with soothing tones. Her patience seemed infinite. Five minutes passed and then ten. More people came to the scene. The rescuer, finding the current tactic wasn't working, laid her body parallel with the tree. The tree bowed more precipitously as her lithe frame stretched further along the branch.

"Be careful!" the king warned sharply, his body tense.

Men lined up underneath the length of the branch. Collective breaths held as the girl inched closer and closer to the child.

The limb complained loudly, and the mother cried out.

"That is far enough," the king commanded, his voice more subdued.

The girl stopped her progression and reached out her hands to the child. There were six inches separating them.

"You just have to take my hands," she cajoled the child serenely. "You're so brave," she reiterated. "Take hold of my hands." The child that was tightly gripping the branch slowly inched his way to the girl. Two inches apart. "C'mon sweetness, you are doing so well," she praised. "Come to me."

The child hesitated and gripped the branch beneath his legs once again, releasing his right hand first, extending it toward his rescuer.

Though frustration and fear choked the air, the girl continued on, seemingly unruffled.

"Try one more time," she spoke encouragingly. "I will give you the first bite of my pie," she sweet-talked the child. That seemed to get the child's attention. The girl strained to hang on to the branch with her legs, all the while stretching to reach for the terrified boy. The child reached forward, fingers stretching ever more, and the girl finally grasped onto one and then both of the boy's hands.

Not very gracefully, she wiggled backward on the branch, pulling the child with her.

It could not have felt good on her legs, Mason thought, noting the many sharp twigs that ran along the branch. When it seemed stable enough she sat up and pulled the child into her arms. They stayed that way for a moment, the girl holding the child and stroking his back, murmuring praise and consolation. The dark-haired young woman shifted her focus, taking stock of what was happening below, and directed a place for the men to stand with the blanket. The child protested, but the girl took his hands and carefully lowered him through some branches and then released the child, who fell safely onto the blanket, having brushed by only a small branch. People cheered and clapped as the mother wiped away tears and gratefully lifted the child from the blanket.

The daring woman deftly scaled back down the tree, to where the king, the young man named Luke, and the light-haired boy that had grabbed the blanket stood waiting.

The king drew the girl into his arms the moment she dropped from the tree. He held her for a long moment. "What were you thinking?" he questioned as he finally pulled away from her. The smile stayed permanently on her face from the victory she had just landed.

"When I saw the child up there, there was no one around but Thaddeus and Luke. Luke could catch the child if he were to fall, Thaddeus went for blankets, and I was the lightest. It just made sense." She looked at the king, who gaped at her incredulously.

The young woman finally noticed Mason and his men watching the scene play out.

Her dark hair fell to her waist with the sides pinned up. She had a smear of dirt on her rosy cheek and a bit of perspiration on her face from the excitement. Her eyes held his gaze, which looked thoughtful, and she pursed her full lips slightly as he continued to look at her. She was stunning! A vision, really, of some mythical angel, though she sported no halo nor wings.

The king interrupted his reverie when he spoke.

"Arabella," King Garrett spoke, while he let one hand go of the girl and held the other toward Mason. Mason continued to look at her. She was probably sixteen years of age, older than he had first thought.

"King Mason Kiefer of Chilton, may I present my daughter, the Princess Arabella," King Garrett spoke formally.

Mason felt his air whoosh out of his lungs as though he'd been punched in the stomach. Arabella, Daniella's daughter? The princess of Anchelle. It was hard to digest the kaleidoscope of emotions that slammed into him. The princess of Anchelle mingling with the people, climbing a tree, her dress pinned in a rather unladylike fashion. He didn't know what he had expected, but this wasn't it. The daughter of the woman whom his father had never stopped wanting or comparing Mason's mother to. The irony was not lost on him. Mason for the first time felt some measure of understanding of his father. For truly he had in that moment never felt such an overwhelming compulsion to own another person's soul. It was so clear that she was meant to be his!

CHAPTER 1

Six Years Later

S he stood behind the stone parapet. Her black gown and dark brown hair billowed like a banner floating on the wind. The fields before her seemed to stand sentinel to the approaching army. The deadly mass of invaders wasn't far out. They would be at her gate in a day's time. A heavy sigh escaped as she tried to take in every tree branch, every curve of every hill, and the beautiful orchard only a quarter mile out. The spring blossoms looked like confectionary clouds of pink frosting, the only color to contrast the dismal overcast day.

Her gaze was inevitably drawn to the recently expanded cemetery where hundreds of newly turned earthen mounds created a blanket of black, rich soil with only tiny tendrils of green weeds slowly starting to crop up. The horror of the past months replaying yet again in her mind caused an audible gasp to leave her throat and her chest to constrict painfully. How could she leave the people? Her eyes became traitors as they let loose a small stream of tears.

"Arabella," a soft voice spoke behind her. "You must take your leave now." The normally cultured voice was strained.

Quickly wiping away the tears with her sleeve, she took a cleansing breath and turned around. She would cry no more. Plenty had been privately shed already, and it was time to put the past a little further from her heart and think of the thousands of people who still depended entirely upon her. Duty to her people would always come first; her personal life mustn't interfere with the demanding responsibilities of her station.

Edmund, the grandfatherly figure standing before her, held out his hand for her to take. He ushered her through a maze of halls of sturdy gray stone to her parents' room. Pulling a decorative cornice just to the right of the fireplace revealed her great-great-grandfather's secret passage, which would take them four furlongs from the castle.

It was a dark tunnel her father had shown her when she was a girl of eight. Though she had been so pleased to be let in on the closely guarded family secret, it would have been very scary if not for her strong father's hand in hers. At the time, there had been lots of spiders and vermin inhabiting the tunnel, giving it a rather unpleasant smell. Today, it was no different. Still, sometime later, it led her to the safety of her waiting faithful guard.

The Anchellian people could little afford the veteran soldiers that would accompany her, reduced now to just a dozen, but the men had insisted. Bending down to one knee, they placed their right fist to their heart in unison. They did it to relieve the tension that hung heavy in the air, and she loved them for it.

"Stand up, you fools!" She laughed. They tried to treat her differently—as befitted their recently made queen rather than as the princess they had known since childhood—but they all felt like brothers, fathers, and grandfathers to her. Every last one of them she had known since . . . well, forever. She rode with them, fought in the lists with them, worked in the orchards with them, and sat by their sides when their loved ones had died alongside her own. In fact, she was sure that Thaddeus or Luke had put them up to saluting. Her two dearest friends.

Thaddeus, with his auburn hair with small waves of curls that made him look more boyish, contrasted with Luke, who had blond hair, a full beard, and blue eyes that made girls sigh when looking upon him.

She looked over at the two of them, and whereas Luke winked at her, Thaddeus's face remained solemn as any good knight would be with their queen. Luke was a little too saucy with her; she might just need to leave him behind. She gave him a stern look, which only made him smile. *The handsome devil.*

George led her horse up to her. He, like Edmund, wouldn't be going on this ride. He was left as the commander in her absence and would surrender Anchelle to Mason's army with what she prayed would be no bloodshed. In light of the devastation that had wreaked havoc across Anchelle, there was no way for the people to defend themselves against Mason's army. It was not but the last harvest season they'd boasted the best army in all of the Norlans, including the countries of Theron, Chilton, Lassiter, and Anchelle, but alas, their army had been reduced sixty percent in a matter of months.

The big, sandy-haired man placed his right hand on her right shoulder as she did to him, and they lightly touched foreheads. The familiar custom touched her heart deeply, knowing what lay ahead of both of them.

"Your highness, I shall do all I can to keep our people safe until your return."

"I know you will, George."

Stepping back, he put her Anchellian cloak around her slight frame and tied it under her chin as if she were still a little girl instead of a woman of twenty-one.

Arabella tapped on Palachio's neck, and the big palomino knelt down on both front legs. Looking around one last time, Arabella was grateful that only the men were there. She didn't know if she could get through this if her people were watching the forced exile of their queen. She felt like a traitor as it was.

With a small leap she flew into the saddle and lightly put her heels to Palachio.

Taking the lead, Arabella galloped away from Anchelle— away from her people. Her throat ached with unshed tears. She only prayed it would all be worth it. To Saldanzia then: her mother's birthplace.

CHAPTER 2

Arabella's heart sank as she saw Benton from a distance running his horse directly toward them, despite the treacherously slick ground. If Benton was running his horse, he had good cause.

"Spread out," Garner ordered as he inched his way closer to Arabella, checking all directions several times.

They watched the rider close the distance. Benton came directly to his queen. Arabella noted his dark brown eyes continually searching for danger and the tense position of his powerful, slender body. His presence always made her feel safer.

"Mason anticipated our flight and had men posted only two miles ahead of us, but they're advancing," Benton spoke while trying to catch his breath. "They don't want us slipping through in the dark."

"How many?" Garner asked.

"Forty."

So many! As the queen's guard, these men were the best Anchelle had to offer. But they were outnumbered more than three to one, and how many were behind them yet? They dare not turn to the right or the left, or they'd never gain entrance to the Unglars. The narrow channel was the only way through within fifty miles on either side. Her brain, sluggish from the cold and sleepless nights, tried to quickly come up with something, anything. She scanned the men looking for an idea. They didn't have much time.

"Harold! Come here!" Garner ordered.

Arabella looked at her commander as Harold reined in his horse next to him. Harold wasn't small, but he was shorter and slenderer than the others.

"What are you thinking?" Arabella asked

Garner laid out the plan quickly. Arabella was incredulous. She felt horrid. She knew what he expected of her, he had told her as much this morning and persuaded her to agree.

She wasn't able to think of anything else, and as bad as she felt for Harold, it *could* succeed.

"Come, let us get this done," Thaddeus directed, grabbing Arabella. It was amazing that as much time as she had spent in the lists, she had never worn armor like this before, and had no idea how to don it to her frame. Over her dress wasn't an easy task, but with the help of Thaddeus, she managed it. There just wasn't time to take off her dress and don breeches. The other men seemed to find something interesting in the other direction, affording her some modicum of privacy. The exception was Roland, who was busy putting all her gear on a bay horse.

When Thaddeus finished, he grabbed her hands in his and waited for her to look at him. Determination filled his countenance as he spoke. "By my troth, Arabella, Luke and I will make sure no harm befalls you."

"'Tis not for my own wellbeing I fear!" she replied. Her stomach roiled with thoughts of her loved ones being in danger. She squeezed his hand. "Ride well, my friend. God keep you safe." It probably wasn't very proper of a queen, but she threw caution to the wind and gave Thaddeus a firm hug, whispering to him, "Please be careful. Take no unnecessary risks." Knowing that two of her dearest friends were there to protect her was both comforting and terrifying.

"Ride well," he replied with a smile. "Don't worry your head, I shall find you."

Arabella put on a brave face and returned the smile.

Luke had found a headdress with a veil that belonged to Arabella and was studiously trying to apply it to Harold. It didn't look perfect, but it didn't need to.

Garner put his hand on her back and walked her to her other mount. She saw the concern etched in his fatherly face as he spoke. "I don't care to have you so far from me, but in order for this ruse to succeed—"

Interrupting him, Arabella fervently replied, "I know what's at stake." She spoke softly but firmly. "I will make it to Saldanzia." Withdrawing herself, she mounted swiftly.

Thaddeus and Luke were mounted by her side immediately, Luke giving her a wink.

Harold mounted Palachio. The palomino was the most distinct of all the horses and would serve to draw Mason's men. Luke gave a little catcall, and she could see the older knights trying to rein in a smile as Harold gave Luke an angry look. As dire as the situation was, Arabella couldn't help but smile. Luke had served to calm her nerves somewhat.

Garner and Benton were the first two in the line with two men behind, Arabella and Luke bringing up the rear. When Mason's men came into view, Garner rang out the command to form a parallel line, with the opposing soldiers. Arabella pushed forward with Luke till they were on the far left flank of Harold, six on either side.

Seeing Mason's men in full body armor, coming at them in a full gallop, made Arabella's stomach clench in fear. Self-consciously, she pulled her helmet lower and sat up, attempting to look bigger in the saddle. She was downright dwarfed amongst these brawny knights.

"Don't crowd me," she commanded through the helmet to Luke and Thaddeus, positioned on either side. Her best friends since childhood, she knew that they would protect her with their lives. She just hoped it wasn't necessary. "They might suspect something if you get too close."

The rain had let up, and the sun had fallen low on the retreating horizon. It wouldn't be light for much longer. The earthy smell after rain had always seemed so pleasant to her, but for once the scent offered no comfort.

Nerves wracked her as she sat atop the bay gelding, having never been in battle, at least not as one of the participants. But as Harold raised his sword in the air, as would have been the queen's right, she removed her sword along with the men around her.

The horses had started to gallop, sensing the anticipation in the air. Not daring to look to the left or right, her eyes trained on the advancing enemy. The man directly in front of her had to be twice her size.

"Steady," Luke spoke, sensing her doubts. "I'll be right behind you."

"For Anchelle!" Garner yelled as Mason's men were only twenty feet out.

"Anchelle!" the men hollered back.

The Chilton soldier in front of Arabella advanced boldly, slicing his sword toward her chest. Arabella blocked the blow— just barely—as she found herself being pitched backward. Desperately, her legs clung to the horse and her left hand reached for the pommel. Her nails bit into the leather before finding a handhold. With blood like wind coursing through her veins, she regained her seat. Her right hand seared with a numbing pain from the clash of the steel. Nevertheless, Arabella grasped her sword tightly.

Arabella let her mount have its head as it rushed past the fray. Casting her eyes to the right she could see the majority of men congregated to the middle. Garner and Benton wielded their swords with a fierce determination as they kept Harold between them—preserving the charade.

Her gut wrenched in anguish as she left the battle behind. Though she was scared, her heart bled to leave the men to their fate. The torment she felt running from the fray was almost paralyzing—these men were fighting for her!

Arabella scarcely noticed the gelding she rode or the greasy mud beneath his shod feet; all she could do was keep her seat as she tried to determine what was taking place behind her whilst stretching her distance from the battle.

Harold was surrounded, and at least two of Mason's men were following her, with another sporting Anchellian colors. It appeared to be Thaddeus giving them chase. The two enemy riders raced neck and neck before one was thrown from the saddle, an arrow protruding from his back.

Arabella had to keep telling herself to continue, that's what she had promised, but it was bleeding her. The battle in her head was as real as the one behind her.

The Unglars loomed ahead, an eerie beacon of safety, as she continued to push her horse. The mass of men locked in battle had diminished in her vision. They were several miles away and barely seen in the fading gray light, except for the two fixed in a race toward her.

The gelding had already endured a hard two-day ride but seemed to understand the need to keep pushing. In only a quarter of a mile, they would meet the Unglars and the shelter of the Hoodoos with the welcome cover of night.

"Just a bit further," she leaned over the horse's neck and whispered into his ear. It was getting harder to see those behind her, too dark to see what would have been evident minutes ago, but the outline of the Unglars rose high, like a stone fortress wall.

Arabella reined the horse to a canter. The animal's sides heaved, and his breath could be seen in the air as he stepped onto the path for the pass.

A dark coldness enveloped her as Arabella slowed the horse through the long tunnel-like pass of the Unglars into what was known as the Hoodoo formations. She glanced back and thought maybe she could see a figure. It could have been her imagination; with so many shapes and shadows it was just too hard to tell. Her heart gave a small jolt.

What was she to do now? It would be treacherous to continue, knowing what lay ahead, but the thought of pursuers close behind kept her persevering. The clopping of the horse hooves echoing against the rock walls sounded eerie, making her feel vulnerable. She couldn't really see ahead, but there was no stopping. Only a few minutes passed before the sound in the tunnel had a distinctive change. It became louder as another horse and rider entered. Surely if Thaddeus was the only one, he would make his presence known.

Thoughts swirled through her mind. She needed to put some distance between her and the person pursuing her, but she could hardly see, and she worried the gelding would lose his footing and injure himself. Arabella could fight, but she was loath to in the dark.

A moment later, the echoes of the tunnel ended and only the soft footfalls of what she believed was sand could be heard. Had the rider dismounted and left his mount to pursue her on foot, knowing that her horse picking his way across the foreign landscape was making noise enough to follow?

Arabella tried to recall everything she had heard of the Hoodoos. Her father had described the massive, elongated rock formations many times. Despite detailed accounts of the landscape, darkness didn't allow her to comprehend what lay before her. Her father had described tall columns of sandstone with a corresponding rock table atop to connect them. Thousands, maybe millions ran from the ground to the tabletops, creating miles of maze. Something she would use to her favor.

Listening intently for any sound, Arabella jumped as her shod horses' hooves struck a rock. Her hand went to her mouth to stifle a scream, then to her heart that beat madly, her other hand gripping her sword tightly with her cold, sweaty hand. Arabella trusted her abilities in a fair fight to defend herself; it was the thought of the enemy getting a drop on her that gave her concern.

As she continued to ride, the chance of meeting an assailant declined the further she went into the Hoodoos. As many twists and turns she had taken, there was little chance they could follow. So she kept on, breathing a bit easier with each turn.

Riding the horse took all her concentration and what little physical strength she could muster. The bay was advancing up and down hills like the waves of the sea, causing her thighs and legs to ache from the exertion to maintain her seat. It was treacherous. Nerves stretched taut as she wondered what had taken place at the battle. Worry for her men, for the people at Anchelle, and for her own horse became paramount in her mind. Did Mason know yet that his soldiers had let the Queen slip through his fingers? Had she?

The hard riding of the day and deluge of emotions had taken its toll physically and mentally. Had she put enough distance between herself and whoever had followed behind? The adrenalin had long worn off and exhaustion settled in. No sound had reached her in a long while, save the cooing of an owl and the scurries of small nocturnal animals. Desperately she longed to stop the horse and sleep till midday. Telling herself she couldn't fall asleep, she forced herself to give attention to riding the horse through the never-ending dips and inclines.

Despite the uneven terrain, so great was her exhaustion that she found herself slipping into an uneasy slumber. There was no way to tell how long it had been before she felt herself instantly awake and plummeting from the saddle. Arabella didn't know what she hit, it was too dark, but there was instant pain as the left side of her body took the impact. Befuddled, she realized her head was lying down a slope with her torso and legs angled up.

She wanted to curse herself, now quite awake and feeling the bruises from the crown of her head to her left hip, with the blood rushing to her head. The pain was so intense for a few minutes that she had to bite her lip to keep from screaming. Tears came to her eyes. Removing her helmet with only her right hand, she was able to wipe away the tears. At least she had been wearing a helmet. Her wounds would have been more grave if not for the protection it offered. Gingerly, she probed the left side of her body. Though she didn't think she had broken anything, her body throbbed ferociously.

Carefully swinging her legs down to her body to stand was a dreadful experience; both her head and her hip cried out cruelly to stop. The rubble beneath her shifted. She couldn't see, feel, or sense her horse anywhere. Where was that beast? It was carrying food, drink, bedroll, and clothing. Wanting to wallow in pity, but knowing it was useless, her mind set to the task of trying to find somewhere to safely bed down for the night. The waning moon provided only minuscule pinholes of light through the thick canopy, so the only way to know how to move was to feel.

She took a few tentative steps, knowing she had to go down the slope. Gingerly taking another step downward, she cried out in dismay when the shale-like ground crumbled beneath her weight and she unceremoniously fell on her backside. Standing slowly only to slip and fall again, this time damaging her hands, she allowed a few tears of frustration to fall. Fatigue threatened to swallow her whole.

The armor made it difficult to walk, restricting movement. The steel made more noise than she liked. Debating its usefulness, she longed for its removal, before realizing the trail it would leave for enemies to follow in the daylight, and it would be more awkward to carry. For now, she would focus on making it off this hillside.

As painful as each step was she squatted down closer to the ground as the armor allowed and took baby steps. It seemed as though hours passed, trying to make it off the hillside alive. Exhaustion couldn't begin to describe how she felt. She fantasized of finding a place to lay her head and kept her feet moving.

It was a huge relief once she made it off the hillside. Feeling her way toward a smaller looming shadow, she discovered some kind of prickly tree and climbed underneath the dense covering its boughs offered. Energy depleted in entirety, she fell asleep in full body armor.

CHAPTER 3

A rabella woke stiff and so sore that she wasn't sure she could stand. Light penetrated spots here and there where holes littered the broken canopy, but for the most part it was quite sheltered. Crawling out from the protection of the prickly tree, her eyes viewed the landscape, amazed to note that somehow she had found the only tree in a large radius. On and on stretched the sandstone formations. The columns were like extremely long legs that reached up to meet a flat stone top. Few plants inhabited the land, and no other living creature could be seen. The grand landscape left her feeling so small and isolated, turning her thoughts to where Thaddeus and Luke were. Though she handpicked each of the men for this trip and knew each of the guardsmen, she was with Thaddeus and Luke on an almost daily basis. They would be worried for her, like she was for them.

Her throat ached for want of a drink. The priority to find some source of water among this land of sand and rock became apparent. Looking back the way she had come the night before, she was stunned to note the rugged terrain she'd survived in the darkness. It was incredibly steep, and the footing was impossible—as her backside and chewed-up hands attested.

Finding the borrowed horse would put her in much better shape. The animal had everything needed for a week's worth of travel. On foot without supplies would be a different matter entirely. She'd read that the Hoodoos lasted about a half a day by horse, and the Unglars tapered to plains for a while before meeting large mountains. To Saldanzia was another week, with a barbarian-like people in between. They called themselves the Cronan. And from what she had heard from her father and the few others who had ventured out of the Norlans, they were people she never wanted to meet.

If she was with the bay gelding, he would likely have found them some water. Certain the animal had to come through the area, she searched for signs of his passing. Thanks be to Benton, she could track an animal.

As she went back to the hill to see where he had made it down, her thoughts turned to her people and her men once again, wondering if any had survived the largely outnumbered attack. Guilt ate at her as she thought of fleeing from them as they met the attackers. Would the enemy follow her? Dread curdled within her. Mason wasn't going to let her slip through his fingers.

Though she didn't like to think of it, she knew of Mason's obsession with her. Their initial meeting during a harvest years ago was the first time she truly recognized a man's desire for her person; she'd been just fifteen years. The man, though several years her senior, was intensely commanding, attractive in build and complexion, and a newly crowned king. At that time, she had felt flattered. Arabella remembered his regular visits to her home each year following the harvest. He had remained with them for a fortnight each time. At every turn, he'd sought her out, offering walks in the garden and rides through the countryside. He would bring her lavish gifts of jewelry, perfume, and pets. Though he was always the perfect gentleman with her, and going above and beyond for her comfort, she had felt a trepidation about him she couldn't articulate. Each year and each visit that feeling grew. There were little misgivings of intolerance with people, the way he would speak of others as inferiors. The way his eyes seemed to devour her began to put her on edge whenever he was in close proximity. That, coupled with Thaddeus's and Luke's vehement dislike for him, made her wary.

The year she turned eighteen, per his usual sojourn, Mason came but left suddenly on the fifth day, without speaking with her—to Arabella's immense relief.

The day after his departure found her in the solar, making a botch of a needlepoint her mother had never finished three years earlier before her untimely death. She should not have tried her hand at this particular one, she lamented. Needlepoint was not one of her strong suits. At the sound of the door opening, she put the cloth away from her body and looked at her father, his own guilty countenance reflecting her own. He walked in, his steps hesitant, hands behind his back, head hung slightly.

"Dearest," he said to Arabella, taking a seat next to her. She was instantly concerned. "I have a confession to make." Arabella noted the anxiety in his eyes, though as always he looked impeccable with his crisp white tunic, black breeches, and black polished boots.

"Mason asked for your hand in marriage," he spoke without further preamble.

Arabella sucked in her breath and sat up straighter in her favorite deep blue chair, looking for him to carry on. "What did you say?" she asked, believing she already knew the answer by Mason's hasty retreat, but she wasn't quite sure. Her parents made it clear that Arabella would have the choice to marry whom she chose, so she was surprised she wasn't consulted.

"I have to admit that my judgments may be colored, so before I answer I would like to ask you first whether he has found favor with you. Do you care to marry him? I'm sorry, I should have asked you first," he stated again, looking at Arabella. "You are of age to know your mind." His concern for her deeply touched her.

It was an easy question to answer. "Nay father, I do not," she spoke. She watched the worry leave his face, and he took a deep breath.

"You are certain?" he questioned.

"Yes," she responded. "I must admit that for some time now he has made me uneasy."

Her father tightened his grip on the chair he was sitting in, his face not hiding concern once again.

"How so?"

"I do not want to speak evil of him, when he has remained a perfect gentleman with me," Arabella spoke, watching her father's grip lessen. "I know that his lifestyle and customs are different than our own."

"How so?" her sire interrupted, seeking clarification.

"He has spoken nonchalantly of . . . having . . ." She could hardly say the word. "Slaves." She took a large gulp, looking at her father, a frown appearing. "I know," she spoke vehemently, "'tis evil, yet he thinks it deserving of his station." Arabella knew her father wanted to say something, but he held his tongue in check and allowed her to continue.

"I'm not sure how to put it into words." She could hardly stop now and continued. "His soul doesn't have light. It's vexed or tormented. He is not well, and I don't mean physically." Arabella looked at the concern on her father's face and hastily replied, "I am not making sense."

"Unfortunately, you are making perfect sense," he replied sadly. "I declined the betrothal agreement." Her sire gently took her hands from her lap. "Mason was"—her father took a moment to gather his thoughts—"very displeased with my answer. I am not sure that we have seen the end of this topic."

Her father then stood up, dropping her hands and beginning to pace. "I have gone back and forth trying to determine whether I should speak of it, but finally I am convinced it bears discussion." He stopped his pacing and turned to her. "Mason's father, Dorian, was an evil man. Abusive. I heard tales of his cruelty to his people and family alike." Arabella sucked in her breath, feeling compassion for Mason that she had not before. It would explain his coldness where others were concerned.

He continued. "Dorian was obsessed with your mother, even after we were married and he was married to Mason's mother. Though your mother was not easily frightened, she was very much scared of Dorian. I detested the man," he said vehemently.

"'Tis why we didn't have a relationship with Chilton before Mason was made king."

Some of the puzzle pieces that Arabella had not even considered earlier were falling into place. Her mother and father's reaction when Chilton was spoken of. The country they did not trade with until Mason was made king. Now she was beginning to understand.

"I did not want my judgment of Mason to be colored by what I knew of his father. I did not think it fair. Though I have no proof, I am beginning to suspect he is just like his father."

They had not talked of it further until the attempted kidnapping of Arabella.

Stop! she scolded herself; she couldn't even think of that. She needed to find the horse promptly. She couldn't let her fears hinder her.

"Ah hah!" she squealed out loud, finding the horse's tracks. Determining that the bay was slowly moving northwest, she gratefully followed his established trail. The more she walked and stretched out, the less her body ached, to a certain point at least. Annoyance with the armor had her finally removing and caching them under a sandstone overhang, using precious energy to try and cover up the metal with the sand and rock at hand. Sliding her sword into the scabbard at her waist, a knife in one of her boots, and the other strapped to her thigh, found her feeling immeasurably better about defending herself and cursing the time it took her to come to the realization. The knock to her head was likely dulling her thought process.

Although she longed to run once she was free from the restrictive armor, her hip was biting her viciously. A headache also tried to claim her sensibilities, between the need for nourishment and the blow to the head. Not daring to stop despite the pounding pain, she plodded on, tracking the horse. Food, water, and a horse were everything she so desperately needed to continue this journey. There was no way she could go through Cronan territory without a horse. It was hard not to grind her teeth in frustration with her current circumstances.

That was an immediate problem, but almost worse was the unknown. Did any of her men make it out alive? If so, where were they?

What were the chances that Saldanzia would come to the aid of another country they'd had a strained relationship with since her mother chose an Achellian king? Some of the Saldanzians could even be hostile toward her.

The daylight waned on as she continued to track the horse. The terrain changed somewhat as the tabletop became less table and more just spindly sandstone legs. The sky could be seen and the sun beat down with a warm spring heat. The temptation to lay down and rest her wearied mind and aching body was a constant battle. Alone in this sand-covered foreign land, with only the occasional bush rabbit, jooper, or bug in sight, discouragement was hard to keep at bay. Never had she known such thirst or hunger. The exhaustion and pain from her injuries was making her nauseous. But her guard had put their lives before hers, and she would honor their sacrifice with her last breath.

Rounding a bend, she came to a small clearing with the most welcome sight—a small gurgling creek and the bay. He, of course, had found water. A smile lit her face as she increased her speed to the creek.

As she gingerly bent down to scoop some water into her palm, the sound of footfalls alerted her to someone's presence. Reacting instinctively, she dove across the creek. She landed jarringly on the opposing bank, her hip screaming as she clumsily stood and drew her sword. Her heart thundered in her chest as she saw four soldiers whose uniforms identified them to be Mason's men. They were advancing slowly on her like they were trying to corral a horse, with their arms empty of weapons and opened wide, just fifty feet out. Blood rushed to her face. How was it possible that in this maze that she had come across them? Had she been so focused on the horse and the water?

"Well, hello there, darlin'!" the one in the middle spoke up, like he was the leader.

They were grinning, every last one of them too, dang them anyway!

"We figured we would wait to see if anyone came looking for that there horse, and it looks like we hit paydirt, boys!"

"Woohoo!" a bearded soldier hollered in response. "We sure did!" Steadily but cautiously, they encroached, spreading out to form a ring, intending to discourage her from running. The sword held aloft, she scanned the area, moving the blade in a dancing arc, one of the many warm-up maneuvers that came naturally after years of practice.

"Well now! No need for that, m'lady! We ain't going to hurt you!" Their sneers and raucous laughter belied the syrupy, exaggerated words. One with a hat on sidled up next to the horse, where they had remained hidden when she leapt across the water. He grabbed a lasso from the horse.

Arabella knew it was a long shot, but—determined to take the chance—she pivoted and ran with adrenaline fueling her weary limbs. Zigging and zagging in an effort to keep the lasso at bay, out of her peripheral vision she saw it land harmlessly. The initial burst of energy was already waning. The whole side of her body protested and she groaned in agony. There was no way she could outrun them, not that fighting four at the same time would have worked either.

Arabella had only run a short distance when she saw a single rider galloping straight at her. Eating up the distance, he beckoned her to him, shouting encouragement to keep moving. The throbbing in her head increased. She squinted, unable to see whether the approaching horseman was friend or foe. She had little choice. The sound of one of Mason's men directly behind brought out a fresh spurt of fear, propelling her to not slow despite the screeching protest of her body. Taking the lifeline the stranger was providing, she grabbed onto his outstretched hand as he passed and swung up behind him in the saddle.

The stranger's horse knocked down the man directly behind her and continued down the path she had just come. Two of the soldiers dove to the side, not to be trampled by the horse. The one with the lasso stepped aside, then let fly the rope. It snared the horse's head, but the stranger put the spurs to his horse, and the rope slid through the soldier's hands, bouncing innocuously to the side of the horse's head. The horse lunged across the creek, making Arabella latch her arms firmly around the stranger's waist.

Looking back, Arabella could see Mason's men running toward their animals that the escaping duo were almost to. Were they slowing? The stranger, she noted, had a long blade in his hand, and leaning forward with a few quick motions had the rope cut that held the group of animals together from the horse's neck. The rescuer smacked one of the now-skittish animals' flanks that was within reach while hollering. Then they were off, pounding down the trail.

Her rescuer looked back, and Arabella noticed two things at once. One, that he was extremely handsome, with cinnamon-brown hair and vibrant green eyes. The second was that he wore the colors of Saldanzia, red and gold with a falcon. Strangely enough, the thought that followed was, *Why was a Saldanzian this far west?*

"We won't be able to outride them double," his deep voice spoke, bringing her back to the present. They had passed right by the bay, unable to stop and pick it up by the creek in their flight.

They looked behind them in unison. The horses hadn't scattered out of reach, and already some of the men were climbing into saddles. Sensing his decision, she spoke: "I will fight too."

He didn't say anything; there wasn't time. Rounding another curve, he stopped his mount quickly and turned around, drawing his sword from the saddle in one fluid movement. After several seconds the first soldier appeared around the bend. With only three strokes of the sword, he dispatched the first of the four of Mason's men.

"Grab his horse," he commanded Arabella, grabbing her arm and dropping her from his saddle to meet the next soldier head on. The remaining two went straight for her.

Rather than mounting the horse, Arabella met the leader and the bearded man with her sword in her right hand and her smaller blade in her left. The approaching soldiers had dismounted their horses, and advancing they came together at once, trying to throw her off. If she hadn't practiced this precise thing in the lists hundreds of times with her father, Luke, and whomever she could persuade, she would never have been able to keep her wits and do what needed to be done. Mason had obviously commanded she was to be unharmed, which gave her an edge she would use without regret. When they were in range, she threw her blade at the leader. It lodged deeply with a thud in his chest. The bearded man was so surprised that he paused for just a second, giving her the advantage to swing her blade toward his body. He blocked it at the last second. But Arabella came at him again as quickly as she could swing, trying to keep him on the defensive.

The horse spooked next to Arabella, and she had to catch herself, losing the upper hand she had gained with her offensive. As she locked blades with the dark-bearded man in front of her, he reached out and tried to grab her. Instead of falling back, as most men would have expected her to do, she pulled him into her and headbutted him. Having seen the men do this maneuver successfully numerous times, she was greatly disappointed to find the effect wasn't the same—her head swam, water filling her eyes. The brute latched onto her arm and squeezed till she was forced to drop the sword. Arabella threw a left hook that landed solidly, but the foul-breathed man just looked at her and grinned.

"Feisty little kitten, aren't you?" he admiringly admitted.

Arabella forced her eyes to stay engaged with her attacker, though she itched to pull her knife from her boot, to not give away her rescuer as he carefully advanced behind the bearded man. The Saldanzian soldier wrapped his arms around the bearded man's neck, sufficiently cutting off his air supply until he blacked out, allowing Arabella's arm to be released.

Breathing heavily, Arabella gasped for air, feeling like she had been the one to lose her breath. Her rescuer was scanning her body intently, checking for harm. Now off the saddle, his height showed that he was quite tall, taller than most. Somewhere between her father's and Mason's height, she thought.

"Thank you," she finally managed to speak, her throat dry. The pounding rush of blood in and out in her head increased— or was it her ears? He tilted his head in acknowledgment but continued to regard her. "I don't think I'm going to faint," she added, wondering why he was watching her so.

He smiled. "I would have caught you," he roguishly claimed.

Arabella had to force a small smile in appreciation of the light humor. The fighting had been a small skirmish, but killing that man had been a huge battle. A war of emotions played through her head.

She walked away from the scene, putting her sword back in its sheath, momentarily wondering whether she should retrieve the smaller blade from where it had lodged. A shudder moved through her at the thought, and she decided it would stay where it was embedded. Waiting for the barrage of questions that were sure to come from the man, she briefly halted, still unwilling to turn back to the carnage.

When no words broke the silence she found her shaking legs carrying her back toward the creek, her body knowing she needed a drink more than any nourishment. The thudding in her head and ears eased as she cupped and drew in a cool swig. A moment later, her stomach revolted as her mind reviewed the past fifteen minutes.

"Never been in battle before?" he asked softly. Though she hadn't noticed him following, it hadn't startled her to find him at her back.

Arabella shook her head.

"Are you from the Norlans, then?"

She was hesitant to tell a total stranger who or where she was from in such perilous times, but it was obvious by the colors on her cloak and speech alone. "Indeed. Anchelle."

"And your escort?" he questioned.

It was a simple question, and it was obvious she was alone. "We were attacked yesterday." She left it at that. The guilt and pain flared yet again at the memory of leaving them.

Arabella tightened the cinch on the horse she'd ridden away from her men on, then grabbed the reins.

"May I assist you to where you are going, milady?" he proposed.

It was a generous offer. The Saldanzian people weren't avowed enemies, but there were certain Saldanzians that wouldn't likely care for her sudden appearance either. The man may have rescued her, and even shed blood in her honor, but how did she know that he didn't have his own designs? She longed to trust him. Saldanzia was a long way to go, especially considering she must cross Cronan territory. To go through by herself would be treacherous at best. In the brief moments of combat, she had witnessed his very impressive fighting skills. He would be an extremely intimidating opponent.

Arabella could really use the help. Could she really ask a complete stranger, she didn't know the name of, to help her to Saldanzia?

The reins were clutched tightly in her grip. She sent a small prayer up and moved toward the horse, ready to mount and be on her way.

"I'm for Saldanzia," she finally admitted. "The offer of aid is noble," she replied, "but I am being pursued by Mason Kiefer's men, men of the king of Chilton, and I don't believe they will stop hunting me." It would be immoral to not present the grim facts. "'Tis imperative I reach Saldanzia with all haste."

"There is no way I would consider leaving any lady to make that journey alone," he fervently declared.

Arabella inwardly sighed, a swelling of gratitude that he would act with honor, yet the reality of their dismal chance to succeed weighed heavily upon her.

The heavy weight and grief of her recent choices with regards to her personal guard pushed her to speak. "'Tis not necessary," she said, trying to provide him an out, if his honor demanded it.

He took a few steps closer to her so that only a foot separated them, locking eyes with her. Arabella's heart sped up. His closeness was compelling.

"I'll accompany and see you safely there. 'Tis not a question!" he quietly maintained. Steel laced the words with finality. She was acutely aware at that moment that *this man is dangerous*, though the thought that followed on the heels of that revelation was that she was in fact not afraid of him. They looked into one another's eyes for what seemed a long time, then he picked her up and carefully set her in the saddle, successfully ending the debate.

"By way of introduction, my name is Ethan," he said, turning his back and walking to his own mount.

She took a deep breath, trying to change directions. "I have heard it said that in Saldanzia, 'tis proper to address a person by their given name?" she inquired.

"Indeed, you may call me Ethan. However, in the Norlans, I would call you Lady . . . ?" he questioned, reining his horse next to her so that they were side by side.

The moment of truth! Should she say her true name, or would he treat her differently to know she was a queen, or even take advantage of her in some way? Or would he even know or care that she was a queen in Anchelle? Deception was a slippery slope, one she had no desire to engage in, but in her position it was foolishness to not take extra care.

"Bells, you may call me Bells." It was her name, not a lie, just not her full name. A woman, a queen without her guard on foreign soil, could never be too careful.

"A beautiful name, pretty enough it could be that of a princess."

Arabella's heart beat rapidly. Did he know who she was? It took great restraint to stifle a gasp and keep from looking up sharply to see if he had a knowing expression in those deep green eyes.

CHAPTER 4

B *ells.* Ethan had to admit, she wasn't like any noblewoman he had before encountered. Though wounded, obviously stiff, and sore, she looked like a goddess regally sitting astride a horse. She was small and lithe of frame, but she exuded strength. Thick, deep-brown hair streamed down to her waist, the rich color accentuating the deep sapphire blue of her eyes framed by dark lashes. The clothing she wore and her bearing spoke of aristocracy, but her movements moments ago were that of a well-trained soldier. Just thinking of her headbutting that soldier made him want to laugh out loud. It had been a bold move, one that she probably still felt the effects of.

That a woman was forced to defend herself made him want to rage. Scouting the area that morning, he'd crossed paths and settled in to see what Chilton soldiers were doing so far from their borders. Mason's men lay in wait for over half an hour, luring her in with the horse. A fiercely protective feeling had all but swallowed him, leaving him stunned by the savageness that reared up.

Ethan and Bells had gathered all of the soldiers' horses and headed east. She didn't seem in the mood to talk, but what he had just witnessed had been an act of war. One didn't attack a lady from another country and follow her into another hostile area. Might she not be from Anchelle as she had claimed? The colors of Anchelle adorned her cloak, as well as her horse, emerald green and silver emblazoned on the chest strap with a leafy tree. At this point he had no reason to believe otherwise.

As he rode pondering the events, while scanning the area reflexively, he noticed her rummage through a saddlebag and produce an apple and some salted meat. "Would you care to share a light repast?" she kindly asked. *Modest fare for a lady*, he observed. He declined her offer, and she quickly ate while they rode.

Bells broke the silence after consuming the simple food. "I'm not familiar with the rank on your uniform." She looked at him curiously, paying particular attention to his shoulders. "It looks like the famous ranger's uniform, but is there more?" she questioned. He waited patiently to see if she could cipher it. As it dawned on her, she looked at him with a measure of awe. "You're the ranger commander."

Ethan smiled and nodded his head, but inside he was chuckling. What lady of the Norlans would know the insignia of the uniforms of Saldanzia? He was the ranger commander, sure, but he was more than that. "In fact," he revealed, "some of my command is about a hard two days' ride from here. We may catch them about halfway through Cronan territory if we're blessed. 'Twould make for safer travel."

She nodded her head in agreement. "Will you share with me what life is like in Saldanzia?" she inquired.

He noticed her unconsciously rubbing her leg, alerting him to her discomfort.

"Are you in pain?" he questioned. Ethan felt a need to take care of women in general, his mother had taught him that, but he felt strongly about this one and he was unsure why. Had he ever been so aware of a woman's every move? It was disconcerting to be sure.

Bells managed a smile, and bravely said, "'Tis nothing. I'll be fine."

"We could take a respite, if you would like?"

"Please, not on my account" was her melodic but firm reply.

Ethan wanted to insist they halt for a brief rest but recognized her need to keep moving. Their scuffle was bound to draw others. Saldanzia it was, then. The Golden City.

"Saldanzia is a beautiful city," he began.

Ethan watched her closely as he spoke, aware of the concern etched in her eyes. He was intrigued by the way she pursed her lips, trying to capture and name the various emotions that crossed the exquisite canvas of her features. A grimace flitted past and he wondered if it was from the pain, or was it a response to something he'd shared? A half-smile formed as he related a clever story, which motivated him to want to make her laugh. He was surprised to note that, like him, Bells continuously scanned the countryside, alert to their surroundings.

The last of the Hoodoos fell behind their caravan just as dark fell, but they continued onward, blessed with a full moon to provide enough light to travel. The soldiers' horses proved a great benefit, allowing them to switch to fresh mounts. An hour before midnight they finally stopped to make a dry camp. A fire would warm her aching body but, alas, would also be a beacon to unwanted eyes. Before he could offer assistance she'd dismounted the horse, untied a bedroll, and limped to a large tree where she spread out to sleep.

"I can take the first watch," she bravely volunteered.

"Allow me to take it. Please take your rest. I'll awaken you on the third watch."

Ethan expected some resistance but it seemed she was too tired. Lying down quickly, she seemed to instantly find sleep. Though he was weary, his brain kept replaying the day's events, over and over again. After four hours, it became difficult to stay alert, and though he internally railed at the thought of waking her, he capitulated, knowing the territory they would cross on the morrow would demand his constant vigilance.

Arabella woke still fatigued and sore in so many places but grateful for the time allotted to take her rest. Walking a distance from the camp, she made a circuit around, taking note of their position. The moon was making a steady descent, stretching shadows. The walking served to warm her during the coolest part of the night while simultaneously serving to stretch her aching, bruised muscles, relieving some of the pain.

She couldn't help but wonder how Thaddeus and Luke fared. Concern so heavy for them, as it was for the rest of her knights, took her breath away, leaving an awful ache. Had they made it through Mason's contingent of soldiers? While circling the campsite, she fervently prayed that the men were ahead of her.

The search for her horse had taken the better part of the morning. Could they have made better time and be found a day ahead of her? Dare she entertain such a notion, or would their continued absence destroy her soul, so weary from the losses of those littering the hills of her home? Would they be pushing hard, thinking she was ahead of them going into Cronan territory alone? Or backtrack, searching for her, further raising the likelihood of contact with additional Chilton forces?

Arabella's turbulent thoughts finally settled on the figure of her rescuer lying asleep close by. Honorable, kind, and those eyes—had she ever found someone more handsome? It made it hard for a girl to breathe steadily.

She had desperately wanted to question him about the affairs of Saldanzia but had hesitated to do so, reasoning that he probably didn't know the intricacies and minds of the Ruling Five families of Saldanzia and would therefore not be able to know if it was possible that Saldanzia could come to her people's aid.

Quietly she puttered around camp, trying to stay alert and warm. The spring night still held a chill. She detangled her hair and braided it down her back, then retrieved water from a canteen and washed both her hands and face.

Scanning the horizon once again, she caught sight of something drifting toward them. Focusing on it for a minute, her heartbeat quickened as she finally identified the silhouette of a horse in the gray dawn. The animal seemed to be heading toward their camp. Initially, it hadn't looked as though there was anyone on the horse, but as it approached, she could tell there was something in the saddle, but it was an odd shape. As her bay horse whinnied, the incoming animal picked up speed toward them.

Recognition flared as she spied the horse's distinctive markings and deduced the rider. Heedless of possible danger, she ran headlong down the grassy embankment. The animal nickered softly, familiar enough with her that it didn't spook.

A strangled cry escaped her lips as she spotted an arrow protruding from Thaddeus's back. The next thing she noticed was his marred face as he hung to the side of the horse, bloodied and bruised. Though his eyes appeared lifeless, she frantically grabbed his wrist, desperate to feel for a pulse. She could see and hear the flies but ignored them. Arabella held his wrist, desperately feeling for a sign of life, setting her hand to his chest, praying to feel it rise.

"Thaddeus!" she cried out. Nothing. Grabbing his body, she frantically tugged on him, but he wouldn't budge. It was then she saw the ropes that tied him fast to the horse. Frantically she pulled on one of the knots, having a hard time seeing with the pools of tears in her eyes. She hardly noticed Ethan working on another knot. When the rough cords were all untied, Ethan pulled Thaddeus off the horse.

"Over here!" Arabella exclaimed, seeing a flat place to lay him. *No, no, no, no, no*, she chanted. She couldn't believe, she *wouldn't* believe it. *Oh, heaven help me. Please let him be alive.* This couldn't be happening. As soon as Ethan laid him on his side, she put her ear to his chest, waiting to hear the steady thump of his chest. *Please God!* She pleaded over and over in her head, *Please don't let him be dead. Not Thaddeus.*

Thaddeus, her sweetest friend and fierce protector, the boy who had grown up next to her, more like a brother than any brother of flesh would be. This couldn't be happening! Heavy sobs wracked her body. How was she going to tell Luke? What if Luke was dead and she never saw him again? The sobbing worsened. She could hardly catch her breath. What if she'd lost them both? What lies she told herself, believing she could command and her body would obey the charge to never again cry; but the pain was so acutely similar to losing her father six months ago to the shivers. In some ways it was worse, because Thaddeus died defending her. An awful sound rent the air. Moments passed before she realized the horrific sound was emitting outward from somewhere inside her. Must death be her constant companion? To love so many, only to lose so much.

Warm strong hands wrapped around her, and she turned, burying her face in Ethan's shirt. Raw pain enveloped her in waves. Arabella could hardly get a hold of herself. Memories flashed of the many escapades she had with Thaddeus as a child, pranks on some of the knights, and the tournaments they had participated in as youths. A scene rolled out in her mind's eye of a trick they played on Luke one autumn day in the garderobe. *Saints be . . .* A world without Thaddeus alongside her was unimaginable.

The warm comfort of Ethan's arms around her was palpable. It was something she desperately needed.

The sobbing lessened as she gained control of her emotions, some half-hour later. Ethan handed her a kerchief, and she tried to discreetly wipe her face as she turned away from him. She couldn't look at Ethan, not wanting to face anyone.

Arabella still hadn't spoken when at noon they'd each placed their last rock over Thaddeus's grave. Her body hurt, and she longed to go crawl under a nearby quakie, go to sleep, and pretend this nightmare wasn't her new reality. Instead, Ethan helped her mount one of captured soldiers' horses. Floating on a sea of loss, she was barely aware of anything around her.

⌒

Ethan's eyes scanned the landscape constantly, his senses on full alert. The enemy could be anywhere around them. Having just crossed into Cronan territory, they could find themselves facing off against the clansmen as easily as Mason's soldiers. They would need to change mounts every few miles, just in case they needed to try to outride any adversary. In the open plains, their enemy could be seen for a considerable distance, but so would they.

He glanced over at Arabella for the second time in the same minute, concerned for her well-being. Holding her today had felt innate, right, and agonizing, all at the same time. Ethan knew he shouldn't be so very invested in her, but he already felt a stirring in him to ease and help take away her pains and sorrows.

He wanted to take her to a physician to see why she was limping around. The anger and determination to pulverize and punish the King of Chilton grew as he catalogued the injuries marring her form and the red brimming of her eyes.

The note that was held in place by the arrow protruding from the young man had blessedly gone unnoticed in Bells's grieving. Instinctively, Ethan had pulled it off his back and tucked it in his tunic. Later he read the sinister message.

Arabella
How many more will have to die before you are mine?
Mason

What were the chances that the note would end up where it did? How many more were out there? The note was intended for her to see. Arabella. Though he'd felt fairly confident within minutes of speaking to her that she was the queen of Anchelle, the truth stared him in the face. He was escorting the newly coronated monarch of Anchelle to his own country. One thing was for sure, the tales of her beauty were not an exaggeration.

Ethan couldn't help but wonder if the dead man himself had been as much of a threat to Mason as the note itself was—perhaps a suitor? Had she been in love with Thaddeus, and Mason was eliminating the competition? Her reaction to his death gave credence to a close relationship; it was clear she'd cared a great deal for him. It had been gut-wrenching to see her reaction. Last he had heard, the queen remained unmarried, though not from the lack of suitors.

The question he asked himself was, what did she hope to gain by coming to Saldanzia? Three possibilities seemed most likely. Two of them had a great deal to do with him.

While she looked straight ahead, Arabella broke the silence. "Thank you," she spoke, so soft that it was just above a whisper. She seemed to recognize the need to be quiet in enemy territory. Arabella turned her face so that she was looking him in the eyes. Her piercing blue eyes were red rimmed, puffy, and looked tired. She gave a sad smile.

He quietly responded, "'Twas my honor to serve."

The pain in those sapphire eyes was still evident.

"We've been inseparable since childhood," she finally admitted a minute later. "I can hardly believe it."

"'Tis understandable," he replied, thinking of his own experiences with sudden violent death. As a soldier, death became a reality. As a commander, he put men's lives at risk constantly. One minute they were there and the next gone forever. The weight of decisions and their consequences was unavoidable in leadership. Still, he wasn't sure how to comfort her or what to say that wouldn't cause more pain.

"What are the chances of not seeing any Cronan on our way through?" she asked, abruptly changing the subject. Her gaze was direct, unflinching. "And please tell me plainly."

He would have to be candid. It was all too likely they would come across one or more, and he wanted her to be ready.

"Not very likely," Ethan admitted. "With only two of us, we are more of a target. Having the extra horses will be an advantage but also draw more attention. We'll move swiftly through their region, hopefully reaching my company in the next twenty-four hours. I know you are exhausted, but if we can push hard, we have a more favorable chance of reaching my men."

"Indeed," she answered back.

A couple hours later, Ethan and Arabella spotted a lone warrior silhouetted atop a rocky ridge watching them. The enemy was too far away to identify any features; one minute he was there, and he was gone the next. Ethan couldn't see any others, but it was only a matter of time. They were in the heart of Cronan territory now, one of the most dangerous places to be found. His pulse quickened, as it did every time he went into battle.

"Time to change mounts," he said, voice even and steady.

She didn't argue. Dismounting before he could help her, she grabbed the bay horse she had been trying to track the first day they had met, which in reality was only a day ago. Why did it seem as though ages had passed? With practiced hands she adjusted the stirrups. Before she mounted he walked to her side and grabbed her hand. The gesture seemed to startle her.

"Just a moment," he demanded, feeling a warm sizzle up his arm, from where her hand rested in his. She turned to look at him, giving him her full attention. "We may be able to outride them, but if you're caught, and they let you live, tell them you want asylum in the Dalmenzie clan." She took a deep breath, hearing what he was telling her. "Though they don't respect most people, the Dalmenzies respected your father. You have a fighting chance with them."

He could tell she was only slightly shocked he knew who she was, and also that she knew now was not the time to ask questions. Grabbing her around the waist, he lifted her into the seat of the bay.

"Ride well, Ethan," she said, showing her Anchellian roots. It wasn't an expression that Saldanzians used, but he liked it.

"Ride well, Arabella."

They had only gone a mile when seven warriors bearing the markings of the Wolf clan came from the North and an eighth appeared from the West. Wolves were known to migrate through this region, as they lived by the southern border. Various colored furs served as rudimentary clothing upon their extremely pale bodies—skin so pale it seemed almost blue, with swirls and garish markings made with blood on faces and uncovered limbs adding to the predatory look. Most warriors wore their hair short and used animal fat to create the illusion of spikes, with clumps

worn straight up several inches and various directions. Ethan had
encountered the Cronan many times, but he never got used to
it. However, the most chilling issue he found was the shrill cry
they made when in pursuit, a fiendish howling at their prey that
grew louder as they neared. The blood curdling sound rent the
air, and Ethan noticed Arabella squeeze her eyes shut. He knew
she had to be terrified, but she doggedly pushed her horse into a
full-out run.

It became quickly evident that they wouldn't be able to retain
all the horses. Ethan couldn't afford to slow down. A blade made
quick work of the lead ropes of all but two. Luckily, they followed
him well. Looking behind him and to the side, he could see that
the Wolves had not gained any ground. They were holding them
off at about a furlong, and two of the warriors had split off after
the extra valuable mounts Ethan had just released.

Arabella looked magnificent as she put all her weight on her
stirrups, lifting her off the horse to allow the horse to stretch
more, using her hands to artfully rein the bay faster. Her much
smaller body riding low over the neck of the animal, combined
with the power of the thoroughbred, gave her an advantage.
Serving in the military, he'd seen every class and skill of horseman, and Arabella was an exceptional rider. Ethan would be
hard pushed to keep up to her; both he and his horse each carried seventy pounds more.

With a glance over his shoulder, he was pleased to note
they had gained some ground over the Wolves. A concern that
weighed heavily on his mind was if the Cronan had positioned
a force ahead of them, and they were being herded into a trap.
Arabella and Ethan couldn't keep up this pace forever, but neither could the Cronan.

Within ten minutes, they were compelled to bring the horses
back down to a canter. The Wolves, though falling back, were
not deterred, steadily plodding on behind them and trying to
wear them and their horses out. The mountains loomed in the
distance. They would be leaving the rolling plains in a matter
of hours.

Ethan advised they switch horses, and Arabella pulled to a stop and swiftly dismounted.

"They won't cease following, will they?" she questioned as they started to ride once again.

"No," he answered honestly. "We will need to ride on and hope we make it to my company before they reach us. If it looks like we aren't going to find reinforcements, we will have to make a stand," he said grimly, trying to prepare her. By his calculations he could take down half of the raiding clan with his bow before they were in close fighting proximity, but he didn't want to be in archery range knowing the risk to Arabella. So they would need to run till they couldn't any longer or find cover somewhere without being a target. He continued to scan the land for any advantage such as a defensible perch where Arabella was secure and he could pick off those that stalked them.

"They look as scary as I have heard tell," she admitted. "Just like the stories to frighten children from wandering afar."

"They're just men," he reassured her. "They bleed and die like anyone else."

She nodded. "Know that if the time comes to face them, I'll fight."

"I know." He had seen her fight; he had no doubt. It was obvious her muscles and reflexes were memory-trained, which bespoke years of dedicated practice.

They kept a careful eye on their pursuers and plodded on. The hours stretched on, worry a constant companion, as was the fatigue. Arabella rarely spoke, though she ate a little and drank when he suggested. Though she had had a rough pair of days, and the outlook didn't look to improve, he had yet to hear any complaint pass her lips. He prayed his company was not too far ahead of them.

Switching mounts again, they took no time to stretch their legs. The enemies continued onward, pressing ever pressing. The mountain's cover was finally before them. The sun was making its final retreat as thick clouds rolled in. The Wolves were on their heels.

CHAPTER 5

A rabella couldn't believe that she was in almost the same predicament she had been in forty-eight hours ago. The irony was not lost on her. She felt like she was in a bad dream that just kept repeating itself. The only improvement was having Ethan alongside her. He'd literally proven a lifesaver.

The pain. She was in so much blasted pain her throat thickened and tears threatened. There didn't seem to be a place on her body that wasn't complaining. Still sore from the multiple falls she had taken, added to rock hauling for Thaddeus's grave and saddle time, her body was viciously protesting. Worse than the physical pain was the ache that seared her heart and refused comfort. Thaddeus's lifeless body had broken something inside of her. Shaking her head, Arabella commanded herself not to think of Thaddeus; it could get her and Ethan killed.

Turning in Thaddeus's saddle for the hundredth time she looked back. Arabella could barely see the Cronan for the darkness that was descending, as well as the trees that hid them intermittently. They were within two furlongs. Ethan and Arabella had steadily started to climb out of the plains for the last four furlongs on a game trail, and the wind was picking up. The smell of rain made it seem imminent. It had already started to cool down the higher they climbed. The thought of rain was not a welcome one. Without dismounting, they grabbed their oilskins.

The wind's tumultuous force made it almost impossible to put them on.

Thunder rumbled, then lightning flashed on the hillside lighting it up. In the brief moments of light, she never saw the Cronan. The wind continued to increase, lashing her hair to her face and making it difficult to see anything. Ethan closed the gap between them and shouted over the wind to look for somewhere to find shelter. He no sooner said it than the rain began to fall in earnest. Thunder and lightning increased: the mountain sounded angry to be disturbed. It was imperative that they find shelter immediately. The rain turned to hail and the ground quickly covered in white, yet no shelter of any kind could be found.

The cold was seeping into her tired body, and streams of water found little places through her oilskin. The hail was pelting her so hard it was sure to leave welts.

The darkness encompassed them, and the hail was so loud that she was having a hard time staying with Ethan. As if he was thinking the same thing, he pulled up beside her and plucked her off her horse and into the saddle in front of him, holding her in place with a brawny arm. The mount didn't care for the additional weight after the strenuous ride and crow-hopped several times before settling down. Ethan grabbed the reins of the horse she had just been on, and they trudged up the muddy mountainside.

Lightning flashed again, and when it did, Ethan reined the horse up a steep embankment. The horse lunged and struggled up the incline, trying to find footing on the rocky, greasy ground. Arabella held the pommel tightly and felt every jolt through her body. Ethan firmly held her with his left hand against his chest. They climbed for several minutes. She hadn't seen what Ethan had, but she trusted him. They stopped when the ground leveled off, and Arabella could barely make out a small overhang, directly in front of them, hardly enough room to house two people and two horses. They would need to squeeze in.

Ethan jumped down, collected her off the horse, and deposited her inside the rock overhang. Her legs and hip would hardly hold her; they were screaming in pain. The weather at least had allowed them to stop. The grassy ground was damp, but the water wasn't moving through the overhang as she had glimpsed outside when the lightning lit up the sky. It had looked like streams pouring off the mountainside. She hadn't seen another living soul, but it was hard to relax, wondering if the Cronan, too, were seeking shelter nearby.

Ethan grabbed their bedrolls and brought hers back to her, then removed two of the four saddles and stood them up as a small wall where the wind was blowing through.

"I'd sure like to let all the horses have their saddles off, but I don't dare; we may need to make a hasty exit." He spoke close to her ear to be heard over the torrential downpour.

Hurriedly taking off her oilskin, she grabbed her blanket and wrapped it securely around herself, feeling chilled to the bone. She then sat down on her bedroll, her back against the mountain wall. Her view out front was nothing more than black.

Ethan watched their surroundings for over thirty minutes before he sat down next to her. Watching her shiver for only a moment, Ethan didn't hesitate to put one arm around her and pull her close to himself, his other hand still holding his crossbow.

She could feel the heat from his firm body against her own, acutely aware of the man holding her.

"You might as well take your rest, I don't know when we will get a chance again for a while," he said.

"You didn't sleep much last night," she stated. "You first." She tried not to think of why he hadn't gotten much sleep.

"Nay," he emphatically spoke. "Go ahead," he encouraged when he sensed her hesitation.

"Very well," she acquiesced as she snuggled into his arm just a little more. Though physically and emotionally exhausted, Arabella didn't know if she could fall asleep; she was so cold. The mountain air was chilly, and she was damp where the oilskin had not protected her entirely. And if she was being completely honest with herself, it was a little disconcerting to be in such close proximity to such an extremely handsome man. Though she'd had plenty of suitors over the last pair of years, none had held her attention for long. She couldn't help wondering what it would be like to be called upon by Ethan.

She pulled her blankets up tightly to her chin and rubbed her legs together, causing Ethan's arm to tighten around her.

"Don't allow me to rest long," she tried to insist. "You need some sleep as well."

"Aye," he said, not at all convincingly.

Arabella didn't know how long she had been sleeping for, but the initial gray of morning was making its first appearance. She could hear the rain still coming down in a light drizzle.

She bolted up to a sitting position to find Ethan, wondering why he had let her sleep the entire night; he stood just outside the overhang, scanning the countryside, his hair charmingly disheveled. He turned and looked at her sleepy eyes with a small grin.

"Were you awake all night?" she asked incredulously in a whisper. She noticed an extra blanket on her, and she felt deliciously warm.

"Nay," he said, coming over and giving her a hand up.

Accepting it, she was pulled to within inches of his face. He looked at her for a long minute, seeming to study her face. She was very aware of how close she was to him. Though she was constantly with men, this felt very different; her heart wanted to beat out of her chest. He dropped one of her hands and reached out and took a loose tendril of her hair and put it behind her ear. Her stomach did a little somersault.

Then something crossed his face, and he took her remaining hand, bringing it to his lips; and he looked at her and kissed it. Arabella's stomach took flight, and all she could do was offer a small smile as she took a ragged breath.

"I stayed awake for the first hour or so, and then I decided the Wolves had to find shelter somewhere as well." He shrugged. "We might as well both get some sleep while it was pouring. The weather couldn't have been better if I had planned it. The rain is just starting to let up. We best be on our way," he said, grabbing a saddle blanket and throwing it on the first horse.

Arabella felt his loss at once.

"Do you think we will reach your company today?" she asked, hoping her voice sounded normal, because she was having a hard time breathing. Her hand still tingled where he had kissed it as she rolled up her bedroll.

"It's hard to say for certain, but mayhap by midday."

"My thanks for the extra blanket last night," she said, handing back his blanket.

They were in the saddle in less than five minutes, their oilskins keeping the water off their heads and backs. A short time later, going over the next rise, they spotted the Wolves a half-mile below them in relentless pursuit, but only half of them. Yikes! Where were the others? She didn't dare hope they had given up the chase. More than likely they were trying to circle around to box them in, or they had gone for more men.

"Only half of them," she finally voiced, wondering what Ethan's assessment was.

"We better move quickly." His face and tone were grave. No doubt they are trying to head us off."

It was as bad as she thought. If they could just keep ahead of the Cronan. It was the only way they were going to make it.

Once they reached the summit, she hoped to see the other side with Ethan's company of men. But the top of the mountain splayed across for at least a few miles that she could tell. Pine trees and spruces dotted the landscape, as did spring flowers, making the dangerous place seem almost welcoming.

"I've a mind to turn one direction," Ethan said, viewing the landscape. "No doubt that the four missing Wolves will be in front of us if we don't turn. I imagine that the south side is the easier one to circle and head us off. In addition, if they came from the south they would push us further into their territory." He spoke his thoughts out loud as he looked all around. "The four missing Wolves are probably headed that way right now."

"Then we turn south as well, toward them, and we wait for them to pass and go behind them," Arabella concluded.

"It will be tricky!" he stated, coming to the same conclusion. "But it might be our best option."

There were a lot of things that could go wrong with this plan. At least the rain had stopped seconds ago.

Putting their heels to their horses, they headed into the trees to the south. They rode that way for a bit, and then west, back the way they had been coming from Anchelle, hoping the four missing Cronan had already passed by. The only sounds that permeated the air were the horses' footfalls and the birds.

Arabella saw their tracks first and immediately pointed them out to Ethan. The tracks were probably only fifteen minutes old, but they were moving fast considering the mucky conditions. Arabella and Ethan turned and followed their path. They had only been on it a short time when the blood-curdling howl of the Wolves pierced the air from the way they had just come.

"They're on to us," Ethan exclaimed. He dug the heels into his horse, as did Arabella. Once again, she was running in treacherous conditions with no choice.

Arabella had no way of knowing if the Cronan ahead of them knew they were behind them by the call the other Cronan had made, but she wondered. They were beginning to see the expanse beyond the mountain when two warriors appeared before Ethan, who was in front of her. Ethan raised his crossbow and shot lightning fast, hitting the first one in the chest. This was followed by an axe to the next Wolf.

Arabella had her bow in her hand ready but couldn't get a shot off with Ethan in the line of fire. She couldn't come around to his side to get a shot off either, though he seemed to not need the help. Ethan loaded his bow quickly as they ran past the two dead Cronan. She briefly looked behind her and was pleased to see no one there. They would take what they could get.

The howling rent the air again, raising Arabella's already racing heart. The sound did little to help her know where the enemy was coming from, though it should have.

The mountainside turned and went back to the north, but rather than follow the trail the Cronan had taken, Ethan went headlong down the east side where there was no trail. When he dropped over, Arabella could finally see the sweeping valley. Ethan's company was in the valley all right, but probably five miles away, giving her a glimmer of hope. Arabella took it all in a glance as she started the treacherous descent. The side was steep and littered with boulders that she had to weave through as her horse followed the lead horse. She had to concentrate on riding, but when Ethan looked back with concern on his face, she couldn't help but look back as well. Two more warriors were right behind her. They must have come back with the other two.

There was no way she could fight them as she descended this mountain. They didn't have a chance. If the warriors just stopped and took aim with their arrows, they were well within range. Even a youth could pluck them off at their leisure.

She expected the arrow in her back for maybe a full minute before she turned around and saw them descending behind her. The Cronan must want them alive. It was a relief and scary all at the same time. She couldn't imagine being their captive. The stories she had heard gave nightmares to children and adults alike. The other four Wolves were now on the downward trek following their companions.

Out of her peripheral, she could see the lead Wolf was coming around, forging a new trail and hoping to cut her off. She couldn't even raise a weapon while trying to hang on at this rapid rate of descent that had her leaning back to not fly forward out of the saddle. As soon as Ethan made it to the bottom, he turned around and raised his bow up. He took out the one to her right first, then got off another shot that flew right past her and then an additional shot. She couldn't see what was happening above her, but she suspected that the one right behind her had taken an arrow or two and that the others were scattering.

Ethan waved her on as she passed him, and when she looked behind he was right on her heels. They started across the valley at a dead run.

Riders coming straight at them, hidden behind a stand of trees, made her heart stop. She pulled her sword before first recognizing the sorrel horse with a bald face that Luke rode and then his distinctive figure upon it. He still lived! Gratitude swept her soul, and she had to take a few deep breaths not to weep for the joy that consumed her.

Not allowing herself to be distracted from the Cronan threat, she turned in her saddle to see only Ethan behind her. The Wolves, seeing the army a small distance away, must assuredly have thought better of pursuing the two. Either that or Ethan's lethal marksmanship had dissuaded them from following.

As they closed the distance to the advancing riders, Arabella was able to identify Roland, Benton, and Garner. *Thanks be, they all yet draw breath.* Relief hit her like a wave when they finally reined in their horses a few miles later. Arabella couldn't help but smile.

As they greeted her each put their fist to their chest, and as she made eye contact with Luke, he winked at her. Blond hair, blue eyes, and a beard that had grown full with age—Arabella knew that the ladies liked him, but as he winked today it was a much more serious wink, like a *good job, I'm glad you're alive* kind of smirk that filled her with the relief of an enormous weight being removed.

"Well rode, Your Highness," Garner spoke. He was the senior knight and therefore the first to address her. "Most joyful to see you hale."

"And I you, Garner, and to the whole lot of you!" She smiled at each of them, feeling the heavy burden eased yet to an even greater degree.

"Ethan," she said, smiling at him. "'Tis Sir Garner," she stated, indicating Garner, and then she pointed to Roland, who was the second senior knight. "Sir Roland, Sir Benton, and Sir Luke." She pointed to each one.

"Gentlemen, 'tis the Ranger Commander of the Saldanzian army, Ethan," she presented.

She paused, letting the information digest. Here was an important figure that they needed as an ally. Each nodded his head in greeting.

"Ethan," she spoke, feeling overwhelming gratitude for the man that had stopped what he was doing to defend her time and again, who seen her honorably delivered to her men, "saved me from Mason's soldiers and then the Cronan. I would not be here now but for his valor."

"'Tis nothing, Your Highness," he spoke, using her proper title.

Each of the knights put their fist to their heart for him. She didn't know if Ethan knew what an honor it was that they had shown him such great respect, but he returned the gesture.

She couldn't help but glance back one more time. The landscape was empty of the enemy.

They cantered toward the army that was situated down the valley, the knights in a tight formation surrounding their queen. Ethan was soon met by several of his men. They all saluted him and maintained a distance to the side of Arabella and her men, giving them some autonomy.

After the initial euphoria of seeing her men, she found it increasingly difficult to make eye contact with Luke. The heartache of telling him that Thaddeus was dead formed a lump in her throat and seemed to make it difficult to draw breath and swallow.

Garner, as befitted the senior knight, rode on her right and filled her in immediately, all quiet business. "Charles, Harold, Timothy, Schofield, Titus, and Bron died in the initial attack." *It was a massacre,* Arabella lamented, seeing each knight's face flash in her mind as Garner spoke their names. *So many died protecting me.* It gutted her. "Bridger died yesterday, Thaddeus is still missing," Garner finished.

The words lodged momentarily. She mentally shoved the lump down—down—down and drew in a ragged breath.

"Ethan and I buried Thaddeus yesterday," she said, trying to keep the tears in. The lump was gone, but it had left an aching, raw throat. Determined to not weep in front of her men, she avoided looking at Luke, knowing it would set off a flood.

They all knew what a personal loss it was to her, and they wisely remained silent. Their combined loss bound them together even more. Yet being reunited there was some measure of comfort to be found for each.

Roland finally broke the silence a mile later. "I have Palachio," he spoke solemnly.

Joy fluttered in her breast amidst the turmoil. Leave it to Roland to find her horse and reunite them. A man of medium stature and weight, with strawberry-blond hair, he was the grandest horse trainer in all of the Norlans. The horses he trained went for more money than any other, and for good reason.

Though he was several years her senior, he had kindly taken her under his wing when she was a girl of ten and schooled her in the art of equestrian care. Together they had trained Palachio into the magnificent creature he was. She adored Roland and felt such solace to know that he still lived.

"Thank you," she responded wholeheartedly.

The Saldanzian company came into sight, and Arabella sighed. These were her people too, she realized.

CHAPTER 6

They rode close to a hundred furlongs before stopping for the night. After consulting with the major for a time, Ethan sought out the cook.

"I am in dire need of good food," he said to the lean man standing over the fire.

The man looked up and smiled at Ethan. "Right away, sir," he replied.

"Did you get that basin of heated water to the queen's tent?" he asked the man.

"Yes sir, just as you ordered. Grateful and sweet as can be for such a wee thing that I couldn't hardly believe she be a queen."

Ethan could well imagine the interplay; truly she was an enigma.

"Brought it back herself as well, and I got to feed her. Can you believe it? Regular old Jimmy got to feed and bathe a queen."

Jimmy realized his mistake immediately and turned two shades darker. "I'm sorry sir, I didn't mean it disrespectfully, honestly."

"'Tis all right, Jimmy, I know what you meant, just don't speak of it again."

"No, of course not, sir," he replied, truly humbled. With his head down in embarrassment, Jimmy shuffled around quickly to gather supplies to feed Ethan. Eating the slightly warm meal felt heavenly: definitely better than average soldier fare.

Grabbing another biscuit, he went to see if he could find Arabella. He wanted to visit with her about tomorrow. Outside her tent, he spoke with Sir Roland, who directed him east toward the woods. Roland said she was in need of stretching her legs. Walking east, he saw her on the arm of Luke, the younger knight he had seen wink at her. He couldn't believe the knight's audacity to show such familiarity. She leaned heavily on Luke's arm as she limped beside him.

There was a distance that separated them, and he didn't care to yell across camp.

"Sir?" a soldier to the side of him asked. Briefly detained, Ethan lost sight of them as he listened to issues that had arisen in camp in his absence, though he found himself watching for her over and over again. When finally the problem was resolved, he headed the way he had last seen her.

A need to make sure she was well after everything she had been through drove him forward. It had been a thoroughly arduous passage. A taxing journey for anyone. And yet, if he was being honest with himself, he just wanted to see her and be near her. Why did it feel strange not to be with her? They had only been together for three days, but it had seemed longer. Which was odd in of itself, something he wasn't sure he was ready to examine quite yet. Surely he'd never formed an attachment in so short of time?

Ethan glimpsed Sir Garner, so she must be close. Once rejoined with her guards, they kept strict observance of her whereabouts. After fifteen more minutes of aimless pursuit, he gave up hope, determining that morning would have to suffice. He would walk the perimeter and check on the watch before taking his rest. The sight was a familiar one for his own army, making the circuit with a word for the watchmen as he passed. Climbing a small knoll, he looked around him. He saw a sentry in one direction, but then he glimpsed the light blue of her dress.

Walking swiftly toward her, he realized his mistake immediately. She was standing in the arms of Luke, her head against his chest, and Sir Luke was kissing her forehead.

Feeling guilty for witnessing such a private moment, he pivoted away, almost running into Sir Benton. The slender, wiry man was like a ghost. *Where did he come from?* Ethan had been in that spot just moments ago.

"Good eve," he said to Benton as he walked past. The man just nodded his head, his face a complete mask.

⟡

Early the next morning when he walked past Arabella's tent she was already outside. She was applying some kind of ointment to Sir Roland's left arm. When she looked up and saw him, a smile found its way to her face.

Curious, he walked over to wish her a good morn. It wasn't every day that a queen helped a knight with a wound. Ethan was continually astonished to see the way she interacted with her men. How did a young queen find ease with soldiers and time to listen attentively to what they had to say?

Her clean dress was simple, her hair plaited down her back, yet she looked regal and glorious. It was hard not to stare. But at closer inspection, he noticed the swollen eyes, like she might have been weeping.

"I think I'm jealous of Sir Roland," Ethan said. Arabella looked at him quizzically. "I wish I had a wound for you to take care of," he spoke playfully.

She smiled graciously. "I don't think you would care for the smell," she said, holding up her hands for him to take a whiff.

Ethan grimaced as he leaned in; it smelled like chicken dung. "Remind me not to ride by Roland today." Arabella and Roland both chuckled.

"I must thank you for the heated water yesterday," she warmly spoke, once she stopped laughing. "'Twas most heavenly, and very much needed." She finished wrapping Sir Roland's arm with a bandage, and then gave Ethan her full attention, which he was shocked to find made his heart race.

"You're welcome." It hadn't been much, but the small metal tub was the best he could do in the circumstances they found themselves.

"Roland said that you came by last night to have a word with me?" she inquired.

"Ah, aye. It wasn't anything important, I just wanted to see how you fared?"

Sir Roland excused himself and walked a short distance away and stood waiting for his charge. The hustle and bustle of camp being broken down took place all around them.

"I am feeling remarkably better today," she said. "Thanks in large measure to you." She paused for a moment, then spoke again looking up at him. "'Twould seem I am forever to be expressing my appreciation."

Ethan didn't doubt her authenticity. Her gratitude was tangible. "Glad to be of assistance." He smiled back at her.

"Do you think the Cronan are still a concern?" she said, changing the subject.

"Yes, unfortunately. We have another two days of vigilance before we are in Saldanzian land, and then a pair of days to the city of Saldanzia. Best to be on our way as soon as possible. We've been here overlong, too likely to attract unwanted attention."

Behind them men were dismantling the tent that had been provided for the queen. The provisions of camp were almost completely gone.

Luke rode up on a horse, holding the reins of a stunning palomino behind him and halting their conversation. "Good morn," Luke spoke first to Arabella, who returned the sentiment. "How did you rest?"

His look was that of concern, and there was a decided undercurrent, like he was asking more than if she slept well. It was definitely an odd way for a knight to address his queen.

"I slept like a rock," she answered with a sigh, clearly not wanting to talk about whatever was truly bothering her. She moved swiftly to the horse and started to talk to him. "How are you, big boy?" she asked the horse, rubbing his head, then putting his head next to her own.

It was amusing to watch. Delicate hands moved with practiced ease over the animal.

"Good, you needed it." Luke spoke rather teasingly, changing the mood entirely. "You look especially fetching this morning."

Arabella continued to smile. "Thank you," she said, gently stroking the horse's head and seeming to breathe the horse in.

"Good morn to you." Luke finally acknowledged Ethan, then gave him a measured look Ethan had seen all too often among men.

"Luke," Ethan spoke.

Luke looked at Arabella before replying firmly, if not a little hard. "Ethan."

The reaction was uncomfortable, but Ethan knew the horse was intended for her, and without too much thought he held his hand out for Arabella to take. She gave it in return, and Ethan grabbed her small waist into his hands and set all one hundred and twenty pounds of her on top of the horse. He decided he liked to take care of her, though he would not think further on that. It might lead to other thoughts that couldn't possibly bear fruit.

The rest of the knights were mounted and waiting for her a short distance away. She bade him farewell, then nudged her horse and rode to her men, who quickly surrounded her, one on each side.

He saw her on and off during the day. Her men were constantly by her side each time, except when Benton would leave intermittently. On Benton's second return, Ethan cantered his horse over to intercept him.

"See anything?" Ethan asked.

"Two young Wolves four furlongs to the north, but elsewhere 'tis naught but quiet."

Ethan's own scouts had come in a quarter hour earlier and had reported similarly. Though a relief, it didn't mean they were clear as of yet.

"Mind if I ask you a few questions?" Ethan asked

"You can ask," the scout replied warily. Benton seemed like the solitary sort—the sort that made the best of scouts, one who often did not care much for conversation.

"Fair enough." He paused for a moment. "What can you tell me of King Mason of Chilton?"

"He is a real snollygoster," Benton replied without hesitation. "He rules with fear. No one in the Norlans has stood up to him excepting Arabella's father, King Garrett. Strong, brutal and a fair hand with a sword." He shrugged. "He will not stop till he gets what he wants."

"What's that?" Ethan said, figuring he already knew the answer but wanting to clarify.

"Queen Arabella and Anchelle."

"Do you think he would come through Cronan territory and march on Saldanzia to get her?" he asked incredulously.

"She doesn't think so."

"But?" Ethan questioned.

Benton shrugged his shoulder, not meeting Ethan's eyes before heading back to Arabella.

⁓

When Ethan made the rounds at the camp that night, he spied her holding onto the arm of Garner whilst visiting with a group of his soldiers. The men were all laughing. One of them was wiping at his eyes with mirth, obviously charmed by the lady. Though she wore a sweet smile, he noted she rubbed her leg absently.

As he walked by she looked up and made eye contact with him, waved, and continued to smile. Not being able to resist, he headed in her direction.

As soon as he stopped, the Saldanzian soldiers looked at him, their grins replaced by a serious expression. "Sir," they said, saluting him.

He saluted them back and they quickly dispersed. "I think perhaps I ruined their evening," Ethan said, not feeling bad in the least.

"Would you mind?" he asked Garner, motioning for her arm, who like any good man looked at Arabella for confirmation.

She nodded, and Garner gave a slight bow before dropping her arm on Ethan's and stepping back a few paces.

"Care for a stroll?" he asked

"Aye," she replied. "I was hoping to stretch my legs after the long ride today." The reason she was rubbing her leg became all the more evident.

"What was the merriment about?" He was curious to see what a queen would say to cause the seasoned soldiers to laugh with abandon—besides the fact that she was talking to mere soldiers of Saldanzia.

"I dare not speak of it," she replied, color tinging her cheeks, only increasing her allure.

"I have to hear it now!" he tried to coax her, more curious than ever.

She hesitated. "You must take into consideration that Thaddeus, Luke, and I were much younger when this came about." She pressed her lips like she was still considering whether or not she should tell him.

"Aye," he agreed, satisfying her.

"The three of us grew up together," she began. "We were inseparable, maybe even insufferable. We gave our parents a hard time. Thaddeus's and Luke's fathers were my father's closest friends, you see?"

Ethan nodded his head. This was beginning to make more sense, the relationship with Luke and Thaddeus. She continued: "Luke was and is such a tease." She paused for a second. "I can't believe I am speaking of this to you," she laughed. He found it ever so endearing. "Thaddeus and I had had enough of his teasings, and so we initiated a caper. I don't know if you know this about the people of Anchelle or not, but we all lock the garderobes from the outside at night because twice in our history invaders have come into the castles from the sewage."

Her face was a bright red at the mention of garderobes, and Ethan chuckled inwardly, then shook his head indicating that he wasn't aware of this, but scrunched up his face at the thought. It would take a hearty assassin indeed.

"Well, from my home, there is an underground water system that carries away the refuse." She paused, looking at him and wondering if he was going to give a reaction to the topic of conversation. But he looked at her expectantly, smoothing his expression, a questioning eyebrow raised.

"Well, one day I went into the garderobe and started screaming, like I was dying. I yelled for help, and when Luke came through the door, I pretended to be struggling with a person coming up through the hole. Thaddeus, of course, came right behind Luke, and when Luke reached in to save me Thaddeus picked up his legs and shoved him through the hole."

"You did not!" Ethan exclaimed, an incredulous smile on his face. "Are you telling in jest?"

"I swear 'tis true," she laughed, covering her smile with her hand.

The image of her young self wreaking havoc in the castle had him laughing harder than he had in ages. Ethan couldn't believe it. With each passing interaction he realized that she was unlike any royalty he had ever met. He was delighted that she would be willing to share the story with his men and him, especially in light of Thaddeus's recent death. What a wonder. He knew her loss had been devastating, knew that the weight of her kingdom was upon her young shoulders, yet she sought to improve morale.

Her wistful smile dimmed after a minute, like she too was thinking of the loss of Thaddeus. Her lips turned down and she quickly wiped at a tear that had come from her right eye. Taking a deep breath, she forced a smile on her face again, like the moment had never happened, then quickly asked a question, changing the subject.

Ethan longed to draw her in close and comfort her, to tell her it was all right to laugh and cry as she remembered a dear friend, but he didn't know if she would appreciate such familiarity. The wound was likely still too fresh.

A few minutes later, when there was a pause in conversation, he remembered there was something he wanted to talk to her about. Why did it seem that his thoughts scattered in her presence? "I'm sending a runner ahead tomorrow. The Blakes will need proper time to ready things, in anticipation of your arrival. The country will want to celebrate." He paused when Arabella stopped abruptly and watched as her expression changed to studious before she looked questioningly at him.

"The Blakes?" she asked, looking shocked. "Truly? 'Tis the Blakes who are in power?"

"Aye, Cleve Blake." He could tell she didn't like the thought any more than he did.

"Were they not in power ten years past? How long has been their term thus far?" she continued to interrogate him.

"They were in power ten years ago, and they have four years and eight months left on their term." Ethan thought of the Saldanzian hierarchy. There were five ruling families: the McKennas, the Graces, the Lorrings, the Surreys, and the Blakes. Each family had a turn to rule for five years, and it would go in succession so that after twenty years they would come into power again. The family member had to be between the age of twenty and sixty. Each person was permitted to rule only twice, and if no direct children came from them, the family would forfeit their right to rule. They would remain a council member, but they would have no last say in any matter.

"How is that possible? Weren't the Lorrings to be the next family in power?"

"Aye, they would have been, but for an accident a few months ago that killed the eldest son. Lord Lorring has already served two terms, and their daughter is but eighteen. She will not rule till their next allotment." Ethan continued to watch her, as she looked at him expectantly.

"The Graces were next and likewise had to forfeit with no heir . . . available." He was sure that one stung a little bit. "The Surreys served the last term, and the McKennas are next in power."

She was silent for a minute, digesting this new information. Realizing that when the Blakes had come into power, Anchelle was being ravaged by the outbreak of the shivers and that information had not made its way to her, with normal communications halted in fear of spreading the sickness.

Though there hadn't been much travel between the two countries in the past quarter century, the shivers had completely shut down travel. This had been Ethan's first personal expedition to gather intelligence on their southwestern neighbors since they first heard of the shivers and tightened borders. Though he had separated from his scouts three days earlier to gather information from different countries, his course had taken a very different route when he had crossed paths with Arabella.

Ethan couldn't help Arabella if he didn't understand what she was seeking in Saldanzia, though he had wanted to ask since the first day of their meeting. With the fighting, the constant running for their lives and sustained losses, it had never seemed the right time to introduce what was sure to be a difficult subject. Drawing closer to the destination forced his hand.

"What do you hope to gain by going to Saldanzia?" he gently questioned. Ethan caught movement and could see Luke and Garner moving in closer and was surprised to note it was almost dark. Time moved far too quickly, it seemed, when he was with Arabella. They were never too far away, but hovered like watch dogs.

It took her a moment to answer. "I need an army," she finally responded, frustration leaking out as she closed her eyes briefly and clenched her fists. "How am I going to get an army from Cleve Blake?"

And there lay the problem. The obvious distress in learning of the recent unexpected shifts in power spoke volumes to him. She clearly understood this singular twist of fate created the greatest degree of challenge to what she sought.

CHAPTER 7

Arabella tossed and turned all night. Though she'd never met Cleve Blake and didn't know what he looked like, he had haunted her dreams, as did Mason, the Cronan, and Thaddeus. All night she would lurch awake, twisted up in the blankets with an oppressing weight of hopelessness. She had come so far and sacrificed so much, to have Cleve Blake be the Ruling Five! Why? Why did more opposition have to continually pile on top of her? Alone, in the dark of the night, the reality of her purpose seemed to grow further away the closer she drew to her hoped-for solution.

There was only one chance. A slim chance it seemed now. The rules of Saldanzia stated that if four of the ruling families were to contradict the one ruling family, a law could be put forth or set aside. Now she would have to win over the other four or face failure. It was a long shot. More than one would likely disagree. As her mind spun, searching for any other avenue, it came up blank: this was the only option to pursue. Finally she settled into a dreamless sleep.

Arabella woke up exhausted, Luke calling her from the tent door. "Get up, lazy bones. The Saldanzians are ready to pull stakes. You are making us look bad."

"A moment, please," she yelled out, her heart pumping wildly. Arabella shot out of her bedroll and quickly dressed, trying to ignore her multitude of aches and pains. Torso and legs were impossibly stiff and sore, though the bruises were fading—just not fast enough to allow for comfortable travel. "Enter," she commanded Luke.

"Sheesh!" he exclaimed, "you look as if you were wrestling with a wild cat last night."

Arabella gave him an indignant look and felt her hair. "Cease speaking and roll up my bed!" she commanded while pulling her braid out. Truly he was the only one she'd speak to thus. Luke was the only one that brought out this side of her, in truth.

"Ethan informed me last eve that Cleve Blake is the Ruling Five," she said without preamble. Pins in her mouth, she began to plait her hair.

Luke cursed, and Arabella sent him a disapproving look.

"My apologies," he spoke unrepentantly. "That was kind of you to allow the rest of us to get our sleep last eve without that bit of misfortune." She nodded her head in agreement. "How is that possible?" he asked.

"'Tis what I asked," Arabella exclaimed, then continued to explain what Ethan had told her last evening.

"What are the chances?" he commiserated with her.

"Truly the very worst possible family to be in control," she responded tiredly.

Even in the light of a new day, which so often brought renewed optimism, it was all she could do to keep from being overwhelmed with grief, discouragement and fear for her people. It was terrible news, but telling Luke about Thaddeus—that had been heart wrenching. They had held each other for at least an hour two nights prior, their pain so acute. Thaddeus's death could drown them. It seemed like they were just trying to keep their heads above the water. Moving forward required them to swim. It was necessary. There was so much yet to accomplish and no time to truly mourn.

Knowing what she was thinking, Luke came in for another hug. Though her throat ached, she pushed back any tears. His warmth and compassion filled her soul.

"My thanks," she spoke as she stepped away from him a minute later. "I needed that."

"Me too," he said somberly.

When they came out of the tent, the soldiers were just starting to pack up the camp. Arabella looked at Luke with disbelief in her eyes.

"My apologies," he said, and for once he actually looked remorseful for the fib.

"You get to ride drag all day today," she said, walking away from him. Food was high on her list of priorities at the moment; she just wished there was something decadent to bite into, soft and sweet—she longed for a sweet to fix the blues. Certainly the warm food of the past few days was an improvement on the hardtack of the ones before, but she had a long habit of snitching a sweet cake or tart when she was down. How often had Thaddeus or Luke brought her a bit of sweet to make up for their foul-ups?

Arabella had known it would not be easy to return to her mother's homeland in glory and have an army from Saldanzia willingly turned over, but she had been hoping for much better odds than that she currently faced. Now she faced mountainous roadblocks. Regardless, she had to win their assistance for her cause.

Midday found them riding onto Saldanzian soil. A sigh of relief seemed to emanate from the entire company. They had traveled through Cronan territory and lived to tell the tale. Arabella was especially aware of this boon in not losing a man to the Wolf Clan.

Studying the landscape that was completely foreign to her, she tried to visualize what life was like here for her mother. Surely her mother must have ridden through this area.

Towns and villages dotted the rolling hills, spaced between rich brown fields that were sprouting tiny tendrils just breaching the rich, loamy soil. It was a dramatic change to the wild lands they had gone through, though both were beautiful in their own way. They passed people on dirt roads as they traveled or worked in their fields. They looked much like those who would be found in Anchelle or in the Norlans. Dirt roads gave way to well-maintained cobbled roads the closer they came to their destination.

Evening found her with her feet in a cold river, deep in thought, as she had been all day.

"Mind if I join you?" Ethan's deep voice broke her semi-solitude. She was never without at least two knights around her at all times, though they gave her peace as they kept watch.

A thrill ran through her. She had been hoping that he would seek her out. He had been doing it regularly and it pleased her so. Still unsure if he felt duty bound—or was he coming to care for her? She longed for the latter. Their time together was ending, and she found it caused anxiety. Though they had had some miserable, difficult times together, she was aware that her eyes continued to scan for him throughout the day, longing to get his thoughts and insights. She had come to care for him a great deal in such a short passage. She was aware of him in a way she'd never been of another man. A tumble in her belly flipped and rolled whenever she was caught in his gaze.

"Not at all." She smiled up at him, welcoming him. Would it change over time? Thus far every time she came in contact with Ethan, there was that heart-pounding awareness of him. If they continued to interact, would it diminish? She hoped not.

"'Tis so beautiful here," she spoke conversationally, tapping a rock next to her for him to sit down.

"'Tis." There was a pause, and he asked, "How do you fare?"

"I am well, a bit nervous, but now I look at this beautiful place and can't help but wonder how hard it must have been for my mother to leave this to go to a land she had never seen before. It made me wonder if any of the people we passed knew her?"

"My mother and father knew her."

She looked at him startled. "Truly? Did they attend school together?"

"My mother did, but my father didn't. Boys and girls don't attend school together in Saldanzia."

"I had forgotten that. What did they say of her?"

"I'll let them tell you for themselves. Would you care to meet them?"

"Of course, I would love to. Is your father in the military like you?"

"Aye, he is."

"Then you are close to the McKennas?"

"Actually very close, why do you ask?"

"My father taught me that the McKennas spent more time on the military side of their duties. All the royal families had certain areas that they were more focused in their service. Could the same be said today?"

His reply was instantaneous. "Very much so. The McKennas certainly spend a great deal of their time in military affairs. What else did your father say of the McKennas?"

"Well, he said that my mother was dear friends with Lady Sofia and quite good friends with Lord Michael. He also said that they even helped my mother escape the city after my grandfather had my father removed from Saldanzia, with a fake letter telling him my mother's affections had changed."

"Really? That's interesting, is there more to the story? Seems with all they have shared of your parents that would have been mentioned."

"Well, it is all very romantic, nothing a man would find very fascinating," she teased.

Again, she lamented their short time together, but she had hope that she would get the chance to work with him. If the Five would rule in her favor.

Ethan liked her playful manner and the set of her lips as she teased him. He struggled to keep from not staring at those full, red lips. It seemed as though gravity pulled him to them, and he had to rein himself in constantly from acting. There were two guards close by who kept a careful eye on their charge. If he was one of her knights, he was certain he would as well. He was further spellbound as she told a funny story of camping out in the mountains with her parents for a few days with Luke's and Thaddeus's family involving a knight in a dress and pilfering the cook's tent of sweets. Arabella, Thaddeus, and Luke sounded like they had been rambunctious youth.

Still laughing when Garner approached, Ethan noted to his chagrin that the magic of her presence had kept him from noting yet again that daylight was fading, and it was time to retire for the night.

"I must be bedward," Arabella sighed. She seemed as reluctant to leave Ethan as he was her.

"May I escort you to your tent? Your Highness." Garner made a short bow in front of her.

She looked at Ethan, who rose up from his sitting position and pulled her up as well.

"I will have Ethan deliver me. Thank you, Garner."

"Your Highness," he spoke, dipping his head and walking back the way he had come.

"They are most protective of me," she said, taking his arm as he led her back to her tent. He knew she was speaking of all of her knights. "And I believe Garner takes on a parental role on my behalf."

"A very good man," Ethan spoke, pleased she had invited him to walk her back.

As they drew near her tent, he felt loath to leave her. Tomorrow eve they would be in the city of Saldanzia. She would meet her peers and the people who could help decide her future.

"With Cleve Blake ruling Saldanzia currently, I know you have a battle on your hands," he said without preamble. Arabella stilled, and it seemed she held her breath, unsure of where he was going with the conversation. "If it is any consolation," he said, taking both of her hands into his, "I will do what I can to aid you." Ethan looked her in the eyes. He leaned in and kissed her on the cheek. She stilled and he inhaled the smell that was entirely her. A flowery scent he could not name, but he had smelled it the night of the rainstorm under the overhang as he held her. It was entirely intoxicating.

Reluctantly he stepped back, and she gave him a soft smile. "I am again in your debt and gladly accept all the help offered," she said almost breathlessly.

The next eve found them a mere mile from the city of Saldanzia. They passed a slow-moving pair of drays loaded down with potatoes, headed to the market of the capital city of Saldanzia.

Ethan was entranced. Villagers came out of their homes as the procession passed and stared at the queen of a foreign place they had only heard stories of. Arabella waved to the women and children as she passed, smiling at them—a sincere smile impossible to mistake. The people in return waved and smiled back at her open-faced enthusiasm.

Dressed in a stunning blue dress that accented her sapphire eyes, she was dazzling. Nestled in her thick dark tresses, she wore a small delicate crown. Palachio pranced, showing off his queen. The horse seemed to like the attention and paraded himself as only royalty could.

Ethan hung back, watching the queen from a short distance. She was majestic to be sure, yet she was easily connecting with the people, not stiff and distant. It was never more apparent that she had been born and raised for this very purpose. Her men stayed close to her side. They, too, had been trained well, but it went beyond that. These men truly and deeply loved their queen. They were attentive and fiercely loyal to her. Royalty didn't get that devotion by just being royalty: she earned it. It wasn't just her looks, though heaven knew she was a rare beauty. Ethan had observed royalty all his life. He had watched the Anchellians all for days and it was fascinating to watch their interactions, so foreign from his own country's circumspection.

She talked with ease and familiarity with each of them as they rode for miles on end, never treating any of them as servants or less than her equal in station. He watched her as she fixed them a sandwich or worked over a wound, only allowing them to guard her or to help her dismount and mount her horse. By doing so, she let them dote on her a very small amount while at the same time making them feel equal. Fascinating. Were all the men of Anchelle like that, or just the queen's guard?

Putting his heels to his horse, he galloped to her side. Her cheeks were rosy and she gave him a lovely smile. The gates were going to be opened momentarily and he wanted to be there to see her reaction. Saldanzia had a large golden gate with tall spires that was rather grand. The gates swung inward before the group could halt, opening to the sprawling city.

She didn't disappoint. "Oh, 'tis breathtaking!" she spoke reverently. Her face spoke volumes. The sun was making its descent, causing the city to look its best, golden and glorious. Hence the appellation *The Golden City*. He had never appreciated how beautiful the city was until that instant. People lined the streets in great throngs. Flowers and streamers adorned the street as far as he could see.

The moment they passed the gate, Ethan was aware that all five of the ruling families had mounted representatives in attendance. Lord Timothy Grace was in the lead. He was a handsome older gentleman, tall and stately. He had a long white beard that came to his chest and his hair came to his shoulders. He openly smiled at Arabella as he walked his horse toward her.

When they were mere feet away from each other, Ethan spoke up. "Your Lordship Timothy Grace, may I introduce your granddaughter, her Highness Arabella, the Queen of Anchelle." Ethan spoke loud enough for those in the immediate area to hear. Though courtesy demanded that they bow to one another, in the case of being seated on a horse a dip of the head sufficed. They looked at each other for a long moment.

Everybody held their breath as the great man dropped from the saddle and made his way to his granddaughter he had never laid eyes on before. Palachio knelt down for his queen as she gracefully slipped out of the saddle and walked toward the man approaching her. As they came closer, he held out his arms to embrace his only living offspring. The audience clapped and shouted for joy as Arabella returned the embrace, and a few tears slipped from her eyes. Spellbound, there was a sigh of happiness from those in attendance, several wiping sleeves across their own faces.

As the two finally released the embrace, Lord Grace still holding a proprietary hand around her waist, Ethan approached with a couple that were closer to her own parents' age if they had been living.

"Your Highness," Ethan spoke while handing her a handkerchief, "may I introduce Lord Michael and Lady Sophia McKenna." Both had dismounted and were approaching.

She wiped her eyes, smiling at these people who had, from her own words, loved her mother.

Lord McKenna reached for her hand, and as she looked into his face it was like a candle in a dark room had been lit.

"Lord McKenna, you bear a striking resemblance to the very honorable man who escorted me here." Arabella looked from Ethan to Lord McKenna and back. He laughed, well knowing they looked so similar it could not be mistaken.

"Call me Michael, and aye this boy is my son," he said while pulling Arabella to his wife, who had tears streaming down her face.

"Arabella." Lady McKenna took both of her hands and looked her over. Then she pulled her in an embrace. They held each other for a moment before Arabella stepped back. His mother spoke again, "I wish your mother was here with you, I have missed her so much. You have the look of her, but I would have to say that you have your very own beauty." She looked at Arabella thoughtfully before turning toward Ethan. "Wouldn't you say, Ethan?"

Arabella and his mother turned to look at Ethan, who had remained close.

In front of all these people, it seemed like Arabella was suddenly very embarrassed, her posture stiff. But for him it was a simple answer.

Ethan looked first fondly at his mother, and then met Arabella's eyes, though she couldn't bear to hold eye contact and looked away. "Aye, mother. She has no equal." He said it with such conviction that her eyes were drawn back as he continued to look on her with approval.

She blushed prettily, took a deep breath, and glanced at the Surreys and Lorrings, who had dismounted their horses and stood ready to meet Arabella. With grace and confidence, Arabella approached them and his father introduced them. Ethan would have gladly watched the whole interaction, but found himself seething inside when he noticed Cleve and Torin Blake were sitting atop their saddles like the pompous buffoons they really were. They were a thorn in his foot that could not be removed. He wanted to yank them off their saddles and throttle them and demand they show a proper greeting to a neighboring monarch. It was clear they had no intentions of getting off their horses and greeting Arabella as their equal.

Ethan wasn't going to allow them to slight her. Solving the problem for her, he took Palachio by the reins and led the great horse to his mistress. When Arabella was done with introductions, she looked at him by her side.

"Your highness, may I?" he asked her quite formally.

"Thank you, kind sir," she replied. She tapped Palachio, who instantly bowed for her, and the whole audience made an exclamation. Even the horse knew she was a queen. Ethan gently placed her on the sidesaddle.

He watched Arabella approach Cleve and Torin, wary of what would take place; however, he was pleasantly stunned, as he always seemed to be with her.

It was the queenly demeanor that was fixed like a shield on her face. It declared loudly that she was a reigning monarch and expected to be received as such. While she had glowed as she greeted the peasants and countrymen, she now was radiant in the knowledge of her identity. *How can she look immovable and yet gracious simultaneously?* Once again his estimation of her rose, and he found it difficult to tear his eyes from her visage.

Her smile seemed genuine as she spoke. "Your Lordship, thank you for the wondrous welcome to Saldanzia. I have dreamt of coming here for years, and I am most enchanted with the people and this beautiful city."

Though his smile was obviously forced, Cleve made a small dip of the head.

"You're welcome," he spoke condescendingly.

Arabella continued unfazed, her head held high, shoulders straight. "Your courtesy, celebrations, and timely congress for visiting officials are world renowned, so I would like to thank you beforehand for every graciousness you bestow."

He stiffly nodded and held out his hand. She placed hers atop his. Giving the horses their heads, the two led the procession through the city, her men ever close behind her.

CHAPTER 8

Arabella sat in a chair gaze fixed on the mirror. Her hair was piled atop her head loosely, with softly curled tendrils, giving her the look of elegance expected in a mature woman. Someone she needed the Five to see her as. No longer a young carefree girl, but rather a confident woman capable of leading a nation.

Dressing in the most exquisite red dress she had ever worn, Arabella marveled and wondered how her grandfather had managed to have it sewn in the twenty-four-hour period she had been in Saldanzia. It had small lace-capped sleeves and tight bodice with yards of fabric that hung from her waist and was fitted with a perfection a woman could dream of but rarely find. A banquet and ball had been prepared in her honor, it seemed from the moment Saldanzia had heard of Arabella's pending arrival.

The McKennas volunteered to host the grand event, given the relationship they had shared with Arabella's parents.

Arabella viewed the picture of her mother that hung in the hall outside her bedroom. The beautiful, poised lady that stared back seemed to infuse courage and confidence into Arabella as she left her suite of rooms to meet her grandfather.

Lord Timothy Grace's home was a lavish sprawling mansion, which sat atop the city, boasting beautiful gardens. Much of the exterior and interior marble had been quarried, she was told, from a fortnight's ride by wagon. Because he was at the far side of the city, his property was hedged with forest. It was an ancient, grand estate that had housed generations of Graces.

As Arabella slowly descended the staircase, Grandfather greeted her at the bottom.

"You are lovely, Arabella. A vision!" her Grandfather complimented. "Having you here makes this place feel like a home again. I am most pleased you have come, finally returned to where you belong."

"My thanks, Grandfather, for this exceptional dress and such a warm welcome," she replied, feeling tendrils of hope that she might build a strong familial connection with this man she was just beginning to know.

"I would like to keep you all to myself, but alas we must be away to the gala honoring your return."

"Yes, we must."

A carriage awaited them outside of the house as did her knights, also bathed and dressed in their formal military attire.

Luke met her at the bottom of the stairs and assisted her to the carriage on the other side of her grandfather. "You look beautiful tonight, Your Highness."

"Thank you." She smiled back. "You look handsome as well." Luke puffed out his chest and grabbed the lapel of his coat. She repressed a chuckle when she noted her grandfather giving a disapproving frown.

"Grandfather, I don't think I have introduced you to Sir Luke." Luke offered him his hand, and Grandfather gave him a hard look before extending his own. "This is Sir Roland, Sir Garner, and Sir Benton. Each is a very dear friend to me." She was determined to smooth the way between the men and her grandfather. It was critical that he understand her need to keep them close without ruffling feathers with his staff.

"Gentlemen, this is Lord Timothy Grace." They each shook hands with her grandfather. There was an awkward silence before Sir Luke took her hand and guided her into the elegant contraption.

She would like to have seen the city, but the confines of the carriage and the dark wouldn't allow it, so she would take the time in learning more of her grandfather.

"How long since Grandmother passed away?"

"Four months ago," he replied. From the hitch in his voice she knew the wound was still fresh. The loss, she realized, connected them; they were all trying to heal from the death of loved ones.

"Tell me of her," Arabella insisted softly.

"She was so much like your mother, headstrong and determined." Grandfather smiled with a glitter in his eye. "Even a little mischievous."

"Really?" Arabella encouraged him, ever so excited to hear of her family.

"Oh yes." He warmed to his subject as he talked of his wife of fifty-two years. He talked of her for almost ten minutes, before he solemnly said, "I have missed her every day since her passing." He patted Arabella's hand. "Glad am I that you have finally come home, Granddaughter."

Arabella wasn't sure how to respond to that. She might have come to Saldanzia, but she wouldn't be here long if she could help it. There was no way she would leave the plight of her people in the hands of Mason. "Yes, well . . . I am most grateful for your kind reception, Grandfather." She was sure her hesitation didn't go unnoticed.

"Of course, my dear. You have always belonged here and finally found the way."

What could she say to that? He obviously missed his family. What great hopes he must have once had that his daughter would have married a Saldanzian and settled there with her family, allowing her to take turns to rule as was her due. It must have been devastating for them to have their only child choose a man from another kingdom.

The carriage came to a halt, and though Arabella knew she needed to address this misconception, now was not the time. Luke opened the carriage door and gave his hand to her. She looked back at her grandfather for a second before accepting his hand and alighting the carriage. As soon as her grandfather was by her side, he whisked her into the large smooth cement home with eight large columns adorning the front entrance. Torchieres lit a wide path to the large edifice. Her father had described Saldanzia many times, but to actually see it was breathtaking.

"Your men can remain by the carriage, I'm sure there are plenty of soldiers stationed around."

"And miss out on all of this, Grandfather? I don't think so." She looked at her men and nodded to Benton, who fell back. Roland, Garner, and Luke followed directly behind her.

With her hand on her grandfather's arm, Arabella took a deep breath as they walked through the large wooden doors, held open by two men in uniforms.

Arabella was greeted with the floating strains of string instruments, laughter, and the tinkling sounds of glasses as hundreds of people congregated in a spacious room. The room was lit with thousands of candles suspended by multiple crystal chandeliers, and along the walls, sconces hung throughout. Lush greenery and white flowers cascaded down pillars and ringed the multiple balcony levels. The floral smell that prevailed was fresh and light despite the press of bodies.

Michael and Sophia McKenna quickly made their way to Arabella and Lord Timothy, the first to greet them as was custom. They were a very striking couple. Attractive and resplendent in some of the finest clothing she'd come across. It seemed the Saldanzian people were exceptional tailors.

"Lord and Lady McKenna," Arabella said, "I would like to introduce you to Sir Garner, Sir Roland, and Sir Luke."

"Welcome," Michael spoke graciously. "Sir Roland, I have heard mention of you."

"Sir?" Roland responded.

"The best horse trainer in all the Norlans, I am told." Michael paused. "'Twould be safe to assume Her Majesty's horse . . .'"

Arabella interrupted him. "Arabella."

"Very well then, was Arabella's horse trained by you?"

"By both of us, sir."

Michael looked at Arabella, his eyes narrowing then filling with delight. "I believe that," he responded. "The product of her mother, I daresay."

It was a lovely compliment. To interact with people who had known her mother made for such a pleasant diversion.

Sophia expertly moved to take Arabella's arm and started to walk with her. "You look lovely, dear. All the men here will be fighting for a dance with you. That dress is sensational." Her openness and smile were charming and made Arabella feel her tension ease.

"Thank you." Arabella's face reddened with the praise. "But I'm sure it won't be a problem."

Lady Sophia smiled knowingly and said, "We shall see."

They had not walked but a few steps when the Lorrings garnered her attention. The Lorrings were a cheerful couple whose family seemed to make up half of the group assembled. They introduced family member after family member, with names and faces she knew she'd never remember. She smiled politely and tried not to appear relieved when dinner was announced.

Grandfather led her to the long table that seated them on one side with the Blakes and the other side the Surreys. A few glances in the Blakes' direction left little doubt that they were unhappy with her presence. It was like walking over the hole of an asp. Arabella had Sir Garner by her side, though her men found places to sit among everyone else. Garner was by far the most diplomatic, and every bit the gentlemen. Though a bit younger than her father, she knew that women found him quite handsome, with his muscular build, blond hair, and blue eyes.

It was a little unnerving to be seated with the two families she was sure would be the hardest to win over. In some ways she felt at a disadvantage. Exhausted from the extended difficult travel, she'd not completely found her bearings in a foreign land, and yet the memories of the horrors she had endured for months were still fresh in her mind. It kept the urgency for forward movement needful. The Anchellian people had suffered terribly, and then to let Mason walk in and take over with no resistance was very humbling.

Arabella calmly answered many questions and deftly diverted many. Her father had been a magnificent statesman and had ingrained in her the art of diplomacy. Sir Garner was every bit as talented and was a veritable wealth of knowledge, versed in the many countries' politics and affairs of the Norlans. He even had several of the ladies blushing and near swooning when he spoke. It was evident that Lord Cleve Blake was annoyed with him, which made it almost comical.

Cleve Blake was not a man to mince words. "Many of us here are concerned about you being here so soon after an epidemic went through your country and killed so many. What is to say that you are not carrying the infection that will kill many of our citizens?" The room went instantly silent, and Arabella could feel the heat in her face.

So concerned that he was sitting next to her? Where did diplomacy go when there was no polite conversation for dinner? No wonder her mother didn't want to marry the man, he was insufferable. Cleve was already launching an assault to sway opinion against her. Most were looking at her, signs of alarm now evident on their faces. Arabella even saw people shift away from Luke and Roland.

"And yet you sit only a breath away from me?" Arabella smiled. "Obviously you are not too distressed." She feigned a light laugh, trying to defuse his fiery accusation as folly in light of their proximity.

Cleve held a tight-lipped smile. She knew she was fueling his derision but was aware his history with her mother had created this enemy long before her birth.

He didn't stop there, merely shifting, pressing harder, searching for a crack in her perceived facade. "How long do you intend to remain in Saldanzia? Or do you intend to take your place in the Ruling Five?" he asked. One could have heard a pin drop, the room had remained so quiet after his first salvo. The question was likely what most the guests had been asking themselves the moment they learned she was coming. One that she had been hoping to avoid for at least a few days. Aware that she needed to tread very carefully, and wishing now she'd taken a few moments in the carriage to visit with her grandfather, Arabella felt the weight of all eyes and ears on her, though the table extended a great distance. It was as if everyone was holding their breath.

Arabella looked at her grandfather, paused a moment to gather her thoughts and looked directly at Cleve, squaring her shoulders. "Anchelle is my priority right now." She emphasized the word *now*, so that no one could assume anything. "As it stands, I will visit with your congress, and then leave immediately for Anchelle." She felt her grandfather stiffen beside her, and Cleve's face hardened even more, which was hard to believe was possible. Exclamations of dismay sounded down the length of the banquet table.

Though she desperately wanted to talk of Anchelle, and a course of needed action, a celebration dinner was not the time or the place for the dire things Arabella would share. There were certain rules of etiquette for visiting dignitaries, and though the rules didn't seem to apply to Lord Blake, she wouldn't stoop to his combative level. It would regrettably have to wait till congress was called, and unfortunately Cleve would need to do that. Ethan had prepared her for the fact that Cleve would likely stall a fortnight to reinforce to all who held the ultimate power, but she desperately prayed he would call for an emergency congress, and start before the week's end. After tonight's dinner, she was certain that he had no intentions of being amiable. The despicable man would make any forward movement difficult. If only it was just the Blake family she had to contend with . . . She was growing concerned that her grandfather might present another issue altogether. She saw him out of the corner of her eye, and his rigid stance spoke volumes.

As dessert was being served, Arabella noticed Ethan enter and sit at the far end of the table. Her eyes had swept the room over the course of the evening, searching for him and wondering what kept him from being present in his family home. Ethan looked her way and nodded his head. A warm smile shot a tingle of awareness through her. Had she recalled just how handsome he was, cleaned up and in his dress suit? She found it difficult to take her eyes off of him. Though he was quickly caught up in a conversation with others around him, the company quieted from their several conversations as he stood and addressed the whole assembly.

"'Tis regrettable to be joining you all late to this lovely reception, but having just returned to the city, I was required to see to those things that have happened in my absence." Ethan stood with his glass in his hand. Several women tittered, and men chuckled in delight, and it was obvious this crowd favored their army's commander. "I heard before arriving this evening that congress was called for tomorrow, and I wanted to toast our leader, Lord Cleve Blake, on his decisive and cordial welcome of her Highness Arabella of Anchelle." He nodded first at Cleve before turning his attention to Arabella and nodded yet again.

Ethan maintained an even, pleasant expression through the whole speech, making it hard to believe that he had contrived a meeting of congress with such ease. Arabella looked at Cleve, who tried to muster a smile, but it came out as more of a grimace. A silence lay heavy in the air.

She had heard no such thing and was positive Ethan had just forced the point in her nation's behalf. He understood the urgency that most people sitting at this table did not. When was the last time these people had worried that their family was going to die from some horrible virus, or had a large imposing army at their gate? As far as Arabella knew, these people had lived in prosperity for some time. The Cronan, their only enemy, had never launched a full-out attack on the capital—ever. The outlying cities were another thing, but those that lived within these walls?

"Hear, hear!" several people spoke around her, their glasses raised, including Garner.

Her grandfather was, however, conspicuously silent. His features tightened even further.

Arabella knew the situation was tenuous. Cleve's disdain for her was fixed and unchangeable despite the fact he had never laid eyes on her before her entrance days past. Such pettiness irked her. Engaging Cleve in conversation, she graciously thanked him for agreeing to hold congress and then asked him multiple questions about himself. For the rest of the dinner, that was all he spoke of, his achievements and vast holdings. The Blakes' wealth extended across the country, and he continued to prattle on interminably, while Arabella found herself drifting and struggling to pay attention as so many concerns rattled around in her thoughts.

After dessert, Garner started to help Arabella from her seat, but her grandfather quickly stepped in.

"Sorry, my lord," Garner spoke while bowing, "didn't mean to step on toes. We are quite used to taking care of your lovely granddaughter."

Her grandfather grumbled a response before capturing her arm and leading her away from Garner and the others they had sat next to. They were stopped almost immediately by cousins to the Lorrings who had seen Palachio yesterday as Arabella had entered the city. The Lorrings were known for their own horse breeding with fine stables and had endless questions about the magnificent creature. Arabella made eye contact with Roland, who swiftly made his way to her side. She made introductions and visited for a time, aware her grandfather was not pleased with the discussion. She was relieved some time later when the sound of musical instruments being tuned reached everyone's ears.

She knew it was a signal for her celebratory first dance in Saldanzia, but she found herself unsure of whom she would dance with. Cleve Blake was the ruling Lord of the Five, which would make him the obvious choice, but they were all guests in the McKennas' home? Michael or Cleve? One was infinitely better than the other. Not that she had a choice; she would be a gracious guest regardless.

Arabella turned when she felt a firm hand on her back. The relief and the thrill of seeing Ethan holding out his hand with a devilish smile on his face made her heart quicken exponentially. She returned the smile, very aware of the dashing figure he cut in his black suit with military insignia.

"May I?" he asked, looking intently at her.

She placed her hand on his, and he began to walk with her to the center. With all eyes on them, the music played lightly in the background.

"I had to arm wrestle my father and Cleve for the first dance. 'Tis obvious I was the winner," he whispered as they walked.

Her smile got bigger as he turned her to face him. "I don't believe you one bit," she whispered back.

"You look stunning," he said, a moment before he took her in his arms. His eyes seemed to tangle with her own.

What could she say to that? She was out of breath the moment he had taken her hand. The music tuning stopped for a breath and then began a traditional lilting waltz. Moments later, he led her gracefully backwards. He never took his eyes off of her, and she was powerless to do any differently.

Arabella knew she shouldn't be caught up like this, shouldn't be thinking of him as anything except as a dear friend—but the feeling inside of her made her feel like she had wings to fly. He grabbed her waist and lifted her in the air, twirling her with practiced ease just to prove her point. They continued to glide across the room, their eyes only on each other.

Others finally joined the dance and Arabella could finally speak as he brought her especially close. "You are a very good dancer," she said, breaking the intensity of the moment. She couldn't allow herself down that path.

"Are you surprised?" he asked

"Perhaps a little" was her coy response.

"To be completely honest, I rarely attend any event that includes dancing," he admitted.

"Really?" She couldn't hide her disbelief. His dancing was much better than average.

"I have a little sister that blackmails me all the time into dancing with her," Ethan said with a smile, then dipped Arabella down so that her body was parallel to the ground, within inches of touching, a dance move she had never experienced before. When he brought her back up, especially close, his devilish smile reappeared. "What she doesn't know is that my parents know of those escapades she is blackmailing me with, and I just can't tell her no," he admitted with a rueful smile.

How adorable! Arabella thought. The big strong warrior had a weak spot for his sister.

"So you let her blackmail you into coming tonight?" she questioned.

The music set was coming to a close and Ethan brought Arabella down so that she almost lay on his knee, his face inches from her own.

Arabella held her breath, and her heart felt like it was going to come out of her chest. He held her there for a long moment before bringing her up. "I didn't come for her," he stated, before he bowed and then took her hands into his own, then kissed each one. *Oh help me!* she thought, wanting to fan herself and the heightened color that was sure to be staining her cheeks.

Applause exploded in the air, and Arabella looked all around her, noticing the mixture of faces. Most were smiling, some held shock, and Cleve Blake held a sneer. Something she was coming to expect of the man. She couldn't analyze it too much, wanting to just enjoy the fleeting moment. All too soon the weight of her world would press back upon her.

Still holding one of her hands, Ethan led her to her grandfather, who gladly claimed her for a short time, before Lord Lorring asked for a dance. Thereafter followed dancing with many of the Lorrings' relatives. There were so many of them that she knew she couldn't dance with all of them before night's end. But most were very gracious and a happy lot. It was hard not to like them. However, after an hour of dancing, she was ready for a break.

She felt relief as Luke snatched her away. He led her out in the middle of the floor against her protests, and an Anchellian folk song began to play. Arabella opened her eyes wide at Luke, and she shook her head at him. The dance was daring and had a much different feel than the dances thus far. Besides, there was the fact that she was in need of some rest. Luke smiled and nodded. People cleared the floor, but Garner had found a partner, and Arabella found courage as she saw Michael and Sophia McKenna come out onto the ballroom floor.

The beat picked up and Luke pulled her to him and began the close intricate moves. Arabella didn't have to think about it, her body just responded to the tempo, as it had many times in the past. Their feet were in unison as they jumped, stepped, and stomped to the music. They were perfectly matched and synchronized to perfection because they had practiced their whole lives together.

She glanced over at Michael and Sophia several times to see them mostly keeping up. Sophia's head lay back and she was laughing. People around them were tapping their toes, watching the proceeding with great interest. Pretty soon a cute, blonde-haired girl had pulled Ethan onto the ballroom floor, and to Arabella's astonishment, and it seemed others' around, they, too, began the quick-paced dance. The audience whooped and hollered and others tried to join in the foreign movements. As the song wore on the music got faster and faster. The skill level in performing increased, the part that Luke really liked to show off. Picking up Arabella, he lifted her over his shoulder and then down around the front, barely missing the floor. She had complete trust in him, though those around them gasped in surprise and then applauded. Luke smiled from ear to ear as the tempo increased. Sophia and Michael backed away, as did Garner and his dance partner, though Ethan and his partner stayed in.

Arabella and Luke were breathing heavily when the song concluded. She definitely needed a break after that one. Luke took her arm and they laughed merrily as everyone cheered loudly and clapped their hands.

Laughing Luke put his head close to her own. "Hopefully that swayed people's opinion in our favor." Arabella nodded her head. Everything she did and said would form people's opinions, and right now, she needed people to favor her and the cause of Anchelle.

There was a short intermission while Arabella sought out the Surreys and visited with Lord and Lady Surrey as well as several adult grandchildren. Arabella's father had told her they had a prosperous mining and jewelry business, so she inquired as to the practices that allowed for safe underground mining and to their success in securing skilled artisans. They obviously were very proud of their accomplishments and spent a great deal of time educating Arabella. Their grandson, a goldsmith, had the entire family wearing his jewelry at the ball, which they wore with pride.

The music started up again, and Arabella danced with Lord Surrey, and then a few other gentlemen that were also close to her grandfather's age. She was grateful that they were very sedate dances; her feet were getting tired and she was trying not to limp as the night wore on. Arabella's dance with Luke had made her healing injuries shout out in protest.

At last she grabbed grandfather's arm and made her way to Ethan, who had a girl on each arm. A small twinge grabbed her heart as she saw the girls' arms linked possessively on Ethan. But she owed him a thank you, at the very least. The night had been a success because of what Ethan had accomplished at dinner this night, neatly boxing Lord Blake into action.

The long blonde-haired girl that had danced the Anchellian folk song with Ethan stepped away from him with a wide smile on her face. She darted a small shy glance to Lord Grace, who it seemed intimidated many of those of the younger crowd, before proceeding to Arabella.

"Your Highness," she spoke with a small bow. "I've been ever so excited to make your acquaintance. Mother told me how she and your mother were the best of friends." The blonde-haired, brown-eyed girl was possibly a year or two younger than Arabella.

Arabella smiled at the lovely and vivacious young lady and gave a questioning look to Ethan.

"Your Highness," he said, bowing. Arabella wanted to correct him and tell him to call her by her given name, but she doubted her grandfather would approve the departure from protocol. She was treading in unsure waters with him. And she wasn't at all sure if in this kind of setting it was appropriate to use familiar names. "Lord Grace." Ethan inclined his head to Lord Grace, then turned back to Arabella. "May I present Lady Claire McKenna, my sister, and Lady Lacey Andrews, niece of Lord Surrey."

The two women were a study in contrasts, where Claire was light haired with a tall, thin, regal frame and a smattering of freckles across her patrician features, she yet exuded an air of innocence. Lady Lacey was petite with stunning raven hair and curves she'd once heard knights wax on in describing the feminine ideal. Claire's eyes were filled with open delight while her companions narrowed on Arabella before turning and taking a leisurely and sultry examination of Ethan in his well-fitting attire.

Lady Andrews clutched possessively at Ethan's arm while Claire took Arabella's in her own hand as a warm welcome.

"You are as beautiful as we have heard tales of," Claire gushed. "I didn't know if I wanted to believe them, but now that I've seen you, I don't think the girls of Saldanzia can doubt."

"They are extremely exaggerated, obviously, look at you both." It was always uncomfortable to Arabella when anyone made mention of her features. Hardly seemed truly subjective that often the people were biased, as though having the station of princess or queen made you beautiful regardless of the actual form.

"Ethan, I am so glad you are finally back from your travels abroad." Lady Lacey turned her back on Arabella to speak to Ethan only. It was a shocking breach of etiquette. "My uncle was just saying he hoped you would be available to join us again for a visit at his country estate."

Luke's boisterous voice interrupted the unveiled proposition. "Ethan, you are keeping all the pretty women to yourself tonight. Please make the introductions." It was all Arabella could do to not roll her eyes at Luke's outrageous attentions to the attractive women.

"Lady Claire, Lady Lacey, this is Sir Luke of Anchelle," Ethan cordially introduced.

"Enchanted, ladies!" Luke first took Lady Claire's hand and kissed it, looking her in the eyes the whole time till she giggled. "Your beauty can only be compared to the summers in Anchelle," he exclaimed. He spoke solemnly, making Claire's smile stretch and cheeks redden.

Arabella watched as Ethan smoothly removed the arm of the raven-haired beauty and turned his frame and attention solely to her person. Verdant green eyes traveled again down her person and back to her eyes, and she saw the message in the movements. A flush crept up her neck, with the sure knowledge that she was the only woman in the room of interest to him. *How can such nearly imperceptible actions speak with such clarity?* she marveled.

As the night wore on and she found herself struggling to focus on the conversation, a soft sigh escaped. It was hard to keep a smile on her face and her shoulder and back straight. They still ached from the journey and the dancing. It was exhausting to be diplomatic, and she was tired of the shallow compliments, though she knew was in great need of their respect before any would agree to send an army to Anchelle's aid. All of this spectacle was a necessary evil. One she longed to avoid. Arabella would like nothing more than to crawl into a nice comfortable bed at the moment, but she had one thing left to do before the night was through.

"Lord McKenna, might I have a word with you?" Arabella asked.

"Ethan," he said seriously. "I'm definitely not Lord McKenna." He held his arm for Arabella to take hold of.

"Grandfather, I will only be a moment. If you don't mind, I would like to retire for the evening. Could I have the carriage sent back for you?"

"Nonsense," he insisted. "I am ready as well. I will just give the host our appreciation and meet you at the carriage."

Arabella bade farewell to Lady Claire and Lacey, and Ethan led her around the crowd of people still milling. He took her past Cleve so she could thank him again for starting congress tomorrow. His facial expressions were not very encouraging.

Ethan and Arabella didn't talk till they were outside in the crisp spring air. The stars were making a brilliant show this evening. She turned to look at him, releasing his arm and leaning her head back to look into his green eyes. Her men were close, including Benton, but they gave them some space.

"My thanks, my lord," she spoke, and she reached up and kissed his cheek.

He was still for a moment. "Whatever for? I might have to do whatever it is more often, so that I might get another kiss from the beautiful queen of Anchelle."

"Mayhaps for saving my life and escorting me safely here." She raised her eyebrows at him. "For tonight . . . I think you know well to what I refer."

He smiled then leaned in and whispered, "I think Cleve might be plotting my demise even as we speak, but the look on his face was priceless."

She laughed out loud.

⌒

As the carriage left the drive from the McKenna's estate, Grandfather came right to the point. "You can't possibly be thinking of going back to Anchelle, Arabella!"

"I am," she replied firmly, and she wasn't backing down.

"Arabella, 'tis madness. You managed to escape before the Chilton king could capture you. 'Twas the most intelligent thing you could have done. Now you must stay here, be protected, and take your rightful place in our family."

Arabella looked at the man who had been her mother's father and could hardly believe what she was hearing. Though it wasn't completely unexpected, she had hoped he would understand.

"Grandfather, I am a queen, a protector. I love my people, and they all look to me to free them from Mason's tyranny. I shall do it, or I shall die trying. Nothing is of greater importance than they. It is my duty."

She wanted to tell them that she *had* a family. She had had an adopted family for her twenty-one years: so many people had loved her, trained and taught her, so many dear people in her life. But she knew that would only be a slap in his face. It wouldn't help him to understand Edmund, who had been an adopted grandfather to her, or George, who had remained with the people when she fled. Their faces were etched in her mind, she feared for them, for so many that she loved were in grave danger with Mason's occupation. How would they be treated? She knew that if required, she would give her life for her people and their freedom. That was what leaders did for their people. They served their people, as had her father.

"What of your duty, to the people of Saldanzia?" he hissed. His voice continued to increase in volume. "Your mother would be leading these people right now if she had stayed and done her duty!" He yelled in his fierce anger, and it was like a physical blow to her face.

He instantly calmed down and lowered his voice. "It needn't be you, to rule Anchelle. You could crown one of your favored knights to be king and let them rule. I'm certain they have much more experience in warfare than a newly made queen. I can see that you care for them. You are devoted to them. Surely one of them is qualified to rule Anchelle. Would it not be better for the country to have a king that was a military man, a sea-soned knight?"

The radical thought took her aback. Would Anchelle do better to have Benton, or Garner, or even Luke lead them? Would they have fled to another country for help? Could they have saved Anchelle? She looked into her grandfather's eyes. "You speak of my inexperience and yet you would have me rule Saldanzia?" she spoke boldly, unwilling to let the blatant hypocrisy stand.

Silence was her answer.

CHAPTER 9

Ethan watched Arabella's carriage drive away. What was he getting into? She was magnificent tonight. Never had a woman occupied so much of his thoughts. He knew he was falling hard for her, but could he really ask his own people to go to war for another country? Could he lead subjectively? It was the worst of times to consider splitting up his forces with the Cronan stirring up trouble in the outlying cities and in places they hadn't seen them before. The Cronan were nothing if not unpredictable, but he knew it wasn't impossible to go to her aid, or he would never have brought her here. It would take some maneuvering, but it was possible. His army was well trained and very capable. After all, should a tyrant rule a neighbor it likely wouldn't be long before the tyrant was looking about for more conquests.

A part of him longed to ask her to stay here with her grandfather and help rule Saldanzia, to allow him to officially court her. But he knew this was wishful thinking. He'd witnessed the way she had cared for her people and knew that she chafed at the delays that kept her away. Arabella belonged to the people of Anchelle. Her duty was foremost to her lands and the people, and he couldn't fault her for it. Had he not felt it every day of his life? Raised and prepared for the purpose to serve and see to the safety of his own countrymen. He already knew what her decision would be. It would be his as well in her place. As he pondered on the players and politics it was sure to be a struggle in Saldanzia, Arabella had a fight on her hands from multiple fronts, which he knew as a military strategist was the most difficult of all to navigate.

Sleep eluded her. She tossed and turned all night. Grandfather's words ran over and over in her mind. Never had she allowed such doubts of her ability to lead be entertained. From the moment of birth, her life had one course and one purpose to strive and prepare for: the day she would rule as queen of Anchelle. Never blessed with siblings, it had always been known to every citizen that one day she would rule. Since she could remember, her days and life were a round of deportment lessons, sewing circles, horsemanship lessons, academic lessons, menu planning, reception planning, husbandry for the land, war room and defense meetings. No, it had never been a question of *if* she would lead; it had only been subject to *when* her reign would begin. Her eyes smarted with a cascading remembrance of her losses. The dark earthen mounds that had covered the view as she fled her home. Too soon, much too soon, that day had come. She lamented yet again the loss of her parents, who should still be alive, to see her married, to meet her children. The injustice of their premature parting was devastating in the dark of night, in a foreign land, with a battle on the horizon to secure aid for her people. If Saldanzia refused their assistance, she very well could have lost her country already, mere months after being crowned.

Before the dawn, she finally arose, dressed, and went to the stables. Roland and Luke followed her. She didn't know how they all knew to gather. It was a mystery, but the whole of her guard were in the stables minutes after her arrival. They tacked and mounted their horses and rode in silence for some time, heading toward the gates of the city.

"Garner?" she questioned her senior commander, seeking his opinion.

He read her mind and spoke his own. "I'm hesitant to speak of it, but 'tis obvious to all that Lord Blake is against you. He doesn't want you here, and he'll do what is necessary to make your life miserable should you stay. I can see only one way to use it to our favor."

It was a blow to have Garner cut straight to the heart of the matter. Cleve Blake's disdain was evident to all who shared the room with him and Arabella.

Garner paused, creating a dramatic effect as he rubbed his chin thoughtfully. "If you were to claim a desire to remain here, as one of the Ruling Five, it might motivate his bitter soul to send their army to help instead."

"Hmm, it may work," Arabella slowly spoke. She saw the validity of the suggestion. If it became necessary, could she pull off the subterfuge? Loathing even the appearance of a lie, she dreaded the very thought of playing a part. Would plain speech render the same result?

"It may be our only chance," Roland spoke up. "Though I think some of the Four would side with you, your grandfather may be your biggest challenge." There were multiple grunts of agreement from the men. It squeezed the breath from her lungs. Had her initial hope for a close kinship with her grandfather been a dream? True, her parents had never reconciled before her mother passed away. The angry words from the carriage ride played through her mind.

Had they heard his angry tirade? Though Grandfather's demeanor at dinner had probably been a good indicator, as well as his seeming detachment at every turn in regard to her guard. Though he saw to their housing and care for their animals, he'd not sought out or engaged any of them in conversation.

"Should they deny our request we could ride from kingdom to kingdom in the Norlans and raise a banner to gather an army.

Surely those nations must be nervous that Mason is coming for them next," Luke said, changing directions.

"Mason may already be in the other Norlan countries," Benton stated quietly. "If that be the case, the other Norlan countries may already be lost."

"If we fail here, we won't have another choice," Luke argued. Like a dog with a bone, he couldn't let it go.

"The Norlans have already failed us," Arabella interjected, putting a stop to the circle they traveled. "None answered our messengers and pleas for assistance. We did not come all this way and lose good men to fail to secure an army. I will make it so."

The edifice held very few people, though the building itself was massive. Arabella looked over the assembly that had gathered. These people would decide the fate of her nation. She looked at each person, gauging their reaction to her. On the first row sat the five families. On the far left Cleve stood, the epitome of arrogance, every movement meant to convey his supremacy and the power he wielded. Following down the line, her eyes came to Lord Surrey, who made eye contact with her and solemnly nodded his head, respectful but giving her no indication of his feelings toward her. The Lorrings didn't look up but talked among themselves. Her grandfather gave her naught but a stern look. And finally her eyes settled on Ethan, whose head tilted and a flirtatious wink and wide smile served to bolster her flagging confidence. The entire McKenna family sat on one bench, a handsome formidable unit.

Cleve stood in front of the group and called everyone to order. He spoke briefly to thank the families for answering the call to congress quickly, though it was sure that all in attendance were aware of his disdain at being forced to meet, then turned the floor over to Arabella.

Arabella took a measured breath, releasing it slowly as she rose. Meeting the eye of each person in attendance, she didn't say anything for a moment, needing to gather her thoughts and emotions in a way that would be compelling, disciplined, and not like an overwrought young girl. If she were too emotional people might think she was exaggerating the case. The heavy silence was beginning to become uncomfortable, with people shifting in their seats.

"Ten months ago," Arabella began, "a runner came from the kingdom of Theron requesting my father's help."

All those assembled in this room knew Theron was a very small country in the heart of the Norlans that lay between Anchelle and Chilton. A very peaceful country that raised sheep and cotton.

"Mason Kiefer, who had succeeded his father as king of Chilton, had gone into Theron's southern border cities of Acropolis and Minerva and taken control of them. He claimed they were part of Chilton since the one-hundred-year war, but they maintained that Acropolis and Minerva have been part of Theron for five hundred years.

"My father helped drive the Chilton army out of Theron. A month later, Mason's army went back to the cities and razed them to the ground, butchered the livestock, and burned the crops, leaving them completely desolate. Those he didn't kill he took back to Chilton as slaves." Murmurs were heard throughout the room, and peoples faces were a mix of shock and disbelief. Slavery was an evil long rooted out of the continent!

"My father was readying his army to help take back those enslaved when the shivers ripped through our country," Arabella explained. "Anchelle boasted the largest army in the Norlans. With the shivers . . . well, it has been reduced drastically. The king, my father, along with over half of the people of Anchelle, were lost to us." She stood resolutely, her voice steady, though the pain in her begged for release.

"What makes you believe that Anchelle still stands?" Lorring asked. "Why wouldn't Mason burn it to the ground in retaliation?" A fair question, considering the awful reprisal in Theron.

"Our spies determined that Mason wants Anchelle intact. Besides the crop production, our precious ores and infrastructure are the envy of the Norlans. 'Twould seem he fancies to make it the capital of his conquests."

What Arabella omitted was that not only was Anchelle the principal target, but so was she. But that wasn't something she intended to tell those present; it was ancillary to the fundamentals of the conflict.

Arabella was never sure if Mason truly wanted her personally or he just thought it was the easiest way to get Anchelle. Thaddeus held firm in the belief it was the former, but Arabella had never questioned or asked for any details on how he knew this. It was unnerving enough to know that a man of Mason's caliber had his eye fixed on her.

"If you would like witnesses to any of these accounts, Sir Garner and Sir Benton were at Acropolis and Minerva. They would be willing to answer any questions."

"Were there any survivors?" Lorring asked.

Arabella looked to Garner to speak.

"There were fifty-nine women and children from Minerva that escaped into the mountains when they saw the army coming again," Garner replied.

"How many were enslaved?" Ethan asked, the disgust in his voice evident.

Once again Garner spoke up solemnly. "Over three thousand, m'lord."

A few more questions were asked before Arabella resumed talking. She pleaded with their basic humanity to help her stop Mason before he got any further in his quest for power and dominion. Though it was plausible to suggest that the tyrant would come all the way to Saldanzia, in his quest for domination, she knew the lack of proof would only weaken her credibility.

"I realize that it is very expensive to maintain an army, and we would gladly compensate the men that are leaving their families to help in this cause." She looked at each person again to gauge their reaction. It would be most indelicate to name a price. Not wanting to offend anyone by suggesting they were paying them off like mercenaries or undervaluing the life of their soldiers, it seemed to be more appropriate to deal with the army in determining compensation, in needed foods and medicines. The primary goal was to raise her voice to a moral issue, rather than a financial issue to benefit Saldanzia.

"How could you possibly promise us funding when Mason has taken over your city? Your treasury has been sacked by now." Cleve's lips moved into a hard line, his eyebrows lifted in clear disdain.

"Though I am bound to not disclose the details, I ask that you trust my word as the sovereign of Anchelle." Arabella calmly spoke and clearly as though she was talking to a child. Though she found it increasingly difficult to remain calm around the infuriating, arrogant man. "I swear to you with an oath that your men will receive half of the agreed-upon wages once they reach the Meadows of Glory in Anchelle. This should provide assurance that they will be compensated. Should the funds not be paid as stated, our deal will be void before the men ever see battle." She let that sink in before she added, "My only stipulation is that every soldier be given the choice to participate, this must be a volunteer basis. I don't believe that any man should be made to go to war for something they don't believe in."

In Arabella's thinking they would be practically useless if they were forced to be there. Additionally, they would have to be paid well. She hated the need for hiring foreign men for battle. The money aspect had initially felt wrong to the young queen when it was first suggested. It had seemed reprehensible, but her own soldiers earned a wage, and money would be needed for food, clothing, medicine, weapons, and to compensate for time away from their loved ones when they could not earn other funds. War campaigns always carried a heavy expense. Funds were critical to secure victory; in truth it was a necessary evil she had come to understand.

"On behalf of the country of Anchelle, and those of Theron, I express my gratitude for your willingness to hear our plea. We shall remove ourselves forthwith, to allow all you time to deliberate."

Head held high, she walked with determination out the doors of the chamber, down the long echoing halls and out into the warm spring morning, and kept walking and allowed her mind to review. It was her first foreign address as monarch, and though she felt guided in her words she yet played over each word, searching for a missed fact or other weakness. It would seem her heart was determined to come out of her chest, so hard did it pound in time with her head, which made for a spectacular headache, making further reflection difficult. It was a most terrible feeling to be at the mercy of foreigners. The pounding changed to an oppressive pressure on her body, which served to slow her forward motion.

Cleve would probably squash the idea, and her own grandfather could second the motion. That was all it would take to shut down any support. Though she despised the negative thoughts they threatened to swamp her. Was there and had there ever really been a chance at success? Had she been wasting precious time on the impossible? Could all their efforts be for naught? Her people, abandoned by their own queen and who were being ruled at this very moment by a wicked man who cared not a whit for them. The least amount of time under his rule, the better.

Despair gripped her. Should she have allowed his hideous suit to preserve her people? The sources her father had sent to Chilton had described hungry peasants in squalid conditions, and that was before he'd taken the people of Theron as slaves. No, had it simply been a matter of marrying a monster—though the very thought made bile rise, she would have. To keep her people healthy and prosperous, she'd have made the necessary sacrifice. Those who led with cruelty and control through fear and enslavement would destroy a kingdom and eventually force an uprising. A warmth settled over her entire frame. Her actions, decisions, and desires were always to the welfare of her people. Her course had been right. Now she prayed fervently that the Saldanzians would be guided to action.

⁓

Ethan watched her walk away once again, and he didn't like it one bit. Every moment in her company was enlivening, yet ever so brief it seemed, with her always leaving him in want of more of her time and person. What a powerful vision she'd been, stating the cause of Anchelle and the Norlans in whole. She made a play on their humanity, and in his case it worked effectively. He had travelers' reports on the cities of Acropolis and Minerva, but before he could send out scouts to get an accurate description, the shivers had shut down travel for an extended time. His disgust and disquiet for King Mason continued to grow. History was riddled with men who craved power, and rarely was it ever satiated in the lust for more. His gut said that once the kingdoms of the Norlans were all under his control, his army replenished, it was only a matter of time before the tyrant set his sights on Saldanzia. In retrospect Ethan recognized that if all he knew of Mason was the harm that had come to Arabella because of the king he would have relished the opportunity to meet him on the field of battle. Personal feelings in this case would align with his military role in defending the weak and maintaining their own sovereign borders.

The room was in utter turmoil, with people shouting and talking over others for several minutes before Cleve brought everyone to order.

"We will go around the room and hear each of the Five's thoughts before we cast lots. Lorring will go first." Cleve stretched out his hand to indicate the man.

Lorring rose from his chair in one smooth motion. The man, though short, had an air of confidence. With the loss of his firstborn son, Ethan had seen a more sedate Lorring emerge that brought a no-nonsense attitude.

"Lords and ladies," Lorring began, the room now completely silent. He halted for a moment, seemingly to decide how to best proceed. "I for one cannot rest easy knowing that a man such as Mason Kiefer exists and exercises authority over others as I've heard today." He looked first at his wife and then at his daughter, who would be the next to rule from the Lorring family. "If all I had ever heard today were the deeds of Mason Kiefer, it would be enough to satisfy me that he needs to be stopped."

His position was of no surprise to Ethan. He watched Surrey and Cleve closely to see what their reactions were to Lorring's statement. Cleve was definitely displeased, but Surrey was unreadable.

Though giving Lorring a chance to speak his mind, Cleve had to inject his own thoughts. "That is if they are not lying." Cleve couldn't hide his contempt. "We have no way of knowing if she speaks the truth." This brought a growl from both Lord Grace and Lord McKenna.

Cleve turned to Ethan. "What exactly did you see, when on your last scouting mission?"

Though Ethan believed every word of what Arabella and her guard had shared, he was keenly aware of his own lack of first-hand knowledge of the charges they had laid against Mason: only rumors, though from multiple sources in different kingdoms.

"I saw four of Mason Kiefer's men attack Queen Arabella." Ethan knew he needn't articulate; that alone was an act of war. Saldanzians held strictly to this code, as did other nations.

"And how do we know for sure she is who she says she is?" Cleve asked.

Ethan looked to Timothy Grace, whose face looked like a thundercloud.

"I found a note intended for Arabella on the back of one of the dead Anchellian soldiers. It was a malevolent warning from Mason to Arabella that she return or more damage would be done."

"I demand to see this evidence!" Cleve snarled.

Having anticipated this very thing, Ethan had put it in his pocket that morning. He handed it to Timothy; her grandfather deserved to understand. Lord Grace looked at it thoughtfully before passing it on, finally making its way to Cleve.

Cleve, clearly piqued that his position at the head meant he read it last, spent a mere moment reading before tossing it to the desk. "First, this does not prove that she is Arabella, Queen of Anchelle. Secondly how do we know that 'tis not a ruse to pull our army from Saldanzia so that invaders can come in?"

Though Ethan knew in his heart that was not the truth, today he could not prove otherwise. Cleve did not like or want to help Arabella in any way.

"I think the note is proof," Lorring interjected. "What was her response to the ghastly message, Ethan?" he asked.

"None," Ethan replied. "She never saw it."

"Could this woman have put the note on the dead soldier's body before you conveniently found it or met up with the girl?" Cleve asked derisively, determined to call Arabella an imposter and thus beneath their notice.

Ethan found the line of questioning ridiculous. Cleve seemed to be pulling at shadows.

Timothy Grace finally stood, raising his hand for everyone's silence. "I have a proposition." This seemed to garner the attention of everyone in attendance, and the body assembled quieted down. "I truly believe my granddaughter, and also believe the threat is real." Cleve tried to interrupt. Timothy silenced him with a look that Ethan found quite humorous and had to hide a smile. "I understand that you don't," he said, looking at Cleve, "but I have a solution." He looked at all those sitting in the room, looking at each one as his granddaughter had done over an hour ago. Everyone waited with bated breath.

"Let's give Arabella the option, she can remain here, and rescind her throne as queen of Anchelle to one of her countrymen, and we will send a third of our army. If she were to give the throne to someone else, she would prove that she loves her country, and wants the best for it, assuring us this isn't a ruse and Mason is who she claims he is. With two-thirds of our army remaining, we would be sufficiently strong to any onslaught." He looked pointedly at Cleve.

Ethan looked at Cleve's apoplectic, spluttering face. Questioning her heritage was a petty insult meant to cut Lord Timothy and sever a growing attachment for a girl, knowing he had never before met his own granddaughter. Lord Blake didn't want to aid Arabella, but having her as a Ruling Five would be even worse. When Lord Timothy died, the Grace family would not have an heir to continue their place, therefore forfeiting their right to rule. Ethan knew that Cleve was counting on it to increase and consolidate his family's position. The Graces, Lorrings, and McKennas often voted similarly, leaving the Blakes and Surreys on the opposing side. Reducing the Ruling Five to Four would lead to two against two with no deciding factor. Such a shift in their well-balanced system would require a change to their government, one he was sure Cleve had been preparing for decades.

Ethan believed wholeheartedly that Arabella spoke fact and if anything was understating her position, certainly her own welfare. The king of Chilton meant to have her at any cost, yet she hadn't even mentioned the constant threat to her own person. No, she spoke the truth and Ethan was willing to bet the lives of his own people. Thankfully, they had a sufficient army to defend and aid Anchelle and the Norlans. Cleve would put up as many roadblocks as possible. Lord Blake's focus had always been on the governing and power to affect the laws, but the man had no comprehensive understanding of military operations, never having spent time going through the inner workings of the military, likely finding it pedestrian and beneath him other than to command the safety of their borders.

Ethan felt confident that Arabella would rescind the throne if it meant her people's liberation, and though he had dreamed of her remaining in Saldanzia, he didn't want her to be forced to make that choice. From observing her every interaction, it was evident that though young, she was a competent and strong

leader who had the full support of her people, if her guards were
to be believed.

Cleve interrupted his train of thought. "I would only be willing to go along with Timothy's idea, if she were to set aside her
claim to the throne of Anchelle." To clarify, Cleve spoke again.
"Anchelle would be annexed into Saldanzia, and their governing
would be under the Rule of Five."

Surrey nodded his head immediately. "That would be most
beneficial to us."

"That would make us the tyrants," Michael McKenna
injected. "Were we in a similar position begging Anchelle to
help us, how many of you would welcome a queen? Would you
willingly hand over our form of government, our identity as
Saldazians?"

"Ridiculous. We would never be found in such a weak position, and it's not like she wouldn't be ruling Saldanzia for a time
as well one day," Cleve spat. "If we verify her claims."

Ethan felt his anger rise precipitously.

"Aside from the question of governance, if we have proof of
Mason's treachery would everyone be willing to send an army?"
Ethan asked with a decided steel edge.

"We don't have proof," Surrey pointed out.

His father stood up claiming the attention of those assembled.
He waited patiently for the noise to die down. "The McKennas
have yet to speak," he challenged Cleve, calmly looking at him.

Cleve could only acquiesce and dipped his head in approval.

"I kept in regular contact with King Garrett of Anchelle
throughout the years." Michael began. "He was a trusted friend
of mine," Michael said without apology. His feelings evident
for the man laid plainly for those around him to see. "In a correspondence from Michael I learned of Mason Kiefer's invasion
into Minerva and Acropolis the first time, and King Garrett's
subsequent expulsion of Chilton's soldiers from the country.
I also learned of the shivers first entering their country, as
Arabella has stated. Though I can't claim any knowledge of the
massacres that took place following the missive arriving here,

everything else Arabella claims parallels the letter I received from Michael."

Michael nodded at Ethan to continue. They had talked of this before coming. Even though Ethan had never read the letter, it was what had inspired them to send spies to the Norlans, after the shivers was contained. It was what lead Ethan to Arabella.

"I have scouts all over the Norlans right now, including Anchelle, Theron, Lassiter, and Chilton. I expect them back in as soon as ten days. Could we all agree if evidence from our scouts confirms Mason's perfidy? Furthermore," he looked at Cleve and Surrey, "if Mason is found to be a viable threat to our own sovereignty, will you send our army?"

"What if we are attacked here while our army is away?" Cleve pushed again.

"We will leave a significant force here to maintain Saldanzia," Ethan firmly answered.

"Are you willing to bet your mother and sister's lives?" Cleve asked heatedly.

Ethan looked at his mother and sister. Both nodded at him, letting him know they trusted his leadership. "I am."

There were a host of questions about how long it would take the military to mobilize and how long of a campaign it might be, and the distances that might need to be traveled to rout the usurping Chilton king.

While Cleve had been the first to question the readiness of their military, it was evident he did not care for the direction the questions were leading and moved to shut down any further speculation of support. "'Twould seem we are at an impasse. Commander, you have a fortnight to produce evidence. Then we will reconvene to decide on the matter."

Ethan was wary for Cleve to concede that easily to delay a decision. Surely there was an agenda. Letting out the breath he was holding, Ethan had, for a second, felt like he must choose between his mother and sister or Arabella. It wasn't the case, but he truly felt responsible for the protection of all of them. War was not new to him. Fighting was something he knew all too well.

Under no circumstances would he want his mother, Claire, or Arabella to ever see any of its horrors. When he'd seen Arabella being chased by Mason's men, the small woman forced to defend herself against them, something had nearly come undone in him. Had fighting for his own life or fellow countrymen ever awakened such an all-encompassing, visceral response?

Arabella would not be pleased with the delay. She was chafing to act, and he couldn't fault her in that. But he knew that what his scouts reported would be the best chance to secure his nation's aid. Ethan would take her the news himself, not wanting her grandfather to find her first. Truly he was gravely concerned with her grandfather's motives at the moment. Did Timothy Grace act out of a love to protect her, or was it a selfish motivation, a desire for his legacy in Saldanzia to live on? Perhaps both, but that he would try to pen her in and force her to abdicate the throne hardly seemed to even acknowledge the woman she truly was, a beloved capable queen who alone ruled a kingdom.

Slipping out the door before anyone noticed he was missing, he went to find her. Roland leaned casually against a pillar but sighted him immediately. He nodded eastward. Throwing himself upon his mount, Ethan pushed his horse to a light canter. It wouldn't do to go racing through town, but he was anxious to reach her. Minutes later he spied her guard at the doors of a church.

The stately old church dated a thousand years before his own birth. It was his favored place of sanctum. The well-crafted, sturdy rock exterior would continue to withstand the elements for another millennium, but the interior was the true crowning glory. Priceless works of art, depicting God and His creations on this planet in murals, graced each wall. Ethan was delighted to find that she had come to this magnificent place of worship, one he had always cherished. He believed in God, and in this place His presence had filled Ethan with peace and direction.

Striding into the chapel, he glimpsed her head bowed in the act of praying. The echo of sound from his feet striking the large flagstones had Arabella lifting her head. Her eyes sought his face as he covered the remaining distance for any clue to how the congress had ended. He gave her a small smile of encouragement, and then folded his lengthy body onto the hard wooden bench next to her as she scooted over.

He gathered his thoughts as she continued to watch him for any clue.

"The answer is not yea or nay," he finally began softly, aware to keep his voice low and preserve the reverence.

A weighted sigh escaped her, and he quickly continued. "The Five need time to gather enough information to make a decision, and it will take time as we wait on scouts to return, in all likelihood a fortnight.

"I'm not at all sure what Cleve has up his sleeve, but I would bet my horse that he has a trick up his sleeve. 'Tis something I will look into immediately, because we don't want him getting the upper hand. When I suggested we wait for my scouts to get back from the Norlans, he conceded much too quickly."

"You have scouts in the Norlans? Is that why you were in the Hoodoos?" she calmly asked. He marveled at how composed she was in the face of more delays, knowing how anxious she was to return to her people.

He nodded his head. "I thought it best to see what Mason was undertaking. I had heard rumors and was in the act of sending out scouts when we heard of the shivers going through Anchelle, so I held off. They remained here till last week, when the wet season had passed enough to allow for travel. That is when I met up with you. I expect to start seeing scouts back, as early as ten days."

"I'm glad you did, though I'm not sure they will have too much to report. Does the Five just want an account of Mason from somebody from Saldanzia to collaborate our story?"

"Yes, they do, but for me it's more than that. Call it a hunch, but I think there is more going on. The Cronan have been very unpredictable of late. We have found their scouts along our southern border." What he didn't add was he was pretty sure they were trying to find weaknesses in their southern border. "One would expect raids from the Cronan. They live by feeding off of others' labor. But never have we seen them so far south and east, as what we have seen as of late. The western and northern border villages have historically been forced to fend off small bands of the pillagers, but southern Saldanzian lands? Never."

"They've been raiding in the south?" she questioned.

Ethan shook his head, sure she was thinking of their recent encounters with the Cronan, and the near catastrophe it could have been. He felt her shiver beside him and was given further evidence. "Not yet."

Though the issue of their southern border seemed ancillary to Anchelle, he told her of a conversation he had recently had with his first-in-command about the Cronan's behavioral changes. They had been keeping a tight lid on their theories. However, it was sure to leak out as he had added additional deployments to the southern border. It was disconcerting to be facing a new threat from a known enemy and to have the Norlans and their continent in upheaval.

"Do you feel like you can tell me about your hunch?" she asked. "Or is it against Saldanzia's policies?"

"Yes, and no. You are a leader of a foreign kingdom, but you are also the direct descendant of the Five, so by all accounts you're one of us. Just indulge me for a handful of days, and I will share what I can when able. You are anxious for action, I know, but nothing can proceed until we learn more."

Ethan struggled to know if he should share the particulars of the congress; did he warn her of her grandfather's desire to separate her from the land of her birth? Or that she might be asked to renounce her crown? He didn't believe it would come to that. Once the scouts confirmed Mason's treachery, surely the Five would see reason and assist Anchelle in return for earned wages and strengthening trade relations that had been somewhat stunted since her mother had married the king of Anchelle. Knowing the weight she bore, he decided to hold his tongue and do what he could to bring some levity from the burdens.

He also desperately wanted some time with her away from the prying eyes of the Five. She could do with some respite, he was sure. The waiting while trying to keep her world from collapsing had to be arduous; the next two weeks would be very trying for her.

"Would you permit me to share some of Saldanzia's beautiful countryside with a picnic tomorrow?" he softly asked, her blue eyes holding him captive.

"I feel guilty even contemplating a day of pleasure in the countryside, and with a dashing Lord of Saldanzia," she admitted, bumping his shoulders playfully. "But somehow I don't think I can say no." She smiled up at him with a smile that reached her eyes, the one he was always trying to garner. Slowly he took her hands into his own, feeling a slight tremor in them, and kissed them softly. He couldn't help his own smile as he stood up.

"May I walk with you? Accompany you to your grandfather's home?"

"I need a few more minutes here," she said a little breathlessly, pausing for a moment. "Of praying," she continued with a slight blush. "I will make my way to my grandfather's home. 'Tis high time to have a frank discussion with him. Perhaps you could ask your parents when I could call on them?"

"I can speak for my mother when I say, for you there is always an invitation."

"My thanks. I shall see you tomorrow then?"

"Aye, you will."

As Ethan exited the church, Garner approached him, followed closely by Luke. Though pleasant of face, he sensed a different undertone, as though taking his measure. Thus far, he had felt a comradeship with these men who protected their lady so fiercely. To that end, he realized that was exactly what they were doing. He was their concern, especially as they noted his more familiar interactions with their liege. Stopping, he waited for them to take the last few feet.

Garner spoke first. "My lord." He bowed his head deferentially. Luke stood behind Garner with his arms folded across his chest.

"Ethan," Ethan said. He respected them and hoped to gain their trust.

"Ethan," Garner acknowledged. "The gents and I wanted to invite you to come spar in the lists with us on the morrow."

I bet they did.

His face now quite stoic, Garner continued. "We want to ensure that you are fit to court our lady." He was not at all intimidated by Ethan's status and being on foreign soil.

Pleased by their honesty and forthrightness he felt his estimation grow. No subtlety. Direct and unapologetic with their duty to protect Arabella. Ethan felt the corners of his mouth turn up at the opportunity to meet them across blades.

⌒

Before the cock crowed the next morning, Ethan was riding to the Grace estate. It was still a bit cold; patches of fog permeated the air. The sun was yet to be seen, though there was enough light to make his way. Luke met him at the stables, a devilish grin on his face.

"Right glad you could make it," Luke began. "I spoke with Garner this morning and suggested that we shouldn't push you too hard this first time. Mayhap just Garner, then Roland to begin with your first time out."

Ethan smiled at the insinuation that one or two of the Anchellian guards could handle him. He didn't doubt they were fit, well-trained knights. The fact that they were the queen's personal guard would suggest superb skills. He threw his head back and laughed; ah, how he loved a challenge in the lists. True, his family was in the Ruling Five, but Ethan didn't get to be the commander of the Saldanzian army because of his parents; that he earned by sweat, blood, and considerable preparation.

Not rising to the verbal bait, he indicated that Luke should lead the way.

On the designated grounds, Garner and Roland sparred, no doubt warming up for the match with Ethan, as well as a dozen of Timothy's personal guards. He watched Garner and Roland closely for any weakness as the sun started to glow on the horizon, causing the fog to dissipate.

As Ethan approached, Garner stopped and greeted him. "Good of you to join us," he said, extending his hand, his waster in the other. As a general rule, soldiers sparred with a practice weapon: a wooden sword, or as it was often called, a waster. Frequently one used a heavier weapon than their own to make their movement quicker and more precise when in real battle and building the body's muscles. He doubted the Anchellian's had brought their own wasters from Anchelle. They undoubtedly borrowed from Timothy's guards.

Garner's grip was almost painful as Ethan applied an equal amount of pressure to their greeting.

His presence was creating some interest. Lord Grace's guards stopped practicing to see what their commander was doing there.

"I'm honored!" Ethan replied, and truly he was. It was a right of passage, to take the measure of a man. One he was glad to know was observed by Anchelle.

Not one to mince about, Garner got straight to it. "Shall we?"

"Indeed," Ethan encouraged.

Waster in hand, Ethan watched Garner advance. Pushing out any distractions, Ethan focused on Garner.

With only a few feints by each man to find openings, they quickly took to an exchange of blades and were soon in the rhythm of a fierce battle. Garner, though older than Ethan by at least a dozen years, was agile and powerful. The broader man had twenty pounds on Ethan. From the vibrations that ran up his sword arm Ethan guessed it to be pure muscle. Garner hadn't been named the queen's commander resting on any laurels. Ethan would push hard with an offensive salvo, and just when it seemed he was gaining some ground, Garner pushed back, finding his reserve. On it went, over and over again. Half an hour passed before Roland came into the fray, advancing at the same time as Garner. One of the Saldanzian soldiers, obviously watching the match, threw Ethan his waster so that he could meet both Anchellians with two wooden blades.

In that brief moment, Ethan felt supreme exhilaration, as though he could do this for hours. To meet two extremely well-trained soldiers in a competition of strength, technique, and endurance was a heady rush. Ethan had practiced and fought frequently with two blades, a particular skill that had taken him many years to become effective in. The feeling of intense discipline of mind and body, pushing oneself to do the impossible. His arms were on fire, but seeing Garner starting to pant bolstered his energy; Roland still had plenty to spare, and it showed.

"You are passing good!" Garner spoke, his breath labored.

"As are you," Ethan panted in return.

"Sir?" Luke called from the sidelines to Garner. "Perchance you let a younger lad have a go at the Saldanzian."

Garner chuckled and halted his advancement on Ethan. "Roland." He commanded the other to cease as well as Luke ran onto the field, anticipation and cocky smile affixed.

"Let's leave the old men out of it, shall we," he taunted. Ethan saw Garner roll his eyes. One of Timothy's guards ran out onto the field as well, a jug of water in hand. Ethan gratefully took it and downed it, preparing for the next onslaught. Luke was of the same build and height as Ethan. Same reach. More energy at the moment. But Ethan was just getting warmed up. Or at least that was what he told himself, not allowing himself to even consider flagging.

"Ready?" Luke questioned. "Or do you need a few wee moments to catch your breath?" he baited Ethan.

Ethan put the jug down, his thirst quenched. Lifting the waster with his right hand, leaving the one he'd used in his left on the ground, he nodded for Luke to begin.

As he advanced, Ethan asked, "Who taught Arabella the sword?"

"'Twas I," Luke preened, locking swords with Ethan. The sound of knocking wood pierced the air throughout the field once again. Timothy's soldiers had given up all pretenses in their training and were gathered about.

"Well . . . to be fair, 'twas her father to start in the lists," Luke clarified after trying to take off Ethan's head with a powerful swing.

"Though there are several of us that continue to spar with her," he said as he dodged one of Ethan's thrusts to the midsection. For the next half-hour, the men parried, pushed, and connected blow after resounding blow. Sweat dripped off Ethan's face and his arms had begun to complain in earnest. Though he had taken a few well-placed hits, he'd delivered as many if not more to every opponent. Luke, though, seemed like he could battle the whole of the day, but he hadn't just taken on Garner and Roland at the same time. Another half an hour gone.

"You're smiling," Luke stated, though he could hear the question in it.

"'Tis a grand time I've been having this morn," Ethan said gleefully. "I'm being sincere when I say the queen's guard are some of the best I have had the pleasure to cross blades." He stepped back and let his weapon drop. "A right good time," he reiterated. "But I've a meeting shortly, and need this horrible stench off of me first," he said, chuckling between breaths.

Luke didn't seem like he wanted to be finished yet, but lowered his waster anyway. He ran his hand through his longish blond hair and gave a slight huff, then closed the small distance between the two men. With a lowered voice he spoke so as not to carry to Lord Timothy's men.

"See now, Arabella is family to me, to us," he said, indicating the guardsmen behind him. "I am not ashamed to tell you

I love her like my own." Ethan felt the sincerity and determination of Luke's words as he looked Ethan in the eyes. His face hardened. "Under no circumstances will I, nor those men, see her hurt."

At last they were to the crux of the matter. Ethan felt the weight of Luke's words echoing the thoughts in his own head.

Ethan could see Garner and Roland at the edge of the field watching the exchange.

"I understand," Ethan said, truly comprehending the knight's stance. The commander of the Saldanzian army was being threatened on his people's land by foreigners and he wouldn't have it any other way, he realized. Ethan knew he was no threat to her, but she was definitely a threat to his heart. Was it the same for her?

Luke's serious tone went from menacing to jovial seconds later when he asked, "Same time tomorrow? We didn't quite get to finish and some of the lads haven't had a go yet. Och, and there is one other matter to be discussing . . ."

CHAPTER 10

When Arabella was summoned to the door of her grandfather's house to greet the commander, his eyes sparkled in amusement as he deftly took her hand and guided her to Palachio. She didn't know when it had been arranged, but Luke sat his horse next to Lady Claire, a devilish smile on his face as he winked at her. She greeted the two and found herself riding next to Ethan, with Claire and Luke behind. Flanking them were several knights, including Roland.

"How did that come to be," she said, indicating the pair following them.

"Let's just say that Luke and I had a heart to heart this morning."

"And you aren't going to tell me more?" she questioned, completely intrigued.

"Nay," he replied. "Mayhap, but it is a tale for another day."

Ooh, that was even more curious. She wanted to press him further, but finally settled with, "'Tis a beautiful morning."

"Aye, perfect for the day I've planned," he spoke.

"What do you have planned, may I ask?"

"You may ask, but I won't tell," he said mysteriously. Ethan led their retinue away from the grand estate. Rather than going toward the city, they followed the hillside moving horizontally, toward the forest.

"Tell me of yourself, Arabella," he asked.

"What would you know?" she replied.

"You know: the seemingly ordinary, what do you like, and things you dislike?" He laughed at himself, and she couldn't help but follow along. The simplicity of conversation put her immediately at ease. Sometimes she felt so comfortable with Ethan, and other times, her heart pounded in her chest and she felt heat in her cheeks.

"I love springtime in the apple orchards of Anchelle. I love the harvest, it's probably my favorite time of the year. My father and George, that's Thaddeus's father, and Burt, who was Luke's father, and Charles, have a large apple orchard. When 'tis time to harvest, families come from all over the kingdom, and we camp, eat, and work together. 'Tis rigorous work, but when the harvest is done for all of Anchelle we have this amazing festival." It really was the best. Thinking about it made her wish that she could share it with Ethan. "I dislike pretenses and pickled squash." Her nose scrunched up as though she'd just taken a bite of the dreaded dish.

Ethan laughed, intoxicated by her open expression as she shared, then asked after her to share a bit about her reign as queen of Anchelle.

"Let's see." She was thoughtful for a moment. The circumstances of her coming to power were still painfully fresh. Perhaps she could respond to how Saldanzia differed from Anchelle. Though the area of her kingdom was quite large, the population was relatively small compared to Saldanzia. Even more after the shivers devastated Anchelle. She thought of all the work she had been doing before leaving—all the time and energy that went into serving her people in the wake of loss. To Arabella, Anchelle was the embodiment of the people she loved, like Thaddeus, Bron, and Charles She couldn't allow herself that train of thought, so she firmly pushed her mind another direction. She couldn't yet speak about being a queen with any ease.

He asked her a few followup questions about Anchelle, and Arabella willingly shared with him the facts and figures of her nation.

"Now, I've done all the talking thus far. 'Tis time for you to take a turn," she insisted.

"Not quite yet, you have talked much of Anchelle, but not yourself, give me ten favorite things, and five things you dislike. Then I will take a turn."

She paused for a moment, "Well I did tell you two of my favorite things, spring and harvest, so eight more?" she questioned.

He nodded his head.

"Fresh bread."

"Mmm, me too," he mumbled.

"Strawberry tarts, mmm, I think I must like food," she commented. "Let's see, a trip to the ocean, freshly laundered sheets, that smell of spring. Did I tell you I like spring?"

Ethan nodded his head with a grin.

"Growing up, I would have said a day in the lists with the knights would be my favorite day, but since my father's death, I don't think I have the same zeal for it. Somehow 'tis not the same."

"I can only imagine," he responded.

All right, just happy things, she told herself, coming back to the present. "Sunsets from my bedroom window, training horses, spending time with Luke and Thaddeus." She paused for the moment, allowing herself to only think joyfully of Thaddeus. She would dwell on the good times, not on the inability to never again behold him in life. Rounding off the list, she added, "And riding Palachio." She ticked off each item, then started another list.

"Dislikes, this should be easy, I already told you squash—ugh. Mushrooms, gathering eggs—much worse than mucking stalls in my opinion as far as chores go."

"Because you have had experience?" he asked incredulously.

"Of course," she said. "My father had me do most things a son would have done. He wanted me to be well rounded and fully able to understand my people."

"'Tis not what I was finding hard to believe that you could, but rather my sister has never had to do any chores." He looked back at his sister for a moment making Arabella turn her head as well. Claire and Luke were riding close together, and Claire was leaning toward Luke and laughing in amusement.

"Truly, I never imagined any princess or nobility having to do such labor aside from embroidery or such," Ethan said, bringing them back to their conversation.

"Oh, I was getting to that," Arabella exclaimed. "I abhor embroidery, or any form of sewing. I can do it, because my father insisted, but I'm not very good either, I'm actually quite poor."

Ethan chuckled.

"I very much detest Mason and all that he represents, and I dislike not having any siblings. I think I would have really liked having at least one, if not seven or eight." He could tell she was very passionate about the last two things, and it made him feel an ache for her and the loneliness of her childhood, which made her closeness with her guard understandable.

"What about you?" she asked, not even giving him a chance to give any more remarks on her dislikes.

"Well, I have to say that I am very fond of a certain queen that does not like to gather eggs."

She laughed. Ethan was becoming quite flirtatious with her. "Is that because she can muck out her own horse's stall? I am sure that must be very appealing to a man." Her heart was beating frantically. She wanted to believe him but knew it would be dangerous to her heart to take it too seriously.

"Aye, 'tis," he said with a warm smile.

She had a puzzled expression on her face. "Ha, surely not?"

"I think your father was a very wise man."

They rode in silence for quite some time. She hadn't known how to respond to all of it. Her heart felt so beaten up with loss and hope trying to share space, and found she desperately wanted him to have genuine affection for her, but how realistic was such a wish? Not very, but it made her hunger for this simple day away from the weighty cares.

"Tell me more of yourself," she gently demanded.

And so he shared of growing up, in a beautiful city, with parents that were good to him and challenged him to be great in his own works. He told of some of his funnier escapades and troubles he had gotten in. Though largely obedient, there seemed to be a wee bit of mischief. Such as the time he "accidentally" gave Torin Blake, Cleve's son, a mud bath. Ethan told her how he and Torin had always been rivals in school. The two competed at everything. It was an unspoken rule.

While they talked, they took in the beautiful morning, appreciating the time they had to spend in peace and quiet. It was high noon when they arrived at their destination. Wrapped up in a story about Ethan's youth and drawn to capture the emotions that moved across his face, Arabella hadn't been as attentive to the surroundings. Having come to a halt, she scanned the area, and though she had never been to this place, she knew instantly where he had brought her.

She looked at him with incredulity. A feeling of awe and wonder settled over her.

"You brought me to the place my parents met?" He nodded his head. Joy thrummed through her, and had they been standing, she knew she would have thrown her arms around him. She signaled Palachio. The beautiful stallion knelt down, and Arabella slid off his back, unaware that Luke and Claire hung back, as well as the guard. Moving forward, she took in the sight. A memory washed over her, her father telling her the story of meeting her mother colliding with the sight she was seeing. It was a most romantic story. She heard herself sigh, just as she had as a little girl when her father repeatedly told the story.

He had come to Saldanzia, a reckless young man, trying to prove to his father that he was his own man and could make his own decisions. He wanted to see the world and experience things before he was to be king. Coming to Saldanzia in disguise, pretending to have no money, he was alone without even a guard. A week after being in the city, he had seen Arabella's mother, and he later learned she was coincidentally in disguise herself, training a horse for a jumping competition against her father's wishes. Garrett had stopped when he spied a small, daring rider jumping rails with fluid ease. It was apparent the rider loved the challenge and was a remarkable horseman. Later learning that she was practicing in a place far enough from the city her father wouldn't hear of it, Garrett had watched them for some time before the horse had spooked and landed poorly, dislodging the rider from the horse and injuring her. Arabella's father went to the aid of the "poor devil" but soon realized it was not as it seemed. The young lad was a woman and had *stolen the breath from his lungs,* he'd oft said. Upon assisting her to her feet and learning of her ambitions, he was so charmed by her he was helpless but to go along with her scheme. He remained at the Graces' estate for a year, serving as a stable boy so that he might keep her near. Arabella's mother, Daniella, fell in love with him and against the family's wishes committed to marry him, before he had even told her of his kingdom far away. Garrett loved her all the more for her acceptance of his seemingly humble past. It was likely why he had insisted on Arabella mucking out stalls from an early age.

Arabella took in her surroundings, letting loose a wondrous laugh, her entire body radiant with this moment of connection. Fingers trailing along the tall grass, marveling that the place was exactly how her father had described it. It appeared as if this remote jumping course was still used regularly, perhaps not surprising with Saldanzia's regular equestrian competitions. A sport the Saldanzians favored above all others, she recalled learning. The barn was worn, and a lazy river meandered under a covered bridge; it was the picture he had described, remarkable considering the passing of three decades' time.

She turned to Ethan, who was watching her intently. "I didn't . . . that is, how did you know?"

"'Twas my mother, of course. Those two really were like sisters."

"I shall have to thank her personally," Arabella commented. "'Twas most thoughtful."

"What about me?" he asked, allowing a note of petulance to enter.

"What about you?" she answered laughingly.

"Don't I deserve some thanks, perhaps another kiss?"

Arabella's face darkened a vermillion shade, and Ethan, thrilled at the effect, laughed outright.

"My father warned me to not be free with my affections." She pretended dismay, playing along, delighted that he would tease her so.

"As I recently mentioned, your father was a wise man."

Ethan offered her his arm and tapped his cheek as though waiting for a kiss. Arabella laughed, then gave him a peck on the cheek. Though truly it wasn't an obligatory kiss and lasted but a moment, she had drawn in his masculine scent, fresh and woodsy, which was decidedly becoming a favorite. Heat seared through her entire body, his proximity thrilling. Breathless and blissful she marveled anew; had her mother likewise been struck with butterflies when near young Garrett?

When she pulled away, it took her a moment to look at him, but when she did, his eyes met her directly and mirrored the longing she felt. Her stomach did a little tumble as she returned his gaze. Could they really be sharing such intense feelings?

Ethan grabbed her hand and put it on his. She dared a glance and he smiled charmingly. They walked to the bridge, in silence. Arabella wondered if his thoughts matched hers. Did his heart hammer against his chest? Did he long for her company and search for him in every room? Arabella couldn't say *love* to even herself—she couldn't. Their time together, though riddled with tension, had at times been tragic and difficult, yet she realized it was most precious to her. Finding her in a place of desperation as she fought off enemies, well knowing she'd presented a tangled mess from their introduction. That this incredibly handsome, thoughtful, kind, and strong man could look at her thus was inexplicable. Recognizing her own desire to see that look remain was telling to the state of her heart.

While taking in the sight of her parents' past, she marveled at his attention and the feelings he elicited. Ethan directed her to a meadow where Luke and Claire were setting out the noon-day fare.

The group lingered in the area for several hours conversing, walking, and even skipping rocks. It was a day filled with the magic of a burbling brook and an attentive suitor, one she was sure to draw on in the coming struggles. Claire was a delight to visit. A beautiful, pampered, yet sweet and vivacious girl. The blond beauty adored her family, and Arabella could see why: she was starting to hold high regard for the family as well.

"Shall we take a walk, and let the gentlemen gather everything up?" Claire suggested to Arabella as she jumped up. Arabella looked to the aforementioned men.

"Off with you, we will see to it," Luke said, "and the two of you can get it next time."

"'Twould seem a good arrangement," Claire said, eyes only for Luke momentarily before she grabbed Arabella's arm and led her away from the men.

"'Tis difficult to believe that you rule a country," Claire said almost immediately as she plucked a wild rose from a stem and brought it to her nose. Then turned a bright shade of crimson when she realized what she said. "Oh, I don't mean that as it came out."

Arabella held up her hand. "'Tis fine," she reassured the girl.

"No, what I mean is that you're so real, not pretentious like the girls who are related to the Five are, you're genuine." The girl rushed on, "I overheard Ethan tell Father and Mother of finding you, and . . . and shared with me the tale of when you found your guard." She twisted her hands together. "How relieved you were that they were yet alive, and how you mourned those that were lost. Well, I may have been eavesdropping, if you want to know the truth."

Arabella was taken back by the compliment, and also by the memories. The relief of reunions and the horror of loss. Still she ached thinking of finding Thaddeus, her mind recalling how Ethan had held her, offered comfort, and then aided her in his burial.

"Did you love any of them?" Claire asked quietly, leaning into her.

She was taken aback, not in the least offended by how personal the nature of the question. Claire was inquisitive and not for mere fodder. "Aye, 'tis true I love them all dearly." She looked away, but couldn't help it, a small tear rolled down her cheek. Too fresh and raw with loss.

"Oh, my apologies, look what I've gone and done now." Claire handed her a lacy handkerchief. "I'm always making a muck of things, Mother is constantly telling me I need to learn the art of discretion."

Arabella had to smile at the admission and mumblings of the girl. She quickly wiped away the tear, abruptly turning the conversation to questions. To learn of Claire and keep her talking about herself till the men came for them with the horses.

"Think you the scouts will find anything of use?" Arabella asked Ethan on their return trip. "I find myself wondering if Mason's army is even now marching at the doors of Lassiter."

"'Tis possible. He might want to take them in a swift campaign, but 'twould leave his army spread out, especially if he thought you successful in returning with an army . . ." He didn't finish the sentence, assuredly in deep thought.

How far was Mason willing to go? Did he just want Anchelle and Arabella, or was there no end to his greed? What was the size of Mason's army, now that he had pressed the people of Theron into servitude and Arabella's own army under his control? These were questions that he prayed his scouts could answer. He didn't believe that even with his conquests, Mason could match the Saldanzian army in numbers. His mind was sorting and trying to see all the worst possible outcomes, including the unlikely event he were to form an alliance with the Cronan. None had ever succeeded in that regard, and Mason didn't seem like a team player but a conqueror. Most critical was the question of if Mason would be satisfied after taking Anchelle. Was that his ultimate achievement?

He was so lost in his own thoughts that he hadn't noticed how quiet Arabella had become. Now he noted a forlorn look upon her face. What was he thinking? He had planned the day to bring her some amusement, a diversion from the horrors that she had faced for the last year and would be facing for an unknown time yet. He scrambled, searching for an opening to change the atmosphere.

"Have I yet mentioned how becoming you look this day?" he said sincerely. She was so beautiful that it was hard not to continually stare. The compliment shifted the mood with light coming back into her eyes.

"Thank you," she said graciously

And so they left the serious matter or armies and invasions behind and spoke of pleasant topics till he dropped her off at her grandfather's estate. Once again despairing to be leaving her presence, and that was not a drop in the bucket to what he feared of watching her leave forever. He was becoming very attached to her.

Upon arriving home he went straightway to his father's study. There were concerns building that he needed to discuss with a trusted advisor, someone who truly understood the complexity of his position. Michael McKenna had led the army for many years before Ethan had taken over the duties only a few years past.

His father stood behind a desk, poring over maps. His lean, tall body stooped low to get a better look. He raised his head as Ethan approached and waved him in immediately. His face was a mask of concentration.

"Come, come. I figured you would be here soon." His voice couldn't hide his enthusiasm. Ethan wasn't surprised to find him working through and studying the terrain of the land. His father may have formally retired his command, but he would never lose the passion of defending and helping his country. It was in his blood. Though he no longer practiced daily in the lists, he was still spry with a sharp mind that had not diminished in any capacity.

"I wanted to show you the letter I received from Garrett shortly before his passing," he stated, gesturing to his son to join him on the sofa, away from the maps.

As commander of the military and one of the Ruling Five it was critical to know what was going on in neighboring kingdoms. One of the first lessons he recalled at his father's knee was the adage that *knowledge was the power that leads to correct actions.*

Of course, having a good friend of a neighboring kingdom helped.

"I really thought highly of him. He was the greatest of men."

"I should have liked to meet him," Ethan admitted. "Arabella revered him."

"Ah . . . yes, the fair Arabella. Has a lot of her mother, Daniella, in her, who likewise was a spirited filly. And if I am not mistaken, some of her father is in there too. I assume you have visited with her in great detail to learn everything she knows of King Mason? Regardless of how Saldanzia responds, 'tis a singular opportunity to gather intelligence, our network has been stymied when the shivers hit and then the passing of Garrett."

Michael continued to press forward, not waiting for a response "You should visit every member of her guard if she will allow it. 'Tis most critical to get every bit of information we can before the scouts return. We can begin on formulating various strategic responses." The older man got up and started to pace. "I was going through the letter from her father again, and something interesting struck me. The last letter I received from Garrett says that the first affected by the shivers were the soldiers. Listen here," his father commanded, grabbing the letter and finding the spot he was looking for before reading aloud to Ethan.

"It seemed simultaneously that my soldiers stationed to the south, to the west, and in the city were the first to contract the illness we have come to call the shivers," his father read from Garrett's own words.

"Wait . . . how can that be?" Ethan asked.

"I'm not sure." They were both in contemplative silence for a few minutes. "Would it be all right if I read the whole of the letter?" Ethan inquired. His dad handed him the letter and he read it through twice. He was struck by the personal nature of the letter, one of a close friend, and it was certain the Achelleian king counted Michael as one. The king's tone was that of fear, and it was clear he was anxious for his only daughter. With a neighboring madman named Mason Kiefer who was greedily expanding his kingdom into the neighboring nation. Garrett feared the worse, having rejected Mason's offer to join their kingdoms through marriage. He spoke a great deal about Arabella, mentioning his implicit faith in her ability to rule a kingdom. The letter held a finality. It seemed the king knew it might be his last correspondence, like he knew he could die in the wide sweeping illness.

"Hmm, I don't know if my other news might bear a connection." Ethan finally came out of his reverie, remembering the reason he sought him out this night. "A village north of Frine was raided and the entire inhabitants destroyed."

"I had not heard that," his father exclaimed. His father sat down for a minute, dumbfounded. "When was this?" he questioned.

"Just now. A runner was here when I returned with initial information. Call it a hunch, but I don't believe it a coincidence that Mason's army has led a campaign through the Norlans recently seizing control of Anchelle, and now Cronan are suddenly increasing their attacks on our border towns.

"That isn't all, there have been several sightings of the Cronan near Capri and Peligree." Ethan joined his father sitting and removed his hat to wipe the sweat from his forehead.

His fathers face reflected further shock. "'Tis strange indeed."

"Should we send a large force, it would put us at the opposite side of our border to Anchelle. While Cronan are known to
cross borders, to raid we haven't lost an entire village in decades."
Ethan paused. "I cannot know for sure that they are related, but
my gut is determined to find the connection. Blake will use this
news to keep us from sending aid with Arabella, but I think by
helping Anchelle we are protecting ourselves."

"I pray I'm seeing shadows where none exist but the timing is
unnerving," Ethan went on. "I've sent thousands of men to Capri
and Peligree. I think the village by Frine is a smokescreen and
they mean to attack on the south."

Ethan watched for a reaction from his father. He didn't want
to be wrong, and it went against the history of the Cronan. His
father held his gaze steadily, so he continued.

"In Capri and Peligree, I have men even now digging trenches
and fortifications around each city that will make it hard for an
army to penetrate. We've cleared the surrounding forests so that
the enemy will be easy to see from a great distance—and no
cover to shield them from our archers."

"'Tis impressive. Those cities have always been our weakest,"
came his father's suddenly weary response. Had he aged while
they spoke?

Ethan nodded his head, "'Tis the plan for the Cronan to find
this as well, at least that is what I am betting on."

"So you don't think the Cronan are taking advantage of the
timing with what's going on in the Norlans, to make preparations to attack?" his father reiterated the question.

"I do, but what the Cronan are doing isn't their style. When
have you ever heard of Cronan scouting incursions on our southern borders? Small raiding parties elsewhere, yes. What if . . ."
Ethan hesitated, then dropped his voice. "What if the Cronan
are the puppets, and Mason the puppeteer?" He let that sink in,
hardly believing it himself. When was the last time the warring
Cronan had come together in any significant number—centuries? They were divided in clans, and kept to their own territory, rarely able to get along outside their own clan. What could

Mason possibly offer the Cronan that would motivate the clans to not only put aside feuds within but to be under the reign of a foreign monarch? Ludicrous, surely. It was much more plausible the Cronan were aware of Mason's machinations in the Norlans and decided the southern area was ripe for an attack with their focus on a weakened Anchelle, where regardless of whether they aided, they would still reinforce that border.

"Even should a Cronan army exist, how does Mason think to remove the threat of our army as well?" his father asked, giving credence to a theory that still remained highly improbable. Wisdom to explore all possibilities, and in reasoning often the correct answer would become apparent—that was a method taught from father to son. "Surely it would be months before his power is consolidated enough, the resources gathered to marshal further land expansion?"

"I don't know," Ethan said with frustration lacing his voice. And that was what had him worried. It didn't seem likely that Mason could just march in and take over country after country. The supplies alone would be insurmountable. He couldn't possibly have the numbers in his army to continue an expansion and also retain the lands taken.

CHAPTER 11

An uneasy truce had been agreed upon between Arabella and her grandfather. Neither was to speak of Arabella staying in Saldanzia or returning to Anchelle. Though it had been awkward at first, they'd found common ground in discussing Arabella's mother and grandmother and learning the history of Saldanzia and all that the Ruling Five oversaw.

Ethan had been gone nearly a week, and she desperately missed him. What kind of torture was she putting herself through? There was no future with him. He was the next in line to rule Saldanzia. Their military commander was a patriot and wouldn't leave his people, just as she couldn't forsake Anchelle. To take her mind off of him shouldn't be so difficult considering what she had come here to accomplish. She kept herself busy training in the lists, counseling with her men, and one-on-one time with her grandfather. But when a missive had come last eve asking Arabella if Ethan could call on her on the morrow, she found it difficult to concentrate entirely in anticipation of his arrival. She attempted to console herself that her interest was merely to receive any update but she well knew it was a lie.

Arabella walked Palachio through the ancient city of Petri, her grandfather by her side. Benton and Roland held position a furlong out. The Saldanzians had abandoned the city a century past, when the city's well had dried up and they were unable to secure another water source. The rubbled ruins gave her only a smattering idea of what the city was like in its full glory. Awe filled her at the enormous skeletal remains of marble pillars with parts still bearing intricate carvings that spoke of great skills and prosperity. Mounted, they rode clopping as their horses' hooves struck the remains of a cobbled roadway just as those that had gone before her. What had it been like to move a city?

"'Tis city center," her grandfather claimed, stiffly dismounting his horse. Arabella nudged Palachio, who obediently knelt down, allowing Arabella to slide off.

"I've got to train my horse to do that too," Grandfather pronounced, "these bones are getting too old for all of this galavanting about." He spoke brusquely but softened it with a wink. He strode to a large well that showed the unremitting wear of wind and rain. Loose rock was spotted with lichen yet formed a circle around the hole.

"Alas, the famous Petri well," Grandfather pointed out. "The well actually dried up during one of my grandmother's reigns. I have her journal that describes the event in great detail."

"I should love to read that," Arabella exclaimed, wondering if her great-great-grandmother was anything like her, and if she might have some wisdom to help Arabella face the issues of her own day. She was thrilled with the idea of learning of those who had gone before her from her mother's family. Had she not read all of her father's ancestors' records multiple times? That she hadn't thought to ask her grandfather about records told of her great preoccupation with removing the usurper from her home. Her father's records had become companions when she was younger, wishing for siblings and feeling bereft of familial connections.

"'Twas an insurmountable issue, the shortage of water. The whole city was forced to leave. 'Twas much too far to haul water. Some citizens remained for time hoping for a solution and unwilling to leave behind centuries of their history that was carved upon buildings and filled their graveyards that could not so easily be moved. Within a decade of the well drying up, all had fled.

"Now we have safe aqueducts systems that can carry water to great distances, though 'twould be foolhardy to ever have a city of this size dependent on water being carried such great distance, a glaring vulnerability," Grandfather stated. He then pointed out a smooth rock on top of the piles. "This is where they brought up the buckets." The rock was worn from constant rubbing of ropes.

Arabella brushed up to her grandfather, and reached out her hand to the smooth surface of the well. The flash of a childhood image playing through her mind caused her to jerk her hand back like she had been stung. Her heart beat raised a notch, as a dreadful thought welled up inside of her. No. No. No. Could it be? Surely not. She chided herself for her overreaction and dark thought. It was a legend, a story to entertain children, not anything that held truth, and yet, why did she feel so uneasy?

Grandfather, unaware of Arabella's reaction to the well, continued to talk of the people of Petri. Determined to reject the malignant thought, she linked her arm through her grandfather's and listened attentively to his storytelling. It couldn't possibly be real.

⌒

Walking along a garden path at her grandfather's estate, Arabella waited for Ethan's arrival. While she had attempted to press her growing feelings off as merely high esteem and gratitude, she felt for his actions in helping her, she now had to admit that she was, in fact, falling in love with him. Why must it be impossible? Love should be liberating and celebrated but instead she was filled with despair once she had acknowledged the emotion. Never would she consider remaining in Saldanzia. She would return to Anchelle, and he would remain here, the next in line to Saldanzia's rule and the army commander.

Stretching her neck and rolling her shoulders, Arabella was rewarded with a satisfying pop in her neck. It released a small amount of tension her body was carrying. Still, a sigh of frustration escaped her lips. Around and around her mind spun, searching for elusive solutions.

Turning about, she made her way back. Stopping for a moment to dislodge a pebble from her boots, she looked up to note Benton, who remained a discreet distance from her, nod his head toward another path. Eyes followed the directions and there she spied Ethan walking toward her: his gait, though not remarkable, was forever etched in her mind already. His confident stride ate up the space between them.

Arabella couldn't contain the smile that emerged. Ethan's own smile was as welcoming as the hands he held out to her as she slipped into his embrace. His strong arms wrapped around her and she felt like she was in heaven as she breathed in his masculine and clean-smelling fragrance.

"Mmm," he sighed. "I have never missed anyone more in my life," he declared, matching her own thoughts. Her heart hammered in her chest and her stomach flipped; how could she be so at peace in his arms? Did his own heart speed up, did he feel this zinging along his spine? Half a fortnight had passed, had the distance and time spent apart changed what they had? She didn't have to wonder long.

Ethan's eyes were fixed on her and there was no doubt of his intent. Maintaining eye contact, he lowered his head, closing the distance between them, his eyes searching for any indication that she didn't want this. The air in her lungs stopped for a moment, and she found that as his lips finally met hers she was completely unprepared for the feeling that exploded inside of her being. Euphoria! It wasn't like anything she had experienced before. Would she ever get enough of this man? Arabella matched his fervent kissing, knowing her world would never be the same.

All too soon Ethan stopped the assault on her lips, though he tenderly kissed her forehead and drew her close. Arabella put her overly warm face to his hard chest, hearing his heartbeat race, and feeling hers join in the frantic pace.

"I am in so deep!" Ethan exclaimed. His arms tightened around her.

Arabella smiled, knowing they were in harmony on that notion, wishing she could halt the world and live in this singular moment. Utterly content to be held within the protective circle of his embrace.

"I've heard that love is complicated. But I think this goes well beyond that adage," he spoke, his voice rough with emotion.

She gave a small gasp, had he just spoken of loving her?

At a loss, the word bounced around her head. *Love. Love. Love.* "Indeed, m'lord," she agreed breathily. Her own voice sounded strange. Longing filled her, a desire to pledge her love and life to him. He owned her heart and yet she was in no position to give it to him.

Neither spoke, both reeling with the impact of that first kiss. He steered her deeper into the grove that bordered her grandfather's lands. The blossoms on the orange and lemon trees were in full bloom and smelled wonderful. Neither of them wanted to break the euphoria that they felt, it was far too precious.

Ethan could see Luke and Roland not too far away, but they wisely kept their distance. "What did you do this week?" Ethan asked, finally breaking the silence.

"The mornings I spent training in the lists with my men." Ethan raised his eyebrows at her incredulously before she continued, "But only in the mornings, before Grandfather awoke, and only three hours."

"Oh, is that all?" Ethan said in a playful tone. This beauty was a study in contradictions. Delicate in form and steel in strength. It angered him that she should need training, but it was also a comfort to know that she was capable of taking care of herself, as he had witnessed the moment they met.

"Then I spent almost the entire daylight hours with Grandfather, riding around Saldanzia. 'Twas healing for both of us. Though I'm not sure what will happen once I leave. He is still as much against it as he was with my mother." Her shoulders dropped a fraction before she straightened them and continued. "And in the evenings," she continued, "I spent endless hours with my guard going over battle strategies. They are . . . inventive." She laughed

"Truly, they are exceptional men," Ethan agreed. "What did you see on your rides? I want to know everywhere you went." Though there was much to discuss, he wanted just a few more minutes to bask in the wonder.

Her hesitation caused Ethan to push her. "What is it?" he questioned "Did something happen this week? Did someone bother you?"

"No, no, all is well," Arabella tried to reassure him.

"What?" he asked, and when she didn't speak. "Please?" She looked up at him and he could see concern written across her face. "You can tell me," he said gently.

"I keep thinking about something." She hesitated, not sure where to begin. "You may think me mad." She looked up, craning her head to meet his gaze, struck again at his formidable height. She gave him a questioning look.

Ethan smiled reassuringly at her. "I will not think you mad." His breathing calmed. How quick his emotions flared, and he wanted to battle her unseen demons the moment he saw something amiss in her countenance. Now he was fairly intrigued, determined to learn what she was having a hard time expressing.

She nodded her head and her lips gave a quirky little sideways move he found adorable.

But she finally took a deep breath. "There was an old man that traveled through Anchelle when I was a child, he was old and unkempt, but for some reason Thaddeus, Luke, and I befriended him. He was only there for less than a fortnight, but he told us glorious stories, make-believe stories of giants and magic powers and such. We loved to listen to him, and we would bring him food and drink, to get him to tell us the stories.

"One day he told us this fantastic tale that he insisted was true. He told of a very evil man who wanted to rule a kingdom and was determined to marry the princess." Arabella looked up at Ethan and blushed when she realized what she had said, then hurried on. "The king did not like the man and had him expelled from the kingdom. I can't remember all the details to the story, just the essence," Arabella apologized. "But after a time, the man made some kind of vile concoction and one night he snuck into the city and put it all over the wells of the city. Not in the wells, but over and around it," she emphasized. "According to the story-teller, it wasn't anything that could be seen with the eye. 'Twas invisible. When the people went to the well for water to drink, it would taint them, and they carried it home . . ." She paused for a second. "It made all the people sick and had eventually killed all who came in contact with those that drew the water."

Ethan was trying to process everything she was telling him. Something about the tale made a stone settle in this stomach.

"The entire city died, and so even though the evil man had made himself king, he didn't have anyone to rule, even the prin-cess was lost," she added softly.

They were quiet for a moment. "I know 'tis naught but an old tale meant to instruct children, and of course we know of poisons that can kill people." She continued, "Indeed there are weeds capable and even others that can create noxious poison-ous smoke when burned, but an entire population by something invisible? Surely 'tis just a fable," she repeated, "but let me tell you something that sounds crazy, but 'tis true.

"When Anchelle came down with the shivers, do you know where it started?"

"The soldiers," he stated matter-of-factly.

"How did you know?" she looked at him questioningly.

"Your father wrote a letter to mine, some months before his passing," he spoke apologetically.

"He did?" she questioned longingly.

Ethan responded with a nod. The story had obviously rat-tled her and he felt similarly alarmed. He had a vague recol-lection of a similar tale from a boy when he was a lad in the schoolyard. Ethan couldn't remember the boy's name, but as he pondered realized the boy from school hadn't told it as a tale but had claimed something like that had happened in his village! Ethan hadn't interacted much with the boy, as he had been circling the crowd with Torin Blake at its center. The more he thought on it, the more wisps of details came back. Hadn't the boy sworn it had happened where he'd lived in a remote region to the far east of Saldanzia?

"Did you know that the army was stationed in several different locations, great distances apart, and that all came down with the symptoms near simultaneously?" She sat on a fallen oak and looked up at him. Fear danced in her eyes. When he had read the letter in his father's study he had assumed the army had been somewhere and brought a sickness home with them, which in fact could still be the case. But she was implying that it could have been intentional and targeted their military?

"The army," he emphasized. "Same day in different outposts?"

"'Tis hard to know for sure, but aye, I believe within a few days at least," she confirmed quietly.

"Did you ever become sick?" he asked.

"Nay, I didn't." Her head bent down and he could tell she was reliving the memories.

"Were you in residence in the castle when others came down with the shivers?" he asked quietly.

"Aye," she sobbed. She seemed to be bombarded with the memory.

He'd known she'd likely seen the horror of it all, but to hear her say with such depth of emotion was heartrending. Sitting beside her on the log, he wrapped her in his arms and held her while sobs wracked her small frame. The daylight was fading when she quieted, and he needed to get her inside before she took a chill. He looked around and saw three of her men had tightened in on their location, no doubt in seeing their queen distressed.

"I'm probably too close to the situation to see clearly," she sniffled. Her eyes were red rimmed and her lashes were moist. "But I can't help but wonder if Mason has somehow made the shivers. I've never heard of a sickness that is made by man. Is that even possible?"

A shiver ran down Ethan's back. It seemed so unlikely, it was unheard of. A poison that if put in the right place could target specific populations? And yet if that were the case . . . Hadn't his dad and him just discussed this subject a week ago? How could Mason think he could march into Saldanzia and take over the city even with the help of their neighbors, the Cronan? The same way they took over Anchelle. Ethan's blood ran cold. The idea answered their unanswerable question.

He stood up suddenly. If that were the case, how would they ever protect themselves? Ethan had assumed that Mason would compel the countries in the Norlans to fight for him with fear tactics and brutality, which he still could, but some kind of unseen poison that could kill the fighting forces of a country? Something that could take out the hearty and hale men but still leave enough people to rule. Truly diabolical!

Ethan looked at Arabella, who had a worried expression on her face. "I saw the well at Petri and the thought occurred to me. I revolted at the idea, and can't believe that any soul could be that cruel, or even have the knowledge to do so. I can say that 'twould be unwise to underestimate Mason, he is . . . an evil man," she declared as a shiver wracked her body. She wrapped her arms around herself.

The sun had gone down and a chill now permeated the evening air. He was anxious to see to her comfort. Even though his mind was racing, sifting and sorting, he stood taking her arm. "Lets get you inside right away. It's probably time for dinner."

She tugged on his arm and made him stop and looked him in the eye, "Do you think I'm mad?" Her insecurity was troubling, which made him swell with pride that she had chosen to trust him with her fears.

Taking both of her small hands, he swept them gently with his thumb, catching on the raised calluses from her daily practices in the list. He smiled reassuringly down at her. "I could never think you mad, and as much as I pray that you are wrong, I am likewise unsettled. From the perspective of military power I'm afraid it makes sense: sadistic, but cunning were it possible."

He wanted to assure her and himself that it was contrary to reason and evidence. Mason marching on Anchelle, and a jittery group of Cronan, were not conclusive.

"Ethan," she gulped and he could hear the pain in her voice, "'twould explain why the other countries in the Norlans never came to our defense." She spoke quietly. "Maybe all this time when we were sick, they were also battling the same plague." They walked quietly toward the house, each deep in their own dark thoughts. "Anchelle completely shut down with the shivers. Though I sent runners to the other countries of the Norlans for aid when we knew Mason was marching on Anchelle, not a single runner returned."

Ethan hated for the evening to end on such a terrible note, not when the night had started with such a joyful reunion. Galled he was that Arabella should be so distraught and he could not simply fix her every trouble.

Taking her arm once again, he pulled her short of the door. "As much as I would like to kiss you senseless under the stars tonight," he said, giving her a squeeze and watching her face turn a lovely shade of pink, "I'm afraid I must see some scholars to see if your theory could be true. But . . . " he said, a roguish smile on his handsome face. He wrapped his arms around her middle and pulled her off her feet so that her face was level with his own. "Mayhap you would give one more kiss to see me off on the long evening ahead." She smiled, and that was all the encouragement he needed.

He had indeed kissed her senseless before, with a heavy sigh, he left her outside the wide porch. Was it strange that she had fallen so hard and fast in love with war looming in front of her? The pendulum swung so hard in shattering loss to only hurl in the opposite direction with blinding joy. Would it end with her bereft and alone?

Arabella had retreated to a bench near the opening of the gardens, her thoughts whirling. Her body was chilled and quaked but she couldn't go in as yet. Luke slipped beside her and laid her own cloak across her shoulders without a word. "My thanks," she said, giving him a tired smile. He nodded his head but remained mute. After a few minutes, she finally asked, "What am I to do?"

"Ask him to come with you," he stated firmly and without hesitation.

Sighing, she commented, "If only it were that easy."

"Mayhaps 'tis just so," he said, raising his eyebrows, challenging her to say differently.

Ethan rode hard for the family estate. He wasted no time with pleasantries, but called for his father and was right down to business, foregoing a reunion with his mother and sister. Once returning to the city he'd cleaned up at the barracks and gone straight to the Graces'.

The story poured out, and his father's face stretched tight, even fearful, as he relayed what Arabella had shared. "If there is any truth to these ideas, I believe it would it be safe to say that your scouts in the Norlans may seen something similar there," Michael stated.

"Absolutely. If Mason has marched on Anchelle's neighboring cities, he could have used the same method as Anchelle. I know 'tis madness to consider, but if Saldanzia is in Mason's sites, the sickness could already be here. That man is determined to have Arabella and he knows she fled here. It may push up his timeline. Of course, this could all be conjecture and totally without merit."

"But you don't think so," his dad stated.

"I think the tactic is genius," Ethan spoke with dread. "Evil! But genius."

His father nodded his head. "I will go speak with Spinter and Creeker."

Ethan nodded. The Saldanzian men were leaders in the medical field from all over the continent. Men and women came from all over the continent to study under them. It was a great privilege.

"I'll track down . . ." There was a brief pause as Ethan once again tried to remember the boy from school. "Howard," he exclaimed, pleased with himself for remembering, when he could have only been six or seven at the time.

Gathering a group of soldiers to accompany him, Ethan set out to find his schoolmate. It took Ethan two hours to track down Howard's home on the east end of Saldanzia, in a seedy part of town. His wife came to the door, none too pleased to be answering the door at midnight. It was safe to say Ethan had awoken her. Grumbling in almost incoherent sentences filled with mumbled coarse epithets, Ethan finally deduced Howard was at the corner pub, just a few buildings down the street.

The pub was heavily occupied as Ethan entered. An initial sweep proved unproductive. He purposely walked in a counter-clockwise circle, making a round in the establishment. Finally spotting a much thicker Howard in the corner, nursing a tall ale, Ethan sat down next to him, pushing other men out of his way.

"Howard," Ethan spoke to the man next to him.

Howard's glazed-over eyes gave no indication that he recognized Ethan.

"What?" Howard bellowed too loudly, like he couldn't hear himself talking.

"I need to talk to you, now," Ethan demanded.

Howard swore, then added, "Leave me to my drink!" very loudly, causing others to stop what they were doing to look at Ethan and Howard. Still no recognition that he knew who Ethan was. Either that or he just didn't care.

"Come on, Howard," Ethan said, grabbing the man's arm and hauling him from his seat.

The man swore again at Ethan.

Ethan hadn't wanted to cause a scene, but Howard's belligerence left him with no choice. As Howard tried to wrestle his arm free of Ethan's grasp, Ethan, in a quick move, put Howard's arm behind his back and pushed him none too gently toward the door. Grabbing a bottle of coulais from the bar keep and dropping a generous payment, they exited the building while corralling the drunk. The cool brisk air would help Howard to sober up, but the coulais would work better. Though Ethan wasn't entirely sure that the man would be any more compliant once sober. His filthy mouth still had Ethan's ears ringing.

Ethan took Howard back to his own hovel, and sat him down at the rough kitchen table. Grabbing a glass from the dirty kitchen counter, Ethan poured a glass of coulais, and shoved it into Howard's surly face. Howard looked at Ethan defiantly before putting the shot down. His wife came out to the kitchen, but wisely removed herself after taking in the scene.

Ethan wasn't sure how coulais worked, only that it did, reversing the effects of alcohol in minutes. More often than not, it made one sick to the stomach. Handing Howard a bucket, the man immediately left his guts' contents in the wooden bucket.

After one more shot of the coulais, and additional curses, Howards eyes started to lose the hostile animal-like gaze. Recognition followed.

"Ethan?" the man finally acknowledged. "What are you doing in my house?" he demanded, hardly more amiable in sobriety.

"I have some questions for you," Ethan answered calmly.

"And it couldn't wait till morning?" the man bellowed.

Ethan felt irritation flare at the man's attitude, but realized the dominating emotion was pity for the crass man. That was not the life that Ethan wanted. "You do realize that I am awake as well, and on duty to keep you and yours protected?" Ethan returned, an edge sharpening his tone.

Howard huffed, and folded his arms. "What do you want?" he demanded again, yet the volume was lower—they were making progress.

"I want to know where you're from originally, and what happened to your town."

"Can't help you. I made an oath to not speak of it," Howard said with a smug look on his face.

Ethan opened the door and called in two soldiers. "Haul him down to the Bridge Street jail, and make sure he gets put with the Cronan prisoner," Ethan commanded.

"Yes sir," the men spoke in unison and grabbed Howard's arms.

"Wait, now just wait! Okay, okay." The man's face looked penitent for the first time.

"Tell me what happened," Ethan demanded again.

It took Howard a minute to start speaking. One of the guards took a step forward and words started to pour out. "A traveling caravan came through our town, Gerda, when I was about seven—lots of trading, as expected. Days after they moved on people started to get sick. Didn't seem like there was any pattern till someone pointed out that it was only the people who had bought from the caravan that were dying. Not many days after even those that hadn't purchased from them were sick too." He swore and his hands trembled as he swatted his eyes angrily. "Most everyone was sick within a fortnight—high fevers, bodies would shake violently." He shuddered, lost in the dark memory.

"How many perished?" Ethan asked, bile churning in his stomach.

Howard scratched his chin. "Our village had about three hundred people when the sickness came. A small fraction were living when it ran its course."

Ethan asked question after question. How long had it lasted? How long to run its course? What were all the symptoms? The answers were horribly familiar.

Ethan rode away from his schoolmate with yet a host of unanswered questions. Was the sickness manmade or did it come from the environment, like influenza? Did it even matter if man could capture and use it to his advantage? And how did you fight an unseen poison? A shudder ran down his frame. It would be an entirely new battlefield that he was woefully ill prepared to meet.

Praying it was all conjecture, Ethan's mind whirled with the ramifications it could have on Saldanzia. If Mason had brought or was bringing a poison or sickness to Saldanzia, their fighting force could be decimated before the fight even started. That was assuming that Mason had his eye even fixed on Saldanzia. The image of the Arabella flashed in his mind, followed by the note he had recovered from Thaddeus's body. Arabella's guards were all concerned with the tyrant's obsession with their queen.

Returning home, Ethan found his father with both Creeker and Spinter in the study, waiting for him.

He shook hands with both men, and with the worried looks on both men's faces, he knew that indeed, they were in trouble.

Brusque greetings aside. "Tell me!" Ethan demanded, his patience waning. He was exhausted, hungry, and he had the safety of an entire country to worry about. Never mind the horror of investigating the Cronan's raids on the west and sightings in the south.

The two scholars of healing were masters, preeminent in their field of study. A long look passed between the men before Spinter began to speak. "When the village of Gerda was heard to lose almost the entire population twenty-one years ago, the Surreys, who were in power at the time, sent me to investigate."

Ethan looked at his father, who shook his head like he was disgusted. "The council was told that the influenza had gone through the village and killed most everyone. I ignorantly believed Surrey, as 'twas possible and could explain the deaths. There is a pattern in our histories, every century or so the influenza is especially fatal."

"Aye, 'tis true," Creeker echoed.

"But in this case," Spinter contended, "it wasn't influenza. I didn't know what could have worked through an entire population with such devastating losses. The symptoms didn't match influenza. I believe there were only two souls with the initial symptoms who recovered. The other few remaining survivors never became ill. I'd certainly never seen nor heard of anything like it before, and searched in all of our healing scrolls and tomes with no success. The only whisperings similar were lore, mere tales. Lord Surrey appointed me to further research, but I was forbidden to speak of it. I'm frankly stunned you knew of it at all, Ethan. Surrey was concerned of mass panic and it seemed contained to one area. I agreed with him, because thankfully 'twas a single isolated incident, and upon my return weeks later not another case was reported. 'Twould seem he had it aright, we haven't seen anything of its like for twenty-one years."

"Loose lips of a child is how I learned of it, though my young self thought it likely overdramatized to attract attention and make friends. Please tell me your studies have yielded answers and there is some way to prevent it or at least stem its spread?" Ethan asked.

"I could, perhaps with time, stop *it*." Spinter emphasized *it*. "But who's to say that the illness that struck Gerda is the same sickness that struck Anchelle? I have no firsthand knowledge of the symptoms—patterns, if you will—of Anchelle's plague. From what I understand that hellish disease has already run its course and the borders are reopening for trade."

"Please bear with me, do you believe it somehow manmade, a poison, or was it an act of nature? And can it be replicated?" Ethan queried.

"I believe it came of nature, but . . . I fear 'tis possible that man could . . . gather . . . 'bottle,' as it were, the contagion and then thus effect its spread," Spinter replied grimly. "Let me explain. A theory existed that the traveling caravan that came through Gerda carried the sickness perhaps in the foods or on the goods that were traded, this . . . plague was highly contagious, only a few people would have had to buy the products to have contact with this illness, and then, they too were contagious, spreading it like brushfire as they were unaware. More lethal than anything in records, the mortality rates were abysmal, young, old, healthy, or weak, those affected were likewise stricken, in mere days dead! There was nothing to suggest this was intentionally shared, blessed be no other villages closest to Gerda were affected. We hypothesized that the caravan's people got sick perhaps while still there or immediately after leaving and they all died. Regardless, no sightings of the actual caravan ever came back to us and no neighboring communities reported them stopping. Odd that considering 'tis their livelihood, hence our belief they all perished. But going back to your original question, yes I fear it could be collected and thus replicated.

"In searching for answers in the years that have passed after Gerda, while no mention of such a contagion was found, curiously, we did find a scroll that spoke of a process centuries past as a method of treatment. But in our lifetime and that of our recent predecessors it's not been taught. Perhaps the passing of time without a need of this method relegated it to be dropped from study and forgotten.

"As it is, we worked to isolate it, so as to identify and in order to create an antidote . . . a treatment. However, the other major problem lies in the fact that even if the two illnesses appear similar, 'tis the nature of these minuscule bacteria to alter or change from year to year. So, the treatment Creeker and I devised from years ago likely wouldn't be as effective today, and though we were thankful there was not an outbreak it meant there was no way to measure if our solution would work. So, my lords, though I cannot say with any certainty our formulations would work I believe the process is true, we've developed what we call an inoculum."

Creeker interjected anxiously, "Hypothetically, any such spreadable illness could be reduced in such a way and diluted and then the most minute of doses would be given so as to allow the body's humors to learn from and combat the contagion. It must be a minuscule amount, not enough that it could overwhelm and attack the body. Of a truth, from what we learned we have created and successfully used this method a decade past on infants to prevent an issue with the lungs that would seasonally see the loss of many wee ones. All midwives administer it across the kingdom."

"We must secure posthaste a sample and carefully study this contagion to create an inoculum."

It was worse than Ethan could ever have imagined. The story confirmed what Howard had just given, but it contained additional horrifying information. He looked at his father, who motioned him to a map of Saldanzia. "Before you arrived, we were hypothesizing as to the most likely spots that would spread quickly to produce the most damage to our population." Michael grimaced and motioned him to the maps. "If we aren't jumping to conclusions, and the king of Chilton is a threat to Saldanzia, the obvious place to my thinking would be our army, the same as Anchelle. 'Tis pure evil if we have it aright, brutally effective, and utterly diabolic!"

The sun was but a few hours from rising before Creeker and Spinter were on their way with direction to call upon Queen Arabella first thing in the morning. They needed firsthand accounts of the illness and prayed someone in the party had recovered from the illness so that they might obtain samples to create an inoculum.

Ethan, Michael, and Sophia summoned the Ruling Five for an emergency council and were in deliberations as soon as all could be gathered. While not the usual time of year for active sessions, all had agreed to remain close by while waiting on evidence in the matter of aiding Anchelle. As usual, the council under Lord Cleve's direction was a frustrating, chafing experience for Ethan. The first two hours, it was as though an explosion had gone off. Only Lord Surrey had known, leaving the remaining Five and all the people of Saldanzia unaware that any malady existed that could kill so many people. None had ever considered it could be used for warfare. Such a frightening idea was a hard thing to swallow.

Accusations were made, mostly against the Surreys, but of course Cleve had to get some digs in undermining Arabella that made Ethan's blood boil. After pontificating over his own stellar leadership and reiterating multiple times his opinion that they could not now consider lending aid to Anchelle, he demanded to know where and what the military was doing. Ethan gave them enough information to satisfy them, while holding back a bit. Cleve was not to be trusted.

When everything had come to a cooling point several hours later out of necessity, they put action to a plan for everyone's safety, and the time was more wisely spent.

Everything was conjecture at this point, which made action and preparation difficult to decide upon. Was Mason's plan to take over Saldanzia as well as the Norlans, or was he only after Anchelle? Was the malady his making, and something he would use on Saldanzia, or was it all an act of nature, and Mason was just using it to his advantage? With no scouts back yet, which heightened Ethan's ever-growing unease, it was decided that they plan for the worst-case scenario. Could Creeker and Spinter create an inoculum that could protect Saldanzia before such a threat arrived at their borders?

If the Ruling Five families split up, it would make it more difficult should Mason target them. This would mean all decisions would have to be made by few rather than the whole body. And the army . . . well, the army was Ethan's problem.

❧

Two days passed in a blur. Ethan didn't get any more than a few hours of sleep the first night and little more the next. He'd briefly seen Arabella in a council meeting as more intelligence was gathered, but not in a private setting. Not quite a fortnight ago, though it seemed longer when he'd brought Anchelle's queen, the problem seemed relatively simple: looking back, help a neighboring country or not. Now there was a huge uproar and turmoil over their citizens' safety. Could Saldanzia already be under attack and they were not yet aware? There was so much that they didn't know, too much speculation and unease. They must prepare for any eventuality, and Anchelle's problems were left to simmer in their static state.

As a precaution, the Five's families were dispatched to different parts of the country with one hundred guards per family. Ethan's own family went to a remote cabin in the mountains, where only his father and he himself knew the location. Ethan had tried to talk Arabella into going with his family, but she had adamantly refused.

Only one member of the ruling family members would stay behind to help in the potential crisis. Each one of the remaining Five had specific duties to fulfill. Lord Blake, Lord Grace, and Lord Surrey worked together over the possible shivers crisis. Lord Lorring would work with Ethan on all aspects of the military and safety.

The first action taken was to close and seal their borders, not only to halt all trade and commerce but alse to suspend all entry. The only people to be permitted to enter through the border were the scouts, leaving most of his military to the southern borders, and authorizing a few more be brought into the capital. He was spread out to be sure, but there was hope that if a sickness ripped through the land, all would not be lost.

Would the inoculum made years ago by Spinter be effective? They had indicated they needed samples from Arabella's people to compare. How long would it take to have enough for thousands of people in Saldanzia to distribute to the entire kingdom? Did they have enough time if the threat was valid?

Ethan's head pounded from the lack of sleep as he guzzled an herbal beverage to keep him alert. He knew he wasn't getting any sleep soon, and it was already midnight. Standing over a map, Ethan looked over those with him in the war room. Thomas, his first-in-command, Lorring—and he'd included Luke and Benton; all provided valuable insight to what might lie ahead. After another sip, a knock was heard at the door.

"Open!" Ethan commanded

A dirty, disheveled man entered, his body slightly hunched. His dust-covered beard hid his face, and it took Ethan a moment to recognize him.

"Forrester," Ethan exclaimed when he saw the man that looked like he was on death's door.

"Came . . . . as fast as I could," the man exclaimed. His eyes looked wild as they adjusted to the light, but seemed to stay that way.

"What news have you?" Ethan demanded, signaling a man to get Forrester a drink and some food. He grabbed the scout a chair and had him sit down, then another for himself.

"King of Chilton . . . he is on his way here." Forrester was gasping as though he had run the whole of his journey.

"How far out?" Ethan asked, his voice not wavering though his heartrate hiked up considerably. He had a million questions flow into his mind, but could only ask one at a time. Standing quickly, Ethan's chair rattled but kept from toppling.

"They were entering Cronan territory, when I left."

"How many days past?"

"Three, sir." The man held his gaze.

Ethan was incredulous. "It took you only three days from the border?"

"Aye, sir, I rarely stopped. My horse died 'bout fifty miles from our border, and I borrowed a horse in Frine."

Arabella entered the council chamber, her eyes widening as she took in the scout's disheveled appearance. Garner and Roland followed on her heels.

Ethan dispatched a runner for the remaining Five to come immediately, then succinctly caught Arabella up to date, before having Forrester continue.

The weary scout took a sip of water to relieve his parched throat before he launched on. "The Cronan were assembled waiting for them."

"The Cronan and the army of Mason are combined?" Dread pooled in Ethan's gut.

"How many total?" he asked, struggling to keep his tone even.

"Thirty thousand, sir."

"Thirty thousand?" Luke sputtered, coming into the conversation. "How is that possible?"

"Are you certain?" Ethan asked, sitting down next to him again. Hadn't he considered this very narrow possibility? It was unimaginable, and yet so was the thought of the controlled release of a horrific illness to decimate kingdom after kingdom.

Looking at the group assembled, then at Ethan he spoke, "I'm sure."

"How is that possible?" Luke asked again, though they were all thinking the same thing.

The scout seemed to see Luke for the first time, then looked at the group as a whole, stopping at Arabella.

"What is it?" Ethan asked. His voice held exasperation.

"Mayhap we might speak in private, sir?" Forrester spoke, his voice hardening. He seemed to be reviving from the journey.

Ethan looked at Arabella, who shrugged. "My men and I will leave if you wish it?" Arabella spoke.

"You can speak freely with them here, Forrester," Ethan, spoke, wishing the man would hurry. Ethan wanted to know everything the scout knew three days ago.

Forrester didn't seem happy to talk but continued, "Some of the men were wearing various Norlan colors, including Anchellian."

Arabella gasped, and Luke came unglued as he lunged at the man. "You lie!" Luke roared. Garner pulled Luke back as Ethan leveled a glare at Luke.

"Sit or leave Luke," Arabella commanded, in a voice he'd never heard used. The two starred each other down, before Luke dropped his shoulders and walked slowly to a chair and sat down heavily.

"I'm not surprised by the news," Ethan spoke, meeting Arabella's eyes, with a pained look.

Arabella regarded him as though he had blasphemed. Ethan held up his hands in defense. "I'm not saying that your people are willing. You are not going to like this, but, I'm sure he is conscripting your men to battle for him. Mason holds all the power, your own commander stayed to surrender. He forces them to march alongside his own soldiers anyplace he has already conquered. It is twofold in nature: first so he doesn't have to leave as many trusted loyal men to maintain the country taken, and moving forces he can't yet trust to conquer and complete his grab for domination. I'm sure your sister countries of the Norlans are in the same predicament. The shivers ravaged their country and then Mason brought his army in and pressed them to service?" Ethan looked to Forrester for confirmation.

The beleaguered man only nodded his head.

"We unfortunately had considered the possibility," Ethan responded, his eyes on Arabella, he watched as she processed his statement as realization flooded her face.

She was the one who further explained. "Mason has left his own appointed leaders to keep those remaining from rebelling, and taken all the able-bodied men to war. Their fear for their families at home would compel them to follow that monster's command."

Arabella started to walk away from the assembled group, her face downcast, her fists clenched. Ethan went to her and grasped her scrunched hands. Her visage looked up at him, her blank face which upon catching his eyes contorted. "You should have said something!" she accused.

"I hoped I was wrong," he answered, gently squeezing her hands and willing her to feel the truth of his words. She tried to pull free of his grasp, when Surrey, Cleve Blake, and Timothy Grace came through the door, questioning looks on all their faces. Cleve locked eyes with Arabella, a derisive smirk upon his face. Unable to hide her disgust of the man, she returned his gaze and straightened her shoulders. Ethan watched the exchange, feeling both furious toward Cleve, and proud of the way Arabella responded, righteous anger rolling off her frame.

Blake, unable to hold her gaze, turned and in scanning the room settled his gaze on the scout.

"Tell me everything that you just told them!" Cleve demanded.

The scout looked for permission from Ethan, his commander. Cleve, seeing the exchange, glared at both men, annoyed at having his question not answered immediately. Both men stood their ground which only infuriated him more. Ethan finally nodded his head in answer.

Forrester rehearsed what had already been said, and Cleve looked at Arabella with a smug look on his face. "So you be a traitor after all, just like your own mother! Fleecing us! You were putting blinders on us this whole time, so you could come in and take over Saldanzia. Naught but a conniving little witch!" Cleve stomped toward Arabella with spittle flying everywhere as he screamed at her.

Every man who had been present in the room prior to Cleve's arrival moved toward the current leader of the Five intent on damage, but it was Luke who was nearest that landed a solid punch, which resulted in the distinctive crack of a nose shattering. It knocked the man clear off his feet, landing abruptly on his buttocks. There was a heavy moment of silence before Cleve lifted his face, blood streaming from his nose. At any other time it may have been amusing but for the mottled rage that filled his face. He looked like a demon.

"Guards!" Cleve screamed, with a murderous look that he aimed at Arabella.

Guards poured into the room, a look of confusion on their faces. They looked between Cleve and Ethan.

"Arrest those men, and that woman," he yelled while pulling himself from off the floor. Cleve indicated the Anchellians. He touched the blood on his nose with his fingers before using the side of his sleeve to wipe away the inordinate amount of blood coming out, which only served to wipe the blood across his apoplectic face.

"Halt!" Ethan's firm command stopped the soldiers in their tracks, who had moved forward to do the ruler's bidding.

"I am the Ruling Five!" Cleve shouted at the guards. "I will see you all hanged if you don't do what I bid, this instant."

The guards shifted uneasily, but ultimately they looked at Ethan who motioned them out of the room, and they obeyed quickly.

"I will have your family taken from the Five forever for this, McKenna. This is an irrevocable act of war, all here must witness it." He looked at Lorring and Surrey to back him up. Surrey looked affrighted while Lorring looked mildly amused.

"Gentlemen," Timothy spoke, drawing everyone's attention. "Such maligning of my granddaughter's character would warrant any man in this room responding thusly, Cleve! It has been a very trying passage of days, we are all on edge and most are in desperate need of sleep. 'Tis critical now more than ever that we work together to overcome the common and real enemy here, Mason Kiefer. He has slaughtered a great many people, including the people of Anchelle by sickness." It looked like Cleve wanted to add his two bits, but Timothy gave him a pointed look. "If we don't stop bickering right now we might as well give him a parade and toss flowers at his feet while he marches down our streets.

"Now," Timothy spoke like he was talking with children. "We have more information than we did yesterday. Mason is coming, this is no longer conjecture. Each of us has our assignments. Let's get to work."

It looked like Cleve was building to argue, but after sweeping the room with his gaze and taking stock, he seemed to realize he had lost the vote among the Ruling Five. Spluttering expletives, he stomped his way out of the building.

⁓

Grandfather took Arabella's hand as he helped her in his waiting carriage. He did not speak until they were a distance from the other group.

"Have you ever had an inoculum, Arabella?" Timothy asked. She hadn't expected that after everything they had just experienced. Her mind was still thinking of the way Cleve had looked at her. Loathing was maybe not a strong enough word for what he felt for her.

Arabella tried to bring herself back to the question her grandfather had just asked her.

"Ah, no, until the recent plague the only real sickness my people had experienced was the seasonal influenza, and our healers have been very successful with herbs to ease it and eradicate many other illnesses. Why?" she asked, perplexed.

"Your blood samples are . . . different, than a couple of your men."

"How so?" A furrow between her eyes deepened as she looked to her grandfather.

"Spinter will visit with you, we spoke but briefly, I had just been coming to the council chamber as we had word of the returning scout. He needs you to call on him first thing in the morning."

"What about?" she asked, befuddled. She had spent so much of the past day at the healer workshop, she and her men answering hours of questions and providing a collection of blood from each of them.

"All I know is that Spinter believed you may have received what he called an inoculum, some sort of treatment, and indicated 'twas the only thing that could explain his findings."

"But I haven't," she said, feeling defensive. She would know if she had a healing treatment, wouldn't she? Her people didn't even utilize the method that had been described. Looking at her grandfather, she wondered if he believed her or not.

She needed sleep desperately.

Several hours later and without an update in information, Arabella sat with her men in a tidy sanatorium that served as a workspace for Spinter and Creeker. Though a few other healers worked around the room, none seemed to pay them any attention, but were busy moving with a frantic determination, measuring and mixing substances. There was a solemn feeling of those assembled. Sleep deprivation was the least of their shared concerns.

Her men fidgeted in their chairs, clearly wanting to be anywhere but present. It was a far cry from their normal knightly duties and news of the impending army made them anxious to see to such preparations.

The questions had been nonstop since they'd sat down hours previous. "Is it possible you all ingested or drank something that the others did not?" Spinter asked. *The others*, meaning those who had died from the epidemic. Arabella sighed, they had all been through this at least a dozen times. Spinter, Creeker, and the Anchellians had had numerous discussions over the last few days on the things they ate and drank and medicines they used. Endless hours trying to find something that linked them all together. Garner and Benton had gotten sick but had pulled through; most were not as fortunate. But Arabella, Roland, and Luke had never gotten sick, while everyone else around them eventually had.

"So between all of you, you collectively know of only about a few dozen people that never exhibited symptoms?" Creeker asked incredulously.

They looked at each other, then Arabella nodded her head. Still after all this time, they had no idea how come they had not come down with the shivers. It was truly mystifying even now, knowing that so few had escaped the illness. In the horror of the grueling days of death when they all worked to see to the overwhelming needs of their people, she'd not thought of the oddity that so many of her inner circle had not fallen ill. Everyone present had lost many in their families; no family was unscathed.

"Let's try something different," Spinter suggested. "Why don't all of you take me through what a typical week would be for each of you, or rather the fortnight before the first death?" Everyone looked at each other. They wanted to help, but this seemed useless. "Please, perhaps we might discern what you all have in common, most especially Arabella, Roland, and Luke.

You never got sick, so let's see if there is any type of variance." Momentarily distracted as one of his assistants spoke to him, he bent over a paper and lifted his glasses to see better. The group from Anchelle looked to Arabella, who shrugged her weary shoulders. Reliving the bleakness and the minute details of the illness that ravaged their kingdom was sickening.

"Garner, Benton, would you find Ethan and see if he has learned anything new, and return posthaste with updates, unless we meet aforehand?" Arabella asked. They looked only too happy to comply with her directive. Luke rolled his eyes as Roland tried hard not to smile.

Garner and Benton somehow must have missed the commander, as mere minutes after they left, Ethan appeared. He looked tired and weighed down, but was extremely welcome and most handsome to her beleaguered sight. Handing her a brown box tied with a red ribbon, with a very cute grin on his face, he placed a brief kiss on her lips before speaking. "For my sweet. Have we discovered anything new?" he asked.

Spinter, seeing the commander, finished with the assistant and walked over. "Aye, some disconcerting news." He didn't wait to be asked but dove right in. "The sickness from sixteen years ago is near similar to the shivers of Anchelle; however, the strain is different."

"And that means?" Ethan asked.

"The shivers, once passed to a body, will react more quickly to incapacitate. The inoculum we made for the last one may prove helpful, as 'tis certainly related at an elemental level, but not enough that people with the inoculum may still get sick. Some who receive it may still die, mostly likely the elderly and I'm sad to say the little ones."

Ethan took a large gulp, his face visibly paling.

"But at least we have the original inoculum," Ethan said. "'Tis better than naught. How many people can we give this treatment?"

Spinter didn't seem too excited with the question. "Only about five hundred, my lord," he stated, wincing as he found the commanders' forlorn eyes.

Ethan seemed dumbfounded but pushed forward. "How soon can you make more?" His subdued voice was rough.

"We can start immediately, but we were hoping to get a better version, one from their blood samples," Spinter said, indicating the Anchellians.

"We are out of time, Mason's army will be here in five days." Ethan's frustration was plainly echoed by those listening. "How soon till the inoculum will take effect?"

"Almost immediately, we believe, sir."

The relief was palpable, they were all desperate for any news that could be considered favorable. Chances were high the sickness was already here. Mason hadn't marched on the other cities until the shivers had run its course. That he was marching here so soon meant that he knew word would get out, and he didn't want to give Saldanzians a chance to protect themselves. Though it was possible that he would forgo the devastating illness, secure in the knowledge that he possessed an army equal to that of Saldanzia.

"That being said," Spinter injected. "If the sickness is already here or within days as suggested, we won't be able to create the inoculum quick enough to help anybody."

Everybody was quiet and disheartened. The awful reality was that there was little they could do to protect themselves against the virus as the invading army continued their approach.

Other council members arrived hearing the news. It was decided to move forward with mass production from the old inoculum with time so limited. Who knew when the virus would strike? The big question was: who would receive the five hundred vaccines first?

Cleve, sporting blackened eyes, argued that only the Ruling Five families received the vaccine. That messengers be sent out posthaste to the families with the available inoculum. Others argued that the healers and several of the key figures in the army should all be beneficiaries of the treatment so as to protect and create additional treatments.

Arabella listened to the news, knowing it was all vitally important, the box all but forgotten in her lap as she listened and followed the heated discussion. Once the comments started to repeat, she had closed her eyes in contemplation. It was beginning to mash together and her body felt heavy with the strain. While she had opinions, it didn't matter, this wasn't her country. Her grandfather would heartily disagree, but no matter the outcome, she would do all in her power to return to her birth country.

Leaving the laboratory, she went outside to get some fresh air. With all those people clamoring to be heard with their varied opinions, the air had become suffocating. She needed to be able to think clearly. Garner and Benton had taken up post outside the building, and as she began walking her men shadowed behind her. It was sometime before her head was clear enough that she was ready to hear what her men had to say. "Garner?" she invited.

The guard shared opinions and updates as they walked. Their feet, she realized, had carried them to what she had come to think of as "her sanctuary." The light drizzle had turned to a deluge as they entered the quiet hush of the stone church, and she prayed that the inclement weather here would mean the invading army was delayed. Rain that slowed their preparations would also likely slow an army. The peace of the place was a balm to the chaos that had seemed a constant companion of late. She marveled anew that she could still feel God's presence here after the contention and pressures of the council chambers and sanatorium.

Arabella and her knights settled on a few plans of their own shortly after they had gathered, which resulted in her sending Benton out on a mission.

Another hour passed in the sanctuary when Luke came and sat down by her. He lifted the box that had been sitting on the pew and handed it to her, his eyebrows wagging at her playfully, encouraging her inspection. It was a welcome distraction, but was it proper to open it up without Ethan present? He'd given it to her without fanfare and with many watching. Desperately wanting to know what was in it, she peeked in the box, a smile stretching her face.

She looked up and saw that Luke was still watching her, and wagging eyebrows again questioning her.

"'Tis candy," she whispered. "Just what I needed."

"Me too," he whispered back.

"Who says I'm sharing?" she asked smirkingly.

Luke rolled his eyes. "When have you ever not? Remember those candy from your secret admirer?" he asked, laughing too loud in the place of worship. "'Twasn't very good."

She put a finger to his lip to quiet him. He looked a little sheepish. "'Twas a most kind notion, everyone knows of my sweet tooth. I . . ." She didn't know if she should say his name out loud, it was still too painful. "I think Thaddeus gave it to me."

Luke grimaced but washed it from his face before he spoke. "Most assuredly not. Thaddeus had a honey," he stated while rolling his eyes. "What makes you think 'twasn't from me?"

"Mayhap because you had three 'honeys' of your own at that time," she said, trying not to laugh at his choice of words. He grinned sheepishly again.

"Said 'twas from an admirer, but I think Thaddeus was just being thoughtful. Don't you remember? Mason had stormed from the keep after my father declined to allow a marriage. Thaddeus knew how upset it made me, and was just trying to cheer me up."

"Mason is determined to yoke the earth or burn it down, isn't he?" Luke spoke, anger thick in his voice. He loosened up after a few moments. Like he just remembered he was trying to cheer her up, not make her more miserable. "That does sound like Thaddeus though," he agreed wistfully. "But," he said, perking up, "no reason not to try these out."

She handed him a hard pink candy as he smiled. "Don't mind if I do."

Standing up, she popped one in her mouth. A smile unfurled across her face as she moved toward the other guards.

"Mmm!" she moaned. "'Tis delicious."

Joining them, they shared and stood just inside the narthex, watching the driving rain, each in deep thought, but every so often each would indulge in another candy, until the box was empty. The camaraderie she felt with these men had been healing. This snatched moment of quiet filled her with an inexplicable peace it would be impossible to describe in the blatant face of opposition, yet she felt it! Arabella sent a silent prayer to her maker for this precious gift amid the storms.

They had been unable to help Spinter but perhaps all was not yet lost. Surely this peace was evidence that God was with them and there was always hope to be found in Him.

When the rain finally diminished they set off to the Grace estate and straight to the lists to burn off the pent-up energy and sugar.

CHAPTER 12

After making it out of Spinter's workspace, Ethan seques-
tered himself with several of his top commanders in the war
room, including Thomas, his next in command. Inoculums were
administered to each man, Ethan took his first and watched the
solemn expressions as each man received his own. They assuredly felt as guilty as he. Each had wives and children at home
or family they would gladly give it to. But they each had a grave
responsibility in maintaining the safety of their nation.

Ethan sat down at the table, then nodded at the soldier by
the door to have Forrester brought in.

Freshly shaven and in clean clothes, Forrester did not look
like the same man Ethan had seen the night before.

"You appear remarkably improved," Ethan stated.

"I feel better. Thank you, sir."

"We need every detail that you can give us," Ethan said.

Forrester began from the moment he left Ethan in the
Hoodoos, which had only been a couple of hours before Ethan
had first met Arabella.

They were interrupted an hour later by a pounding of the
door. A white-faced Creeker was shown in, his expression grim.

The man looked directly at Ethan. "Sir, 'tis just confirmed,
the shivers are in Saldanzia."

An audible gasp was heard. Ethan, who had stood when Creeker entered, now sat down. The room was silent as they all looked at Ethan.

"Thank you, Creeker. Please do all you can to contain the spread as we discussed previously, and keep me informed on the dispensing of treatment. If you need anything else or have information you think might be of import to our cause, send a runner with the messages. Your time is of great value and will be needed at the infirmary."

Creeker nodded his head.

"Did you receive the inoculum?" Ethan asked just as the man turned to leave.

"Aye sir, thank you."

Ethan nodded his head in dismissal. He felt a twinge of remorse that one of his first thoughts was how Arabella would take the news, followed by how the people of Saldanzia would take the news. What did it say of him that with an invading army and a plague that could kill many people, that his first thought was of her? Ethan hoped that his family's departure from the city had got them ahead of the sickness.

It was a continuous effort to keep her from his thoughts. Despite the approaching army, he thought of her safety first. Everything that happened now, he wondered how it would affect her. He wanted to be her knight in shining armor; he was determined to save her. When Cleve had torn after her the night before, Ethan had gone for his blade, ready to call him out. Luke had unknowingly saved the wretched man's life when he had punched him.

Most of the lights were off in the Grace home when he pulled his horse to a stop in front of it. He hesitated, wondering if he should awaken her. She would need all the precious sleep she could manage. He could use some sleep himself, but he desperately wanted to see her.

Luke walked out from the shadows and approached him.

"Is she asleep then?" he asked her protector, wishing it were him.

"Aye, finally."

"I'm sure it was a rough day for her. I'm glad she can get some sleep."

"Me too," Luke said solemnly.

"Will you tell her I will be here by sunrise tomorrow? Ask her to stay till I arrive?"

"Aye."

Ethan started to turn away, but Luke stopped him as he grabbed the horse's bridle. "You won't let her walk away, will you?" he said seriously.

Ethan looked at Luke and measured him up. "I would definitely be a fool if I did, wouldn't I?" For a time Ethan had wondered if Luke loved Arabella, because who in their right mind wouldn't? He now knew that Luke loved her, and that Arabella loved him, but it was familial, like brother and sister, true and devoted as any sibling could be. They did have a special bond, and he was happy for that.

Luke smiled. "That would be an understatement."

"I would never ask her to stay here. I know she has a duty, but 'tis much more than that, she really loves Anchelle and all of you."

"I said naught of her staying," Luke scoffed, walking back to the shadow's embrace, leaving Ethan wondering if he just said what he thought he said. Deducing that the only solution in this matter was for Ethan to leave Saldanzia? And had he just been dismissed? By a knight?

⁓

Early the next morning Ethan was shown to the Grace family gardens, where Arabella appeared to have the bulk of her guard surrounding her, though they quickly dispersed as she stood to greet him. Dressed in breeches and a long-sleeved linen shirt, she was unlike anything he had seen before. He fought to not stare or linger over her legs. A blade swung from a hip and another was strapped to her thigh. It seemed she was headed for the lists. The smile she gave him made him feel as if the world had stilled. Stopped. Moments before his world had been a jumble of lists as he sorted through tasks and strategies. Last eve he'd returned home certain to find immediate sleep, but it had evaded him. Even with everything that was going on, what bothered him the most was Luke's parting shot, the night before.

She stood still, prepared to greet him as he made his way through the tall green evergreens. "I've missed you," he whispered while he gathered her in his arms. She smelled of fresh flowers, or perhaps a fruit, he couldn't readily identify, but it was something sweet and tantalizing, the scent different and intoxicating as nothing had been in the past.

"And I you," she sighed into his chest.

"My thanks for the sweets," she said, touching his arm. "'Twas most delicious, I've never tasted the flavor afore. What do you call it?"

"Touret. My mother shared 'twas your mother's favorite candy, and we wondered if 'tis found in Anchelle or not. I guess that settles the question." They removed to the stone bench.

"I shall have to fill my saddlebags full when I go," she said laughingly. "'Tis divine. Actually, now that I think on it, saddlebags won't be enough. Sir Roland and Luke will have it gone afore we reach Anchelle."

"You shared?" he asked, as though wounded, while inside his stomach clenched at the casual mention of her leaving. It served as a cold dousing of reality.

"'Tis gone," she said sadly. "Luke had some, and then of course I had to share with Roland . . ." There was a long pause, and her body tightened, and her eyes went wide in shock. She appeared to look at Ethan but he was certain she wasn't seeing him. "The sweets . . . the candy." Her eyes darted around, then looked at Ethan again. "'Twas the candy!"

"What was?" he asked, confused. He attempted to capture both her hands, but she shot to her feet and called out to Luke.

She paced back and forth furiously till Luke arrived, a little out of breath. Luke gave Ethan a wary look before he gave his attention to Arabella.

She dropped suddenly back to the bench, her knee bobbing in another sign of her agitation. Luke sat beside her, and Arabella waved Ethan over to join them. She had both of their undivided attention. She looked at Luke. "The candy I thought from Thaddeus, I shared with you, Thaddeus, Roland, Abigail, and Cook." She articulated each name.

Luke's eyes went bright with understanding, leaving Ethan still in the dark.

"Who else has been giving you candy and why is that significant?" Ethan spoke, feeling quite confused and irritable at the thought of another trying to win her affection.

Arabella turned her attention to Ethan. "Because we were the only six to not get sick in the whole of the castle." She let that sink in. "And . . . I received the candy from a secret admirer, a day after another marriage proposal from Mason. The candy came from Mason, when all this time I thought 'twas from Thaddeus, meant to cheer me from the dread of Mason's visit."

The thought of marriage proposals from that monster was wholly unsettling. "What was the candy?" Ethan tersely queried.

Arabella looked thoughtful. "'Twas not anything we had afore tasted, so I took it to Cook, to see if she knew the flavor. After tasting a piece she said 'twas something she had eaten as a little girl, in her village of Tilken. Cook hadn't had it since we didn't grow saysee in Anchelle."

"Could it have been any ingredient Mason mixed in, not the saysee?" he said, though he didn't want to crush the hope radiating from her. It was a likely conclusion.

"But," she said with a twinkle in her eye, "saysee is only grown in the Tilken hillsides, hundreds of miles from Anchelle. 'Twas another reason I thought Thaddeus was my secret admirer." Arabella turned to Luke. "Thaddeus had just returned from Tilken. Do you remember? My father sent a few scouts to see what Mason was doing so far from his home."

Arabella turned her attention to Ethan. "Father was always wary of Mason, and had him watched," she said.

Luke's face lit up with some remembrance, and then his face morphed into that of regret and misery. "How did we not remember this afore?" Luke groaned in frustration.

"How could we have known?" Arabella stated. "Seemed fairly benign at the time. And then we were all fighting for our lives. None could have imagined a sickness delivered by a man to kill our people. He is the worst sort of evil imaginable."

They were all deep in thought for a minute as silence hung in the air. Ethan's mind was running unchecked. Was it possible? Would this herb saysee really be the cure or a treatment to the shivers? And if so, how fast could they procure some? How soon would it take effect? Could a simple ingredient of a candy be the cure to his people's devastation?

"Is this saysee grown all year round? I've never even heard of it," Ethan questioned Arabella

"I don't really know, Thaddeus was there in the summer months. And now we are in the spring months . . . I'm not really sure," she acknowledged. "I'm sorry. But we could leave immediately and try to bring as much back as possible?"

He took a minute to think it over, mulling the pros and cons over in his head. A really fast rider could be in Tilken in two days. But getting an appropriate amount and hauling it back by wagons would take much more time. The fighting could be done by then. She would be out of the city, but then again, he would still bet the city would be a safer place for her to be. Arabella was a good negotiator, and her opinion held weight, but Tilken might already have an alliance with Mason, and it could get ugly. In that case, she would be safer here.

Might it also have been when Mason formed an alliance? Tilken land bordered Cronan and Saldanzian borders. It would make sense.

He shook his head. "No, as soon as I've talked to Spinter and Creeker, if they agree tis a plausible solution, I will dispatch men immediately.

"Can I have a moment?" he asked Luke, who gave him a pointed look before disappearing the way he had come. He took Arabella's small, callused hands into his own and turned them over, gently touching the hardened calluses. "I'm guessing you are for the lists?" She smiled and nodded her head. "Do you wear breeches oft?"

"Just to the lists, 'twas the only time my father allowed it," she remarked, leaving him no doubt that was a disappointment for her.

"You are a queen now," he taunted. "You can wear whatever you like." Bringing her hands to his lips, he gently kissed the calluses of her palms. "But alas, once again, I can see his wisdom."

"How so?" she asked innocently.

"Well, to any man in existence, you look much too enticing." Her eyes went wide, as her lips formed a perfect O followed by a spectacular blush stealing across her delicate cheekbones.

"I need to leave," he spoke with regret. "Will you promise me something?"

"Depends on what you ask of me," she replied with concern.

"Can you remain here at your grandfather's estate, until I come for you?" he asked her so very softly, compelling, all but begging her to agree.

"When will that be?" Her voice held a slight edge, wary.

"I'm not sure, but Arabella, I *need* to protect you." What he didn't say but troubled him was that while there were a lot of good people in this city, there were a lot of terrified people right now, and even rational good people liked to blame others for their misfortunes no matter how unfounded they really were. He didn't know if he could trust the people to do the right thing right now, namely Cleve.

"I know the people are scared and some even angry with me. That I came upon heels of an illness with a tyrant following. Should I hide, they will believe the story all the more, regardless of its veracity. No. I'm a queen and must have the strength to defend my people and my actions!"

The inactivity of the past few days, with only time in the lists that could temporarily alleviate her desire to act, was beginning to wear on her, he could well surmise.

"I know well, sweetheart," he said, looking her in the eye, and bringing her hand to cup his cheek, "but I don't know if I . . . can take it," he grumbled.

"Listen, I will come see you, or I will send Thomas for you, but please don't leave. Your grandfather's estate is well protected, doubly so with your extraordinarily well-trained men."

She nodded in agreement of her men's superior skills, but still didn't say yes.

"Please? Arabella?"

"All right, I will endeavor to stay here, and be a good little girl," she retorted impishly. Concern melted from him. This woman had no idea the power she held over him. He would do anything she asked, if she would only ask . . . He pulled her into a tight embrace and kissed the top of her head, and groaned. "I've got to go."

"I know," she said.

Leaning down, he poured his heart into a kiss he knew would be seared into her heart and mind forever. At last breaking free, he petitioned huskily, "Be safe, Highness."

He bowed and she added breathlessly, "Aye, you as well, my lord." The way she pronounced *my* had a grin erupting across his face, and then he turned and walked away with purposeful strides.

~

As Ethan gathered up the reins to mount his horse to leave the estate, he was caught up in the memory of their last kiss. Those luscious, sweet lips would be the death of him. He was taken by surprise as Benton led his horse up next to him.

"A bit of woolgathering?" the man questioned dryly.

Ethan hadn't blushed in a long time, but he felt his cheeks heat at being caught. The commander of the Saldanzian army woolgathering?

"Aye, you have me dead to rights," he admitted, chuckling.

Benton chortled along.

"I thought you left the city?" Ethan questioned.

"I was, and am headed out again," the scout replied, not adding any more information than that.

They mounted their horses and rode in silence for a moment, Ethan patiently waiting for Benton to speak what he had come to say.

"You once asked me concerning Mason."

"Aye," Ethan encouraged.

"To give this story perspective, it must needs start thirty years ago." Benton paused in his consideration. "Garrett and Daniella had fallen in love here in Saldanzia, though she was engaged to . . ."

"Cleve Blake," Ethan filled in for him. "An arranged marriage." Ethan spat the words out, grateful his parents had never done anything as antiquated as that.

"Yes," Benton agreed and continued, "Garrett felt it was time he return to Anchelle, and Daniella agreed to go with him as his betrothed. Somehow Lord Timothy found out about it and fabricated a letter to Garrett saying that Daniella had changed her mind, and felt strongly her duty was to remain in Saldanzia and she would marry Cleve.

"Heartbroken, Garrett left without speaking to Daniella. Of course, Daniella had no idea and thought that Garrett had changed his mind and left her heartbroken as well.

"Cleve and Daniella's wedding was planned, and as these grand weddings go, all dignitaries far and wide were invited. On the day of the wedding, Daniella found that she couldn't go through with it, and she went to your mother for help."

"I had heard a little something of this from Arabella," Ethan acknowledged. "But my parents haven't ever told me the story."

"I'm not surprised," Benton said. "Can you imagine if Cleve or Timothy were to hear of it? Where you are all so closely tied together, I'm sure they haven't told anyone."

"I can see how that would go very badly, considering how everyone feels about the integrity and need for the council."

"Just so. There was a search for Daniella everywhere, but she was not to be found. Your own parents had hidden her away until those who had come for the wedding left. They secreted her with the party of the king of Theron, a very good man who understood Daniella's plight and was happily married to a lady of his own choosing. The good king said he would assist Daniella in her journey as long as she needed.

"A month after they had left, Garrett wrote a letter to your father. Garrett had heard of the canceled wedding and the disappearance of Daniella, and wanted to know what he could do in the search for Daniella.

"Lord Michael was furious with Garrett for abandoning Daniella, not knowing anything concerning the letter. It took almost half a year for the men to clear up the misunderstanding," Benton chuckled.

Ethan could well imagine. Letters took so long to travel from one country to the next.

"Daniella always said 'twas the longest year. One whole year till Garrett found her."

"Daniella told you this story?" Ethan asked.

Benton wiggled his head side to side. "I lived it. I was Garrett's squire."

What? A monarch that did the knight's training? Ethan could hardly believe it. But hadn't he done something similar, refusing a rank he hadn't earned to start his career, though it was his right to claim?

"I will admit that Garrett was an unusual knight, being heir to the throne. But as I am sure you are coming to understand, Anchelle's monarchy is nothing like other kingdoms. Daniella, the angel that she was, had a soft spot for me. I was with Garrett when he arrived in Theron, frantic, in his search for his love.

"You can understand why this has been kept secret for so long? If Cleve or Timothy were to learn that the king of Theron harbored Daniella, what fractures might it cause the tenuous relations? Especially in light of the recent massacres in Acropolis and Minerva."

"For certain. What a mess," Ethan agreed with a shake of his head.

"As you well know, Daniella and Garrett were married. A happy marriage they had." Benton was looking off to the south. His face had a soft smile from the memory. "However . . ." A dark look replaced the smile. "In the sojourn of Theron, Daniella made the acquaintance of the king's cousin. The man had become utterly obsessed with her. Can you guess who that was?"

"No, who?" Ethan asked.

"Dorian Kiefer."

"Mason's father?" Ethan questioned. He was aware only that a relative of King Theron had married the female heir to the Chilton kingdom. Maybe Mason felt he was owed the Theron kingdom and that was why he had attacked it, or he felt slighted, but that would be another story, and as fascinating as this story was, he was two furlongs from his destination and needed to visit with Spinter on the possible validity of the saysee herb.

"Aye," Benton confirmed. "He was absolutely fixated on Daniella. There were even attempts to kidnap her once afore, and once after they were married. Even though he was married with an heir already. Possessed! It seems he just couldn't let go of her."

"And you believe Mason to be of the same ilk as his father?" Ethan knew where this thread was taking them.

"Aye, without question!" Benton said. "Garrett was determined to not hold his father's sins against him, insisted Mason be given a fair chance, hoping he was different, but he just isn't.

"Actually, I misspeak. He is different. He is much more calculating, stronger, and one of the best swordsmen I have seen. In some ways he is rigid in discipline, but when it comes to Arabella, 'tis entirely different matter. He wants to possess her! He wants her fierceness, her sweetness, and all things that are uniquely her." Benton's face was dark with disdain.

"Mason sought Arabella's betrothal twice. He was firmly denied. There was the kidnapping attempt afore the shivers took hold. One of the reasons it didn't succeed was a decoy that had been put in Arabella's place a week earlier."

"Hold . . ." Ethan said. "Mason tried to abduct her?" Of *course* he had tried to take her, just like in the Hoodoos.

Benton nodded his head. "Once his true colors were revealed, I was ordered by King Garrett to cross into Chilton and gather as much information as I could on Mason after the failed abduction. I secreted into his castle while Mason was on a hunt."

Naturally. No one could disappear like Benton. Ethan would very much like to develop that skill further.

"What found you?" Ethan finally asked.

"Maps and notes, but his plans were coded, and I couldn't decipher any of it." Benton shrugged his shoulders, a wistful expression on his face. "'Twas most unfortunate. Perhaps if I'd managed it, it might have saved us from the shivers. So much death."

Ethan was getting anxious; they were almost to the destination. There had to be more to the story. "And," he prodded.

"In his bedchambers," Benton said reluctantly, his face hardening and his knuckles tight, "I found a lot of paintings and charcoal drawings. Probably thirty total. All of them were pictures of Arabella, with the exception of one of Mason's mother." Benton stopped his horse, causing Ethan to halt his own. He got up next to Ethan, looked around, and lowered his voice substantially.

"Some of them were beautiful depictions of Arabella, showing her tenderness and kindness, others of her fierceness and determination, fighting in the lists, and riding Palachio. And then there were the pictures of Arabella and Mason being married in an Anchellian church and another of her pregnant beside him. More troublesome than those were two more that I have told no one but her father and you. They were, let's say," he said, his face hard with anger at the memory, "decidedly indecent in nature."

Ethan couldn't hide his shock and fury.

"In another room, I found similar drawings of Daniella." Benton let that sink in. "I stole them and burned them at the first opportunity." Benton matched Ethan's look.

"As goeth the father, so goeth the son." Ethan whispered the old adage.

Benton nodded his head.

They walked their mounts the remaining distance to Saldanzian headquarters, but before they got within hearing of the guards at the gate Benton concluded: "'Tis my opinion that Mason is brilliant. The shivers alone prove that. Theron proves that. He may or may not want to rule the world, but nothing— and I mean nothing—will stop him from making Arabella his own, save death alone." Finality laced his bitter words.

"Why share it now?" Ethan strove to remove the disgust from his tone. The whole of it sickened him. There had been other opportunities to have this discussion, so why hold it till now?

"Any man to whom Arabella chooses to plight her troth must fight that demon afore they can truly have peace. Our queen deserves a worthy champion for a companion."

Four days later, Ethan paced next to his father in the southern border town of Capri as one of his sentries alerted him Mason's army was a mere two hours' ride from their border. Michael had taken his family safely to the mountains but couldn't assuage the need to help his country. Feeling his family was as safe as could be maintained, Michael came back to lend his expertise.

Though Ethan had been very careful in his concealment of his men throughout the area, he had recent information that one unit had come down with the shivers. All were isolated with the hopes of halting the spread. Not knowing when and how the illness had been spread initially, nor how long it took to show signs of it, made these decisions difficult.

Ethan had sent Lord Surrey with a company of soldiers to Tilken, praying they might secure some of the herb and that the efforts would bear a treatment for the deadly plague. However, they could hardly expect to see them for several days regardless of their success. Sprinter and Creeker had created leaflets to be dropped at every household. Riders were sent out with directions across the kingdom to warn and advise how to treat and separate those that became ill. Cleve had argued against it, but the rest of the council had been fully united that the people be made aware of the threats.

There were numerous ways that this plague could have been triggered in Saldanzia. Quickly they had realized the futility of trying to determine it, and chose instead to prepare what they could.

In his soul, Ethan felt like Mason would head to Capri first, it having been the weakest city historically. The Cronan raids were no coincidence. Their small military campaigns to draw soldiers from the smaller cities were to see what kind of fighting force the cities would produce. Ethan felt in his bones that the slaughter of the civilians in western borders had been premeditated in serving to draw their armies to that location.

For the invaders to get to the capital of Saldanzia, he was sure to use their direct roadways that would allow the army to travel with greater speed and access to pillage food and resources as soldiers passed through several small cities. Ethan would know shortly which city Mason planned to attack first. He just prayed that everything he had implemented would be enough to hold back the attack. If he was wrong, they would have to turn their army about and make haste to another position. He was evaluating his land's security critically to understand how the enemy would perceive their defenses to know where their attack might be most successful.

From the top of the parapet Ethan could see a rider stirring a dust cloud in the distance. The late spring morning was already starting to feel warm and there was a small shimmer in the air. The ground around the city already looked like a battle zone. The earth was dug out around the whole city, creating deep, gaping trenches. The rough-hewn spikes protruding from the hole, though barbaric, were most deadly. And the treeline was pushed back to provide no cover for the advancing army. The reality of war was upon this landscape afore the enemy had even arrived. He prayed it was enough.

Field glasses were fetched and Ethan finally marked the distinct black gelding of one of his own scouts, who had the animal in a full out gallop, and he knew he would soon have an answer. If Mason was coming to Capri, this was the scout that would be sent to the capital to give the needed information. Mason was headed to Capri! Ethan let out a breath he hadn't realized he had been holding. His father clapped his hand on his shoulder.

"You read the terrain aright, well done!" his father exclaimed.

Not yet, Ethan thought. There was still the fact that Mason marched with his thirty thousand on his ten thousand, who at any point could become sick. Ten thousand were stationed with Thomas at Peligree and another ten thousand were stationed in Saldanzia. Perhaps those numbers were already significantly decreased; unknown to him were the number of sick. The people had worked alongside the army in making the defensive changes to the outer wall. He sent up a prayer that it would prove a grave deterrent.

The day grew warmer and the men started to become restless. The wait seemed to go on and on, though in truth was only a few hours. But in an eerie wave, barbarians appeared through the expanded treeline. Their heads shorn, blood-red streaks across their faces and pale bodies: the Cronan. It was unheard of, them fighting alongside one of the civilized kingdoms. A piercing howling rent the air, the sound of thousands of vicious wolves hungry to attack.

The men next to Ethan began to murmur. The sound was so disconcerting and feral it had struck fear into his men. The look alone of the Cronan would make most women swoon in terror. Ethan had seen his enemy many times but had never gotten used to seeing men look so inhuman. Everything about them was meant to intimidate the enemy. They looked evil, black smudges around their eyes and the blood of animals or humans on much of the exposed, whitest-of-white skin. *How does skin stay so pale when they live under the sky?* he marveled. Their battle array, he realized by focusing his magnifying glass; he noted they wore the complete hide of animals to cover their vital parts. The hair from the animal was still intact, making them look like the hairy beasts they had echoed with their screams.

Ethan notched an arrow at the one that was the leader, identifiable now by the elaborate necklaces of tooth and bone, and let the arrow loose. It hit the man in the torso, causing him to fall back swiftly. Ethan's archers followed suit, effectively stopping the noise as they pierced the unprotected bodies of the Cronan. Archers that had stopped in the security of the new treeline volleyed shots back at the Saldanzians as the Cronan retreated. The shots fell just short of the city walls, causing Ethan to grin.

Mason watched the volley of arrows that halted the Cronan advancement from atop his mount. Capri was a complete surprise. The Cronan scouting parties had all reported that the isolated city would be easy to take. When, in fact, it looked from the outside like it might take more troops than had originally been told would be needed to defeat it. The gouged earth and rough-split green timbers bespoke the recent work that had been put into fortifying this city. Noting with frustration the evidence of recently cleared land that put the wall outside their archers' range, his anger was building rapidly. Mason's campaign thus far had been swift. His strategy and planning had been meticulous. How would they even know he had planned to attack here?

No matter, the cannons were on their way, a bit behind his men, not traveling nearly as fast. But they would prove useful tools yet.

Previously, Mason had met with little resistance in his rampage. The different countries of the Norlans had fallen easily, with few losses amongst his own troops. Not that his opponents had a chance. So many were dead that they had never even had hope to launch any sort of counterattack. The shivers had worked with deadly efficiency. He wondered if most in the city of Capri were sick, and the outside was just a facade.

"Send out the archers!" Mason bellowed. "Two archers for every shield."

His soldiers huddled under their shields as they left behind the cover of the trees and scampered closer to the city's wall.

At a command, the archer holding the shield removed the protection so that the other could fire.

Anticipating the tactic, the soldiers in Capri responded with a volley in response. The sky seemed to darken under the barrage of a blanket of arrows crossing the sky. Many of Mason's archers dropped like flies, while others remained protected beneath a shield. There was no way to tell what damage had been inflicted by Mason's archers to the Saldanzians.

This might take much longer than originally calculated, he thought to himself. Which, on reflection, might not be all bad. Obviously they were better prepared than foreseen, but time was his ally. More of them would become sick and unable to fight. Either way they would die, but Mason didn't need to lose his own men in the process. He would need a strong healthy army to maintain all the countries. More time meant fewer to fight. Calling his men back, he split his army in half, leaving half to take the city of Capri. They would lay siege to the city, and in due time, with the sickness soon to take its toll, they would defeat it.

Meanwhile, he might as well proceed to the next city. He considered himself a patient man, but he was fast losing that tightly wrapped control he so prided himself on. Had he waited another week this would have been a simple exercise of taking control of those left. Arabella had led him on a good chase, and he loved the challenge the girl provided, because it led him to where he was today. The most powerful man in all the kingdoms of the Norlans, and soon Saldanzia. That woman was a worthy prize, one he felt pulling, compelling him to act.

His father had been too weak to take what he wanted, but this further proved to him the rightness of his own path. He would rule the entire continent in his bid to have her.

⁓

Ethan walked the entire breadth of the parapet, taking note of Mason's army that was surrounding Capri. As he returned from his starting point on the west side, he was rewarded with the sight of a large group of Mason's soldiers detaching from the main group and heading in the direction of Peligree. Was Mason leaving half his force to lay siege to the city? It would effectively cut the men off stationed here to the rest of Saldanzia.

He wished it were the biggest obstacle he faced. Ethan's men were dropping in large numbers—and it was not to the arrow or sword. The shivers had somehow made its way into the city. Perhaps it had been there all along. Though the city had drastically improved their defense in the past days, if there were no men to fight, there would be no one to hold it. How could he, a man who had trained his whole life to defend his country, protect it from something so insidious? The monster was waging war on more than just another army, but upon every man, woman, and child. That kind of evil could not be reasoned with nor amicable treaties made. To have such blatant disregard for life was unfathomable to him. It gave him great pause to think that Arabella had earned the attention and obsession of the madman. It shook him to the core to think of her strength and sweetness under the power of such a beast.

As Mason's army made camp for the night, it was bittersweet. Had they attacked now, they had a decent fighting force to repel the onslaught. If the enemy settled in to wait for the sickness to decimate them from within, the only way they might survive, was if Surrey's force managed to find and return with the saysee, which he desperately prayed was an effective treatment. The only other option they had was to attack Mason in an all-out hand-to-hand combat. The idea didn't sit well with him. He was disturbed about having to fight those from the Norlans, knowing many had been pressed into service. Was there any way to turn them to fight Mason? Arabella might have such an effect, but there was no way he was bringing her here.

Next to him, he noted another one of his soldier's hands and body go from almost indiscernible tremors to violent shaking, while another beside him was bent over, vomiting.

Hours later, after the darkness banished the day, Ethan lay abed shaking uncontrollably. *So cold, why is it so cold?* He couldn't seem to get the blanket to stay atop him. What was wrong with the blanket? It was like it had a mind of its own. He saw his dad come and look down at him. "How fare you, son?" he asked.

"Well, if I could get this stupid blanket to cooperate, I'd be fine." He chattered. "'Tis such a cold night! It's been a bad winter, hasn't it?" He squinted, his father's face blurring.

His dad looked worried. "Aye, it has. Rest, son," he commanded.

CHAPTER 13

Arabella spent the morning in the lists but continued to make careless mistakes over and over again. Ethan had been gone for five days and she was going out of her mind. She had told him she would endeavor to stay out of the fight, especially knowing some of her countrymen were forced to fight in Mason's army. Not that she wanted violence—but she wanted to aid the efforts, to be of use, to not feel like she was under house arrest.

Disgusted with her performance, she'd returned to her room and was just changing into a dress when she heard the sound of a horse coming down the lane. Arabella peered out her bedroom window while tying a sash around her waist. Benton's distinctive figure galloped toward the stables. Anxious to hear what he had to say, Arabella hurriedly thrust her feet in sturdy boots and tied them up, then swiftly descended the stairs and out to the cobbled path that would take her to the stables.

"Benton? Hello?" Arabella called out in search of the rider as she entered the stables. The odor of horse manure was quite pungent in the rising heat of the morn.

Benton had the saddle already removed from his horse and was brushing the animal, but handed over the brush to a stable boy as Arabella drew near.

"Your Highness," he replied.

"Shall we?" she said, indicating that they remove themselves from the stables and go elsewhere, where there were no other ears.

"I've been through Mason's army," he began as they walked. "There are forty-five hundred Anchellian men within it," he spoke sorrowfully.

Though Arabella had known Ethan's scout Forrester had spoken the truth, she had not wanted to believe it. "How many soldiers are there from Theron and Lassiter?" she pressed.

"Fifty-five hundred," he responded.

"The Cronan?" she continued to question.

"Ten thousand," he answered. "I've visited with several Anchellian soldiers, and they said that Mason left a small force at Anchelle. That if the Anchellians didn't fight the Saldanzians, and Mason himself did not return to Anchelle, the army that remained in Anchelle would kill their families."

Arabella's stomach lurched with disgust, knowing Mason would make good on his threat. The depravity sickened her.

Benton's face showed his remorse and pain that he too was feeling. These were men of action, and there was no place they would rather be then defending their people and kingdom. But these, her faithful guard, remained loyally by her side, always seeming to feel a greater need to protect her—they would chafe all the more at this news.

"I cannot take this any longer," she murmured angrily. "You all want to protect me, and I really do appreciate it, but isn't the queen's responsibility to protect her people?" she lamented. "If I were a man, we wouldn't be in this position. We would all be out on the battlefront." They had had this discussion before, but with little success.

"Not all kings go to the battlefront," he reminded her.

"Anchellian. Kings. Do!" she emphasized.

He acknowledged with an abrupt nod.

"Our countrymen would listen to me. If I could just speak to them . . ."

Luke rounded a bush holding a plate of sandwiches and a few cookies. He seemed oblivious to the frustration she was feeling as he held the plate in front of Arabella's face, trying to get her to smell the desserts. After the news she had just received from Benton, food didn't seem appealing. Food hadn't been appetizing at all of late. Taking the plate, she handed it to Benton.

"Really?" Luke questioned, "I went to all that trouble to get you a treat, and you don't even accept my gift." Luke attempted to feign offense but his smile after the tirade said otherwise.

"I'm sure Benton will do better justice to your offering than I would. If you did indeed make the sandwiches?" she challenged with a lift of her eyebrows and pursed lips.

"*I,*" Luke emphasized the word, "went to all the trouble of getting all of us some food." He took the plate from Benton, who had already started to help himself, and pushed the plate in front of Arabella—who shook her head.

Luke's face lost its charm and became serious. "Really, Arabella, you are becoming as skinny as when the shivers struck. Eat some food!" His stern order shocked Arabella.

His concern for her was touching, and feeling guilty that she was worrying him, she grabbed one of the sandwiches and bit into it. With a self-satisfied grin, he handed her a cookie as well.

Sitting down on a rock wall ledge, the trio ate in silence for a moment. Before Arabella continued to question Benton, Garner arrived with some food as well, holding it out to Arabella. Apparently Luke wasn't the only one who noticed her eating habits, or current lack thereof. Though she had no interest in the food, she took another sandwich from the plate, earning their relieved smiles.

Arabella hardly had the sandwich finished when Roland came into view. She didn't think she could eat another sandwich. But the look on his face said he had something entirely different in mind. In fact, his serious nature made her heart speed up. "We need to hurry," he said, taking her elbow and rushing her along the treeline. What could possibly be going on that had Roland in such a lather? It had to be important; he was rarely ruffled.

"Cleve and Lorring are headed to your grandfather's even as we speak," he spoke urgently.

That was unusual. In fact, it had never happened while Arabella had been there. Grandfather was always summoned to a council room. What would be so urgent that they would come here to his estate?

"We have to be able to hear everything that is said. Where will they meet? And where can we hide?" Roland didn't bother to look at her as he rushed her to the house.

This wasn't like Roland at all, this urgency. She reviewed in her mind all of Grandfather's formal rooms to determine where he might receive the guests. Since Benton had been scouting the Anchellian army, Arabella had Roland watching Cleve.

"You will have to stay close, but we all can't hide in there," Roland told the men. "You will have to stay outside, but don't become visible. We don't want them to know that Arabella is inside," Roland directed.

The men disappeared around the wall, as Roland and Arabella quietly went through a back entrance.

"Quick!" Roland whispered. Where would they go? Roland started to remove his boots and indicated Arabella should as well.

They could hear Grandfather greeting someone in the front foyer.

"Grandfather's study," Arabella whispered back, hoping she was right. The house was quiet, and luckily they didn't see anyone as they sprinted to the study.

"The drapes!" Roland commanded.

Arabella quickly slid behind the drapes, her heart racing. It felt so clandestine, and if it wasn't Roland, she might have been laughing. As it was, it unnerved her enough to regret the sandwiches trying to remain in her stomach.

She heard their footfalls as they entered the study and firmly closed the door.

"Sit down, gentlemen," she heard her grandfather speak. There was a moment of rustling as the men took their seats.

"What's this all about?" Grandfather questioned.

"A runner made it from Capri," came Cleve's immediate response.

"Through the secret tunnel Ethan had built in case of siege?" Grandfather clarified.

"Aye," Lorring spoke. "Peligree has one too. Ethan was spot-on with where Mason would launch the initial attack. There was an initial skirmish, an exchange of arrows, but the Chilton army wisely withdrew, having no cover. Our men were prepared to fight, they just weren't prepared for the sickness."

"Nay!" her grandfather ground out. "Are they sick then?"

"Aye, it seems that Commander McKenna has contracted the illness as well," Lorring provided.

Arabella wanted to scream in horror, instead creating half moons as her nails dug into her closed fists.

Cleve's angry voice could be heard easily to exclaim, "He promised on his mother and sisters' lives he could defend Saldanzia!"

"No one could have predicted everyone getting sick!" her grandfather exclaimed. "Let alone him getting sick. His father is at least there, we have that to be thankful for. Michael competently led this country for many years."

Arabella gasped, her mind reeling. Ethan was sick. Images of her father dying, as well as her friends, came instantly to her mind, and she couldn't help but think of Ethan lying in some lonely bed with hundreds of other men dying. There were never enough to help with the sick.

"Mason left half his men surrounding Capri and marched with the rest onto Peligree last night, starting a campaign early this morning. As of yet Peligree hasn't seen sickness, but I wouldn't hold my breath," Lorring continued. "Commander Thomas is holding Peligree, and I have great faith in him."

"As do I," Grandfather acknowledged.

"Our remaining ten thousand are holed up here outside Saldanzia. They've created a line of defense miles long. Ramparts have been built to secrete themselves behind and provide defense." Cleve held some begrudging approval for Ethan's strategic moves.

"Let's pray that Surrey can find the plant and return through enemy lines, and quickly." Grandfather gave a heavy sigh. "Or Spinter gets a more effective inoculum made quickly. We might have the fortifications, but they can't be held without men to man them."

"I feel it's my duty to tell you that Creeker, who you know is in Capri, told me through the messenger something important." Cleve paused for a minute, making Arabella even more curious. "I can't tell you how accurate this is because the messenger was sick by the time he got here and was bumbling on and the other information that he carried was from Michael in the form of a letter. This, however, was a verbal communication between Creeker and the messenger to me. This is what he said, 'Ethan's sick, 'tis possible Anchellian blood could cure him.'"

"Go on, surely that is not all?" Grandfather commanded.

"Aye," Cleve answered.

"It's not even reliable information then. Michael's missive had his seal on it, correct?" Grandfather asked.

"That's correct," Cleve said. "I don't think we should dismiss what Michael said."

"Absolutely not!" Grandfather spoke vehemently. "And Arabella must not learn of this. If she were to know, she would certainly go. 'Tis much too dangerous."

"'Tis a shame." Lorring lamented. "Did he happen to say if one in particular could help? If we could just send one of her men . . ."

"I'm afraid not," Cleve said.

"Nay, absolutely not!" Grandfather ground out.

There was silence for a moment, and then Cleve spoke up. "I guess 'tis decided then, I know to have Ethan out of commission is a loss, but at least we have Michael, as you've said."

"The boy is strong," Lorring interjected. "I'll not give up on him yet. He was given the old inoculum. That may lessen the gravity. Spinter suggested it when we met initially."

The men continued to talk, and Arabella could hear the fear in Lorring's and her grandfather's voices. They spoke of "in the event" that Michael or Thomas didn't make it back to Saldanzia before Mason's army came to the capital city Saldanzia. It felt like they talked for hours, though it was probably only half an hour before they had sufficiently divided up tasks to concentrate on.

As Grandfather walked the men to the front door, Roland and Arabella slipped noiselessly back the way they had come, retracing their steps from the house.

With their boots on and a distance from the house, the other men emerged from the trees and made their way to Roland and Arabella.

Luke, Roland, and Garner looked at the two expectantly.

"Ethan has the shivers," Arabella spoke. Her heart was heavy, but she began to make plans in her head. There was no way they were not going to help Ethan if they had a chance to do so.

"Oh, Arabella," Luke said, coming to her and putting an arm around her shoulder. "I'm sorry."

"Something else that is noteworthy is that Torin Blake is still in Saldanzia," Roland said.

Strange, that, when Cleve had pushed so hard for his family to be removed to safety, Arabella thought. It sounded like a few of the families had others stay in the city as well, so that wasn't wholly unusual. But Arabella and her guard had determined early on it would be important to know what Cleve and Torin were doing outside the council chambers.

"I know not if it be of significance, but I followed Torin to the outskirts of the city, where he headed south with thirty men, all in civilian clothes. I made the decision to return to Cleve, rather than follow them," Roland said.

"What do you suppose that was all about?" Luke mirrored her thoughts. "For anyone besides the army to go toward the conflict?"

"Passing strange," Garner remarked.

"'Twas one of the reasons I was so interested to hear what Cleve had to say to your grandfather," Roland pointed out. "I thought mayhap Torin had learned something, because shortly after he returned, Cleve came here."

Though likely that was relevant information, right now, Arabella had to deal with another pressing matter.

Getting around the line of defense of Saldanzia took extra time, but several hours later, the Anchellians with extra mounts were closing on Capri. The next problem lay with a very large enemy army that was surrounding the city, and carefully locating and navigating their small group to the recently created tunnel. They only needed to give Benton enough time and space to track the runner that had come from Capri to Saldanzia this morning. He had been following the scout's sign for the last half an hour.

Her men had wanted to leave her several miles from the city till they located the tunnel, but she wouldn't hear of it. They had done everything together, and they would finish together.

For housing a large army nearby, and a city that was under siege, it was eerily quiet. Placing one's foot took extra care; a breaking twig could be heard from some distance. Nobody spoke a word, and hand signals were used often to keep everyone from being seen.

With Benton scouting and tracking they quietly moved through a forest on foot. Armor was carefully stashed for later retrieval in the need to reduce noise that could alert any sentries from the enemy camp. Everyone was on high alert as they passed large evergreens mingled with aspen, tall grass with scattered fallen trees, which made the route more hazardous to traverse in the dim light of the thick canopy. The trail wasn't very wide, just a game trail, and could only retain one person abreast. It was not a heavily used trail. With a hand signal from Roland everyone became still.

The sound of men's voices could be heard from a road close by. Scrambling for cover, each person found the closest hiding place. Arabella found a scrub bush, just as soldiers from the invading army rounded a corner. A split second was all that she had before she tucked her head in. She didn't dare to look from where she crouched behind the spindly green bush. The only other person she could see from her hiding spot was Luke, who barely shook his head for her to keep down, a deep warning in his eyes. Not that she needed it. She knew their position was precarious.

The sound of soldiers approaching was unnerving. She held as still as possible, worried that if she moved, the enemies' horses would be spooked. Hearing them talking, and more noise as the hooves of the horses fell on the packed roadway, gave her pause.

After a heart-stopping minute, Arabella was worried that the whole army was going to have to pass by them. The sounds grew louder as they began to pass their places of concealment. Her crouching position was uncomfortable to say the least. She desperately wanted to straighten her back and relieve the crink but was terrified to move. If they were all caught, she knew her life would be spared, but not so for her guard. The minutes dragged on as more and more men journeyed on. She could hear little tidbits of conversation, with so many men, but with the noise of the horses she couldn't glean anything useful. All she knew was that there were hundreds of men passing their location.

Cramps began in earnest in her lower back, from twinges to spasms of agony. She desperately needed to straighten her spine. The back of her calves were now, too, on fire. If she could just sit down or stand up. Luke didn't seem to be in any better position, but it didn't seem to bother him that she could detect. Fearful, she tried to remain as calm as she could, willing her heartbeat to slow down a bit. But the army went on and on. It seemed like forever.

Back and body went into a painful numbing mode before the last soldier had passed. But they didn't dare move for some time, wondering if there were any stragglers or rearward guards.

She couldn't have been more relieved when Benton arose from his hiding place. Luke kept his hand up to stop her from moving, and she was tempted to not give heed, but Benton stealthily surveyed the area before Luke gave the signal to proceed and she gingerly and slowly straightened, sighing joyfully in her mind despite her muscles' protestations.

Thankfully they had kept to the game trail the runner had used, rather than the road nearby, so they continued their journey to the besieged city. It would be dark soon, and they would need to find the tunnel before light fled. Arabella was all too happy to be moving and stretching out the quivering muscles in her lower back.

Though they had to move very slowly the last mile, they found the tunnel. The runner must have been overanxious to get word to the capital, for with little searching Benton found the disturbed fauna and the hasty attempts to cover his tracks. They reached the tunnel just as the sun went behind the mountain. They cleared all the signs of both parties passing before entering. Cloaks were put on afore submerging themselves into the cold earth. Luke went into the tunnel first, followed by Garner, then Arabella, Benton, and Roland.

Flashes of a similar memory as they fled Anchelle furthered her desire to return as soon as possible to her kingdom. But what drove her nearly mad with fear was that they might not find Ethan alive. Could he survive it? So precious few who contracted the dreaded disease lived. How soon till Surrey's party returned? From their own costly experience with this plague she knew of many that had come down with the shivers who had suffered for ten days afore succumbing to death. The greatest majority died within three or four. Only a fifth of her people survived it. Not Ethan! He was healthy and strong, surely he could press through it. Arabella's sad experience had been that the disease brought death to all ages, even the seemingly healthy. Still, she prayed he would be able to hold on. It was a selfish desire, she knew, but after losing her family and her home because of this madness she wasn't sure if she had the heart to move on if he was no longer alive. Pushing such dreadful thoughts from her mind, she renewed her petition to God to find him whole.

The walk, though lit by a torch found at the entrance, was still quite dark and seemed endless. Furry and long-legged creatures had taken up residence. Several times she had to keep from letting a small scream escape her lips as she almost stepped on a rat or found a spider on her arm. Shaking her whole body to dislodge any creatures every so often and brushing her arms frequently kept her mind busy in the oppressive, cloying dirt walls.

The end of the tunnel found them being led up several iron stairs to a false trapdoor. Luke rapped on the door to alert the guard, who surely watched the strategic location.

A moment later, the door was opened, several grim-faced men peering down at them with swords and a lamp.

"Her Highness Arabella, requesting permission to be seen by Commander McKenna," Garner barked out.

The exhausted soldiers looked at her and backed away, while a man of rank was brought to peer down at the arriving refugees.

It took only a look and then they backed away, motioning them in.

The room looked to be that of a healer's storage area. All types of glass jars and bandages of all shapes were stacked neatly, but the telltale sign was the smell of antiseptic. Though tidy, it was more closet than room: so small and cramped with the dozen or so bodies within it.

"Please take me to see Commander McKenna," again Arabella asked the sergeant.

"Which one?" the soldier questioned.

"Both, actually," Arabella answered.

"I'm not sure where you will find Ethan," the sergeant said. "Since he has come down with the sickness, I can only direct you as to his father's whereabouts."

"You have my thanks, sir."

"I will have my man accompany you," he added.

The sergeant opened the door and barked, "Williams!"

In the sea of heads, a younger man turned his head. "Yes, sir!" His eyes got large as he looked at Arabella, and he took a big gulp.

"You are to accompany Her Highness to Commander McKenna. I would escort the queen myself, but I have been commanded to not leave my post."

"Aye, sir." The boy could scarcely be called a man. His youthful face probably had not yet seen a razor, let alone battle.

"This way," he spoke, his voice cracking slightly.

When they left the tightened quarters, the scene that greeted them was painfully all too familiar and horrifying at once. The storage room took them straight to a temporary sanatorium. Many sick men lay on the small cots. Arabella put her hand to her face; the smell was nauseating. Bile rose and she covered her face in an effort to stem the acid. Apparently Garner felt the same way, because she saw him pause, then dash outside the room to find a place to empty the contents of his stomach. They all quickly followed.

Torches lit the walkway periodically through the darkness within the city. It sounded eerily silent for a city that was besieged. A few coughs sounded in houses they passed by. Fear seemed to permeate the very air. The inns were quiet as people stayed home, giving an almost vacant feel to all the common areas they passed.

The boy led them down the dark streets to the far side of the city in endless twists and turns. It seemed to take forever before they came to an old wooden door surrounded by rock walls in the city's inner defense. There were a couple of men stationed at the door who announced their arrival.

Lord Michael came to the door, his eyes wide, his worry obvious. He looked exhausted.

"Arabella!" he exclaimed. "How did you get here?"

Arabella had a hard time calling him Michael, but after him insisting several times, she was finally coming around to it.

"We came through the northwest tunnel."

Michael looked at Benton. "I guess I know how."

"We have news from home that could not wait," Arabella said, right to the point. "I don't know if it is accurate or not, but we understand that a runner came through today from you, but also a message from Creeker?"

"I sent a message of course, but no I wasn't aware of anything from Creeker." Michael looked stumped.

Arabella sighed, worried that the messenger could have been delirious from the sickness. "From what we understood, Creeker felt like one of us from Anchelle might be of help to Ethan in some way with the sickness?"

"Well, that would be a godsend." The small flame of hope lit Michael's eyes and Arabella in that moment knew Ethan was not doing well. "We'll go immediately. Let me grab my cloak." Michael disappeared for a moment, returning with his cloak in hand.

They walked out into the night sky again, and Michael briskly gave the rundown on the happenings of the siege and the advancing sickness. Fifteen minutes later, they ascended the stairs to a modest two-story brick house and knocked on the door. A middle-aged woman answered, and Michael and Arabella left her knights in the sitting parlor before following the lady to the back of the house. The home was relatively dark and quiet, as though all in it slept. Arabella was tired but anxious to see him. Her nerves had been a mess all day. She'd hardly eaten anything on the journey and only at the instance of her men. Michael remained in the hall whispering to the woman whom he had left his son's care.

Old oak floorboards creaked as she stepped into a sparse-looking small room with a large bed. No one was in the room but him, and he lay so still! She froze, fear choked: *What if he has already passed on?* A single candle burned, just showing the outline of his body. Her eyes began to water, and her heart leapt painfully in her chest. The acidic smell in the room over-whelmed her senses and brought back so many vivid memories, till only one remained. Her king, her father, wasting away before her eyes to finally succumb to a tortured, rasping death.

Shaking the image from her mind, she slowly advanced, not ready for any more death, but more significantly his.

As she drew closer, the slow rise and fall of his chest allowed her to take a deep breath. Closing her eyes, she uttered a swift prayer of gratitude that she had arrived in time to see him. Moments later Creeker and Michael came into the room and Arabella turned to greet them.

"Glad am I that my message found you," he said, looking at Arabella.

Arabella allowed a small smile of relief. "I'm afraid that I don't know how I can help, but you have but to ask," she said.

Creeker looked at both Michael and her before beginning. "I have studied your blood, and that of your men, under significant magnification. I also had blood drawn from the Ruling Five. I don't know if you know it or not, but there was a lady named Elizabeth Sweeten who lived about a century past. Remarkably bright, she isolated and proved there were but eight types of blood among all people. Since then, we have had enhanced convex pieces of glass layered to see to the very basic elements that make up our blood. Since the virus has made its way here, I have wondered if a person who survived the shivers, because their body created a response for the invading pathogen, could give a small amount of their blood to someone with a matching blood type who didn't have the immunity. My hypothesis is that it would give the person receiving it a formula to replicate and build a defense, a weapon if you will, to battle the foreign invader. I realized that with only two of your men that have survived the shivers, it would never be enough to help with the population of Saldanzia, but if it was only for a few people, critical to the success of our defense . . ." He let the thought hang in the air.

"You think Garner or Benton, who both came down with the shivers and survived, made something in their blood to fight it, and that could help Ethan?" Arabella asked, making sure she understood his reasoning.

The tired man nodded his head, but continued, "Though I can't be sure, m'lady."

The thought swirled and wanted to find purchase in her fearful state. Arabella felt the unfurling tendrils of hope alight in her, weariness fading altogether. Could this really help? "I assume one of them has the same blood type as Ethan, else you wouldn't have sent word?"

"Aye, Garner does."

"A moment please," Arabella said walking back out to the parlor, where all her knights stood when she entered.

"Garner," she said. "Would you come with me, please?"

Returning to Ethan's room, she asked Creeker to repeat what he had just suggested. She looked at Garner. whose aging face remained stoic. He was ever a warrior.

"It would please me to do this, Your Highness." He spoke confidently, without the slightest hesitation.

She smiled gratefully at him and looked at Creeker once again. "Could Garner have any harm come to him, if he were to do this?" There was no way this sacrifice could be tolerated if there was risk to this healthy man who led Anchelle's army and was the family of her heart.

"There is some danger to Ethan, and none to speak of to Garner," Creeker spoke slowly. "I have given blood to others before who have lost significant amounts of blood and have had great success. I don't anticipate anything more for Garner than him feeling tired for a short time till his body replaces what was taken."

An hour and a half later, the doctor had finally completed the transfer of blood and the men and Michael left. Arabella went to Ethan's side and fixated on the singular motion of his chest's rise and fall. A tear slipped down her face, and soon they streamed. Taking his hand in her own, she bent and kissed his cheek. A moment later a shiver wracked his body. Was his body fighting it? Or was this one of the final death throes they witnessed in the last hours of life? Pulling up a chair next to him, she sat with his hand in her own, murmuring nonsensical encouragement to him and sharing details of their journey. Hours passed, and she dreaded to shut her eyes in fear that he would leave her if she broke her vigil. Sleep claimed her at last in the deep of the night, lulled to sleep with her head on his chest, listening to the wondrous rhythmic beating of his heart.

Repeating loud noises in the distance woke her. The sound repeated itself over and over again. Shaking the dregs of sleep, her mind tried to understand the loud percussions. Capri was under a full-fledged attack! Heart racing, she listened to the various sounds, sorting through the patterns of noise and fighting a dark fear that the city would be overtaken. Composing herself, she identified cannons firing from the walls of the city, a steady barrage of incessant thundering cacophony. Worry for the people of the city took root in her mind. The sound seemed to be coming from everywhere, as if the attack that warranted the cannon was on all fronts.

Arabella noted the rise and fall of Ethan's chest before creeping out of the room to spy Luke sitting up on a couch in the sitting room, as though he, too, had been startled from his sleep. The other men were up moving. Some had left to do reconnaissance. She visited with Luke for a brief time, then returned to the oppressive room.

She studied Ethan's face. He seemed unchanged from last night, though she could see him better with daylight filtering through a small window. Whiskers now adorned his face, creating a roguish air. Darkened wells under his eyes seemed to add age. His face contorted. He appeared tormented, shoulders squirming, heavy with fatigue. The battle taking place in his mind and body replicated the sounds of war upon the city walls. Her fingers settled on his brow, so as to smooth the tension from his face, but found his head extremely hot to the touch. Alarmed, she shouted for someone to bring some cool water. A basin was thrust in her hands, though she could not have said who brought it. After bathing his face, she then began wiping his arms and feet, recognizing how critical it was that they bring the fever down with all haste.

No. No. No. Her mind reviewed the litany of symptoms. When the sick reached this stage, they rarely woke, and she desperately wanted, no, *needed him* to survive! Not wanting to contemplate a world that Ethan did not exist in, she whispered tender words of encouragement. Then she pleaded and finally she commanded him to fight, to come back to her.

The day passed monotonously. A tonic was brought, and she called for supplies and applied herbal compresses known to help the lungs remain open. Great fatigue and fear tormented her as she watched Ethan, who exhibited no change. How many times in the past year had she done this very thing? While it kept her hands busy, it didn't help her heartache, which increased with each hour, the hopelessness escalating.

Arabella was constant in her vigil, the sound of the battle outside grating on her already-frayed nerves. The men reported every few hours, keeping her apprised of the situation outside, which seemed to worsen by the hour. Garner visited with Michael several times, but it seemed like many of their ill soldiers were fading and new cases continued to climb with even the sick loading the cannon till they passed out and were replaced with someone still able. Every minute that passed made the defense of the city more difficult. Arabella finally sent all her men but Luke to aid in critical places so as to help the failing city. Arabella bustled around a home she did not even know the owner of, helping servants and people take care of Ethan, and several other men she hadn't learned the names of. Finally, upon asking, she learned that none of the souls caring for the sick seemed to know who they were, as they were soldiers stationed elsewhere in the empire afore this conflict. As the difficult day finally found the reprieve of night, Ethan's body still raged with fever. Sickened by the sinking chances of a recovery, she struggled to recall if anyone in Anchelle had come back after reaching this stage. After a thorough inspection of her experience, she admitted to herself that no one who had suffered with the high fever for such a lengthy duration had not succumbed. The room was dark as she sank into a chair. She began to weep. His breath was becoming more shallow, and she knew it was only a matter of time.

Must she lose another person she loved so much? Raw, hot anger simmered just below the surface as the noise droned steadily on, the pounding of war that incessantly raged. A pounding that she felt through her entire body. Mason was the worst man to be born! To consciously take human life so callously! To war against people for no other reason than greed.

She squeezed Ethan's hand, willing him to take some of her energy and to live, then sobbed in earnest as never before, gutted by it all. Her nose ran unchecked, and her body began to wrack in anguish with her bitter cries. No one disturbed her. She was thankful for the privacy till the thought came that they probably thought that Ethan had died to elicit such a response.

As the tears dried up and her head pounded relentlessly from the thrashing emotions, Arabella put her hand on his whiskery, hot face. "Wake up, darling," she whispered, wanting to hope that it was possible. She leaned over and kissed him on the lips. "I love you!" she said. She had never told a man besides her father that before. Though she loved many men, including all with her, never had she loved any man this way before. It was so much more and ever so bittersweet.

Somewhere after all the raging, she pled with God to spare him: praying fervently that he lived, but keenly aware that everything should be God's will.

Exhaustion overwhelmed her and she fell asleep in a chair with her head resting on the bed.

The feeling of someone smoothing her hair down brought her softly from sleep. She was groggy and at a loss at such an intimate gesture, which should be and yet wasn't alarming but was comforting . . . Where was she? Her head rested against . . . ? She struggled and sat up, concern spiraling as recalled where she was, dreading to look and see and know that he had passed on in the night, without her knowledge, without her to witness his last breath, and now someone was consoling her. She wanted to scream in agony, but she had already had her meltdown last night and wouldn't do it again. It was still dark, but as she sat up, she realized she was the only one in the room with Ethan.

"Good morning, love." His voice was soft, husky with disuse.

As her eyes met his, she found miraculously his eyes alive with light.

"Ethan!" she gasped, as she threw her arms around him, not daring to let go. Tears came to her eyes. Her hands finally went to his head,; he was no longer burning with fever! Leaning back, her gaze traveled the length of his body. How? He was awake! No shaking present, and his eyes were alert and locked in on her.

"I thought you promised to stay at your grandfather's." His eyes were alight with wonder. "Just couldn't stay away from me, could you?"

CHAPTER 14

Mason punched the man in front of him and felt the satisfying response as the man's head flew backward with blood gushing from his face. His anger had built to a boiling point, and this was just the beginning of his response to this man's incompetence. Capri and Peligree were both ready for his attack, and he was losing too many of his men. Though reports had indicated sickness in Capri and Saldanzia, word of mouth still held that Peligree had not been infected. Yet through it all, the Saldanzians had made remarkable preparations for defense, which were frustrating every effort.

Kicking the man in the ribs over and over again, his anger built. In the beginning, all he had wanted was Arabella. If her insipid father had just given her to him, none of this would have been necessary. When Mason had stumbled upon the shivers, it had been his answer to King Garrett's belligerent refusal. Mason would have Arabella and Anchelle, two birds with one stone. But he couldn't have the other countries in the Norlans coming to their aid either. With all the Norlans in his power his closest enemy would be the Cronan. Two years ago, after King Garrett refused his first offer of betrothal, a plan started to form, starting with the Cronan. Mason couldn't have believed how easily he would form an alliance with them. Their hatred toward the Saldanzians blinded them from all else. They never thought of those in the Norlans nor cared. The clans held that the land of Saldanzia was their own, millennia ago, and they had been pushed into the badlands and less desirable areas.

His march on Saldanzia had not been in the original plan. However, his campaign had been swift and successful so far against the Norlans. Saldanzia could be manipulated exactly as the others. His vision grew as Arabella fled to the country of her mother's birth. The Cronan spies were sure that the more exposed southern cities would be easy to pass through on the way to the capital, as had his men he had sent with them, including the man that lay unconscious at his feet. He kicked him again for good measure, then walked out of the tent.

The Saldanzians had somehow predicted where they would strike first. Mason was certain it wasn't a leak from his own people, as he shared none of the information with even his top commanders. Would they anticipate his picking up stakes and moving on? In the middle of the night, he had pulled out most of his men at Peligree and moved northwest into the borderlands of Cronan territory and Saldanzia.

He was gambling there was a sizable army left in the capital city of Saldanzia to protect their city of governance.

Anticipating a swift end to the siege with widespread sickness confirmed in Capri, he'd sent a runner with instructions for them to pull out and make haste to rejoin the main body on the march to the capital.

Oh, he'd left a few thousand men at Peligree to put up a loud fight, to make those at Peligree believe the army still fought there and hold them in. The Saldanzian soldiers and the people of Peligree would be none the wiser. As in Capri, his foot soldiers were getting picked off, while Peligree had sustained few losses, safely behind their walls. The fortifications were impressive, something he would mirror in all his holdings once this last kingdom fell. There was still a possibility of Peligree noting Mason's troop movements and openly engaging, but with the ten thousand coming on the other side of the capital, they would have to split their army, and he was betting they had been instructed to hold that city.

Ethan and Arabella's joyous reunion had been all too brief as a weary Garner entered. Without any pleasantries he spoke to the urgent matter. "Benton has confirmed that Mason's army pulled out last night, Your Highness. No doubt he's anxious to secure the capital." He spoke to both Ethan and Arabella.

"What direction? Are the gates holding? Any word on how Peligree fairs?" Ethan shot question after question at Garner, which he answered. Then, calling for a servant, he commanded them to fetch his father. Aware he had been close to death, he was filled with gratitude for a clear mind, while fully cognizant that his yet-aching body was not so easily restored, his stomach growling with hunger.

Arabella stood somewhat stiffly, marking her long vigil through the night, and squeezed his hand. "I shall return forthwith." She locked gazes with him; in them he saw her love, relief, and resolve before she was gone.

Yet again he marveled at his return from death's grasp. Though grateful beyond ability to express, he was vividly aware that he'd not have the luxury to recuperate whilst his enemy broadened his conquests, slaughtering his countrymen. Whilst he'd been abed, fevered and shaking, he caught remembrances of the fitful dreams, nightmares, as death and carnage raged throughout the face of the land. Mason had a plan in motion, and he'd best figure it out before Mason destroyed and conquered Saldanzia.

"I've brought you some broth," Arabella spoke as she walked more fluidly back to his side. "Let's get some food into your rumbling belly." She held out the steaming liquid to him, which he gratefully accepted.

No sooner had the broth gone down than he slowly removed himself from the bed to the sitting room in the house. Ethan might not be able to stay atop a mount, but he could certainly keep apprised of what was happening and direct orders.

His father entered the home swiftly, interrupting Ethan's discussion with Garner and Arabella. Michael, who was ever tidy, polished, and clean, appeared to have aged overnight; he was weary and worn, his clothing rumpled. His stubbled face visibly relaxed when his eyes rested on Ethan.

"Praise the Maker!" His father's face beamed with astonishment, the smile reaching to his glittering eyes with unshed tears. "You gave us a frightful scare, son," he said, striding to Ethan, pulling him in for an embrace before taking a seat next to him.

Ethan returned the smile and sentiment. "I'm most glad to yet remain."

His dad reached his arm to latch onto his son's shoulder as though to further convince himself of his presence. "I didn't think you were going to last through the night," his father admitted. Written on his father's weathered face was the devastating loss it would have been to lose his son. Ethan rarely had seen such depth of emotion from his father so clearly displayed. "I'm certain you would have, had Garner and Arabella not arrived."

Ethan nodded his head in acknowledgment. A lump had formed in his throat. Arabella had explained the treatment of blood transfer from Garner to Ethan. It seemed quite amazing. But now wasn't the time to dwell on his life being spared. He was sure his father felt the same urgency he felt.

"They left?" Ethan asked.

Michael shook his head. "We were terribly lucky. If they knew how close we had come to not being able to defend this city . . ." Michael clenched his fists. "Another half an hour and we'd have lost the city. If you hadn't fortified this city as you saw to, we would have been at their mercy."

Ethan was visibly shaken. "What do you have planned?" Ethan asked his father.

"I leave with most of the garrison in the next half of an hour. We go directly to Saldanzia. Had I more men we could have come behind the invaders and surrounded him with the troops stationed outside Saldanzia, but as it is, I will enter the city to reinforce the troops as needed."

Ethan nodded his head. He would have directed it thusly. "Garner said that you only have about forty percent of the troops in marching condition?" Ethan asked, knowing that Garner was right but needing to hear it from his father.

"Aye, and from what I hear, that is a miracle in itself. Though I expect loss in the expedited journey," Michael spoke gravely.

Arabella nodded her head in agreement.

"And the saysee?" Ethan questioned further.

"No word," his father responded.

Ethan shook his head, frustrated with his limitations. "I will leave tomorrow and make my way to Saldanzia." He spoke in a way that left no room for anyone to question him on his decision. He rose from his seat. A wave of dizziness threatened and he latched onto his father, who had likewise risen, to steady himself. He hoped to make it appear as affection. He knew his father needed to leave immediately.

"Be careful," his father warned, with a look that said Ethan wasn't fooling him in the least.

Ethan looked at Arabella and then his father. "Aye, we all will."

Without further discussion, his father left as swiftly as he had come.

Awakening from a deep sleep the following morning, Ethan heard loud exclamations come from the street. Rising slowly, he looked out the window as people walked determinedly down the street in something akin to a procession. A thin middle-aged woman bore a hopeful expression as she carried a child on her hip.

He dressed as hurriedly as he could, and when he stepped from the room, there seemed to be none but an empty house to greet him. Ethan opened the front door, hearing the hustle and bustle of activity without and the deep timbre of Garner.

Arabella's tired eyes brightened upon seeing him. She was with a solemn Garner on the porch of his borrowed home.

"They've made it back!" Arabella exclaimed, pointing down the street. Ethan stepped closer to Arabella and saw the little town had exploded with people who were clamoring to the heavy-laden carts being pulled down the street. The carts were laden with what he could only assume was saysee. He released a breath he hadn't realized he was holding.

The townsmen, something like a mob, reached out their hands to excitedly grab the herb and then hastily retreat to their homes. He knew if Arabella were ill with the shivers, he would have been one of the first to seek the herb as well.

Garner explained that the expedition had arrived a few hours past, and as previously determined, should the venture meet with success, the party would split the herb to divide amongst the cities anticipated to be a target. Leaflets had been prepared and dropped at each home with instructions for care of the illness and marking their homes to indicate the number of sick or dead. The sick were to remain at home to convalesce while the sanatorium and field hospitals were designated to soldiers who fell ill or were wounded. The healers were advised of the herb and how it would need to be dispensed and boiled down to drink as a tea.

He held Arabella around the waist as they watched the stream of beleaguered people for a time, observing the hope displayed as some returned clutching the treatment. Fast tiring, Ethan directed her to a nearby bench. For a brief moment he was at peace as he sat with Arabella in his arms and lost himself in the awe of answered prayers. Now if only the saysee was a good remedy for the sickness . . .

Much too soon, the world pressed back in on him, and he reluctantly relinquished the warmth and peace he found only in her embrace. "'Tis time to be away." He felt as weak as a kitten, and not in the least up for a grueling day's ride, but he didn't have a choice.

"I'll ready myself and my men," she responded. He didn't know the safest place for her, but right beside him was his selfish preference. On an unseen signal the Anchellian guard came forth with their borrowed mounts, out of the woodworks it seemed, and set to efficiently pack their meager belongings. Ethan returned to the room he battled death and gathered his own small bundle with the little energy he had and thanked the homeowner where he had been cared for.

The Anchellian band waited atop horses for him. Seeing his own mount had been brought, he felt some trepidation at his ability to climb atop. Panting, and with a clumsiness foreign to his body, he managed the feat. One of his own men strapped down weapons, rations, and bedroll. Under different circumstances he would never have permitted it, but he found he didn't even have the energy to argue.

All but those that recovered from shivers were given a precious dose of saysee should they fall ill in travel. Sir Benton was sent out, as were a few others, to scout the surrounding area ahead of them. Too many enemies now inhabited Saldanzian land, and they couldn't be too careful.

Ethan wanted to be left behind by midmorning; he hurt everywhere, and his heavy arms didn't want to hold even the light reins, he was so confoundedly weak. The morning passed uneventfully, though everyone's nerves remained taut and little was said. The ride was grueling mentally and physically. Knowing that he didn't have a choice, lives depended upon him, was all that kept him moving. Another hour passed and idly he wondered if death would be an improvement to his miserable state. Arabella, who had been riding next to him, looked at him often with concern in her eyes.

It was one of those times that she came closer to him, "I'm greatly fatigued, sir," she said, giving him a wink, which perked him up momentarily. "Do you think 'twould be aright if you rode behind me to keep me on the horse?"

He knew what she was doing but didn't think he could even mount her horse. She pulled up short and dismounted before anyone could help her.

Handing her reins to one of his own soldiers, she forced his horse to a stop and commanded, "Scootch back!" He wasn't up to arguing, and she knew it, and he did as she bade. Quickly adjusting his stirrups, she swung up, hardly slowing the group. "I had something made up for you this morning, which will be most unpleasant to taste, but will help immensely. Would you be willing to try it?"

He looked at her through the haziness fast returning, but with absolute faith in her. "Aye," he said, wondering what she was about, but too tired to really think.

She pulled some parchment from her coat and unwrapped a gooey glob of something that smelled of fish. "Eat this!" she directed, taking the gooey mess in her thumb and index finger and placing it in his mouth. It reminded him of the smelly concoction she had given to Benton on the way to Saldanzia for some kind of scratch.

He grimaced as the smell and taste hit him almost simultaneously. He wanted to gag, but somehow kept it down. Arabella was ready with her canteen to help wash the vile mixture down. "And here I thought you liked me," he complained after taking a long pull of the water.

She turned her body to look at him better in the eyes. "Nay, has nothing to do with liking! 'Tis love. I. Love. You," she declared. He stared at her for a moment wondering if his sickness was somehow playing a trick on his mind. Though they had spoken of love, she had never said directly, *I love you*. A moment later, she demanded, "Now wrap your arms around me, and get you to sleep!" This was something he could do every day, he thought as his hands came around her small waist. She smelled and felt wonderful. And it seemed moments before blessed sleep claimed him.

Knowing within minutes that she wouldn't be able to hold his weight against her for any lengthy duration, Arabella had the men quickly construct a travois. He needed to sleep to recover, she knew this, but she was also aware of the urgency that demanded his presence in Saldanzia. His duty to his people was something she keenly felt for her own people, but also a growing duty to the Saldanzians. As the granddaughter of a Saldanzian, and also to a people that had taken her in, in her time of need, she felt a responsibility certainly, but also an undeniable growing kinship.

The travois was constructed inside half an hour. The men had moved him without him so much as stirring. So deep was his sleep, she found herself once again watching for his chest to rise and fall as they plodded onward. Worry ate at her to not have him seated on a horse should the need arise to make a run for it, but it just couldn't be helped.

Benton came back reporting that the southern route into the city would be impossible to get through, so they altered their course to bring them in from the northeast. It added precious time to the journey but served as the best chance to enter the city unnoticed. According to Benton, the Chiltons were holding their ground just out of reach of the Saldanzian soldiers stationed south of their capital.

They found throughout the day they would have to skirt wider and wider to avoid detection. Benton was unmatched in his skills in scouting, and she had implicit trust in him; where he said to go, she followed. The Saldanzian soldiers followed her lead. The journey took several times longer than it should have, with several Chilton parties cropping up at different intervals.

It took them all day, having to skirt the entire city and coming around the northeast through another tunnel. The city wasn't completely surrounded, as large as it was, but the enemy was definitely knocking at several other doors.

Signals from Ethan's men to those atop the wall sent guards to meet them at the hidden tunnel gate, with a few changes to report. The party carrying the saysee had made it into the city hours ago and it was already being used to treat those sick. Mason's army had yet to attack the city.

As they privily entered into the city, Arabella noted with a moment of cheer what she termed her sanctuary, the bell that hung from the top rafter of the church tower. Though the buildings remained, it didn't seem like the same glorious city. A solemn ache seemed to fuel the air. Not many people were in the streets, but rather closed up in their homes, and those that were out looked tired and disheveled. Dark markings adorned structures, indicating the number sick and deceased. A stench filled the twilight air, causing her to hold a kerchief to her nose. A large wagon was being pulled from house to house, loading the remains of those that had succumbed to the devastating shivers. A tear escaped at the scene that felt terribly familiar. She gazed anew at the still-sleeping form of Ethan and longed to hold him. That he was alive was a miracle. Great relief and gratitude filled her this day that he slept soundly. Restorative sleep had been desperately needed—and there would be no relief once he woke, she was sure of that.

As they neared the business district of the city, Arabella witnessed a mother crying over her dead child. A soldier took the child away to place on an ever-growing pile, bringing fresh tears to Arabella's eyes. A tremendous weight pressed upon her as she thought of the welcome she received on her initial arrival and the dire conditions these people were currently enduring. Was this horror her fault? Every death a mark on her soul? Deep down she knew the blame lay at the feet of one man's obsession, but she wondered if the situation could have been avoided. Could there have been a compromise reached? Her father hadn't believed so, and he had much more wisdom and experience with the ways of men.

The group of Anchellians drew the attention of the belea-guered citizens of Saldanzia; she saw the concern and growing distrust toward them. No one shouted profanities or blame but it was written upon the faces. Not that Arabella could fault them, she might feel similarly in their shoes. The further they traveled through the fear-soaked city the harder it became for her to look directly at anyone.

With deep relief they pulled up in front of her grandfather's estate, just as the stars were winking into view. Ethan finally awoke as they set the travois on the bed. He looked confused momentarily until he locked eyes with her.

Forcing a happy expression to her face, Arabella tried to push the despairing thoughts away. Ethan had enough burden to shoulder, she'd not add hers to his heavy load. She needed to focus on the blessings. Number one, Ethan was alive.

"Where are we?" he asked, breaking eye contact to see Arabella gesture for Roland and Luke to leave. Swinging his leg to the side of the travois, he managed to sit up.

"We are at my grandfather's home in Saldanzia," she whispered. She didn't know who was present or how many of the servants had been sent home to be with family and men to bolster the military.

"Did I sleep the whole way here?" he asked, rubbing his hand over his stubbled jaw and roughly through his hair in an unsuccessful attempt at taming the strands determined to stick out in all directions.

"Do you not remember being miserable this morn, and the struggle to remain in the saddle?" she asked with a smile.

"That's right," he said with his own sheepish smile. "Till some lovely lady needed help staying in her saddle, 'because she was too exhausted to hold on.'" Horror crossed his face. "You didn't hold me the entire time, did you?"

She laughed in delight that he was able to be playful despite the circumstances, before indicating the travois he was still sitting on. "Nay, you're way too heavy. The men made a snug little bed for you," she said, "and you slept like a wee baby."

"Nay!" he spoke, horrified. "Now I'll never hear the end of it. I will be mocked so badly I may need to flee the country. Do you think Anchelle would take in a lone refugee?"

She laughed at him, but wished it were true. "I think one of your men, Seward if I recall, said nearly the same thing. Something about now having two pieces of blackmail on you. Whatever did he mean?" she asked innocently.

Ethan rolled his eyes, but then he seemed to remember where he was, and the levity faded. "What news have you heard. Is your grandfather in residence?"

From down the hall, they could hear him bellow so all could hear, "I am coming this instant. I couldn't let my granddaughter be in a room by herself with a young scoundrel, could I?"

He entered the room, and Arabella scooted further from Ethan. It felt like her dad giving her a lecture on interaction with the male persuasion. Ethan gave her a roguish grin and just pulled her closer again. Timothy's eyebrows shot up as he gave Ethan a look that Arabella had seen him use on the council many times already. Ethan blithely ignored the look and grabbed her hand to hold, turning his own steely gaze to her grandfather.

"Hrumph!" he grumbled before supplying: "Mason is sitting without the city walls as we speak. He made it through the ramparts at midmorning and our men have fallen back to the city. He has not attacked the city as of yet, and decidedly it has made everyone uneasy.

"How in the world did you get through? Nevermind, I already know the answer." Her grandfather shook his head. "Saldanzia needs a Benton." Before Arabella could reply to his monologue, her grandfather continued. "Our scouts say only that Mason looks to be waiting for something."

"Waiting for something." Ethan looked quizzical. "Like more troops?"

"Your father asked the same thing when he arrived. We don't know if he has more troops coming, but your father sent for Thomas, and most of the troops at Peligree, to come behind them and pin down Mason."

"How far out are they?"

"We haven't heard when Commander Thomas will arrive with his troops."

"What is Mason waiting for?" Ethan said again, standing swiftly and running his hand through his hair. His face had a far-off look, like he was trying to bring something to remembrance. She also noted that as nimbly as he stood, he must be feeling a measure recovered. The medicine she had fed Ethan seemed to have done the trick. He had slept for a solid eight hours and seemed to have more energy.

"I need to leave," Ethan resolved.

"I'll accompany you." Grandfather stood as well. "Just in case Cleve has decided to play military man as well." Grandfather feigned a chuckle.

"Heaven help us," Ethan agreed.

"I'll just go get my cloak, some mounts, and a bit of food," Grandfather said. He kissed Arabella's cheek and swiftly left. "Don't think we won't be talking about your leaving at some point." He finally spoke directly to her, though she could see the relief in his eyes. He left quietly, trusting the two a moment to say goodbyes.

Ethan pulled Arabella into a hug. "How can I give my thanks for taking care of me this week? Even that smelly concoction saved my life, after it nearly killed me." He grinned but pinned her with an intensity that had made her stomach dip and roll.

Arabella returned the smile, but somehow a tear slipped out to collect in her upturned lip. He wiped it away with exquisite tenderness and lifted her chin to look at him, his face now serious. "I love you, Arabella," he said, bringing his lips to hers. He kissed her passionately, as though it was their last, and slowly pulled away.

"Do you remember that promise I made you give me before I left last time?" he asked.

"Aye," she said slowly.

"Same?" he asked.

"Same," she said. His mouth was on her again, weaving heady delight, and his arms fastened as though he hardly dared to be parted. One scorching kiss later, he wrenched himself away from her and swiftly left the room.

The only wise course of action would be to seek sleep. The interminable day had been brutal in the saddle, filled with wariness and concern. It seemed as though she was constantly tired. *Will ever there be a time that I'm not tired?* In Anchelle her position was to serve the people and rarely was it convenient. *But what if I never make it back to Anchelle? What if Mason is never defeated, or . . . ?* She couldn't let her mind wander down such dark paths. There was only one option that needed to be fixed in her mind, in her heart, and that was *the defeat of Mason.*

Mason will be punished for the crimes to my people and all the kingdoms. She would see to it.

Climbing the stairs to her rooms, she quickly changed into her night garment and slipped into bed amid crisp, fresh sheets; a moan escaped as she settled.

A persistent knocking at her door woke her from a dead sleep. It took a minute after sitting up to clear the cobwebs away. When Arabella didn't answer right away, a dark head poked through the door, followed by Luke's serious voice.

"A messenger at the door requesting to see you."

Arabella's brain was foggy, and she had a hard time coming to. "What did he say he wanted?"

"He said Ethan had a message for you, and that you needed to go with him," Luke spoke through the slightly parted door.

Arabella was instantly awake. She jumped out of bed and practically ran for the door. "Are you sure he said Ethan requested that I come to him?" she questioned. She opened it further and quietly pulled Luke into her room.

Luke looked ready to laugh at her before he saw her serious face. "Is the messenger alone?" she asked, before going to the windows to look out at her grandfather's vast property. She couldn't see anything.

"Aye, he's alone," Luke said, "he's a little bitty thing to carry a weapon, but so does everyone in this city now; you could take him easily," Luke said. "Why are you so concerned?"

"Ethan made me promise to not go with anyone from Grandfather's save himself or his second-in-command, Thomas, who is hopefully marching from Peligree even as we speak. He said to trust no one."

Going behind the screen in her room, she started to dress quickly. Arabella threw on her breeches and shirt that she wore in the lists; they were the closest to her screen. Who was really trying to get her attention, and why? Roland was with Ethan, because one stayed on with him to keep her apprised of any new developments. If Ethan had needed to send some information, he would have sent Roland.

As she came out of her room, Benton was sprinting up the stairs. As soon as he saw her, he hollered. "Armed men are coming this way through the trees. They're surrounding the house. We have to get you away from here now. Come this way!" he ordered, motioning with his hand.

With Luke at her side, Arabella ran behind Benton. They ran down the stairs and through the kitchen toward the back door. Garner came in the door just as they arrived, startling her.

Garner shut the door behind himself. He looked at all of them, resignation on his face. "We're too late. Too many. We can't make it through them."

"Where are Grandfather's guards?" she asked. She was desperate, dread fast pooling in her gut, knowing they would be here helping if they were near.

"Nowhere in sight," Garner spoke angrily.

Arabella looked at the three men. Her mind raced for any solutions. Hide? It wouldn't work. They were obviously here for her—they knew she was here. More than likely, they had been watching the estate, and once word was sent of her arrival . . . But they might not know how many of her men were with her.

"Benton, you need to hide now!" Arabella commanded, coming to several swift conclusions. If she wasn't getting out of this, someone needed to.

They all knew it made sense. He could disappear better than anyone, and he would have no problem tracking them. "That's a command!" she said firmly. She knew how Benton felt about leaving her. With an anguished face, Benton ran away from them.

Arabella walked to the front door and opened it wide.

She was stunned when a man stepped from the shadows and Cleve Blake's scornful face came into view, followed by his sniveling son Torin. "Why are you here?" Her mind tried to juggle the cascading questions of this surprise visit, proud her voice remained even. "Where are my grandfather's guards?"

He ignored her completely. "Gag them and tie them!" Cleve ordered the large group of men that followed. Each of the trio was summarily bound and viciously yanked from the shelter of the house.

Cleve appeared next to her face, a crazed rage filling his eyes. He spat upon her now-gagged face. Arabella tried to remain stoic, but all the while she was seething in disgust. What was he doing, and who knew of it?

Like he could read her mind, after staring at her for a time he sneered, "I'm finally getting rid of the Graces and the McKennas for good. It should have been done a long time ago. The others of the Ruling Five will be taken care of soon enough. Get her on a horse!" he commanded, his face still inches from hers. "I would see you whipped and then drag you behind my horse if we had time, but alas, we are on a tight schedule. I wish to be rid of you myself, but as it is, Torin will have to do the honors for me."

She looked briefly at Luke, terrified he would do something stupid, knowing he wouldn't watch someone harm her, shaking her head and commanding him with her eyes to not be reckless. Though she could see the seething in Luke's eyes, he didn't move. In that moment she felt relief that they had bound them all and hadn't killed them immediately. The peace was short lived as guards came up to viciously club Luke and Garner on the head, knocking both out.

Arabella was manhandled onto Palachio, who protested skittishly, and the group left almost as quickly as it came. She had to employ all her skills to stay in the saddle, as her arms were pulled tightly behind her back with a rough rope. It required her legs doing all the work to stay on properly. Had they put her on any other animal, she was certain she would have been unable to stay aloft. Though thick with the darkness of night, the moon shone enough through the heavy clouds to light their immediate surroundings. Watching intently, she was able to ascertain that they were headed northwest away from the city. It was imperative that she pay attention to everything. A single detail might prove helpful when the chance for escape came. That, too, seemed highly unlikely with Garner and Luke unconscious. Never would she choose to leave them behind. Though they would be furious with such a notion. Never would she abandon her people again. Never.

She prayed Benton had remained undetected. Surely he had found a place to hide. Knowing Benton as she did, once he escaped, he was a ghost. This single hope gave her confidence that perhaps all was not lost.

Arabella carefully kept track of where they passed, searching for any landmarks to imprint in her memory. Cleve's jeering face repeatedly appeared in her mind, replaying what he had said. It didn't bode well for any of them or the rest of the Ruling Five. How was he to get rid of the Graces and the McKennas? He had her, and yet he hadn't swiftly killed her. What about her grandfather, Ethan, and Michael? From what she knew, Ethan's mother and sister still remained in a remote location heavily guarded. How was Cleve to accomplish this with an advancing army? Of course, he wasn't concerned with an advancing army, because that was Ethan's job. This chaos was an opportunity for Cleve. Ethan, Michael, and Grandfather would be so concerned with Mason, they wouldn't see an inside threat.

It didn't take them long and they were at the city wall, where the gate was instantly lifted as the group approached. There were no guards in sight. They must have been expected, but it was hard to believe considering the state of the city at the moment. There should have been thousands of men stationed along any section of the wall, even in the night. The group rode through the opening quickly, the clattering of the gate indicating it had been lowered as soon as they passed through. Within a mile they entered the dark forest. The clouds had moved enough for her to see the full moon and note the evergreen trees around them and the small road they traveled—not a main artery from the city. A quarter-mile later, they turned onto a narrow game trail and Arabella could hear the gurgle of a small stream.

With no outerwear on, Arabella shivered in the cool night air. Worry ate at her for herself, and more so for Luke and Garner strapped over and tied to a horse while being led by another horseman. They would be used to make her cooperate, or they wouldn't have been brought along. Knowing Cleve disliked her so much, she didn't hold much hope that he was going to let her live, but why this drawn-out ordeal she couldn't reason, surely every mile they passed would have been a risk of being found out with Torin leading. The pieces just didn't fit. She was missing something.

Abruptly Torin came to halt. Everyone else followed. Arabella's teeth were chattering. She was losing feeling, starting with her fingers and moving to her hands. Stopped, she was able to pivot her head around without fear of toppling from Palachio but couldn't see anything of interest along the treeline. An eerie prickly sensation made the hair on the back of her neck rise. Sounds started to penetrate the once-still night. Not the sounds of nocturnal creatures but men, lots of them. She was startled as all around her bodies emerged from the trees in all directions, surrounding the group of horsemen. Some of the arriving men were on horses, and others on foot.

The moon gave off enough glow that as they approached she could see their faces. Her gasp served to choke her with the gag tight in her mouth; strangled coughs brought some air into her starved lungs while horror filled her being as she watched the advancing Cronan. It all came back in an instant, she and Ethan racing from them and their terrifying cries. Crippling fear stole over her. The heads of predators—bear, jaguar, wolf, lion—sat atop their heads like a gruesome party hat. The hide of the animal still attached to its fur was the covering for the vital parts of their otherwise pale white bodies, broken up by the striping design of smeared blood and some type of black dye. Up close they were even more ghastly, and the smell coming from their bodies had her heaving into the rancid cloth that gagged her mouth.

Arabella's heart ratcheted painfully, and she strained to get free from the bonds that held her tight, panic thrumming through her. She frantically scanned her surroundings, desperate to flee. Cronan were everywhere, but mingled with them were men with the emblems of Chilton. From the left she saw the Cronan part, though they faced away from the man who advanced. She squinted. The man was huge atop a coal destrier. Before his face could be seen, she instinctively knew who had come. She was frozen in horror as the massive man and equally large mount ate up the remaining distance. Her abductors were last to move out of the way for him as he approached her. She scoured his face, trying to comprehend how anyone so seemingly attractive could be so evil that it radiated off him in waves. Every remaining ounce of courage was used as Arabella drew back her shoulders and straightened her spine, legs working to balance her. There was nowhere to go, but she would never give him the satisfaction of seeing her broken, knowing it would feed the monster within.

He moved purposefully toward her, a hard smile on his face. How could she ever have considered him handsome, even pleasant? His dark brown hair and eyes and square face held her captive as he advanced on her like a wolf with a lamb. There was a raw power, a depravity there now, that hadn't been present the last time she'd seen him.

Dismounting his horse, he went immediately to Arabella's side, reached up, and pulled her down to stand next to him.

"At last," he said quietly, gently framing her face with his enormous, rough, callused hands. His eyes devoured her form. Arabella didn't move a muscle. She wished desperately for her sword to defend herself with, to stop the pain, the devastation, and the terror that he created everywhere he went. To put an end to his tyranny.

He removed her gag and used a knife to take off her rough bands. "You've given me a long chase, Arabella," he spoke close to her ear, bending down so only she could hear. She could feel his hot breath on her neck and a woodsy, musty smell. "It has been most exhilarating!" he whispered, his lips grazing her neck.

Carefully she pulled away from him and rubbed her sore wrists, stretching her body. She managed to halt the urge to shudder with revulsion, though she yet shivered from the cold.

"Did this man hurt you?" Mason demanded loudly, as he took her hands into his own and examined her wrists in the dark. Noting cold hands and delicate shivers, Mason removed his cloak and draped it around Arabella's shoulders before taking her hands once again.

As much as she disliked Torin, she wouldn't lie either. "Nay, he did not," she answered, trying to gently pull her hands from Mason's, which he wouldn't allow. Longing to scream and yank off his cloak that reeked of him, dark and musty, she was completely disturbed by the whole situation. Over a hundred men stood watch around them, all gazes fastened on them.

Torin didn't look thrilled to be there, and he seemed annoyed that Mason hadn't addressed him yet. Getting close to Mason's face, he spoke haughtily. "I didn't touch the girl, as promised. Can you confirm the McKenna women are taken care of?"

Mason turned from looking at Arabella and looked at Torin like he was a bug he was ready to squash. If Arabella had been in Torin's shoes, she would have trod lightly. He had no idea who he was dealing with and was playing with a fire he couldn't combat.

"The Cronan were more than happy to comply with your wish," Mason spoke calmly. "They left hours ago to go after the women."

The evil in the air felt suffocating. *What?* she screamed in her head. *They are going after Ethan's mom and sister? This is what Torin has been up to. Making treaties with the enemy.*

"If you are certain they will meet with success we can discuss the other part of our deal." Torin spoke imperiously, having taken note of his father's haughty demeanor no doubt. He looked all around him at those that were assembled. "You said that once you had her, you would leave Saldanzia. We expect you all gone with the rise of morning."

"Nay, that won't work for me now." Mason spoke easily, turning away from Torin, obviously done with the traitor. Mason pulled Arabella away from the younger Blake and started to walk away. Arabella looked over her shoulder and could see the Cronan advancing on the Saldanzians, brandishing axes, knives, and swords. It was horrifying. Garner and Luke were among them, hands tied behind their backs. Luke was awake and met her gaze, mirroring the panic in their eyes.

"Don't, please, Mason," Arabella pleaded with Mason in a voice she didn't recognize as her own. Terror filled her and she pulled on Mason's arm to hear her.

Torin started to yell at Mason, "We had a deal! I gave her to you!"

"Please, Mason," she choked as one of the Cronan impaled one of the Saldanzians with his sword. It would be a bloodbath; the Saldanzians were highly outnumbered.

"Don't," Mason commanded Arabella, pulling her face to look at him.

"Mason, please," she whimpered, angry at her own weakness as tears fell. "Please don't let them hurt my men! Please!" she pleaded.

"Mason Kiefer!" Torin shouted once again, "My father will hunt you down . . ." There was a loud grunt, and then the blood-curdling scream of the Cronan that caused Arabella to jump.

"My men!" Arabella yelled, anger fueling her now. She struggled against his hold.

"They will be fine . . . for now," Mason said banally, continuing to drag her away.

"Nay," she said, looking at him, desperate to believe him. "They will be slaughtered."

Mason shrugged, giving her very little assurance. "I said they will be fine for now." He emphasized the now, lending her to believe that Luke and Garner were far from safe.

Terrified with the information, she felt like a little girl being led and feasted upon by a true monster, and she was weak, weaponless, and altogether helpless to do anything about it.

The disturbing sounds of murder rent the air, and the screaming of Torin's men, who were so obviously not trained soldiers, made her long to plug her ears. Then emptiness found her. She was hollow inside, unable to process the sounds and fear that permeated the air.

Minutes passed and she came to herself, noting the yelling of the Cronan had ceased along with the clash of steel. Mason pulled her toward a lone tent. Scary thoughts ran unchecked through her head. Arabella tried to take everything around her in, trying to find any weapon. Her senses were overloaded with so many smells: sweat, blood, food, burning fires. Soldiers milled about, some even wore different uniforms from the Norlans, except Anchelle, which was a relief. They all slowed to a stop and stood respectfully, or perhaps in terror, as the king of Chilton passed by.

Once they reached the tent, Mason pulled her in and sat her on a cot, then sat next to her. Her heart raced and she didn't know if she could withstand such terror and still breathe. His knees touched her own, and he took her hands. She looked into his eyes, trying desperately to put up a good front, to remove all traces of her fear. Arabella didn't want to seem weak, even though it owned her at that instant.

He looked at her for a long moment. "Ah, the fire in your eyes! 'Tis what draws me to you, a moth to your flame," he said. "I have wanted you since the day I first saw you in the orchard!"

"You can't *have* me!" Arabella stated calmly. Though she felt anything but calm.

"Do not doubt it," he threatened. "As soon as Saldanzia is conquered we will return to Anchelle and raise ten fine lads." He smiled at her, his eyes lit with surety. Insane. The man was crazed. One second he was murdering men, and the next speaking of domestic bliss.

She didn't want to be anywhere near him, but she didn't wish Saldanzia to pay the price for her running there either. "Why don't we leave now, then?" she asked.

"Because you are a Saldanzian princess as well, and we wouldn't want them coming for you later." He spoke as though exasperated with the situation. "'Tis your own birthright and will be our sons'. Now I want you to think about this whilst I'm gone." His eyes held a steely glint she was afraid to think on. "I will have you regardless. I will never tie you up or treat you badly; however, if you ever run from me, I will take off Luke's arm first." He spoke with calm that belied that bloody threat. "'Tis his name, isn't it?" he asked her. He waited for her to respond. She nodded her head after hesitating a minute. "If he survives that loss, I will take a leg. If he proves unable to endure your punishment, well never fear, I also have that other knight I could work it out with, and well . . . at last count over four thousand Anchellians, here with me, should you fail to heed my commands and obey me. Do you understand?"

A tear slipped down Arabella's cheek, and she angrily wiped it away before he could. "Aye, crystal clear," she spoke softly, shivering once again and unable to control the tremors. Her blood ran cold at the vivid image he'd portrayed.

"I will be gone for a time. You are to remain here. No one will bother or harm you. They will bring you food. We are in agreement, then, and you understand the consequences?"

She managed a sharp nod. "Good, now let's have a little token of your affection, a kiss to send your king off with!" he purred, an arm snaking around her waist and his hand pulling her face to his own. Arabella's instincts were to kick him in the groin and shove the palm of her hand into his face, like she had been taught, but she didn't think it would kill him, and then Luke would pay the consequences. And so she stood still as he kissed her lips in a passionate way, making her stomach roil with bile.

He pulled away and studied her intently for a moment before marching out of the tent.

When he left, Arabella searched the tent quickly for something to throw up into. She had no sooner found a pail before she heaved repeatedly in the receptacle.

CHAPTER 15

E than stood next to a map, deep in thought. The Ruling Five were congregated in a council room, having recently begun another emergency session. The bulk of Mason's army was camped out at the south gate. He felt confident that they would attack at dawn's light, hours yet away. Still he was restless. Something wasn't . . . right. He shook his head. Nothing was right, they faced an illness, an army. And yet why did it seem he was missing something even yet? He looked carefully at the group assembled and all seemed anxious, to be sure. They pored over maps and documents talking together in bursts and heated tones. He looked at Cleve, who turned and looked at him as well. Ethan couldn't believe it, but the man smiled at him pleasantly. He pinched his hand. Yep, it hurt. He needed to get some sleep, and apparently so did Cleve. What in the world was going on?

He walked out of the room and then exited the building, drawing deeply of the cool night air into his lungs in an attempt to clear his head. Had Cleve just smiled at him? What was the weasel up to? He looked all around him. Stillness permeated. No one walked the city this night. Men were stationed around the city, but here, now, the night was almost eerily silent. The moon had risen since last he had been outside, the stars were bright, and he could easily see under their combined light.

Ethan thought of the sight that had met him as he had rode his horse from the Graces' home hours before. Illness followed closely by death had robbed many people of this city in a short time period. The citizens looked glassy eyed, almost beaten, with so many still sick with fevers and violent shivers. Were there enough to fight the enemy that they would be battling in just a few hours?

Those thoughts worried him greatly, but still something nagged at him, bothering him more. Something he couldn't put his finger on.

"What are you about?" his father asked, as he came out to join him on the steps of the council building.

"I don't know father, but something feels really off."

"There is an invading army sitting at our doorstep this very eve, and we yet wait for them to attack," his dad spoke solemnly.

"Nay. Do you not feel it? Something isn't right. What have we missed?"

His dad paused and really looked at him. "What do you believe it to be?" The silence stretched. The city was quiet as people huddled in their homes, many battling illness and all waiting in dreaded anticipation of the battle. Men and no doubt some women slept with their swords.

"I don't know," Ethan admitted, frustration leaking out.

"They will attack soon," his dad surmised.

"Undoubtedly," Ethan said. "Do you know what, Dad? I looked right at Cleve, and he smiled."

"He smiled?" his dad responded. Ethan nodded his head. "'Tis passing strange," he said, puzzled.

They sat for a moment, both of their minds taking them down different paths. "Where is Roland?" Ethan asked aloud. He worried about Arabella especially, and he realized he hadn't seen Roland for a time. One of her men always stayed by him to give her updates. The council wouldn't have been a pleasant place to be tonight. Now that he thought about it, Roland would have been spelled off by one of the others by now. He didn't know who, but she would make sure to be apprised of anything and everything that was happening. One of her men should be here. What did that mean?

A desperate need to verify that all was right with her warred with the present need that he present himself at the gate for updates on the wall, at a change in shift; it was his obligation. It needed to take top priority. They had pulled their army back to the city sometime before Ethan had arrived in Saldanzia.

"Let me see to the gate," his dad spoke, having once again discerned his son's thoughts. Fear pulsed through him at the thought of losing his father in the coming conflict.

Ethan hesitated. The gate was where the leader should be. He had prepared the area for the attack, and left capable men to command the post, but he must be there before morning's light and the attack began. They were shorthanded as it was, with so many dead or still sick from the shivers. The saysee would surely prove lifesaving to those who were not too far gone with the disease. The army had dispensed the medicine with surprisingly little difficulty. He longed to sit and hear about how the team had managed to traverse the mountain passes still entrenched with winter snow to secure so much of the herb. It had seemed like such a long shot that to have them return with wagons of the treatment that it was truly miraculous.

The city was kind of like a ghost town. Residents not needed for services were directed to stay home to curb the spread of illness and free the line of sight along the roadways.

Why? Why did he feel so compelled to see why none of Arabella's men were close by? If there was something wrong, surely they would tell him?

"Be quick," his dad hissed. "You are worried for a reason. Trust that. GO!"

Ethan ran to his mount and galloped from the building, trying to not give it another thought. The disquiet, the fear, he realized, was for Arabella. Why he would worry about her, he wasn't sure. Her guardsmen were outstanding swordsmen, every one, and she could handle herself, as he had seen with his own eyes on multiple occasions. She was safe as anyone in the city, perhaps more. Clear streets and a fast mount should get him to her within a quarter of an hour. He'd assure himself of her welfare; if all was well, he would have plenty of time to make the gates of the wall well before dawn.

The deep heat of shame filled him for a moment with the thought of going to the home of his love rather than the gate where he was obligated to be. She probably would be asleep and he would feel all the worse. But when he couldn't shake the feeling that it was necessary, urgent even, he pushed on, rationalizing he would just check in with her men stationed outside and be off to the gate before half an hour. Shame was replaced with hard determination at the reminder of his own father's insistence that he follow through with his gut.

The horse's hooves clattered loudly on the barren streets as he passed home after home that likely fitfully slept. The city had a nervous energy, a dark fear that he had never felt before. The people had been sobered: first the shivers, and now an enemy at the gates. There had been some grumbling heard in groups against Anchellians, he knew, but none had dared say anything to him. They were blind, ignorant, if they thought this was her fault.

As he approached the outskirts of the darkened Grace estate, he knew instantly that something was wrong. No one stopped him, and when he drew up to the house, no one greeted him. His heart rate increased fueled with a growing dread. Where were all the guards? People would be asleep inside, but there should have been several soldiers to receive him. Timothy's and Arabella's guard had met him on every previous arrival, even those late in the night. Vaulting from the horse, he dropped the reins and raced up the stairs to the front door, pounding on them before throwing them open.

"Arabella!" he yelled as he began to climb the stairs in search of her room. Ethan wasn't sure which one was hers, never having been in it. "Arabella!" He shouted her name several more times as he threw door after door open. No one? Not even a servant?

What was going on? Where were Timothy's guards that Timothy had left for Arabella's protection?

He found a darkened room, the bed carelessly thrown askew, a night dress lying haphazard, the smell of her lingering in the room. Undisciplined, blind panic was not something Ethan had experienced oft, but he felt well acquainted with it at that moment. He searched the room for any clue but found none. He didn't see her blade anywhere and prayed she still had it.

Running from the room, he wracked his brain trying to think of where to go or what to do. The timing couldn't be any worse. Did he try to find her, or go to the gate? Had all fled? Butler? Maid? Cooks? Stablehands? How could everyone disappear?

A galloping horse broke the stillness and could be heard advancing as Ethan ran outside the mansion. He tried to find the rider in the dark, but couldn't see him. Vaulting onto his horse, Ethan raced toward the sound; it may or may not be a clue. Regardless, at this time of night, it probably was something he should look into. At breakneck speed he ran his horse toward the sound, though it was muffled now that he too ran his horse. He had to stop once to make sure he would intercept the horsemen. A minute later, Ethan pulled on the reins on his horse, as the other horsemen came into view galloping toward him.

Halting within a foot of Ethan's own horse, Benton's face looked pained, and Ethan knew that something had gone horribly wrong. He waited, sure if he opened his mouth a scream of anger would pour out. Benton took no time before he launched into the tale. "Cleve and Torin came over an hour ago with over fifty armed men. Arabella commanded me to hide. Cleve left with a few men before the others, I assume to the council. I followed Torin with Arabella trussed up and Luke and Garner knocked out and strapped to animals. They took them through the city, to a less frequented gate along the northwest wall. Someone was waiting because they let them through and closed the portcullis the moment they passed through. There were no soldiers along the section to present. Took them about two miles and into the forest. Torin rendezvoused with a group of Cronan, and Mason was there. He handed over Arabella, Luke, and Garner."

Ethan felt bile rise. The thought of her in his hands tore at his sanity.

"The Cronan slaughtered Torin and all of his men as though it was their reward and then removed their outer clothing. That northwest gate must still have a handful of men there, but they let Torin out, and . . ."

"The Chilton army, or rather fifty men, now have my men's uniforms," Ethan finished, disgust for the traitors lacing his words.

"Aye. Roland is hidden by the gate. He caught up with me when no one came to relieve him from the council. He will try to hold them off."

"How is there only a handful of men at the gate? There should be near three thousand men stationed within shouting distance?"

"Cleve or Torin must have sent them somewhere else, so he could rendezvous with Mason."

Though they talked of grave matters, securing the city from falling, yet his mind was wrapped up in thoughts of Arabella. "Was she harmed?" he finally asked, not sure if he could bear the answer, while holding to the knowledge that Mason wanted her alive.

"Nay, but . . . I left her," Benton lamented. Ethan could tell that it hurt Benton greatly to leave his queen in the hands of the murderer. "After the massacre I couldn't follow, there were too many. and the Cronan are much more aware of their surroundings. The only way to get her is to defeat Mason, and his army will soon be upon us."

"Stay with me!" Ethan commanded. "We will need to get a company of men to the northwestern gate soon."

"Wait!" Benton said, holding up his hand, and Ethan pulled the reins on his horse, more than eager to be on their way. "There's more. I heard Torin say twice that your family and the Graces would be killed. Mason said that he had the Cronan go after your mother and sister."

Ethan felt like he had been punched in the gut as air rushed out of him. He and his father were always in danger, but his mother and sister? What could that possibly mean? The only ones that knew the location of his mom and sister were his dad, him, and those that accompanied his mother and sister. Did anyone come back with his father and know the location where they were hiding? Could they have given it away? Benton shared Cleve's plan to remove the Grace and McKenna families under the cover of this conflict; Cleve would have their entire families exterminated. They would have spies, he knew very well. Even in all this war, the Blakes let the McKennas take the risk in battle to care for the citizens while they plotted the demise of the ruling families once their lands were secured.

His mind raced to his father, who was even now at the southern gate. Ethan needed to lead a sizable portion of their army to the northwestern gate, to save the city at first light. Thomas could possibly be here within the hour from Peligree with ten thousand troops, but would the enemy be in the city already?

Ethan couldn't go after the woman he loved more than his own life, and he couldn't protect his mother and sister at the moment. How ironic that he had bet their lives in front of Cleve only a few days ago. The anguish of the betrayals was unbearable.

Looking at Benton, he asked, "Could you go warn my father, and tell him everything? When Thomas gets here, send him with half of his army to flank Mason's army attacking the northwestern gate, and to leave the other half with my father. Might manage to surround them."

"Aye."

"Bye, my friend, and my thanks." Spurring his horse, he galloped to where he knew a large company of men guarded another area. He needed soldiers at the northwestern gate to meet Mason's men. His mind whirled with questions, his brain trying to understand where the company of men disappeared from the northwestern gate. Three thousand men. Where were they? Where were the Graces' guards? What had Cleve been doing all this time, besides entering into treaties with the enemy? Apparently, that hadn't gone well for him. Did the man know his son had been murdered this night because of his machinations?

Was there really a threat to his mother and sister? Could somebody find them? While he himself and his father fought the enemy here, was the enemy right now destroying his family? An anguished sigh escaped his mouth.

Cleve would be brought to justice, he vowed. He might currently lead the Ruling Five, but he would not allow for him to win in his traitorous acts. It wouldn't be today, but by the stars and the moon as his witness, Cleve Blake would never again lead the people of Saldanzia. He would be disgraced and hanged for his acts.

His mind kept wandering to Arabella out there in the night with a madman, but he would have to rein in his thoughts, or he wouldn't be able to do what needed to be done. It would be dawn soon, and he knew the strike at the south gate would happen then. Now he was also sure that they would flood in from the north and take the city, while the south was occupied in its own battle.

Pushing his mount to its limits, Ethan hurtled down the avenue that would bring him closest to the northwestern gate, where he knew other men to be stationed. Counting the banners along the inner wall, he was quickly able to ascertain that there were three thousand stationed in the area: not nearly enough. They needed a whole world of luck to hold them off long enough for Thomas's reinforcements. Just as he was nearing from the northwestern gate, an explosion rocked the air from the south. Pulling the horse to a stop, Ethan instinctively covered his head with his hands. The men all around him scrambled for cover. Turning, he saw an enormous cloud raging through the sky.

"Hurry, men!" Ethan called out. "We have to move."

The Saldanzians had never seen anything like it, and it was hard not to turn around and watch the bilious dark cloud forming. Racing their horses hard to the northwestern gate, Ethan watched dismayed as men poured in wearing Saldanzian colors. Yelling to get the men's attention following him, he gave them hand commands. Raising his sword, they poured into the group of horsemen with Saldanzian colors. Driving his sword into the closest enemy, Ethan yelled at the gatekeeper to close the inner gate. Moments later, the gatekeeper fell by an arrow lodged in his chest.

Where the gatekeeper had been moments before, Ethan saw Roland fighting with two men in Saldanzian colors, but more were advancing. Combating his way to the staircase which ran along the inside the wall, Ethan leapt from his horse onto the landing and fought his way to Roland.

"Hurry!" Roland shouted. "They're coming from the woods!"

Approaching Roland, Ethan was able to see what he'd described. Thousands were pouring out from the treeline. It seemed a horde of savage beasts led the charge. The barbaric screeches identified them as Cronan. Their feral yowls were turning the air into a living, breathing tide of piercing, emotional pain that stripped the body of coherent thought. It was a fearful phenomenon that made a brawny man want to turn tail and run. Ethan had seen it himself a few times.

Seeing his men's horrorstricken faces, Ethan hastily battled his way to Roland. In sync, as though they had fought many a battle together, they pushed the men back to the place where the mechanism ran the gate. Together they slammed the gate into place.

The battle below was dwindling as Ethan gave the command for the archers to come to the battlement atop the wall, where Cronan and Norlan soldiers alike rushed the wall. Dismayed by the necessary decision, Ethan commanded the archers to take out the advancing enemy. It was a hard directive, knowing the Norlan men were conscripted to be there, fighting a war they were forced to participate in.

Droves of men rushed the outside wall. Ethan's archers streamed arrows down onto the hosts of men, hardly putting a dent into the masses below. Fiery arrows came from outside the city wall's forest line.

"Shields!" Ethan shouted, followed by several other men repeating the command. Though most of his men got their shields up in time, some were not so lucky.

A huge explosion rocked the air, and Ethan felt himself being propelled backward—a burst of intense pain—and then there was nothing but blackness.

CHAPTER 16

Somebody was slapping Ethan's face and shouting at him. "Wake up! Ethan, quickly, you have got to rally your troops." The muffled words came as though underwater. Another brisk slap to his face wasn't helping the pounding of his head, nor the ringing in his ears. His head spun, his eyes trying to focus on Roland. The side of his body ached, and pain shot up his foot.

His senses felt dull, sounds coming in muted tones, though he knew the air must ring with the sounds of battle. He stumbled to his feet, wobbling precariously. Roland helped him to remain upright. "Hurry, your companies are coming to help, but the Cronan are coming through the wall. You have got to organize them!" he shouted.

Ethan tried to take it all in from his position on the wall of the city, his head spinning. Cronan were pouring through a large hole where the rock wall had once been. He turned in a circle to take in everything around him. From the east, thousands of his men were coming to their aid. The sun was finally making an appearance, coming up and allowing him to see for miles. The Cronan were facing into the sun as they crawled into the city, giving the Saldanzians a welcome and needed advantage.

If only Thomas would come to their aid now, Thomas could flank them, and their enemy would be surrounded. That would give the Saldanzians a chance to end the conflict—and

Mason. Ethan scanned the horizon, but there was no sign of Thomas's garrison.

With Roland next to him, Ethan came off the wall to their horses. The two comrades raced to meet their own army to help the attack on the Cronan and Norlan men. The Cronan's loud cries once again pierced the air. It made one want to hold their hands to their ears to shut out the cacophony. That was maybe the idea.

Thousands upon thousands of Cronans and Norlans poured through the gaping hole in the city's walls, running and wailing. Never had the Saldanzians seen an army of Cronans this size or magnitude. It was unheard of. Ethan knew that they were vastly outnumbered, but the Saldanzians had a few advantages, and yielding was not an option. His men were mounted on horses and wearing heavy armor, giving them an advantage in height and great efficacy in dealing mortal blows against the relative nakedness of the Cronan. Heading to the forefront of his armies, men lined up behind him. Ethan called out commands to his leaders, who rode down the ranks of their men, echoing precisely Ethan's commands.

A couple hundred archers were perched atop buildings with bundles of arrows awaiting the signal, trained to first pick off the Cronan leaders and the handful of Mason's men that commanded the Cronan army. There was a terrible moment of waiting for the perfect time when the distance was just within reach of the archers. On Ethan's command the skilled archers let off a volley, bringing many of the Cronan commanders to the ground instantly.

The remaining Saldanzian soldiers held still as the screaming Cronan drew closer, their javelins held at ready. The stillness of the Saldanzian army was like a masterpiece, something that had been trained in them well, and which they held even in the face of gruesome enemies. "Now!" Ethan yelled. The Saldanzian pointed their javelins at the Cronan, who were immediately impaled. Letting go of their javelins, the Saldanzian soldiers reached for their swords and the work of death continued.

It was a savage and bloody fight. The day stretched and the men still held the Cronan off from in the fields inside of the city. Bodies littered the ground, and blood soaked the earth. Roland and Ethan fought side by side, each covering the other's back. They were both off their horses now, and each had a few minor wounds. Roland had one on his face that looked like it needed stitches, but had at least stopped streaming, and Ethan was sure the back of his leg could use several as well.

The Cronan kept coming, and it looked like there was no end in sight. His men, though fighting bravely, seemed to be losing ground. For the hundredth time he wondered where Thomas could be. Had the messenger not made it through? Had Thomas's entire army fallen ill and were unable to come? He simply needed more men to be able to push back the Cronan. Looking all around him Ethan tried to note anything useful that could be used to their advantage. Thoughts churned. There was no time to stop and assess while a constant unremitting stream of soldiers poured through.

Ethan realized he needed to rally his troops. They were outnumbered, but they were also in the right, fighting to save their families, the entire city from destruction. If he couldn't think of something, and soon, they would fall.

CHAPTER 17

Arabella sat in a canvas tent for a time, stomach relieved of its entire contents. Depression weighed heavily: emotionally battered and scared beyond measure, for herself and her people.

She could only imagine what her people had already met at the hands of Mason. Some of her men would fight against the Saldanzians this day against their will. It was horrifying. All she could do was sit back and allow it to happen. Never had she felt so powerless. Reduced to waiting while the dictator conquered the last resistance. He was such a vile and monstrous man, and the memory of the forced kiss made her skin crawl. Her body shook as wave upon wave of emotions—fear, anger, hatred—engulfed her and threatened to drown her in their depths.

A loud noise rent the air, and she felt certain the ground had shook slightly. Arabella jumped from her bed and paced around the tent. What could make such a violent sound that the earth trembled? Searching her memory, she came up empty. She could only surmise that it had to do with the attack on Saldanzia.

Arabella longed to scream and thrash in frustration, impotent to respond when so many people she loved would be maimed, would die, or would wish for death's release. The thought of Luke being tortured because of her made her want to weep anew. How could she ever make Mason content enough that he would never hurt her loved ones? The thought was sobering. He could never achieve contentment. The realization of this stopped her cold. The obsessed king would never have all that he wanted with his voracious appetite to control. People would suffer because of her all the time. Even should she find a way to liberate those she held dear, there would be others—the maid, her horse, the innocent, the list was endless. Mason would never be happy with her because she could never give him her heart, her allegiance. Nothing she did would ever be enough to satisfy him. It wasn't in him. He was too full of darkness.

What choice did that leave her? Killing herself wasn't an option, but fighting if necessary to her death was. Could she do it? If she failed and people paid the price for her insubordination, could she live with herself? What was the alternative? Every day of their lives the Anchellians would wonder if it was their last. They would look at each day with fear because that was what Mason instilled in people.

If she chose to wait and fight him, she had to be sure to succeed. Failure would mean death to her men. Was there any way to escape with both Luke and Garner? At least she could act, try to learn more so she could plan. Dumping out her water, leaving the pity and depression behind, she flipped open the tent flap and poked her head out, trying to take everything in at once. It was mostly light enough to see dawn was now upon them. She saw a cloud of dark furling smoke in the distance above the treeline. If she had her bearings, it was the south side of the city. Arabella watched it for a moment before the shuffling of feet nearby had her swing her head to find the soldiers guarding her.

Two men stood just outside her door. Both were impressive in height and carried their weapons with such ease it was obvious of their extensive training. She suspected Mason had chosen them for their intimidating presence. One had a little bit of a crooked nose with an elongated face, and the other was like a square, and slightly taller, with raised scars crisscrossing his thickly muscled arms.

"I'm so sorry," she began immediately, seeing the anger on their faces. "I'm not trying to get you into trouble, but I spilled my water when that loud explosion startled me. I was so upset . . ." She aimed to have them think her vapid, frightened, and weak. It wasn't hard to pull off, feeling the way she did. "Is there any way I can get some more?" she said, holding out her can. It looked like they wanted to say no, so she rushed on. "I haven't had anything to drink in a day. We came from Capri yesterday, and the city was low on water. We rode all day. Mason wouldn't want me to fall ill," she added, not sure exactly if it was true.

The men were Mason's men, she noticed. Chiltons. All the men she could see around her were, in fact, from his country of birth. Not one soldier that loitered was from the other Norlans cities, she noted, and no Cronan, thank goodness. Just looking at *them* made her feel squeamish.

"I can get my own, if you want to follow and direct me," she said, "make sure I don't escape." She forced a shallow laugh, hoping they believed her naught but a flighty girl. She needed to see around the camp, try to figure out where Luke and Garner were, before she could settle on a plan. There were a surprising number of men still milling about the camp. Odd, with the battle already begun. More information was necessary, and she desperately needed a blade. Perhaps if she continued to play a silly helpless girl, they would let their guard down. Arabella had seen other girls do it. Mayhap she could pull it off as well.

"Aye, let's go then," the taller one spoke, leading the way. A small path meandered through the trees to an open field, where thousands of bedrolls lay dispersed. The ground was tamped down flat, attesting to the thousands that passed the night here. They led her along the treeline to a small creek. Soldiers warily eyed her as they passed, keen with interest, but none approached or spoke to her. There were around fifty that she could see in her field of vision, but wherever she looked there was no indication of where Garner or Luke were held. Were they indeed alive? Had Mason lied to her and allowed the Cronan to kill them too?

There was no way she would leave without them. At least she had made that single decision, but the problem lay with her odds of success in even locating them. The enemy camp was spread out over too large of a distance. Compared with the tens of thousands of brothers in arms, even the fifty that yet remained would still prove insurmountable for a single person. And those were just the soldiers she could see. Would there be sentries as well?

Stooping down and scooping the water in the pail, Arabella lingered, looking all around her. Though she was slow in her perusal, there didn't seem to be any way out of her current predicament. The men were spread out. Before she could think of any plausible escape plan, her impatient captors directed her back to the tent.

That was a complete letdown. Not even a flicker of an idea. At a total loss, she dropped to her knees by the cot and prayed. She pled with the Lord to save her people, the people of the Norlans and Saldanzia, petitioning God to lead her to find a way to deliver everyone from Mason. Sharing with her Maker her desire to find a way to escape with her men so that they could join the battle.

Still on her knees sometime later when a commotion could be heard, she closed her prayer. It sounded as though a large company of men were returning to the camp. The two guards that had been watching entered the tent with their blades out, eyes hard. "What's going on?" Arabella demanded.

The taller one grabbed her wrist and lifted her up. He tried to turn her so her back was against him, but she elbowed him in the face. Then she chopped his wrist holding the sword with her hand, making him drop the weapon. Diving to the ground, she grabbed the heavy sword and sliced it toward the man with the crooked nose. They both came at her. Using the skills she had honed for the last twelve years of her life, she battled the men, as her life and others' depended on it. Though they were much stronger, she was quick and a much better swordsman. They would rely on brute strength where she had applied herself to the mastery. Near-lifelong training took over, and the one whose blade she held stepped in, planning to wrest it from her. His own blade met his gut and she drove it deep before retrieving it and giving the last man her full attention. Fury glinted in his eyes. A litany of curses and threats poured out of him.

His anger made his powerful swings sloppy and left openings that she took full advantage of, dropping low to her knees as he swung, missing her. Her blade shot up before he could swing back and made contact as she drove the weapon through his gut, angling up. His startled eyes revealed his hopeless state before he crumpled and fell hard, landing on his back, eyes still wide in shock when death claimed him. She was aware of his warm blood on her hands, but the clash of steel outside gave her a moment's pause. She had been so embroiled in her own battle that she'd not realized the camp was under attack! This was her chance! She needed to move quickly.

Though squeamish, she set aside her disgust to search their bodies for more weapons than the blade she still held in her hand like a lifeline. Arabella located a dagger from the scarred man's belt sheath, which was immediately tucked into her boot. She gleaned the other soldier's sword and was pleased to find it a bit lighter. A moment of gratitude welled for Garner's insistence. She'd practiced at times with one of their heavier blades.

With adrenaline pumping through her veins, she peeked out of the tent flap, praying none of the enemy soldiers were headed her way to investigate the battle that had been within. Relief flooded through her at the sight of Benton, followed by soldiers bearing the colors of Anchelle. They were casting back tent flaps, searching. The skirmish was over. The soldiers that had loitered when she was out for water all lay spread across the field.

Arabella made her way out of the tent. At a cry from Benton the men stopped in their tracks, each locking onto her form. One by one they knelt before her, right arm with a closed fist thumped against their left breast. She smiled widely, her heart full of gratitude, as she caught sight of double the number that had been here. They appeared healthy and mostly whole from the short battle. She walked to Benton, and at her command he stood.

Not being able to contain herself, Arabella embraced him. He returned the gesture, and when she pulled back, she whispered, "My thanks, Benton."

The scout inclined his head in response.

"Where are the rest of the conscripted Anchellian soldiers?" she queried.

"Forced to battle with Mason's army. I believe they are engaged at the southern front. I was trying to see if Captain Thomas was close at hand and found these men instead. I hoped there would be enough to take on whoever was guarding you. They were more than pleased to answer my call to arms." He led her toward the men.

"That we be, Your Highness," a young man declared among the crowd gathered. The warrior was not familiar to her. He boldly locked eyes with her and stated. "If you can get to the rest of the army, you can rally them. They will follow!" His boldness surprised her.

"Well, there is no time to lose then!" she said, meeting his eyes. "First we need to find Luke and Garner," she said to Benton. "I'm praying they're here somewhere."

"Here!" The distant sound of Luke's lilting timbre came from somewhere to the left of her. "If you would stop lollygagging over there. My arms feel like they are going to fall off."

"Where are you then?" Arabella laughed with pure joy, finally spying them, out of line of sight from her own tent and the opposite way she'd taken to get water. She ran over to them. Benton beat her there and was cutting their bindings where each had been strapped to neighboring trees. Arabella threw her arms around Luke, and the two embraced for a minute. Her relief that he was well was tangible. She took her commander's hands into her own, and he put his forehead to hers.

"Are you yet well, Your Highness?" Garner inquired, his eyes drawn to the blood still drying along her arms.

"Aye, Garner, my thanks to you for it. A heavy sword took down my two captors. I'll never complain again in practice." The commander's eyes widened and filled with pride as she finished the brief explanation.

"I'd hear of it once we are out of this tangle."

She nodded and called out, "Benton," stepping away from Garner. "What else have you to report?"

"No sign of Captain Thomas," Benton spoke mournfully. The joyful reunion was all but forgotten as they turned their focus to what still lay ahead of them this day.

"Take a few men, make another large sweep and see if you see any sign of his army," Arabella commanded. "He might yet prove our angel of mercy this day."

Stealing through the forest, south of Saldanzia, the small Anchellian band circled the city to the south gate in hopes of finding their comrades. Fighting in the distance could be heard through the city wall. Mason had somehow foregone the gates and breached the city walls to create openings, and had pushed the fight within the capital's walls.

They needed more time and more men! Neither were present. They were desperate to find the battalions filled with the people of Anchelle and the soldiers of the Norlans likewise pressed into service. The city would fall if nothing changed. It would be over before night, she calculated. Saldanzia would serve as the last defense against Mason's tyranny. If she could find those troops and convince them to fight against their oppressor, it could stem the relentless tide and allow the missing troops of Captain Thomas to arrive. Racing, she pondered what she could say, well knowing they didn't want to be here. They couldn't possibly want him to rule their countries, but fear was a powerful motivator. The threat against their own person and loved ones was very real, something she was beginning to know firsthand.

With the south open, they streamed through without resistance. Less than a month ago, she had met her grandfather here for the very first time, in this very spot. The thought was sobering.

She could hear the fighting all over and knew it was close, but signs of the fighting went east and west.

"Do we split up?" she asked Garner. "The troops know you as well as me."

Garner shook his head. "Some of them wouldn't know me. This group we have here isn't nearly enough to protect you from Mason right now. We stay together."

She looked at Luke, who nodded his head in agreement. "If you were Saldanzian, which way would you fall back?" she asked.

They thought about it for a moment. Luke spoke first. "West. They would have the higher ground, and fewer civilians."

"Agreed," Garner said.

To the west the group pushed into the city. Bodies littered the ground from all the countries, but the majority wore Saldanzian colors. Men lay at odd angles in death, some missing limbs, a gruesome testament to the battle waged. Dark blood splattered surfaces everywhere, and there was a distinct coppery smell. Sweat, fear, and illness saturated the air. A combined scent she had never smelt before, but it made her stomach churn.

⁓

Carried atop horses, the scenes of bloodshed they passed further overwhelmed her senses. Men moaned and screamed, with very few around to help ease their suffering. A man reached out for them, and to her shame Arabella kept riding. "I'm sorry," she whispered, knowing he couldn't hear her. It broke something inside her. She longed to stop, to acknowledge each dying man's request to not pass this life with no one present. The reality that there would be thousands more sharing this fate propelled her forward, furthering her conviction in what she needed to do.

The vibrant green tunics of fallen Anchellian soldiers were scattered across the ground. Her heart screamed in anger at the continuous scene of ruin. Each man's life prematurely snuffed out and left as refuse to molder. Iron resolve formed, a silent promise to those fallen that she would do everything in her power to end

Mason. Not just her fellow Anchellians but also the people of the Norlans, and for the Saldanzians that had taken her in. Mason had to be stopped. She vowed to succeed or die trying to rid the world of his stain.

Initially wanting to view and hold in remembrance each green uniform that lay still, her growing-fragile sanity demanded she stop searching bodies. Though it would be a sight that would be imprinted in her mind forever, lest she forget. Battling the compelling need to look for familiar faces among the dead, Arabella forced her gaze from the scene to focus solely on the path straight ahead.

They knew they were going the right way when the sound of fighting became more prevalent. It seemed though the battle had split off down differing streets.

"Arabella." Luke, who had been unusually quiet, riding beside her the entire time, indicated a corpse nearby. "I think you should put on armor." Arabella revolted at the idea of stripping off and wearing the dead soldier's armor.

"I agree," Garner spoke from her left side.

"For the men to be able to truly see me, and know it's me, I need to be visible for our plan to work, otherwise there is no point in being here."

"I don't like it," Luke growled. Arabella looked at her dearest friend and she could see the anguish inside of him. To say that this was dangerous was an understatement.

The man who had spoken to her in Mason's camp chimed in, "Your Highness?" She turned around her mount to see him clearly.

"I, too, worry for your safety, but if you could just find a place to be seen, without getting too close to the fray, the men will follow you. They know that even if Mason were to make it back to Anchelle, life would be horrible under his reign. They would live a life of fear for their loved ones."

Resuming their journey, it was but moments before the sound increased dramatically.

"Close enough," Garner cautioned. They could see people now fighting. The noise would be deafening once they got closer. How could she get her men's attention, and turn them on Mason Kiefer's army?

Looking all around, she spied a welcome landmark. Her pulse increased, understanding the miracle before them. A prayer answered. "There." She pointed. The bell on "her" church tower lay straight ahead through the conflict. Now she just needed to get through the melee of men that were fighting, climb the tower, and ring it. How was she to get through with her relatively small group of men? Saldanzian men would automatically strike against their group wearing the green Anchellian colors. She didn't want her men to have to fight Saldanzians.

The colorful tiled rooftops were spaced far enough apart that there was no way to make it from rooftop to rooftop. Her eyes looked all around. A bakery, a flower shop, and more shops dotted each side of the gray cobbled streets. Behind them, stone houses ran parallel with the streets.

The sewer? Ugh! She couldn't see any nearby, thank goodness. The closest option was an aqueduct that ran along the street. It would take them close to the church, but they would still have a small distance to get from the aqueduct to the church. It was the best option she could think of.

Laying out the plan quickly, Arabella insisted only a few proceed with her. Her hope was that if there were only a few of them on the aqueducts, they could slip into the battle unnoticed. She could tell Garner wanted to argue, but she gave him a firm look, staying his response.

Reining Palachio to the nearest aqueduct, Arabella looked around at her men. "Garner, once we get their attention, bring the men to Saldanzia's aid."

He nodded his head in resignation then reached over and pulled her forehead to his. "Stay safe, Your Highness!"

"And you." Arabella stood atop her saddle as she reached upward for the tubing. Not nearly tall enough, Luke jumped from standing in his saddle and grabbed ahold of the cylinder and easily hefted himself above the aqueduct. Reaching his arms down, he helped her up. She was grateful in that moment that she still wore her leggings; a dress would have been a huge hindrance. The young Anchellian man that had addressed her from camp, whom she still did not know the name of, also climbed the duct, and they lightly jogged the long beam with Luke and herself and a half-dozen others. Arabella had never had a fear of heights, but she felt the heady pulse of blood flow. From this height she could see the armies scattered all around fighting. The noise was deafening.

The vantage presented a bird's-eye view. Mason's army was pushing the Saldanzian army back further into the city. The Saldanzian fighting force seemed small in contrast to the invading army, and had nowhere to go but to retreat.

She couldn't see any indication of where Mason might be amongst the various pitched battles, praying he was not near the area they were. Thoughts shifting to Ethan for a brief moment, she wondered where he was—if he was yet healthy and whole. They passed over men fighting below them of all nationalities, but no one noticed or looked up. They were in a battle for their own lives. Without getting to the bell, they would never be able to draw the attention of those below.

As they came as close to the church as they were going to get, Luke stopped. No one seemed to have noticed them yet. There were men all around below, it would be hazardous to drop into the fighting, but they had come this far. Luke dropped down first, with Arabella and the other man close behind. Luke had his sword drawn and shielded her as she drew the one she had taken from her crooked-nose captor. It wasn't as light and fine as her own, but it would have to do.

A soldier in Chilton colors caught sight of her, recognition flared, and he grabbed a few fellow comrades and came toward them. Luke, Arabella, and the young Anchellian soldier and the few others met them head on. The Chilton soldier that fought against Arabella was twice her size and was skilled with the sword. Though Arabella wasn't by any means a seasoned warrior, years of training kept her movements fluid. She knew that he was only trying to disarm her, which was a complete disadvantage to him. Though she hated to take life, she resolved in her heart that defending her people from tyranny was a righteous cause. The desire for the well-being of her people allowed her to fight with a passion that she desperately needed in battle.

He was so much stronger than her. Not that she hadn't been sparring with strong men her entire life, but she couldn't help but wonder if they had been holding back a bit. All of a sudden a man came from behind her adversary, grabbed him by the waist, and pulled him down to the ground. The man was wearing the colors of the Norlan city Lassiter!

No time to recover before strong arms grabbed her too from behind in a vice-like grip, forcing the borrowed sword to clatter useless to the ground. Thrashing wildly and elbowing him several times proved ineffective. With swift kicks, she nailed him in the shin hard, repeatedly, to where he loosened his grip. Managing to free her hands, she pulled the dagger from her boot. Arabella sliced the man's arm as he let go of her. Cursing, the soldier came at her again, but Luke stepped in front of her and blocked the blow. Pushing with his sword, Luke pulled out his own dagger and thrust deep into the man's chest.

Grabbing her hand, Luke pulled her toward the church only to let go, having only gained thirty feet before they were met again by enemies. However, as she had been embroiled in battle, soldiers around them became aware of what was taking place. Anchellian men had started to withdraw, and several soldiers took up a perimeter around her, including a few men in the colors of the Norlan cities Lassiter and Theron. Men's voices could be heard to say, "'Tis the queen! Protect the queen!"

A smile came to her lips as she confronted one of Mason's men again. Luke on one side, the newcomer on her right, and Anchellians pressing in almost to them.

The man facing Arabella at that moment didn't seem to worry if he killed her. He was brutal as he swung his sword time and again at her. The full anger and might of the man intent on destroying her was awful to behold, and Arabella feared for her life as he swung quickly over and over again. Barely she managed to bring the knife up each time it came down and rattled her entire frame. He faked left then went hard for her right side. She moved quickly to the side, but not fast enough, and the cold steel blade found its mark. Arabella felt the piercing bite of the wound but channeled it away, aware that she needed to be fully engaged or fall. Her attacker's momentum pushed him forward enough that Arabella found the first opening, driving her blade into his stomach. Clutching the dagger, the man backed up, allowing Arabella a chance to move around him. Disbelief etched his face; he'd miscalculated her. But then again, she had miscalculated him as well, as evidenced by the pain in her side. She told herself it was only a scratch. She needed to believe that. She had somewhere she needed to be right now.

With a clear path to the church, Arabella sprinted the last few feet and climbed the steps to the door. Flinging the doors open, Arabella didn't allow her eyes to adjust to the darkness. She bolted to the right, knowing that the stairs were thus located. Darting into the stairwell, she registered Luke had also arrived into the building and was only steps behind her. Flying up the stairs, she didn't dare to stop and catch her ragged breath as she climbed steadily higher.

Arabella heard Luke's boots behind her and took the stairs two at a time. Time seemed to slow in her haste to reach the top, so much riding on this very moment that she intuitively understood the gravity. Vaguely aware of physical pain, she flew up the stairs with adrenalin hastening her every move. Every second might cost a man's life, in this horrible battle that Mason had brought to all these people. Simultaneously her legs, lungs, and side burned as she reached the top. Though the pain in her torso became more present with each passing breath, she felt invigorated, alive, in knowing she was exactly where she was meant to be.

Luke appeared behind her a mere second later, reaching the rope as her own hand found purchase on the rough fibers. Eyes locked, he shouted, "Are you ready?"

She nodded her head, still gasping from the wild sprint up the stairs. They both yanked on the thick pull rope. Once. Twice. Three times before she dropped the rope, and she turned around the city in wonder, then clasped her hands over her ears. Luke tugged once again and the bell pealed out a long, strong chime. People paused for a second, looking up, and Arabella stepped up and over the roof so that others could see her better, and took a long gulp as the bell continued to ring. Her mind raced as she wondered what she could say to turn everyone to fight solely against Mason's army. Would they be able to hear her? Could she inspire them enough to follow? The Anchellian soldier felt certain they would. A hasty prayer she sent heavenward.

"People of the Norlans, of Saldanzia!" she yelled loudly, not wanting to lose their attention and momentum as the bells echoed died out.

"If you fight with Mason's army, you will never truly win. If he wins here this day, he will own you. He will control not only your own life but well you know the lives of your wives and children. *Fear?* His control is fear. He has instilled fear into you to fight for him. Is that how you want to live everyday of your life?" Most people remained still as she yelled out to them. Her voice ached. She could see the Chilton men trying to make a drive to the church, but she continued on. "I ask you to fight for your families and your loved ones, the chance not for them to merely live in bondage but rather free to make your own destiny. Fight instead the fiend that is trying to control you! Mason Kiefer purposefully spread the shivers, causing thousands of deaths in nearly every land!" Gasps were heard by soldiers just now beginning to understand the depravity of the man that led them. "I ask you now, will you fight with me to rid the earth of his tyranny?" Loud eruptions filled the plaza where the church was situated. Men started to pile into the church. "The Saldanzians are our allies! Fight with the Saldanzians. For

Anchelle! For Lassiter! For Theron!" The responding roar made the echoes of the bell pale in comparison.

Right then Garner's men, though few, came pouring up the street, yelling, "Saldanzia! Saldanzia!" Men below her raised their weapons in the air, yelling, "Fight Mason! Fight Mason! Fight Mason!"

"Time to go," Luke warned as footsteps started to make their way up the narrow stairwell. Grabbing the rope once again, he pulled it with his hands and started to ravel it up toward them. Stiff fibers cut into her hands as she helped Luke to pull the cumbersome rope to the outside of the church wall. The din of battle being waged inside the church floated up, and rapid heavy footsteps still continued to climb.

"Hurry," she commanded as she saw a Chilton soldier twenty steps below. As the end of the rope came into view, Luke threw the rope to the outer church wall.

"Now," he yelled, "start going."

The clomping of the footfalls coming from the stairs made her think an army was headed up the stairs. Luke and Arabella jumped atop the wall and Arabella grabbed the rope and wrapped it once around her right foot, then holding the rope between her hands she let a small squeal escape as she descended down the weathered stone wall and a soldier came into view. She knew Luke would probably need a quick exit, there was no way around it; her hands burned as she slid down. The fighting had resumed outside the church, and once again, people fought for their lives below her. Luke was already on the rope then, sliding toward her and moving much quicker than her descent.

The last eight feet she jumped, with Luke only a second behind her. "This way," he said, latching onto her hand, which protested the rough treatment. Soldiers failed to notice their march as they weaved their way through the crowd of people. Those that caught sight of them were too busy defending their own lives. A few of the Chilton soldiers advanced on them. Arabella and Luke were quickly able to defend themselves and move on.

Darting down alleys and through a ribbon shop, they made it far enough that they weren't in the melee anymore. Luke bent over, gasping. Arabella grabbed her side. A stitch had seized it in the exertion, but the wound from the Chilton soldier had begun to throb nearly unbearably. The repressed pain seemed to collide with her awareness and stole the breath from her lungs. Coughing, desperate to draw air in her body, she inhaled only to have the pain respond with heightened awareness.

"I. Don't. Like. Fleeing," Arabella spoke aloud, exasperated.

"Nor do I," he lamented. "But we can't let one of Mason's men get you, or all that you just accomplished could be lost. You did your job as the queen, which was much too dangerous by the way, and now as their queen, you need to remain safe."

Arabella had to think about that for a moment.

"Besides, I think the tide has changed. Come, let's scale this house and see if we can discern the lay of it."

Desperate to see what was going on, she shoved the pain down and allowed him to pull her up on the roof after climbing a rain barrel, though her side ached fiercely as he lifted her to the tiled roof.

Even at the first glance it was obvious a shift had occurred in the area where Arabella had just fled. Mason's men were falling back. However, at the gate, where Arabella had been taken through the night before, smoke billowed heavily. A battle raged there just as it did close to the church. Where was Ethan? Had Thomas's army arrived? It certainly didn't appear as though he had. They hadn't seen any of the Cronan thus far, and Arabella shuddered, recalling the ominous sight in their grisly war accoutrements. The Cronan must be battling at the northwestern gate.

"How long would you have us wait here?" she asked. Well she knew she could leave whenever she pleased, yet she deferred to Luke's judgement. He was a warrior. No doubt he chafed and being drawn out of the battle to see to her protection.

"Not long" was all that he said.

"Where do you think Thomas is?" she asked softly. She was sure that all of the Saldanzian army wondered the same thing.

"I'm betting somewhere between here and Peligree. I fear that the messenger never made it to him, or he would have been here hours ago." Luke voiced what she already thought.

"I'm worried about Ethan and Roland."

"They are fairly resourceful," Luke spoke up.

Underneath his bravado, Arabella sensed Luke's own worries.

"Maybe we can help with the wounded," Luke said.

Arabella felt remorse to have so quickly forgotten the men she had left behind. The face of the man who begged her help when they entered the city was before her. All the unanswered pleas for aid they had ridden past. Though not a trained healer she had been a nurse plenty of times in the last year. Avoiding even looking at the wound across her belly, she felt the world spin, and she feared it would become an issue.

"Do you think we need to keep an eye on the battle, get closer to it?" she asked. The pain was pulsing, making it difficult to reason; she needed to be at the battle didn't she? The throbbing continued and she pushed on her stomach, desperate for the pain to stop. Why was it so wet and how could it be on fire? Her eyes looked at her hands, trying to process the sight. So much blood. It was running out of her belly, rivulets streaming.

"Definitely not!" Luke rebuked her, eyes still scanning the action beyond. "War is no place for a lady."

"What about a queen?" she questioned haughtily. "Especially when there is no husband," she pointed out, and an absurd cackle came out. Why was she even arguing? There was no way she could help anyone right now she needed to change her clothes.

"That is why you appointed a very capable commander," he responded, still fixed on the battles raging. "My duty is to your safety, Arabella. We were lucky before. There is too much that can happen. Come now, let's go see if there is aught we can do."

Arabella relented and gave her hands to him, to help her up. Her mind spun, what had they been talking about? He was tugging her hand trying to pull her along, but when she moved to lift her leg, a blinding pain shot through her. Some recess of her mind said not to scream, that they needed to be careful, but an awful keening noise betrayed her.

"What in the world, Arabella?" Luke's eyes went wide as he saw the blood on the side of her stomach, inspecting it all for the first time.

"'Tis a scratch," Arabella tried to reassure him. He had such a scowl on his face. Yanking her back to the roof, he looked probingly into her eyes and tugged up her tunic soaked with blood and found a grisly gash that spanned half her stomach and was bleeding profusely.

"'Tis not a scratch, Arabella!" He was almost screaming. He needed to stop, it made her head hurt. "I would ask you where you got that, but I think I have a pretty good idea. I'm such an idiot," he said, while ripping off a piece of his tunic on the bottom, then getting close again to examine it. "You need a healer. It will definitely need some stitches. You should be abed." His temper, the sternness directed at her, were so unlike him. They brought the world and pain pounding back into focus for her. Not good, this was not good.

Luke applied his tunic to the wound, and heaven knew she tried to not scream, but a groan emanated nevertheless.

"Nay, Luke, perhaps we can just take a few moments to rest. The healers will rightly be triaging. My wound isn't critical, there are too many men in dire need, and you know it."

"You're a princess of Saldanzian and a queen of Anchelle, Arabella. 'Tis certain they could make time for your care."

"I don't want them to make time for me," she said, exasperated. "And I am not playing that card, end of discussion. If you think I need stitches so badly then you do it." She knew she needed stitches, if for the pain alone. She had gotten a glimpse of it when Luke inspected it and could even yet feel a trickle of the blood running down the side of her body. The running for their lives had taken precedence, and now that the adrenalin had worn off the pain continued to build. The throbbing was becoming so intense that she longed to sob, but knew Luke would force her to retreat to the healer.

They both stared at each other for a time, until Luke finally spoke. "I don't know how to sew," he finally said. "Or I would. Let me go to a few houses to see if I can get a housewife to do it for you."

"Fine," she said, "I will wait here, I can keep an eye on the battle," but mostly because she didn't feel good enough to walk around till they found someone to help her.

He looked relieved. "I will be back in a moment. One of these houses surely has a fine seamstress. I will get you to her, then take up position to keep *us* apprised of the battle."

"Nay! You will not!" Arabella shouted, her side screaming in pain. Luke's eyes widened at her vehemence.

"You will," she repeated, working to lower her tone and appear calm, "hold my hand, so I don't scream like a little girl and ruin my reputation." Arabella tried to smile, but she knew it was more of a grimace. She'd never felt very "queenly" with Luke around. He was so much like a brother. Since being crowned queen she'd struggled with "official" interaction with Luke. It seemed ridiculous, like she was yet a child demanding his respect.

His face turned green, but managed to paste a smirk before capitulating. "Deal." He winked at her, then jumped down to the rain barrel. She had no intentions of him being by her while she was being sewed up, but she bet he spent the whole of the trip focused on how to keep from losing his breakfast. She tried to grin at something to hold over him, but all that came was another groan. The wound hurt like the devil. Luke had insisted she apply pressure from his piece of tunic turned bandage over the laceration.

Relieved to lay back down on the roof, another moan escaped her lips. It was so much pain! She squeezed her eyes shut, as a single drop leaked from her left eye. The pain was all that she could think about, causing her to pant.

The sound of Luke climbing the rain barrel did little to comfort her. How was she going to get off the roof?

"That didn't take you . . ." The word died on her lips as she opened her eyes and collided with Mason. He moved fast and was crouched next to her before she could move, his hand instantly over her mouth.

Worry competing with anger etched his face. "Not a word, if you want Luke to live," he threatened.

"Come now, my queen, let's get a move on then." He lifted her body off the roof, causing agonizing pain. He then set her on the edge of the roof and first dropped to the barrel, then pulled her into his arms. Then again as they descended the rain barrel.

"Just remember my sweet, I have no qualms about killing anyone that should try to help you. If you are wise we will leave the city without anyone else being killed." He had shed all his armor and colors, and looked like a regular, sword-carrying civilian.

She nodded her head in acknowledgment as he made his way to the south gate.

How had he found her in all that had transpired? Why wasn't he with his men, fighting alongside them? Where was Luke, and what would he do when he didn't find her? Had Mason killed him already? Or had he made it down and had time to be away? How would he know Mason had her, or would he think she had gone to find Ethan, or join the campaign, or who knew what else? Why was there so much pain?

Should she try to leave a blood trail for Luke? She would become weak with the loss of blood. Who was she kidding, she was already weak with the loss of blood, and the point was moot; blood littered the ground everywhere. It was hard to think of a way to let Luke know Mason had her, the pain made it hard to focus. Everything was difficult, why was it so arduous to think, it was tough to keep her eyes open . . .

CHAPTER 18

E than sighed in dismay and wiped the sweat from the corner of his eye. The Cronan seemed innumerable. The whole city would be wiped out. Still no sign of Thomas, and at this point Ethan counted him out. He hoped his father fared better than he did.

Pulling his horse back from the main line holding the Cronan, Ethan needed a moment to think. The line was steadily forced to fall back, and they simply wouldn't stay the advance much longer. They would need to cross the bridge shortly. When they left the field behind and crossed the bridge, they would be in residential Saldanzia. People's homes. Densely populated. The plague had made getting the women, children, and elderly to safety afore. Mothers would be huddled in their homes, caring for the sick whilst their husbands were on the front lines.

They couldn't let them cross the bridge, but it seemed inevitable. What could he do? His mind searched endlessly, looking for a solution. Something whizzed by his head. Ethan instinctively ducked. That was too close. He needed to stay alive if he was going to come up with a solution, he thought dryly. With a shield in his left hand blocking the fight, Ethan looked to the left, behind, and finally to the right. The sight to the right was like a beacon of salvation. The gears turned in his head, thinking of everything that needed to be done. To make it work perfectly would take exact precision.

"Hold the line!" Ethan yelled several times. He could see some of his men falling back, and he ground his teeth in frustration.

Finding a lieutenant, he got his attention and asked him to run down the line of men and tell them to hold the line for a little longer. The man galloped to his beckoning.

When he spotted Roland in the melee of men, Ethan yelled for his attention and gained the attention of several of his lieutenants who hung close to him. He had them withdraw from the main body to a patch of trees.

Ethan noted Roland's ragged breathing and those standing round. Roland had several wounds but looked alert, if not tired. Singling out four men, including Roland, he gave them their charge. Not giving the men another glance, Ethan zeroed in on the remaining men.

"Lieutenant Reed," Ethan spoke to the only lieutenant he knew the name of and backed his horse up further. The fight was progressing toward them. "I need that bridge up now." Several faces looked to question him, but one of the men's faces contorted with pain, and he cried out. An arrow had found the exposed part of his leg.

The soldier closest to the wounded man grabbed his comrade to support him from falling from his horse.

"Take him across the bridge with you, and get it up now, then I want it inoperable!" he commanded Reed. Ethan turned to watch the fight. They just needed a few more minutes before he gave the order to fall back. "I need the rest of you placed along the entire back line. When I give the order, I want you to have your men fall back across the canal."

His men looked to the dry canal bed and then a verbal "Aye, sir."

Ethan couldn't directly engage the enemy, needing to remain in position, but he placed several arrows in Cronan he noted to be leaders as he hung back, giving enough time for Roland to get in place.

Each second felt exaggerated as though minutes were passing. Ethan could hardly hold his body still, he was so anxious. He continued to watch the progress of the bridge and the advancement of his enemy. Observing the bridge was up, he finally shouted, "FALL BACK!"

He could see his lieutenants pass down the line of his command, as one the men reined their horses back. "Across the canal!" Ethan shouted, guiding the men and making his way toward the dry canal bed. He pulled up his horse before going down the bank and watched the retreat of his men, who on horses had made a gap between themselves and the Cronan who were on foot. A few hundred Norlan men on horses trailed closer to the Saldanzian soldiers, keeping them within reach.

Not wasting any time, Ethan made the descent down into the canal. An eerie feeling settled in as he rode hard for the other side. The ride across the canal was a furlong and took him only a minute.

High on the bank, Ethan noted many achieving the city side of the bank. His lieutenants ordered them to face the bank and create a line of archers to hold the Cronan at the canal. The Norlan men reigned in their mounts to stay with the Cronan, not wanting to fight the Saldanzians alone. There weren't enough of them.

Archers lined the banks and let off volley after volley at the Cronan, who had only crossed a third of the canal bed.

Waving his red tunic, Ethan signaled to Roland and waited, hardly daring to breathe. Most of his men had made it to the top of the bank, but others who had lost their mounts in the fighting were barely ahead of the fastest Cronan warrior. The Saldanzian runners were getting mowed down by the Norlan men, provoking the Saldanzian archers to target the Norlan men.

The Saldanzian runners were getting close to the bank when a massive wave of water could be seen barreling down the dry canal bed. As the group of Cronan, Norlan, and Saldanzian alike heard the tremendous roar they turned their heads, and then doubled their efforts to make it to the south side of the bank.

Their faces were a mask of fear, and it seemed in slow motion that they ran with all their might.

With a swift campaign the wall started to swallow those on the far west end of the canal, and like a flash it roared past Ethan and continued east, washing away everyone and everything in its path. The few Norlan men that had made the bank were quickly taken as prisoners of war. All the Cronan who had entered were swept away; only those that had not made their way into the canal yet remained. They stood on the far bank howling and jeering at the Saldanzians. There were so few left, that if it hadn't been so real, it would have been comical.

A huge cry of joy resonated down the line of Saldanzian men. The battle had almost entered the densely populated streets of their homes. Ethan turned and saw the smiles and relief on the faces of these men that were protecting their wives, children, and livelihoods. He couldn't help but take a large breath of relief himself, and a silent prayer of gratitude to his Maker.

CHAPTER 19

E xhaustion threatened to drag Ethan down. A deep ache permeated his entire body, most notably a protesting head wound. A few stitches were in order. He longed to give chase to the retreating Chilton army but darkness was upon them, and his men were as beat as he was.

Astonished and relieved, Ethan learned from runners that Arabella had somehow escaped Mason and incredibly managed to rally their Norlan sister countries to change sides and turn the tide. By all accounts, she managed to save the day on the south side of the city. Ethan would have loved to witness the moment, that dark mane of hair blowing in the breeze and sapphire eyes flashing as she called men to choose the righteous path against a dictator. A yearning desire to find her flooded him, but he needed to check in with his father and the council and learn the status of the wounded.

The war was not over. The first battle was ended, but there was still an army out there. His fear for his mother and sister was heightened with each passing second. And then there was Cleve. The man would need to be brought to justice. He wondered about Thomas's whereabouts, and how the people in the city fared if they had been infected and succumbed to the shivers, or if the messengers they had sent Thomas had died in their pursuit. At this point he had no information and only conjecture.

Ethan had gone personally to learn how the healers were managing the wounded and care of the dead. He allowed a medic to only bandage his wounds. He hadn't time for further treatment. Meeting with various lieutenants, he assigned units to gather information. One sent to obtain updates on the state of the arsenal weapons, arrows that would need to be replenished. He sent scouts out, to patrol the whereabouts of all their enemies; the list of things that needed attention seemed endless. Finally having seen to his men's immediate needs, he headed for the council chambers. Roland followed as well as a few other soldiers, needing to testify to Cleve's treason. Leaving them in an outer room, Ethan strode directly to the council chambers.

Scanning the room, he noted every family had a representative present: his father speaking with Timothy Grace, the Surreys, Cleve, and the Lorrings. A breath of relief wooshed out in seeing his father whole. He made eye contact with his father and inclined his head to the corner. Ethan strode toward him, his father meeting him on the edge of the room. The two embraced for a moment, though they both wore expressions of concern. "Did Benton speak with you?" he asked quietly. His father nodded his head gravely.

"What think you?" Ethan questioned his father. "Could anyone know Mother and Claire's location?" He was tormented by the thought that they may be too late, but couldn't make his voice articulate the terrible thought. He wondered what the Cronan knew that would make them think they could find them?

"I don't know how they could know their location, but of course I am worried," his father spoke, the distress plain. "I am planning on leaving immediately. I will need a handful of your best men. I know everyone is dog tired, but we dare not wait."

Ethan knew his father was in the right. Though he wanted to go with his father, the reality of an entire kingdom's continuance was on his shoulders—the weight of defending every life, even scum like Cleve. Duty had never been so terrible before, and though he had a duty to his family, his father was yet capable.

"I know what you're thinking," his father said, looking him in the eye. "You can't come. You well know I would have you at my side. But without Thomas's army here, we've an enemy outside the gates yet and some within. One of us must remain in council, there is no one to be trusted till it's sorted out the depth of the Blakes' perfidy. Emotions are too high, and everyone is in mourning, fear-addled and sleep-deprived. Someone is bound to set off the tinderbox. You must remain."

It stung: the needed choice to set aside his family's safety.

"What plan have you for Cleve right now? He's bound to kill us in our sleep." His father struggled to maintain the equanimity he was so known for. Anger was written in his very posture. "My wife! Your sister! Promise me you will make him pay!" The harsh whispers drew many eyes. Michael McKenna was always composed.

"I swear it, Father!" Ethan answered. "I have several witnesses that will testify against him, and the things he said directly in their hearing."

Some of the anger dimmed, and control once again reined in, his father said, "I'll let you deal with him."

"I will," Ethan rumbled. "I've anticipated your request and have thirty of my best guards standing ready at the north stable awaiting for your command."

His father inclined his head. "Of course you do," he said with a hint of a smile.

"Godspeed, Father."

"Godspeed, Son." The two embraced again. They would not speak about possible bad outcomes. They both had to believe their women were unharmed. Because if they weren't . . .

His father took a few steps to leave then turned back around. "You are a hero today, Son."

Ethan shrugged it off, unwilling to claim anything in the devastation of lives. "Arabella was the hero today."

"You both were," his father acquiesced. "The battle on the north was every bit as crucial today as was the south. It could have gone really bad. Your quick thinking was the only thing that saved those men's lives today, and the city."

"'Twas divine inspiration," Ethan said, thinking back to those moments when fighting for their lives, to keep the hordes without, so badly outnumbered; in minutes they would have been annihilated and then left to wreak havoc on their families.

"We were blessed today," he acknowledged. Things had gone remarkably well considering Thomas had never come. Being outnumbered, and half the population sick, had not been a good start. Truly it had seemed a small chance to hold the day. Now if they could only have a happy ending with his sister and mother.

Michael slipped out of the room, and Ethan signaled the soldier who stood in attention at the open chamber's doors, who in turn directed a handful of Ethan's elite guards to enter. The doors were closed and the guards stood barring the exit. The clink of armor drew all eyes to Ethan. Soldiers and visitors weren't permitted into the council chamber as a general rule.

Surprise echoed on each person's face, except for Cleve, whose mottled anger was evident on his visage.

"What is the meaning of this! 'Tis my right alone to call others to chamber!" Cleve shouted.

Ethan declined to answer him, instead addressing the whole. "I know that we have had a lot to deal with today, but unfortunately, there is yet more and of grave import." Ethan spoke in a commanding voice. No sound could be heard in the room.

"I ask that I be able to speak uninterrupted, and then the accused may state their case." He looked at all the four Ruling, and Cleve looked like he could spit in Ethan's face. But the other three nodded their agreement to his proposal.

"I will not agree to any such thing, boy! I am the ruling family." Cleve sneered.

"Let's not be pig headed tonight, Cleve," Lorring spoke. "That *man* has led and successfully repelled an invader this day. I want to go to bed tonight, you well know the rules, so if four vote one way, then that's that."

Cleve looked even more mad, if that was possible, as a darkened vein stretching from his hairline to eyebrow pumped in strained agitation.

"What's this about, Ethan?" Lord Timothy Grace spoke.

"Treason," Ethan spoke, trying to keep the heat from his words and failing. "I have several men that can testify to the validity of what I will share. When I've presented the evidence you may call them in and ask them your own questions. If you need to track down others, you may do so. Not all who were present are here, but the urgency required I make haste in informing the council. You may need to summon others in the morn."

"Go ahead," Lorring spoke.

Ethan suggested they each be seated and was pleased to note he'd managed to remove the heat from his own tone.

"I left the council last night, and headed to Timothy Grace's home. Arriving there, I did not see a single guard. In fact, not one person was there."

"That's probably because the Anchellian witch was luring Mason into our city," Cleve practically screamed. It took every ounce of willpower for Ethan to not strike down the man where he stood.

The council turned on him with icy eyes, but Cleve did not stop. "She turned up here, and the city came down with the shivers, as well as an invading army yet sleeping at our front gate!"

"We know how you feel about Arabella," Lorring spoke again. "Let Ethan finish."

"Where were my guards?" Timothy asked. "They were given specific orders to protect Arabella in my absence."

"I didn't know, though I have since ascertained that they were slaughtered along with your entire household."

Shock filled Timothy's face. His body drooped, seeming to lose its habitual rigidity.

"Who killed them?" Surrey asked.

Ethan breathed a heavy sigh. This was going to take another full night, and he was exhausted. "Can we save the questions for later, please? We will see the sunrise together at this pace."

"Sorry, do continue," Surrey apologized.

"I heard a horse galloping in the distance, and knowing the situation we were in, knew it couldn't be good, so I rushed to meet it. The rider was Benton, the Anchellian guard to Queen Arabella."

"I told you!" Cleve butted in once again.

Ethan's gaze drilled into the man. "He was running to find me because the northwestern gate was unmanned, and only Roland, another Saldanzian guard, yet manned it, though I myself had ordered thousands of men to that area. Cleve and Torin Blake had kidnapped Queen Arabella, relieved the—"

"What?" Cleve spouted, spit flying. He was up and coming straight at Ethan, his eyes blazing! "You lie!" A huge gasp spread through those assembled.

Ethan's face turned stone cold as he faced the treasonous fool that had now done more harm than good in his rule and would ever be known by the appellation of traitor. Ethan drew his sword, and Cleve instantly saw his mistake. To call a man a liar to his face was one of the rudest statements a person could utter, and he better back up his statement with a sword.

"I would pull your sword if I were you," Ethan calmly spoke, though iron laced each word with promise.

"Let's not be rash," Cleve spoke, almost instantly backpedaling and walking backward.

"Like I said," Ethan spoke coldly, "either pull your blade or sit and I see you gagged."

His voice brooked no argument, and everyone remained quiet. "Torin relieved the regiment at the northwestern gate an hour afore and sent them to be stationed at another gate." Indignant gasps filled the hall. "From there he transported the queen without the city and to Mason Kiefer, our invader. As payment for delivering Arabella, Mason was to have the Graces and the McKennas killed, including my mother and sister in their safe quarters. He said the rest of you would be taken care of later." He let that sit for a moment. "I believe that was why Mason did not attack sooner. He was waiting for Arabella."

He watched their faces closely while he continued. "In exchange, Mason was to withdraw his campaign and leave Saldanzia. We don't know what else Torin had agreed to with Mason, who in turn had Torin executed, along with the men who had accompanied him."

Cleve's face went an ashen gray, like he would be sick. Ethan realized that until that point, Cleve hadn't known of his son's death. He was for once silent.

"From there, Mason's men removed the uniforms from the Saldanzian traitors' backs and then headed to the gate. The Cronan were keeping a safe distance back, to not be seen. Roland and I made it in time to see the gate closed with only a few of Mason's soldiers getting in, giving us precious few minutes to have the guard redirected and spread to the empty section. 'Twas a short though needed reprieve. As we saw on the southern gate this morning, they had some kind of incendiary device that blew up the gate. The Cronan breached the city. As you have been informed, 'twas a bloody battle, and many good men died. I have a half-dozen witnesses outside the door you can question, or you may find your own."

Ethan continued looking at Cleve. "Cleve Blake had several Saldazian soldiers and the people of Lord Grace's household murdered. He personally saw, threatened, and kidnapped a member of the Ruling Five, also the Queen of Anchelle and the guards with her, and handed them over to our enemy. His actions compromised our security at the gate adding more deaths to his tally. He bragged to having contracted each of your families and your own deaths, securing his reign while abolishing our governmental body. All this was done without the sanction of the council and under the cover of darkness. As is stated in our law, any crime of treason is punishable by hanging. That is the McKenna vote."

Ethan walked toward the door. "What?! Where are you going?" Lorring asked incredulously.

"I have already heard the testimony of the witnesses and yet have a country to secure, so I take my leave." He spoke firmly, his disgust evident. "A few of my guard," Ethan said, indicating the men barring the doors, "will take Cleve into custody, if you vote to do so. I advise you to at the very least remand him to the brig till you are decided." He kept walking outside the door into the night air. He was so tired, tired of this, tired of the council. Cleve was corrupt to the core. He didn't know if the council would have him hanged; it might well take days of discussion and further witnesses being called. But at this moment he had made his vote known. His nerves felt stretched to breaking and he was done with the council tonight. If he spent one more minute in that coward's presence he would be unable to stay his need for vengeance.

Drawing cool air through his nose, he slowed. The desire to check on Arabella rose yet again, to see for himself that she was well.

"Commander McKenna." A soldier walked from an alcove off the council building.

"Aye?" he responded, taking in the unfamiliar soldier.

"I have a handwritten message from Sir Roland. He said it was urgent, and to give to you as soon as you left the council."

"Thank you, soldier," Ethan took the paper. He was surprised Roland had left when he needed him to testify, but he was also aware he wasn't one of his soldiers to command, he was Arabella's. He opened the paper as another soldier brought him his horse. "I have word from Captain Thomas," the sergeant spoke. Ethan's mind warred. Which one first, Arabella or Thomas?

"Hold a minute, Sergeant." Ethan opened the letter but walked back to the building to see with a candle. It looked hastily scrawled, hardly legible.

Ethan
Arabella injured during battle, when thought to be safe,
Luke went for help. When he returned she had disappeared,
unable to find her. Thought to have been captured by
Mason's men. Help if you can.
Roland

Ethan's heart jammed in his throat. He thought he had her back, only to have her disappear. She was out there somewhere injured. How bad? Bad enough that Luke left her alone to go for help; that must mean she wasn't able to travel.

"Sir?" the sergeant standing close to him asked. "Can I be of aid?" Awakening from his despair, he turned to the sergeant.

"What is the word from Captain Thomas?"

"He will be here in thirty minutes, and wants to know your orders?"

The path was clear and without question. "We will march on Mason's army tonight!"

⁓

At three in the morning, Ethan, with Captain Thomas's relatively fresh ten thousand men and Benton, raided a small sleeping group of the Norlan army and Cronan, only five miles out of Saldanzia. The army was unorganized, battle worn, and ill prepared for an attack. Few lives were taken as the army surrounded the sleeping camp. Leaders surrendered and were surprisingly willing to share all. The leaders could only surmise that Mason had left with most of his army only a couple hours earlier, because when they returned from Saldanzia, Mason was gone.

Sickened to know that Arabella was most likely gone and under Mason's control, Ethan rode back to Saldanzia dazed, only somewhat aware of his surroundings. He was dead tired and didn't know if he should be making any decisions at the moment. Could the man, his body, even cooperate and function to go after the woman he loved? He'd been at death's door a mere two days afore. The commander that lived within knew it was critical for him to take down the man that could be a viable threat in the future. Just because Mason left didn't mean he wouldn't return. He didn't know how his family fared and wouldn't for a couple days. He had a responsibility to protect his people. Did that mean going after Mason, or was it to remain here? The council, the people, all were in a bad way right now.

His father gone, he remained the only McKenna present, and the need for leadership had never been more critical. The casualties from the shivers were high, bodies had to be buried, and the city walls needed to be repaired. Roland leaving, and the rest of her guard gone rightly to secure Arabella's safety, meant there was not a single witness remaining that had heard and seen directly Cleve's perfidy, though his soldiers could testify to Torin's. Surely there was a gateman to be found that had been paid off to open the gate for the traitors. How to deal with the Cronan? Could they even keep them contained? The list was endless.

There was a slim chance Arabella was still in the city, found wounded as she was and taken into someone's home, not coherent to tell anyone who she was or send word. To be sure there were enough sick and injured in the city that it would prove a massive undertaking to find her amidst the chaos of the city. But his gut told him otherwise. Besides, he hadn't seen any of Arabella's men, aside from Benton, who was even now riding hard for Anchelle mere minutes after it was reported she could very well be a captive of Mason.

Ethan finally crawled into bed when the roosters were crowing and as the rest of Saldanzia was waking up to aftermath of war. Aching and bruised, certain he was the most miserable he had ever felt in his life.

Ethan awoke to a knocking at his door. He practically crawled from the bed, his body protesting all movements in so many places he couldn't count, and wondering absently what time it was. The butler stood outside his bedroom, stiff as a rod. "Sir, Captain Thomas is here to see you." The butler had barely finished talking when Thomas could be seen bounding up the stairs.

"Thanks chap, I shall take it from here." Thomas gave the butler a clap on the back and then turned to Ethan. "You look terrible!" his childhood friend said by way of greeting.

"Thanks," Ethan mumbled, opening the door wider so his friend could come in. Ethan waited for Thomas to continue, but annoyingly the man kept him in suspense.

"We've got a million things—" Ethan began.

Thomas held up his hand, interrupting him. "Cleve is to be hanged in the city square today at noon." His tone was much more subdued.

Ethan stood still for a moment, then nodded, warmed that the members in the council could see Cleve Blake for the real murdering threat he presented to their sovereignty. "That's at least something," Ethan finally responded.

"I thought you would want to know," Thomas said, disappointed with Ethan's response. "I thought you would want to be present."

"Aye, I do," Ethan said, trying to placate him. "'Tis just that I'm leaving," Ethan said decisively.

"After Anchelle's queen?"

"Aye," Ethan replied. "And there is something I need you to do for me," he said.

"Name it," Thomas said without hesitation.

Ethan's shoulders relaxed visibly. He had come to the right person. Actually, the right person had come to him. Ethan discussed the situation with his comrade for over an hour and then embraced him before he left his home.

Oh, one more thing," Thomas said, as he was walking out the door. "Saysee has been a heavenly boon. The physicians have already seen a drastic change and they are optimistic it will reduce the suffering substantially, even be lifesaving."

What a blessing! Ethan smiled for the first time that day.

Within the hour of Thomas leaving, Ethan rode his horse through the heavily secured property of Timothy Grace.

Minutes later Timothy met him at his front door. "I was expecting you sooner," he spoke while shaking his hand.

"'Twas a long night, and as I am sure you have heard, the enemy that remained surrendered." Ethan didn't elaborate, but got right to the point. "I've come to say goodbye," Ethan said.

"I expected as much."

"I guess you know what I'm here for then?"

"Aye, I should say."

CHAPTER 20

Arabella was vaguely aware of motion. Was she being pulled? Groggy, it took several minutes for her to slowly awake from a deep sleep. Trapped? She felt restricted, confined. Panic spurted, hastening her wakefulness; she tried to move, but everything felt tight. She couldn't move her arms, and she felt weak as a kitten. Arabella could hear the steady rhythm of horses' hooves, and she could smell trees and grass. Opening her eyes to the glare of the sun, she had to blink several times before any shadows emerged. Where was she, and what was going on?

When her vision finally cleared, her memory came rushing back in full horror. She was among an army of men. After losing consciousness in the city of Saldanzia, her own scream had awoken her in a tent, thrashing in agony while someone had been stitching her side. The pain had been excruciating, and had caused tears to run down her face, but she had remained silent. Mason had been by her side the whole time, holding her hand, appearing as though he was genuinely concerned for her well-being.

The moment the healer finished, Mason had scooped her up and set her atop his mount with her in his arms as the animal lurched to a start. Naught else could she remember, though she was now secured in a travois pulled by a sorrel horse. Pain as she had never known existed riddled her body, she longed for death's release, she was so miserable, the aching was unbearable and exhausting beyond measure.

Though she'd already passed hours unconscious she found it difficult to stay awake and had fallen asleep several times in the travois. The pain would return to awaken her. Not wanting any of Mason's attention, Arabella remained silent.

When she woke the next morning, she was hot, burning with a fever, and couldn't move. When Mason came to check on her, he must not have liked what he saw, for he forced some type of medicine on her, and she fell asleep.

When next she became cognizant, the haze of fever was held at bay, though she had no way to discern how long she had remained unconscious. As she became increasingly alert and was able to assess her physical well-being, she struggled to lift her arms. She was so weak, but the pain was not near as sharp and all consuming. Her stomach grumbled for attention.

Alone except her surrounding enemies, wounded, and sick with despair, Arabella idly wondered if she might lay broken on the pallet and never rise—to never have to deal with what lay ahead. The thought of being forced to wed Mason was repugnant, unimaginable. How was she ever going to get out of this mess? Did her men know where she was? Had Ethan survived the battle? Did he know Mason had her? Would he come for her? Surely not, his responsibilities were far too great. He had a whole country to keep safe. His mother and sister to rescue. A plague. No, she would need to rely on herself and pray for divine guidance.

What would happen to the Anchellian men that had turned on Mason's army? She hadn't seen any in the caravan, though she had to admit, she had never been very lucid. Nor did she see any from any of the Norlan countries, for that matter, aside from the Chilton colors of Mason's own homeland. Had the others escaped ahead of Mason, or were they behind? Or worse yet, had Mason killed them? The thought brought a heavy weight to her chest.

Her stirring had obviously brought some attention. Mason dismounted his horse close to her and started to walk next to her.

"You have color returning to your visage. I am most happy to see you are improved today. How are you feeling, my sweet?"

"Tired," she replied. There was no harm in telling the truth.

He laughed outright. "You've been asleep for five days. You're probably famished."

Asleep for five days. "Aye," Arabella responded. Had she been close to death to have been that unconscious for that long? she wondered, unable to feel joy in her recovery.

"I'll have someone get you some food and water." He nodded to a soldier hovering close by to secure sustenance. Had the soldier seemed vaguely familiar? He was gone before she could study the face. She scolded herself for even hoping.

"Despite your illness, we are making good time and should be home in Anchelle within four more days," he spoke, his tone even, warm. He almost seemed like a normal man, having a normal conversation with a close friend. Of course, several years ago, she might have considered him a friend. It was very strange and added to her disquiet, knowing the monster that lurked beneath the surface.

Over the past weeks, she had experienced moments of deep longing for home and to be among her people. But she had never considered herself returning this way, a trophy to the tyrant that held them all bondage. The daydreams had always included her victorious return atop Palachio, the guard at her side and her people liberated from the oppressor. Instead she would be returning to bring further terror. Not only had the people of Anchelle suffered, but if she hadn't run away, Saldanzia would have had continued peace and prosperity. So many lost to the plague, and how many lives were taken when Mason arrived to find her gone? How many men of Anchelle were forced into soldiering and even now lay moldering on foreign soil? Was this her punishment? The weight of every single decision she had made since her father's death cascaded through her mind. The bitter agony threatened to destroy her soul.

Though she longed to curl up and never face her failures, or to rant and rave and scream out every frustration, she knew it would serve no purpose and would only antagonize a very volatile man. Right now, diplomatic might be better than emotional. She took a few steadying breaths, but didn't dare speak lest it release the flood of visceral feelings.

They continued to plod on, Mason walking next to her, the reins of his horse in his hands. He didn't say more. A man brought her some food and water. She sat up and ate the salted meal, terrible as it was, and didn't complain. What could she expect on the trail with an army of men? She lay back down. Fatigue had her eyes lowering, and sleep claimed her yet again.

Arabella awoke. It seemed like a few hours later, though she wasn't sure. Looking around, she didn't see any familiar faces. Just a sea of men who looked her way occasionally. Needing to stretch her legs, she pushed away the blankets that seemed to tie her in place. Her wound ached, but it was bearable. Gingerly she arose from the still-moving travois. Men looked at her but didn't object or comment.

She wore the same clothes: her breeches and a torn shirt. Wishing there was a cloak or something to put over herself, she grabbed the stained, bloody wool blanket from the travois and wrapped it around her torso, conscious of her skin showing through her ripped shirt. Surrounded by thousands of men made it more uncomfortable.

Walking, though, still felt wonderful. Arabella was grateful that no one had challenged her walking or had spoken to or bothered her. She wondered where Luke was, and Benton, Roland, and Garner. Had they survived the fighting? Were they close behind them? Was there any way they could help her? Luke would have been frantic when he returned to the rooftop to find her gone. She knew well she was more than a responsibility to him. He was the dearest of all her friends and ever stood as a protector.

She wondered what Anchelle would be like when she arrived. Would the fields be planted, with blades of grain sprouting tendrils from the ground? There should be, but there wouldn't have been much help out in the fields with the dead, and with Mason conscripting so many men. They depended upon each crop.

Arabella walked deep in thought for some time before Mason showed up once again. "You look better," he commented.

She wasn't sure what to say to that, though she knew she felt an improvement. "I feel noticeably improved" was all she said.

He grunted slightly in acknowledgment. "Are you cold?"

"No" was all she would say, unwilling to have a conversation with him about modesty with men all around her.

After an uncomfortable amount of silence, he asked, "Are you ready to ride?"

She was growing tired quickly, especially trying to keep up to the riders. A simple "Aye" was all that she spoke.

A black mount was brought a few minutes later. He adjusted the stirrups as she held the blanket around her waist, then waited as Mason insisted on helping her mount the animal. The gelding was a beautiful horse, not too high stepping, but not docile either. His gait was smooth, which made riding him bearable with her injury, which yet pained her.

They rode the rest of the day in silence, and only made camp when the shadows ebbed out the remaining daylight. Exhausted but pleased to see a tent was erected for her, she quickly hid herself within. Despite the necessity for sleep she found her nerves stretched taut. Though they had been acquainted for years now, she truly didn't know him. Upon meeting him in the orchard so many seasons past, Mason had been circumspect, chivalrous and attentive to her, though she had never been at peace in his presence. Initially she'd been too young and naive to understand the hunger that lurked in his gaze. This threatening Mason, hard, immovable, a man that would destroy others, the one that sought to possess her soul and body, was foreign—and yet she now knew it to be his true face.

Someone brought her food, hard bread and something that resembled dry meat, but she had no idea what. The soldier made a quick exit after handing it off to her. She nibbled on the bread and dared not touch the meat. Desperate to stretch out she crawled into her bedroll and tried to find sleep. The noise of thousands of men seemed to take the better part of the night before it began to die down, and then every noise only served to make her startle and add to her anxiety. At some point weariness finally overpowered the fear and she managed to fall into a dreamless sleep.

Awakening to the sound of the breaking up of camp, she slowly got up, wishing she had a change of clothes and a brush. Her hair felt like it went in every direction. Running her hands through her tresses as quickly as she could, she finally detangled it enough to manage a simple braid. Poking her head from the tent, she saw men everywhere, a hive of activity. Some took down camp, others sharpened weapons, some ate. Several stationed close by looked up at her but didn't acknowledge her, and few even made eye contact. Not feeling very brave, she stood undecided, not in the tent and not out of it.

Her eyes widened as she saw a familiar face making his way toward her. The Anchellian soldier that had accompanied Luke and her as they had climbed the aqueducts. Eyes widening, she tried to tamp down any sign of recognition. His face was a solemn mask; the slightest shaking of his head let her know to have a care. He carried food in his hand and pushed his way into the tent.

"Your Highness," he said, handing her the food.

She took the plate from him, a million questions in her head. Where did she begin? "What is your name?" she asked. She waited for him to tell her something useful, not knowing if people could hear them or not, she would allow him to take the lead.

"Stewart, Your Highness," he said, bowing stiffly.

"My thanks, Stewart," she responded.

Lowering his voice, Stewart spoke in a whisper. "I saw Mason get on a rooftop, not long after you slid from the bell tower. He stayed there for a while. I was sure he was watching you. I tried to follow him for a time, but I lost him. I was too late. When next I found him, he already had you. Switched my uniform to that common soldier of Chilton like I saw him do, and walked out of the city. I followed him till he met his army, then just blended in with the crowd and mounted up. I've tried to stay close to you, but I have guard duty, among other things."

"Thank you, Stewart," she said once again. "Do you have word or know anything of Sir Garner, Roland, Benton, or Luke?" she asked, though she held little hope.

"Sir Benton," he said, "caught me on sentry duty, the second night." She had a hard time keeping a straight face. She knew how stealthy Benton was, and it probably scared him near to death.

"I explained what I had seen and done. That you were sick with a burning fever, but that Mason was seeing to your care. He warned me upon pain of death to watch over you, then disappeared as quickly as he had come. 'Tis all I know."

That sounded like Benton. At least he was alive. She wished that Benton had said more to Stewart, but she would have to be content with that. At least there was a small hope, if only a sliver. It would have to sustain her.

Just then the tent flap opened and Mason strode in. He looked at Arabella, then Stewart. "What are you doing in here still?" Mason boomed, then strode toward Stewart ready to strike him down. Arabella jumped back. Stewart kept his head down, not daring to look at Arabella.

"Sorry." Arabella spoke quickly in the defense of her new friend. "'Tis my fault," Arabella said, looking down. She always had a hard time trying to deceive someone. "My tunic . . ." She jumped to the only thing she could think of. "'Tis torn, and it makes me very uncomfortable to be seen amongst the men." Mason looked down at the shirt. "I asked this man if there was any way for him to find me another tunic, or perhaps a needle and thread. 'Tis unseemly, and I couldn't bear the thought of being wrapped in a blanket again once the heat of the day comes." At least that part was truthful.

Mason's eyes hardened on her for a second before they softened. "I will take care of it." he spoke, his tone dismissing Stewart. When Stewart was gone, Mason took Arabella's hands. "If you have a need, you are to bring it to me, not one of my men." He spoke condescendingly, like he was talking to a child. "You don't know the power you have over men," he stated calmly. "You need to be careful," Mason warned with a stern voice.

Arabella nodded her head. "Sorry," she said, hoping that would placate him. "I didn't think that you would have time to see to something so mundane."

She hardly knew what tack to take or what to expect from his volatile behavior. He was a brutal man. There was the constant fear and worry he would treat her like a dog, a slave, beneath him as she had seen him treat others recently. Thus far, he hadn't turned his anger on her directly. Though she didn't hold out too much hope that this was a permanent position. All their interactions in Anchelle when he would visit had been cordial, if uncomfortable in the intensity of his attention. Unease filled her and she struggled to hold still, wanting to wrench her hands from his, but he held them possessively. His eyes traveled along her face. His left hand came up to her face and brushed an escaping tendril aside.

Instantly freezing, her heart pounded in response to his revolting touch. She knew it would be ill advised to anger him, but she despised having to endure his touch. Wanting to grab his dagger which was strapped to his waist and put it in his heart, she refrained, instinctively rejecting the notion. In her current physical state there was little chance she was faster than him. Taking a step back, she saw his eyes harden once again. Nay, she must be patient, for when she finally struck she must be absolutely sure of her ability or others would be forced to pay the price. As awful as it was to consider, she would need to keep him at ease so that the opportunity would present itself. One day soon he would let his guard down and she would be ready to strike. Angering him would only serve to restrict her movements. It would be a fine line. She knew he wouldn't trust her to be suddenly compliant. After all, hadn't he remarked how he loved her fire?

"I should like to break my fast," she stated, lifting her hand from his and smoothing out the hair around her braid. Anything to distract him. How to be amenable without inviting his unwanted attention or putting him on guard? It was going to be difficult, she realized. Resolve settled into her being. He had to die, or she must escape to fight another day. Bending to him was not an option. Surviving his affections, impossible.

Benton . . . she prayed he was nearby, planning, waiting to move, to give her an opening to strike or escape. Additionally, she prayed that all her guards had survived the battle and were headed back to Anchelle. She was daydreaming that her guard traveled with haste, and were able to make their way to Anchelle ahead of the large army to arrive before Mason arrived, but she knew it was wishful thinking. Mason kept a blistering pace.

"Aye, let's eat together." He indicated that she should be seated, and then he sat close to her. He continued his slow perusal of her. *Great*, she thought.

There was only one plate, but it was loaded with food. She took a piece of bread that looked slightly better than the gristly meat. He grabbed a chunk of meat.

"Are we in a hurry today?" she asked, hoping not to prolong this meeting.

"We have time," he said with a smile, as though sensing her discomfort and finding it amusing.

She nodded her head and continued on, taking a nibble of the stale, near-inedible bread and trying not to gag. "Will we make it to the Hoodoos today?" she asked, eager to keep the conversation on a safe subject.

"Nay, tomorow," he spoke, his eyes not leaving her. "It will be nice, will it not, to have Anchellian food again?" he asked, his eyes unreadable, as the conversation turned back to the food. She felt anger flare when he spoke of Anchelle as his domain, but she took a calming breath before readily agreeing. It would be much better than this food. If she had to live on it much longer she might forego food altogether.

"What will happen when we return to Anchelle?" she finally asked. Arabella had wondered for days, but was equally parts terrified and curious to learn of his plans.

He gave a chilling smile. "I thought you would never ask," he claimed. "Any traitor that fought for Saldanzia will be hanged immediately, as the people must understand that anyone that turns on me will forfeit their life." He spoke while staring Arabella down to let her know that he wasn't happy with what she had done and would punish her as promised through the suffering of her people.

Fingers tightened into fists, Arabella placed them under her legs to keep from retaliating. Indignation and fury ran hot inside of her and took tremendous will to force down.

"Five days after our return," he continued, "we will be married. It will be a huge event that we will host to all of the Norlans. I've sent runners ahead to all the different states to make ready for the wedding. Everyone will see it. We will bring all the Norlans into one country."

She had feared as much, but still felt her gut wrench.

"Your eyes betray you, flashing with heat. 'Tis most intoxicating," he suggested provocatively from across the table. "Have you naught to say, little minx?" he queried, a clear challenge.

What could she say? He was holding all the cards at the moment, and no amount of pleading would change his mind. A war that had been waged for some time to this end would not be changed by voicing her opinion of the man or his ideas. This battle was his. She had time yet. She longed to rail, to shout and scream all the vile churning he elicited, but recognized the glint in his eye. He was looking for a reaction, and this was one battle she need not concede. All she could own and control at this moment was her response.

"I am ready to go," she said coldly, rising from her chair. Wanting to get away from him as fast as she could.

"Och, anxious are you to reach our home, ready to be my wife are you?" he asked. The smug smile and glint left little doubt that he had read her reaction perfectly. Dark eyes locked on her, he languidly rose. It was plainly written upon him how much he thrived on her discomfort and the power to make her squirm.

Her hand, which had been clenched tight to her trouser, started to lift; the need to slap that smirk off his face burned. His eyebrow raised in invitation or question, perceiving her violence. Desire radiated from him and his grin stretched even wider. She forced her face to appear neutral, letting her hands drop, and turned from him, determined to end the futile discussion. But he grabbed her left arm and dragged her toward him. With her right arm she tried to slap his face, but he quickly grabbed it as well. His tight grip sent sharp throbbing through both her wrists at the lack of blood flow. Mason dropped his face to within inches of her own.

"Ah! That is what I was looking for! The fiery Arabella. 'Tis what draws me to you."

Anger surged through her. She knew he was playing with her and still fell into his trap. "Och, your eyes, they're dazzling right now. Come here, dear," he said, pulling her body even closer.

Stepping down hard on his foot, she kicked him in the other shin, but he still held her tight. She thought he would be mad, but he laughed harder. "So feisty! You will find me eager to play."

He pulled her in again to kiss her, just as a sound came from outside the tent.

"Sir!" She could hear a muffled voice. "I have the shirt Her Highness requested."

Mason sighed, then spoke, "Leave it by the tent flap."

"Sir," the man that could only be Stewart spoke again, "would you like me to help with the tent? The men are ready to go, and I think there may be some new developments."

She could tell that Mason's patience was wearing thin with the soldier, but she couldn't be more relieved he had come when he did, though she knew it was no accident. Stewart took his charge seriously.

Mason turned his face back to Arabella's and fiercely kissed her lips in a bruising display of his strength over hers. When he pulled away, she couldn't hide the contempt from her face, but he only laughed with amusement on his face. "Aye, your fire will keep me warm for years to come" was his parting parry as he walked outside the tent door.

She could hear talking outside the door, but didn't really register anything through her anger, until she heard Stewart's voice again. "The tunic, Your Highness." His hand reached inside the tent with the shirt extended, but his body remained without.

"Thank you," she spoke softly, rubbing her mouth against her sleeve in an effort to remove his taste. She approached the tent flap and grabbed the proffered garment. Once she had secured the tent flap, she quickly removed the bloody garment. Pain radiated from the sutures at the stretching required to remove and replace the clean garment. Relief filled her to note that the garment drowned her, covering her entire torso and near to her knees. It did little for her appearance, which was perfect.

Stepping outside the tent, the early morning was already starting to get warm. Stewart was already pulling stakes, and Mason was nowhere in sight so she walked past him.

"My thanks," she said in a whisper with her back to him, pretending she wasn't talking to him. "Are there any new developments?" she asked, worried that he would get in trouble.

"All I know is the scouts came back in a hurry," he said, not looking at her as he yanked on another stake. "It seemed like a good time to say something."

It had been. The young man was endearing. She hoped he made it out of this alive. In fact, she determined that one day he would be trained as a knight if he chose to.

A couple other soldiers came over to give Stewart a hand. It seemed like all of a sudden they were in a hurry. Another soldier brought Arabella the same mount as yesterday, helped her on, and then led her to where most had already started off.

Taking notice of everything around her, Arabella wanted to get an idea of how large Mason's army was now, to try to see everything from a defensive or military standpoint, strengths and weaknesses. She hadn't seen any other colors than that of Chilton. She wondered where the men were that had fought with Mason from the Norlans. Would they desert their homeland? Were they in fact on their way home, maybe some of each?

By midday, the sun hammered down on them with few breezes to interrupt the stifling heat. Still recovering, Arabella found it increasingly difficult to remain alert. She was pleased with herself when she finally managed to ascertain that Mason's army that she traveled with seemed in fact to be around five thousand. She didn't know how many men Mason had left in each country in the Norlans to subdue the people, but she had heard that he had brought thirty thousand with him on his campaign to take Saldanzia. It would seem Mason had sustained devastating losses in Saldanzia, though his soldiers yet remained an army to be reckoned with. Could each of the countries in the Norlans muster a thousand men? Could she somehow get away from Mason, and rally her own people and then the rest of the kingdoms? They would need more than those left in Anchelle. All the countries in the Norlans would need to come together.

Determination fueled her. People would suffer under his reign. She would not legitimize his place in her land with a marriage as his wife. Death would be preferable, and to her last breath she would die fighting. The trick was planning, waiting to find the right moment. Would it be enough if Mason was imprisoned, or must he die? He wouldn't be easy to defeat, as he had proven time and again. But was there another that would step in and take over Mason's kingdom of Chilton were she able to kill him? She hadn't been able to puzzle out the hierarchy of his soldiers, not even to discern who his second-in-command might be.

Had any of her men survived the Battle of Saldanzia besides Benton? She felt fairly certain Luke was alive, and she knew that they would help her to their dying breath. But their ability to gather an army with speed or come up with a plan in the timeframe she would like seemed unlikely, which meant the decisions rightly would fall back on her . . . a plan, with some chance of success and then the means to carry it out. Escape seemed pretty unattainable as long as she was surrounded by Mason's army.

The day, though uneventful, was tiring. Arabella's body yet ached from its injuries and the extended march. Despite the unremitting heat of the day, she believed her fever finally gone. Would she ever find the morning rays welcome and her body not still exhausted? Longing to crawl back into the travois that had been built while the fever raged, she tried to keep her mind active, thinking of possible escape scenarios, ways to defeat Mason, always alert to any signal or sign her men might try to send. They were resourceful, and she knew that they would be looking for a way to help her, and the people of Anchelle. She kept flip-flopping on whether her guard, aside from Benton, might have survived and even now could be traveling to her aid or yet remained injured and broken in Saldanzia. She realized she wasn't even sure she wanted them to come, as they would be targeted before all others as leverage with Mason served to further the tangle in her thinking.

Never once did she spy Stewart the entire day. She made a singular attempt to engage in conversation with a younger Chilton soldier who was riding nearby. But when she did, Mason noticed and angrily sent the young man to ride in the back, to eat the dust of the numerous soldiers, and then took up position near her in angry silence. The message was received loud and clear, anyone seen communicating with her would be punished for her actions.

It was late when they finally made camp that night. Mason pushed extra long to keep their large contingent moving swiftly. Three more days and she would be home.

Weary in body and spirit, she fell asleep on the ground before the tent was even pitched, though she woke on a cot the next morning. It was frightening that in her exhaustion she'd slept through someone lifting her and putting her to bed, and it served to heighten her vulnerability. Elation and dread warred.

They would soon be to her kingdom, and she still had no concrete plan to defeat Mason. It would be hard to return home conquered. Would the people hate her for leaving them in the hands of a monster? Would they know how hard she had tried to rescue them? Would she be able to look them in the eyes with her head held high, as Mason made his way into her city? Mason the victor.

The next day, with five thousand men they marched through the Hoodoos. It was eerie to say the least. Mason never left her side, but it was strange as men would disappear from her view for different lengths of time on different paths, to return some time later. The sound was almost deafening as the tabletop above kept the sound inside reverberating off the walls. The thousands of shod horses' hooves striking rock echoed discordantly off the stone and reverberations through her added to the growing disquiet of all she faced.

The darkened interior made it more difficult to navigate and left her feeling cold. Enough that she would welcome being back in the sunlight as goosebumps covered her arms and legs. Had it been just a day past she cursed the heat of the sun atop her horse? The animals were skittish, likely at the cacophony of sounds and the feeling of being entombed in rock.

Arabella was learning that Mason didn't want anyone near her. He was isolating her. No doubt her stirring the Norlan soldiers to turn on him played heavily in his reasoning. No other man, it seemed, was permitted to address her. They could help her mount, bring her food or things she needed, but no one was to talk to her directly.

The sense of isolation and fear deepened. While she had no desire to make conversation with Mason, she wouldn't want anyone to be disciplined for her actions, so she kept her mouth shut.

The next day passed in solitude, followed by the day she awoke dreading and anticipating the return to Anchelle. It was bittersweet. Longing to be on Anchelle's soil, but sick at the thought of what Anchelle had lost and how she would face her people, failing them yet again. Wanting to be their savior but not being enough was a terrible blow that she felt in every fiber of her being. To her very soul.

Anxiously she would watch for Stewart, that he might give her an update from Benton. Hoping and praying that he had an idea that wouldn't force her to march through the streets of Anchelle this day, a slave to a monster—not a redeemer that they needed. Disappointment filled her when Mason brought breakfast himself. The thought of ingesting any food would be difficult, the army rations were tasteless gruel. Getting food down and keeping it there would be a monumental task.

"Good morning." Mason put the plate down at the small table. "A wonderful day, is it not? We shall finally be home!" He looked eager, excitement radiating as he walked to her and forced an abrupt kiss upon her before she had thought to step away. Arabella pushed against him as he tried to deepen the kiss. He laughed as she shoved him away. "Grr, not much of a morning person, are you?" he laughed. "You were quite exhausted when I put you to bed a few nights past, but we should be home earlier tonight." She hated the way he talked to her, like he was already her husband and Anchelle his home. It was not his home, nor would he ever own her!

He pulled out her chair and nodded his head to have her come and sit before he sat across from her. What a contradiction. He obviously prided himself on ever being the nobleman, but he was selective in holding fast to some manners; the rest of his behavior was deplorable. She thought of his need to help her into the saddle and take care of her physical needs, and then his ordering the death of someone for the slightest provocation. How could any human being care so little for the sanctity of life? She had always despised noblemen and noblewomen who treated her one way because of her "elevated position" and then behind closed doors would beat a servant. Far too many in places of power became heady with it and acted as though anyone below them in station was inferior. Her father had never allowed such duplicity.

She tried to eat, but it was tasteless but for the slightly rancid taste that lingered. She managed to choke a few bites down before giving up. He ate hurriedly, failing to note her lack of appetite, and she was only too grateful for him to leave.

All too soon, she was back in the saddle and on the road again, mashed between thousands of men. Despair battered her even while she caught sight of known landmarks. Everything was so achingly familiar, usually so comforting, like a favorite soft blanket, warm and comfortable, but today it was smothering. Failure. It was bitter, and bile rose in her throat often. She had tried so hard. What had she done wrong? Could evil triumph over good? Life as a princess, though blessed, had also been difficult. She worked hard, trying to deserve her affluence. The king had taught her that those who led were the greatest servants. Yet despite her efforts and intentions so many good and wonderful people had died, and all for what? Greed? Power?

Arabella watched the horizon intently, checking periodically in their rear for any avenues of escape, but it was all in vain. Stewart never materialized with word from Benton. The cavalry hadn't come to rescue her from her captor.

Trees stood tall around them in patches, thick groves that she knew well. She noted that the country had grown green in her absence. Summer had come to the kingdom of Anchelle, and the fruit trees that had held blossoms when she left now held gloriously verdant green leaves.

As the day wore on and they were less than an hour from Anchelle, Mason came back to her side. "I have a surprise for you, my lady," he spoke, as they crested a hill and came upon a tent set up in the middle of a clearing. "I had some of my men leave early this morning to retrieve your lady's maid."

His words barely registered before she spied Hilary. Mason helped her down from her horse, and Arabella immediately embraced her countrywoman. Hilary had worked for her family for as long as Arabella could remember. Close to her grandfather's age, she stood tall, with gray hair ever worn in a fashionable bun. Always the picture of decorum, she was a truly welcome sight that had Arabella's eyes smarting with unwanted moisture.

"Come, Your Highness." Hilary directed her into the tent. When they were alone, the giant tears finally fell. "Oh dear," Hilary continued in her strong accent that only came from having been born in the western Norlans. "I have been so afraid for you," she spoke through corresponding tears broken by a warm smile.

"You've been afraid for me?" Arabella asked incredulously. "I have been so worried for all of you. How do you fare, how does Anchelle keep?" she asked, desperately wanting to know, and yet desperate to remain in ignorance. Scared to learn what had transpired in her absence, Arabella insisted Hilary tell her everything she knew.

Hilary stayed closer to Arabella and lowered her voice. "The first week, 'twas awful, m'lady" she began. "The Chilton army came into the city at dawn." She took a large breath. "No one opposed them, so there wasn't any fighting. Somehow Mason must have known you had fled, because he didn't come with the first wave."

A dagger felt pressed in her heart as Hilary spoke the words of Arabella fleeing. She knew that Hilary hadn't meant to hurt her, but the comment wounded nevertheless.

"George." Hilary choked out tears springing to her own eyes. If Arabella hadn't felt sick already, she did then. A terrible feeling filled her stomach.

"George," Hilary continued, "was taken immediately. The soldiers rounded up the knights as fast as they could. As soon as most of the knights realized what was happening, they fled." Hilary continued, wiping tears from her eyes. "Some made it out of the city." Hilary paused, and looked down, like she was remembering the scene all too well. Arabella felt time slow and stop, awaiting the rest of the sad tale.

"What happened?" she asked.

Hilary looked up. "Slaves in the mines."

Arabella gasped. "George?"

"George," Hilary whispered, and after looking all around her continued, "boldly declared himself your liegeman. And once George confirmed your departure to Mason, Mason struck him down in a fit."

"He died?" Arabella whispered, wanting to clarify the horror she believed she was hearing.

Hilary nodded her head.

Sick to think of George's fate, devastation tore through her battered being to learn he had been murdered so cruelly. It was unheard of to murder someone surrendering. Truly George was the best of men. He was a kind father, husband, and statesman—and now snatched away after having survived the shivers. So much death, and all because of Mason.

"What of Edmund?" she asked about the man who was every bit a grandfather to her. She didn't know if she really wanted to know, but was unable to bear the uncertainty.

"I fear the worst, he hasn't been seen since shortly after you left. I'm afraid that I am of little help. They have kept us locked in the castle, and we have had no outside word. I couldn't even guess the state of Anchelle. How sorry I am, Your Highness." Hilary put an end to the line of questioning. "I fear we have little time," she continued. "I am under strict orders to speedily make you presentable for our people. Before he left, we were put to work to make ready for the wedding." She looked into Arabella's eyes. "Your wedding."

Arabella nodded her head, not daring her voice to respond. If she could find a way out of this mess, she would. Worry consumed her when she thought about who would pay the price if she fled again. Thaddeus, George, and Charles had died because she had fled, as well as many others. Could she do it again? Nay; she had to fight, needed to fight, but who else would pay the price if she failed? How many before she admitted defeat? Could she keep fighting, when another fell in her place?

She allowed the maid to help her disrobe. Hilary fretted over Arabella's wound as soon as she saw it, letting out cries of dismay and distress. Arabella gave her a very brief description of the event, but didn't feel like she could talk yet of her time in Saldanzia. The failure was too raw.

Hilary washed her off as best as she could in the circumstances, given the small tub of water. Then she brushed Arabella's long hair till it shone, and plaited it into numerous braids that wrapped and wove into a beautiful masterpiece. Her mother's crown was settled atop and secured. The corset was strung, though not tightly on account of her wound, before she was fit in one of her own dresses. It was a beautiful deep purple shift with a wide gold trim that bespoke her royal lineage. It was good that they didn't have far to go. It would be terribly uncomfortable to ride in.

All too soon they were done, and Mason was at the tent door, impatient to be on their way. Her stomach was in knots thinking of returning to her own city. Would the people come out to meet them or would they hide in their homes? She didn't want to be seen with Mason, but at this moment, there wasn't a choice.

Mason's eyes examined her from crown to foot and then nodded his head in approval, then dismissed Hilary. He then lifted her onto a sidesaddle atop a beautiful, well-groomed black steed that matched his own mount. A hundred men rode ahead of them in regimented precision, banners streaming, and then Arabella and Mason rode side by side a furlong behind them to keep out of their dust. There was silence between them for a time. That was destroyed when he began to speak of their upcoming nuptials.

She barely listened, all too anxious, watching her beloved landscape pass, thinking of golden or silly memories as they passed various places. The apple orchards were starting to develop fruit but looked unkept and unruly, a condition she had never before seen. The roadways were barren. The flags in the not-so-far distance were raised to Chilton colors. The graveyard could hardly be identified through the weeds that grew over two feet tall. Had she not been certain of its location she'd never know it existed beneath the weedy overgrowth. Part of her was startled to realize she was glad her parents had not lived to see the horror of this day, brought as she was to be paraded through the conquered streets, vinegar to the wounds of those few that yet remained.

In no time, they were at the city gate. Arabella's stomach was in knots. A line of trumpets blew along the city walls, echoing through out the city. At the signal doors cracked open, and people slowly emerged from their homes. Their faces were stoic as Arabella proceeded next to Mason. She could see a tear or two on some faces, but there was no clapping or joy from the people. Arabella wanted to smile and reassure them that all would be well. That was her nature. But she couldn't, it wasn't all well. Being with Mason was awful, and these people knew it. Lowering themselves to the ground, they went down on one knee as they passed, their right fist to their heart. It was quiet as they passed, till in the distance some bold figure yelled. "All hail our liege Arabella, Queen of Anchelle!" Arabella tried to see who had said it, but in the sea of people, it was impossible. Soldiers went in the direction of the solitary voice. She prayed they wouldn't find him.

It was better than she had imagined it would be. She had worried that someone would throw fruit at her, or call her a coward, or worse. She loved these people, this land, and she didn't know if she could take their disapproval of her. Arabella prayed, her heart reaching to the heavens that one day they would be freed from tyranny, and would find joy again. Given the power, she would do it, she covenanted.

The castle, the only home she'd ever known, rose up in her view, and a lump that had formed some time ago now almost choked her. It was beautiful. The lovely modest castle clad in colorful climbing clematis called her mind to reflection of a litany of peaceful times but also of sorrow, of love and tragedy. But through it all, it had been her safe refuge in the wonderful place called home. The staff filed out of the castle as their procession drew near and the servants lined the lane. Dear friends and loved ones came out to greet them in a solemn assembly.

She knew each one of them, and couldn't help but nod at a few as they passed them by. Her heart felt so full at the moment.

Relief and horror fought for supremacy whilst the monster at her side reveled in his dominion over all.

Mason helped her from her mount, holding her around her waist. "You're exquisite," he spoke admiringly, not letting her go. Coming from him, it felt slimy and dirty. It was no compliment. "I don't think I can wait five days to make you mine," he said.

Arabella didn't dare make eye contact. She didn't want to see what his eyes were saying. "You're making a scene, m'lord," she said, trying to push him away from her.

"I should hope so," he said, "they need to know that you are mine." Slowly he let her go, but not before he gave her a very sober warning. "Arabella, mark me well, if you flee again." He looked at Hilary. Her eyes opened wide at his insinuation. "Others will pay the price. And don't think I have forgotten Luke—if I ever find him, he will hang front and center tomorrow, or any day after."

Her heart stopped.

Leaving him, she walked slowly to the assembled people. Her mind had to be told over and over again that it would be alright. Her eyes met one of the stablehands, and she couldn't help but smile at him. Her step might have faltered for a moment, but she proceeded to those assembled, many of whom she embraced.

Locked in her room that night, she looked for anything that resembled a weapon. Her father had insisted on hiding ample weapons in her room. But to her dismay, nothing had been left in her room that could be used to hurt anyone. Looking through the keyhole she spied several guards posted at her door, and counted at least five. Mason didn't seem to be taking any chances.

That night she prayed for hours, pleading for inspiration and guidance before she crawled into bed and fell asleep. The sleep was fitful at best, knowing that Mason planned to round up those that had defied him in Saldanzia, and have them hang. It sat heavy on her conscience. Certain he planned to make her watch, so that she would know the consequences of her actions, cow her into submission. She had been told that outside any public hangings she was to remain in the castle, unless Mason said otherwise, having to "earn his trust back."

Would she take back that moment in Saldanzia, from the tower as she raised the armies against Mason, if she could? Was it fair for her countrymen to wage war on another nation, because Mason forced them to do so? There was probably no right answer to the question, but she dreamt of it all night long as she slept. Reliving the tower over and over again, followed by the gallows in the city square whilst she was forced to watch, clothed in her wedding shroud. She woke early, exhausted and overwhelmed. The dark stitches tugged and itched. Looking at her marred body she relished in the gruesome scars, it seemed only right that she have physical reminders of her failures. Broken, she was broken, surrounded by all her possessions. Sobs made their way out of some dark place inside. This room, her home, all that had represented safety and security was now her ruinous cage, and laying there huddled in a ball as the early morning sun finally rose in the sky, she mourned, desperate to wrench the darkness of loss and hate from her soul out.

The never-ending questions replayed over and over, deepening the despair. Had she made the right decision in leaving Anchelle for help? She would never have met Ethan, and as painful as it was that she would never see him again, was it worse knowing what she couldn't have? Never meeting her grandfather, or seeing the home of her mother's nativity? But the cost? So many good people had died, and many more would over time, all because of her. Could she keep fighting? Did Arabella have the right to fight, when so many paid for her actions?

Arabella didn't want anyone to see her in this state, but she couldn't control the crying. Even knowing she was a pitiful creature in that moment, she didn't find the energy to face the day. In three days the hangings would commence, and she was to witness it; to look in the men's eyes before their death might break her irreparably. To have their families witness it and blame her.

Four days till she was to be wed.

CHAPTER 21

E than crept through the tall grass, his senses on high alert. With his back now against a tall aspen tree he listened. He had seen someone, he knew he had. It still wasn't quite full light yet, but the dawn threatened. Slowly he drew his sword up. The steel whispered and slashed outward, to be met with the ring of steel. Relief flooded him, he let his sword drop down back into the scabbard.

"Sneaky as ever," he spoke to Benton, and clasped arms with the man. "Well met, my friend."

"Aye. I saw you coming and decided to come out to meet you."

Relief at seeing Arabella's guard overshadowed the annoyance at being spotted. "I'm glad you did. What can you tell me?" he said, getting right to the point. He needed to know Arabella was well. Nightmares of her being with Mason had plagued his journey; fear for her had nearly crippled him.

"Mason isn't wasting any time," Benton started. "There is to be a public execution in three days, and the wedding four days hence."

She was alive then. The wound had not been too severe. It was a huge relief. He would take that small win and not focus on all that was against them, time being foremost.

They walked back to where Ethan's small army of men waited, and then mounted up. Benton led the way.

"What word do you have from her of late?" he asked, more anxious than ever to see her whole.

Benton shook his head in frustration. "I have not seen her myself, but I have been within the castle." Of course he had, Ethan thought. If you ever needed stealth, Benton was the man. He seemed to have limitless endurance, and he moved around the world like a shadow.

"I have spoken to a few within the castle. Arabella's room is heavily guarded, but that isn't the problem as much what really binds her. 'Tis Mason's threats. A maid said that Mason has threatened Arabella that were she to run away again the staff's lives would be in jeopardy, and she knows he will make good on his threats."

Ethan had to agree with him. Arabella wouldn't risk other people's lives to flee now. Coming over a rise Ethan met the Anchellian camp of soldiers bustling around a hive of activity. Stunned to see there had to be over four thousand soldiers here, he couldn't contain his excitement.

"You have been hard at work!" he exclaimed.

"Rounded them up on the way here," Benton commented modestly.

Ethan wasn't fooled. The short passage of time—it was a miracle. As he looked them over more carefully, he noted the colors from their sister Norlan countries, Theron and Lassiter.

"Some were persuaded easily to join the cause. Others rode for home, or what's left of it," Benton commented.

Ethan left his own men on the edge of camp and followed Benton to a tent off to the west. Benton held the tent flap as Ethan ducked his head and body in. Smiles and head bumps were met all around as Ethan first greeted Garner, then Roland.

"Sorry to duck out on you like that, m'lord," Roland apologized for leaving Ethan at the council when Cleve was being tried.

"You had your own duty to fulfill, one of much greater import." Ethan waved away the apology. "Besides, Cleve was hanged the next day." He said it without emotion.

"Good riddance." Luke entered having caught his declaration. They clasped forearms before touching foreheads. Camaraderie and joy filled him to be reunited with these men who had become brothers, and he couldn't be more pleased to fight alongside them to protect that which they held most precious. In the short time he had known them he found them to be the most loyal, brutally capable, and good men in spirit.

"Finally came to your senses?" Luke asked.

Ethan gave Luke a smile and nodded his head once. "She is the only thing that makes sense to me."

The guards all smiled knowingly at Ethan.

"What can I do to help?" Ethan asked Garner effectively, cutting off the feel-good moment. They were men of action with the most crucial battle yet before them. Garner stood next to a map and Ethan joined him, followed by the rest of the knights.

By noon, she still hadn't left her room. Hilary had come by, inviting her to breakfast and offering to draw her a bath, but she couldn't be persuaded to leave her bed. Hillary returned at the noon hour, and pled with her to sup, but her stomach roiled at the thought.

She was taunted with the knowledge that she could flee the castle the same way she had a month ago, but there was no way she was leaving these people again. If Hilary were to die because of her, she wouldn't be able to live with herself. Her thoughts were terrible. If there was any way to kill Mason, she would have to do it. It was the only hope for people and her own sanity. Would there be a chance, an opportunity? Mason always carried a weapon upon his person, but she didn't think she was fast enough to pull it off his body and land a killing blow before he stopped her. That would only infuriate him more, and Hilary or anyone she showed preference to would have to pay the price.

All of her thoughts went in a continual circle, and by dinnertime, she still had no idea what to do. However, by six o'clock she was summoned to dinner by Mason, and he was not to be ignored. Hilary came up practically in tears, pleading with Arabella to have dinner with Mason. Pulling herself together, she determined to not let Mason see her beaten.

Arabella allowed Hilary to get her ready. Her eyes were still swollen, but there was nothing to be done about it. She wore her most modest dress and pulled all her hair up into a tight bun, not wanting to look alluring in any way, and walked down to the dining room, one guard in front and one behind.

With her head held high and her posture befitting any queen, she entered the dining hall. Mason immediately rose from his chair and took her hand. His clothing, though fine, bespoke a more rough, masculine look. He looked her up and down, a frown on his face, but finally spoke with a forced smile. "On anyone else, that dress would make a woman look dowdy, and that hairstyle will not do." His displeasure with her appearance provided grim satisfaction. "It looks as though we will need to have dresses made for you. I will have someone brought in immediately who will do your hair properly."

The short-lived victory snuffed out, Arabella glared at the man, but he only laughed at her. "You can't win, I would tell you to accept your defeat, but I love the fire in your eyes and wouldn't want to stamp it out." She couldn't help but glare, which only made him laugh more.

As soon as Mason was seated the first course came out. "Smells heavenly, does it not, my dear?" he asked.

"I'm afraid my stomach has not been cooperating with me this last little while," she replied. She hated the way he always said, "My dear." He was anything but dear to her.

"Is the infection still lingering?" he asked, like he was concerned. "I will have the physician come immediately," he added, lifting his hand to summon one of her father's healers.

"No, 'tis not necessary," Arabella interjected. "Mayhap just a little soup will settle it."

The servant nodded his head and went for some soup. "I hope you will be feeling well for the wedding. I thought five days home would give you plenty of time to recuperate from the wound and travel."

Arabella was surprised he would even consider her health and wondered if feigning sickness might serve to delay the nuptials. It was something to consider. If worse came to worst, and it really did feel *worse*, maybe one of the herbalists could give her something to keep her sick for a while without truly harming her body? "I'm sure with some Anchellian food, I shall be doing well in no time," she lied and allowed a small smile to break. She was going to have to get Hilary to slip her something that would induce vomiting. Who knows how long she might extend their oaths. It was worth a try.

Mason nodded his head in agreement then continued with his largely one-sided conversation. He declared that he had compiled a detailed list of her roles and his expectations. The soup gurgled in her stomach. Perhaps she wouldn't need herbs to induce vomiting after all. The glee in his unholy eyes was revolting! The words he said she vowed to never repeat to anyone ever. It was a painfully long dinner. She gave up all attempts at eating and uttered not a single word, praying this was not her life stretching on for decades trapped inside her mind, her body owned by him.

He personally escorted her to her room and locked the door, but not before demanding she be to breakfast the next morning.

Though she got very little sleep, she was up early as ordered. Mason had a dress brought for her in blue and someone else came to do her hair, someone she had never met before. It frightened her. She wondered where Hilary was. Had her friend already been punished for her careless actions? Knowing someone had slaved all night to make the garment for her, because of her defiance, made her wither.

The dress was beautiful, though the scoop neck was lower than she wore her dresses. She went along with it, wondering if she were a sheep for long enough, would he grow disinterested, or—and more importantly—would he relax enough to miss the wolf rising in her. The one that would take him down.

The look on his face when she came into the room was frightening. The dress and hair served to heighten his obsession. He walked a slow circle around her, then came from behind her to run his nose along her neck, inhaling sharply before placing a lingering kiss on her shoulder. "Much better," he growled.

She pretended to not be interested in breakfast, though it looked and smelled good, to keep him believing she wasn't feeling well. He stared at her all through breakfast, not saying much, adding to her discomfort. It was a relief when a soldier entered and took his attention from her. "Wait a moment, my dear," he said as he stood to talk with the soldier a few feet away.

Not being able to hear what was being said, her attention wasn't really piqued until Mason smiled. It couldn't be good if he was smiling. Mason and the soldier talked animatedly for another minute before Mason returned to the table. She had planned to leave while they were talking, but curiosity kept her in place.

He sat smiling like a cat that had gotten the mouse. "Ah, such a fine day before us. All is as it should be, my love." He made sure he had her full attention before revealing where his joy came from.

"Garner and Luke have been located!" he gloated. "They are not far from here. It seems that they have rounded up some soldiers from Anchelle. We should have him and the deserters in a few hours' time, then we can finally put an end to this rebellion. Begin our lives fresh, build an empire worthy of our sons."

Her first thought was joy to know that they both still lived, but the next emotions rampaged, swamping the joy with fear, distress and hate warring in her mind. This could not be happening.

It was like the straw that broke the proverbial camel's back. "You are a monster!" she railed, pouring every ounce of venom and loathing she felt for him into the words.

Vibrating with anger she stood, wishing she had a sword in her hand to challenge him. No doubt she would lose, but she longed to mar his pleasing visage, to make the monster more visible. His smile never left his face, his eyes alight with desire; he tilted his head back and roared in amusement.

"Och, you must realize how incredibly tantalizing you appear when you are mad," he said, infuriating her more. It was naught but a game to him. It didn't matter that people's lives lay in the balance. He just wanted the challenge, to feed the insatiable beast.

"Come, dear," he said, taking her hand, "I think it would be in your best interest to get some air today, mayhap a brisk walk." He said it like she was the one that needed help. Awareness settled upon her that every time they were together he was playing with her, feeding from her. Everything he said was done to elicit a reaction from her. Exciting and rejuvenating him. She was the mouse that he the cat would harass, play with for as long as the mouse would scurry.

"Mayhap from the top of the castle we may see a little. I will come for you, when they bring them in," he gloated.

As Mason led her back to her room, she wanted to slap the grin off his face, beat her hands against his chest. Frightened by her desire for violence, she determined to remain placid, refusing to play the sordid game. Holding her composure till she was ensconced in her room with only the stone walls to hear cries of frustration.

✑

Ethan's blood pulsed through his veins as he watched Garner and Luke thunder past his place of concealment leading a group of five hundred Anchellian soldiers. The previous eve, the two knights with the five hundred soldiers had stationed themselves close enough to the city of Anchelle to be discovered by Mason's scouts.

Secreted behind a small incline with bushes, and stands of trees all around, Ethan waited with bated breath, as did the soldiers behind him. They watched as the last Anchellian soldier took flight eastward fleeing Mason's army that Ethan had yet to see. Silence followed. Not even a bird chirped. The well-trained soldiers behind Ethan didn't even shift the weight of their feet as they waited for Mason's army. A minute past and then two, but then the vibration of the earth could be felt and the distant roaring of thousands of horses' hooves eating up the ground in a rush to catch the fleeing Anchellians. The wave began slowly and built into a mountainous roar as thousands of Mason's cavalry of gold swept past them in pursuit of the largely outnumbered Anchellian and Norlans men led by Garner and Luke.

Ethan and those around him were dead still as Mason's army took several minutes to pass. The Chilton army was doggedly determined to meet up with the Anchellians ahead of them, bent on their annihilation.

Sweat beaded on his forehead in the early hot summer day as Ethan continued to wait. The need to act thrummed through him, anxious to press forward. He took a deep breath to control the impulse to move before the carefully planned time. This was not where he wanted to be, but Mason's army had to be dealt with if they had a chance of freeing Arabella. A twig behind him snapped, breaking the silence and Ethan's thoughts. Ethan turned to see the chagrined man behind him.

Seconds later, the time was upon them. Ethan put his heels to his horse and shot out toward the road just vacated by Mason's army. Roland and Benton, who had sat their horses not far from Ethan, now were neck and neck as they barreled down the roadway, followed closely by Anchellian, Saldanzian, Theron, and Lassiter soldiers.

Ethan's heart thundered with the sounds of hooves, the anticipation of the chase, and the expected battle. He galloped his horse, watching closely for the moment that the Chilton army realized they were being pursued.

Within a furlong, he noted several Chiltons riding at the rear turning and noting in astonishment they were being pursued. Shouts rang out as they tried to notify their comrades, the concern on their faces evident. From what Ethan could see, it moved up the ranks of the Chiltons quickly, as many turned to look behind.

But it was too late for Mason's army to turn left or right or to stop as Ethan's army came from the rear, effectively creating the final push into the canyon, encompassed with smooth sandstone walls streaked with red hues. The walls reached high into the air. There was no way to climb out of it; the way they entered proved the only access. As Ethan thundered through the canyon opening, he cringed, wanting to put some kind of muffler over his ears as the sound of the army running through it reverberated off the walls over and over again, amplified tenfold. Ethan raced through the short sandstone canyon before the view opened up to a large field with tall rocky cliffs surrounding it. The chase came to a screeching halt four furlongs later, as Ethan pulled hard on the reins to stop their forward momentum.

The battle had already started. Many of Mason's men already lay dead with arrows protruding from their bodies. Norlan and Anchellian archers who had been secreted atop of the ridges earlier that day took out hundreds of Chiltons in several quick volleys.

With an animal-like roar, Ethan led the charge into the enemy. Those in the rear of Mason's army had turned about and were trying to ready themselves for Ethan's charge, but were ill prepared amidst the chaos of attackers above, in front of, and behind them. The deafening sounds seemed to further their agitation and the men of Chilton were surrounded and had no way to turn about or retreat, pressed upon as they were. What had been sure to be a quick route to destroy the Anchellian army led by Garner had turned into an ambush for the Chilton soldiers. Ethan didn't allow them a chance to pull themselves together but attacked with a righteous indignation, swinging his sword with precision over and over again.

CHAPTER 22

At the lunch hour, Arabella was brought up a steaming bowl of soup with dark bread. It wasn't someone she knew, and though she tried to talk to her, the woman merely shook her head and didn't respond. Arabella didn't know if the woman couldn't speak, or if Mason threatened her—in which case, she didn't want the lady to get in trouble.

By the dinner hour, she was desperate for news, but no one came to ready her for dinner. A plate was brought up again by the same mute servant. Scenarios ran circles in her mind, but surely if Mason had captured Luke and Garner he would be here gloating. A tiny seed of hope sprouted.

Pacing the room, the loud booming of Mason's voice outside her room had her instantly on alert. She scrambled around her, looking for anything that could be used as a weapon, but the best she had was a book. If his voice was any indication, Mason was not happy. She did not want to be on the receiving side of his anger. A rattle of keys and the door fairly flew open. An anger mottled his face, one she had not seen before, and it served to heighten her fear.

Reaching for her hand, he yanked hard and spoke only: "Come!"

She wanted to know what had happened, but she was terrified to say anything to further enrage him. He pulled her through the now-dark halls to her father's study. It looked as though he had taken up residence within. Clothing lay scattered and maps lay strewn across the great oak table. Guards had followed them along the hall and remained by the door while he pulled her in, shut and locked it. Grabbing steel shackles from the floor, Mason pulled her to him and fumbled to latch the shackle to her right arm.

"Nay!" Arabella yelled, tugging back. "Don't do it!"

Struggling with all her might, she looked around the room for any weapon. Her father had kept plenty about his sanctuary. But Mason was too quick, and he had it clamped around her wrist. Mason then proceeded to clamp the other manacle to his own left wrist.

"What . . . Why? Why are you doing this?" she asked, terrified as to his reasoning. It was certain he was not in his right mind.

"Keeping you by my side." He spoke angrily, like it was obvious. "No one can take you from me." He was deranged, she realized. Had something happened that had made him think someone could take her from him? Her hope increased, ever slightly.

"We shan't ever be apart again," he claimed vehemently. "Too many times we've been parted, and I will never let it happen again." His eyes bored into her, trying to infuse her will to his.

"But how would you fight?" she asked, desperate to be released from the shackles that already bit roughly into her hand.

"It won't come to that," he said, not taking his eyes off of her.

Would he hide behind her? That didn't seem plausible. He was always ferocious and fearless. Why would he put himself in a situation where he wouldn't be able to fight without being hindered?

"Now, I have lots of work to do. I can't get it done if I'm worried about you."

"But surely with me in the same room, we don't need the shackles," she tried to reason. "I can sit comfortably on the couch, and if I get sleepy, I can go to sleep. You can move about and do what you need."

It looked like he was having second thoughts on the shackles as well, so she added, "It even now cuts into our wrists."

He pulled up a chair for her, and she slid into it. He sat in one himself, and looked over the maps. Violence radiated from him, so she wisely let the issue go. Being so close to him, it was easy to see what he was looking at. The maps were detailed and showed the area to the south and east of the city. Littered around the closest map to him were maps of the other cities in the Norlans. On the maps sat pieces from a game Arabella and her father had oft played. Tiny figures of horses and knights; a king and queen were placed what appeared strategically across the maps. She knew it meant something because the king and queen sat in Anchelle. Two other colors displayed various positions of Mason's army and what she could only assume were Norlan soldiers, because of the limited amount represented in various parts of the maps.

He didn't seem concerned with her looking at the map, deep in thought, so Arabella took the opportunity to study it well. After careful examination, she postulated that the colors of soldiers in different areas indicated kingdom of birth. Looking around the room, she looked for any other clues that might be useful. It appeared as though he had not allowed maids into his sanctum. It wasn't terribly messy, but not as clean as it would have been otherwise.

The darkness of night deepened and after several hours she felt her alertness fade. The crash of adrenaline left her sleepy. Use of the garderobe became necessary. In her sleepy state, a thought struck her. Hidden weapons were put in each garderobe throughout the castle. In her lifetime, her fathers, and her grandfathers from before, had never had to use one. But everyone knew that an enemy trying to breach the castle could breach the castle through the cesspits if they felt so inclined. Not very effective for a whole army, but as an assassin, it could be quite useful. And so all the locks for the garderobes were secured from the outside of the garderobe religiously every night. Arabella had been trained since a wee child and took it very seriously.

Each garderobe held a defensive weapon. The one connected to her room had been taken, but maybe they had not thought to look in the other garderobes. There was a chance, no matter how slim, that a weapon yet remained hidden in the garderobe connected to her father's study.

Meekly requesting the use of the garderobe, Mason unlocked the shackles from a key around his neck. He was still in deep thought as she managed to sedately walk herself to the door off her father's study and shut it behind her. Quickly she searched the small room. She had never had use for one in the garderobe, but she knew where they were hidden.

She didn't know what to think as her hand clamped over the cold steel handle. Elation? Maybe not. The cool metal made the situation real, and though she had told herself over and over again that she would kill Mason given the chance, she found it yet difficult to plot his death. Could she strike him when he was unaware, if he wasn't holding his own weapon?

Over the years she had found ways to conceal weapons in her dress, and she made short work of it now. Finding it fueled her confidence to again have a weapon, one she was very capable and skilled at wielding.

Arabella knew she could climb through the hole of the garderobe and try to make an escape, but the thoughts of those at the castle still held her in check, and the possibility of going through the sewage held a little sway in the decision. Mason was not forgiving, and even though he had not 'hurt' her yet, she had no doubt he would take it out on anyone she held dear, or on anyone unfortunate to be close by when he raged.

When she was finished using the facilities, she had to still her hands from trembling. Arabella tried to appear nonchalant as she left the garderobe. Thoughts of how she might attack Mason warred in her head. The timing must be perfect, and she would need to be close to his person. They were not pretty thoughts. In fact, they were horrible. The thought of deliberately taking another's life was appalling, even Mason's. It would have to be in self defense, she determined.

Having killed men in self-defense already, she knew how terrible it was to live with. Arabella found a measure of comfort in knowing that God valued life and virtue—and Mason would continue to enslave and slaughter. As the ruler of her kingdom, she had pledged to God to protect the rights of her people. Thus God would not judge her too harshly, she hoped.

Arabella sat down on the couch when Mason looked up at her. The shackle was off of his wrist; that was a good sign. Though she could fight with her left and right hand, her right hand was stronger. He only looked at her for a moment, then brought a chair and sat in front of her so their knees touched.

Looking into her eyes, he said, "I know you studied the maps."

She didn't deny it.

So he continued, "Are there any other ways in or out of the city, secret doors, tunnels, anything of the like?"

Arabella tried to school her expression, then looked thoughtful, like she was really trying to come up with something. Of course, she was trying to come up with a lie. "I have heard," she began slowly, "that there are. As a child, the other children asked me. But when I went to my father about it, he wouldn't confirm or deny anything." She looked him in the eyes, hoping her response would meet with his approval. But his eyes burned into her, as though to ferret out the truth.

Rising swiftly, Mason walked back to the maps. Arabella released a sigh of relief when he didn't question her further. She would need to wait for the ideal moment to use the weapon. Scenarios rolled through her mind, and she noted her hands were beginning to sweat. A few minutes later he crossed over to the door and said something to a guard outside the door, then paced the room, his mind seeming to be in deep thought. She tried to relax on the settee, but she felt the climbing fear and tension made it impossible. Minutes later a knock came to the door. Mason walked to the door, admitting one of the younger kitchen staff girls, then shut it behind her and locked it. Leslie's eyes looked down, but it was easily discerned that the right side of her face was bruised. She looked as if she would cry as she carried tea and cookies into the study. Not daring to look at Mason or Arabella, she waited for instruction on where to set the tray.

Arabella's stomach plummeted. Immediately she went to the girl's side. "What has happened to you?" Arabella asked, outrage beginning to take root at the sight of the distressed maid.

The trembling girl kept her head down, and muttered, "I was clumsy and fell down."

Arabella looked at Mason, who only looked amused, but then spoke. "'Tis not the truth, girl. Tell her what really happened." The young girl looked at Mason, questioning him with her eyes. "Go on!" he commanded.

"His Highness," she started, "was teaching me a lesson." The girl took a deep breath, avoiding any eye contact.

"A lesson on what?" Arabella asked with astonishment. Her anger was growing at the mountainous man who would lay a finger on the young girl.

"A lesson on being truthful," Mason said, looking directly at Arabella.

Arabella couldn't help it. She took a small gulp. She was proud of herself when she managed to remain standing in the same place, though she fought the urge to take a step back in fear.

Mason smiled at her, like a cat that had caught a mouse. With swift precision, Mason smacked the girl on the other side of her face, causing the hot liquid and cookies to go spewing every which direction, and making Arabella jump back. Not in the least concerned, Mason quickly grabbed the girl's arm and pulled it back like he would break it. The girl screamed; her eyes looked horrified as she looked at Arabella. Arabella could tell the girl was in a lot of pain as she whimpered and tears came to her eyes.

"Do you want to tell me where the secret entrances are now?" he asked Arabella.

"Of course," she said, head held high, turning her back on him. It was the hardest thing to do, but she wanted him to take his hands off that poor girl. *Direct his thoughts elsewhere,* she thought. Arabella marched over to the maps. With her back to him, slowly she drew the dagger from the folds of her dress. Her hands were shaking slightly. *Oh please*, she thought, *let me be able to aim true.* Practicing and doing were two completely different things. Her heart was going so fast and her mind was whirling.

"You will find over here . . ." Arabella knew her voice wasn't very steady. She pointed with her left hand. "That the well . . ." Taking a deep breath, she waited for him to lean in closer. "See here?" she asked. As he leaned over, she hurtled the dagger at his chest, burying it to the hilt with a sickening thud. He looked at her incredulously, astonishment paramount on his face.

Arabella too felt shock. Time seemed to stand still. She had attacked him! Her own astonishment mirrored his horror. Backing up quickly, she motioned for the girl who Mason had released to move behind her.

Mason's face had morphed, a puzzled look, as though trying to discern how it was possible to be in the current position. Arabella could only stare at him, praying her strike had been true. Finally he cried, "Arabella?" before shaking his head as if to clear it. "Guards!"

Someone tried rattling the locked door, and Arabella scanned the room, searching for a defense. The guards would batter the door down and be upon them in minutes. Grabbing the girl's hand, she pulled her toward the garderobe. Loud thundering sounds came from the door as soldiers tried to breach it. Reaching their escape meant passing Mason, who had as yet not moved. As she darted past, he reached to take her hand, which she easily evaded, but his momentum toppled him to the floor with a groan and thud.

"Quickly," Arabella hissed, as she pushed the girl into the small room and shut the door behind her. Opening the seat, the smell made her hesitate for only a second. "In!" she yelled at the maid. The girl's eyes widened before she shook her head. "Hurry, please, Leslie. They will be in here any second." She had not dared to call the girl by name in Mason's presence lest he think them more familiar, but the appellation seemed to stir the young girl as the pounding continued. "I promise I will be right behind you!"

"Promise?"

"Aye, go, Leslie!" The girl stood on top of the seat, just as they heard the study door be breached. Arabella quickly pushed her in, then climbed in right behind her. A blinding pain hit her side as she came down atop Leslie's head. They sank, and then both sputtered as they came up for air. The stench was awful and she wanted to take a second to let the pain ease up, but she literally had to swim to stay above the refuse. Aware that Leslie was with her, and that they were slowly being carried down the channel of the underground river, she listened for any noise that would indicate they were being pursued. Hearing only the commotion up above for a second, Arabella was unsure if anyone gave chase. They rounded a bend and were carried further away.

CHAPTER 23

E than, accompanied by Benton, Roland, Luke, and a handful of Anchellian Knights, noiselessly crept from the dark tunnel that led into a large and luxurious bed chamber in Arabella's ancestral home. All were on high alert. No one occupied the dark room, but a large commotion without the room had the group instantly concerned. Yelling at this hour was never a good sign.

Like ghosts, they moved swiftly toward the door, where Benton carefully peered out. With hand gestures, Benton indicated half the group go left and the other go right. With swords ready, Ethan joined Luke as they sprinted down a long hallway. No one was there to stop them, and the disturbance was growing louder and closer.

Luke halted and his tight fist indicated Ethan likewise halt. Luke pushed the door of a room open. He poked his head into a room that Ethan could only surmise was Arabella's. Shaking his head, Luke backed out of the room and resumed his run down the corridor. Ethan felt at a distinct disadvantage not knowing the layout of the castle, grateful for his companion yet again.

Rounding a bend, four Chilton soldiers looked at the group of Anchellians with surprise and fear. They stood just outside a room with a door that had been broken off the hinges. It was hard to tell if there were more soldiers inside the room. Benton and those he led came from the opposite direction. The

Chiltons, seeing the futility of a fight, threw down their weapons with haste.

"We surrender," one of the soldiers said.

Ethan continued to advance, his sword still up.

"What's going on here?" Luke said, now within arm's reach of the soldiers.

Benton from the other side pulled the soldiers out and handed them to the Anchellian soldiers behind them to secure their prisoners.

Ethan went around the pile of shredded remains to what had been a sturdy door and drew inside the room, where two more soldiers stood with their hands in the air and swords on the ground. "Start talking!" he demanded.

"This is where Mason and the queen were," one of the two soldiers in the room spoke. His face showed his fear, and Ethan and those gathering around him were drawn to a large pool of red darkening the light wooden floorboards.

"Whose blood is it?" Ethan growled out loud, instantly fearing the worst.

"Mason's" was the quick response.

"Where are they?" Ethan continued to question.

"Mason went that way." The soldier gestured to his right, and Ethan could now see the drops of blood that he hadn't spied.

"And the queen?" Ethan prodded, praying Arabella hadn't been with Mason.

"I don't know," the soldier said, looking first at Ethan, and then the other soldiers.

Ethan looked at the other soldiers, and they shook their heads like they didn't know.

Benton swiftly held a blade up to one of the soldier's throats, and real fear entered the Chilton's eyes.

"I don't know where she went" was the immediate response. "I swear. She was in this room, and then Mason came out, but she didn't."

The other soldier nodded his head in agreement.

Benton released the soldier and studied the room, carefully moving about so as not to disturb things as they were. Ethan watched as the scout swept the room before turning back to the Chilton soldiers.

"What else can you tell us?" he pressed, the urgency to find her overpowering every other thought. If it was truly Mason who was wounded, he would surely be even more dangerous to Arabella. The monster had moved armies to reach her and assure she was taken alive. If she had wounded him there was no telling how he would respond.

"We thought they were hiding in the garderobe, but when we opened the door, they weren't in there either."

What? Ethan wondered. He needed more information now. "Who are *they?*"

"The queen and a scullery maid, m'lord," the soldier replied defensively.

"Start from the beginning!" Ethan ordered quickly, losing patience. Precious time was slipping away. He needed to find Arabella now. He was not yet convinced it wasn't her blood, and until he saw her, nothing would be right.

The frightened soldier took a breath. "Mason, the queen, and a maid were inside the room. We heard Mason shout for us, and the door was locked, so we had to break it down. When we came in, Mason had a knife in his chest and he was trying to get up from the ground. He pointed at the garderobe door, and so we ran over there, but when we opened it, no one was in it."

Luke startled. Ethan watched as an idea took shape on the Anchellian's face. Luke's eyes widened, and a ridiculous smile split his face, triggering a memory in the recesses of Ethan's mind.

"Nay, you don't think?" Ethan asked, though even as he spoke he realized she most certainly had escaped through the sewer.

Luke nodded his head. "Let's go," he called over his shoulder as he started away from the room and into the corridor. "I know exactly where she is."

The relief that swept through Ethan was deep, but he still wouldn't breathe easy till he saw her for himself. Especially with a wounded Mason at large. Where *was* that man?

Descending the stairs, Ethan and Luke ran outside the castle to be met by six Chilton guards. The soldiers seemed surprised to see them, and they looked behind them uneasily as fighting could be heard in the streets. Garner must have made it into the city.

"Drop your weapons," Luke commanded. "And we will let you live."

"There be only two of you." One in the middle spoke for the six.

"We haven't time for this," Ethan complained. These men were in the way of him finding Arabella.

As a group, the six charged Luke and Ethan. Ethan pulled another sword from his back, so that he now carried one in each hand, and met the oncoming soldiers. He stepped back as one tried to impale him on his sword, but the momentum of his attacker allowed Ethan to drive his own blade home, while with his left hand he blocked another sword—only to be joined by another attacker, so that he now faced two men at the same time. Deftly he parried the blows and retreated several steps before pushing back and attacking them.

When the opportunity presented itself, Ethan took care of one, and finally the second man stumbled, opening his side to receive a fatal blow. Luke was finishing off the one who had spoken, and the remaining man wisely fled. Luke, panting, pointed to the stables, and they ran without needing to speak. Their own horses were a mile away where they had left them before entering the tunnels.

They slowed their approach nearing the building, searching for Chilton guards, but they were fortunate not to encounter any. Where were they all? Did Mason send most of his army to destroy Luke and Garner and leave so little at the castle? Or had those stationed near the castle heard the fighting in the city and run to aid?

The stablehands came cautiously out to help them and startled with recognition of Luke. With broad smiles of those who
had been in bondage and were sensing freedom, they helped to
ready the horses with haste. They didn't seem to know where the
Chilton guards were, but they all remained on high alert. When
the horses were ready, Roland and several Anchellian soldiers
were there to ride with them.

"Where's Benton?" Luke asked Roland.

"He said we didn't need him. He was going to track Mason,"
Roland replied.

Kicking their horses into a run, Luke led the way once again,
the only one that knew Arabella's path.

⌒

Arabella stood in the dark night, cold, dripping from her saturated clothes and shivering whilst she rubbed her arms vigor-
ously. Was he truly dead? Had she killed Mason? Or was he
coming for her even now? She thought it would be impossible for
him to find her unless he had someone follow them through the
underground river system that carried the refuse away, which was
certainly plausible.

Would this all be over if she had succeeded in killing him?
He had dropped to the floor like a felled tree as they had passed
around him. The blade had sunk deep, even to the hilt. Blood
had begun to blossom on his tunic, she now realized in reflection.

Had the soldiers been given orders for such a circumstance
as this? she wondered. Would they hunt her down and kill her?
How could she find out? She would have to make her way back to
the city and find someone willing to hide her. Somewhere where
the Chiltons weren't watching. Or would it be better to leave
behind the city, and see if she couldn't find some of the knights
that were believed to be in hiding or at the mines?

Mason had shared nothing with her about this day's battle,
so she had no idea of the state of affairs. Indecision warred, she
settled on the first step, to get out of this wet clothing. They

had scrubbed at their clothes and bodies as best they could in a spring close by. If they could just get off the offending clothing, it would do wonders for the smell. But they couldn't very well run around naked.

Arabella noted the violent tremors of the serving girl's thin frame. Leslie wasn't one to talk, and she remained quietly by her side, lost in her own misery, it appeared.

The distinct sound of horses approaching had both of the girls scrambling for the closest bushes. How could Mason find her so soon? How did he know to look here? Looking all around her, Arabella grabbed a couple of rocks and a small stick. They probably wouldn't do much, but she had no more time to secure something better to protect them with, as the horses were almost upon them.

What would Mason do to her now? Would he finally have had enough of her, that he would kill her himself? Hang her with everyone else?

She tried to remain perfectly still and hoped Leslie would do the same. Her breathing was coming fast and loud. Would someone be able to find her in the dark from her harsh breathing?

"You know 'twas a wee bit anticlimactic—us stealthily breaching the castle tonight, only to find the queen had already made her escape." Luke spoke as though perturbed but even he could not disguise his relief at the situation.

The sound of Luke's voice was such an instantaneous relief that she was momentarily unable to speak! Arabella took a calming breath through her nose to steady herself. Could it really be?

"How did you find me?" she asked, amazed at the drastic turn of events, rising from behind the bush, hardly daring to believe her fortune.

"You of all people should know that I could find you here," Luke spoke with a lightly condescending tone.

Arabella could hear the chuckle of someone close to Luke, and her heart thudded wildly before settling, sure her ears were playing tricks on her. It had sounded exactly like Ethan's.

"Roland even had the presence of mind to bring you a change of clothes and blankets for you and the maid. Thought you might be cold or stinky," Luke responded.

"God bless you, Roland," Arabella spoke, playing along with Luke. "Throw the clothes over here, please!"

A satchel was launched at Arabella, and she peeled off the wet dress.

"'Twould seem we're even now," Arabella spoke toward Luke.

"How do you figure?" Luke asked, offended.

Arabella wrestled the dry garment onto her cold, wet skin and pulled her wet hair to the side so she could button up the borrowed woolen dress.

"Well, I had to ride the river of refuse just like you," Arabella reasoned.

She was faster than Leslie and waited a moment for the girl to finish. Could this really be over?

"That's not how it works." Luke scoffed with indignation, making Arabella laugh as he had meant. It was the first laugh she had had in a long while.

Stepping out the trees in her dry clothing, she easily located Luke's face. The last week had been so taxing, what she really needed was a hug, and yet she dared not, lest the floodgates release and break down. She needed to keep up the lighthearted banter, to keep the horror, the image of Mason's face filled with disbelief, from her brain—the moment when he realized she'd attacked.

"I guess the next man that wants to marry me will think twice," she said with a painful ache in her throat. She was trying in vain to keep it light, but the weight of it all pressed in on her, unwilling to allow the levity purchase after the terror endured.

"Hmmm. I wouldn't say that."

What? It was his voice, but as her head whipped around, she knew her eyes were playing tricks on her now too. There was no way it could be him. The night remained dark, but the light of the waning moon was enough to show her multiple silhouettes, and her eyes zeroed in on the one who spoke.

Off his horse, the ground between them disappeared as long strides ate up the remaining distance. Warm strong arms were wrapped about her, and everything inside of her seemed to stop. All other sounds, gone. No one else existed outside of this singular moment. Her world of a sudden felt whole. He. Was. Here.

Arabella couldn't help but smile as eagerly as a little schoolgirl. She unconsciously clutched him tighter, as though to be convinced he was flesh. His hand came up to reverently cup her face.

His eyes didn't leave her. They held her a willing captive.

"You came! I don't . . . How . . ." She attempted to get out the questions and was overwhelmed with his presence. Standing on her tiptoes to bring her head into contact with his forehead—it was her every daydream. His hand held her face and his head descended toward her own. A featherlight kiss that she eagerly answered and deepened. Ethan answered her every question as he kissed her possessively, as if he wanted her and nothing more. Arabella found herself responding, running her hands through his hair, feeling an explosion of sweetness and joy beyond description. Nothing had ever felt so right as this.

Someone clearing their throat, and the familiar sound of Luke's laugh, had Arabella coming to herself and pulling back from Ethan.

"I can scout the city and see if it's safe to return to the castle?" Roland volunteered.

Arabella gave Roland his leave, grateful for the dark that hid the blush she was sure would have otherwise been evident. Ethan asked the men to set up a perimeter, then led Arabella to a grassy spot next to a fallen tree. Sitting down, he pulled her next to him and put his arms around her and signaled for a blanket to be brought.

"You feel a bit cold," he commented, rubbing her arms.

"'Tis of no concern," she responded, nestling next to his body, already feeling his warmth permeate her own. Could this really be happening? Ethan holding her, when just hours before, Mason held her captive?

She felt unable to grasp the wildly swinging emotions. Tears threatened, yet she wanted to laugh, and then she felt fear. Fear of when Ethan would have to leave her. She desperately wanted to ask how long he would remain, but she couldn't bring herself to ask. She didn't want anything to ruin the moment. She would just have to take everything she could get and hold onto it tightly as a sweet remembrance.

"I am surprised that you smell so good," he murmured.

"Really, why is that?" she responded coyly.

"Well, you know . . . Well," he started, "better yet," he said, backpedalling, "'tis the truth you always smell divine," he finished with a whisper.

She laughed outright. "'Tis some flowers that grow on the bank of the spring, over there," She pointed into the darkness. "I have to admit, I left the offending clothing over there, but my sense of smell is not yet functioning." She nodded with her head.

When she couldn't take it anymore, she finally asked the other question that lay heavily on her mind. "Is Mason dead?" She could hardly believe she had stabbed him.

"I don't know," he spoke simply.

They sat for a time talking. First Ethan insisted on her telling her tale thus far. It was painful, especially watching his face as she told of Mason's brutalities. His jaw and fists would clench, and he looked as if he could kill the man if he could find him. Finally, when she finished rehearsing her recent events, he proceeded to tell of their victory that day over Mason's army. She had wondered and fretted for so long. To hear that Cleve was dead, and that Saldanzia had survived, was a huge relief. Saysee had made it to the capital city and it was expected to save many. All of it had proven a heavy burden that she had been holding onto and unable to divest herself of.

"What of your mother and Claire?" Arabella asked when he had summed up their time apart, and had not once mentioned his family.

"I don't know," he said regrettably. "My father took some good men and left as soon as the battle was over, but I . . ." He didn't finish the sentence. He didn't need to.

"Oh, Ethan," she said. "I'm so sorry!" She was struck anew with incredulity that he would leave when he did, to come help her and her people. That he would leave without knowing about his mother and sister was an incredibly difficult notion.

The night waned as they waited for Roland to return. A fire had been built and Leslie had fallen asleep, curled close to its flames. Ethan held Arabella tightly, and after a time, she fell asleep in his arms, finally overcome with fatigue.

Arabella woke in her bedroom, sunlight filling her room. She remembered coming home the night before, as Ethan had helped her onto a horse and rode with her back to the castle. She remembered the wonderful kiss Ethan had left with her just outside her bedroom door, and she remembered crawling into bed without taking her outer clothes off.

Moments later, a knock sounded at her door, and Arabella opened the door to see several guards outside her door and a smiling Hilary, who was flanked by a host of people carrying large buckets of steaming water.

"Oh, Hilary!" she exclaimed, embracing the older lady as servants swept past to a tub placed in her room.

"You dear girl," she responded in kind.

Arabella stepped back into the room with Hilary and shut the door.

"We best get you ready for the day," Hilary spoke. "There are several men waiting downstairs for you. And everything is urgent," Hilary grumbled, rolling her eyes. "But I think a bath is in order."

"Of course," Arabella smiled, eager to be ready for the day.

Now that she was awake, Arabella could hardly wait to hear what was going on, and see everyone in the light of day, assuring herself it had not all been a wonderful dream.

As soon as she was bathed, Hilary did her hair. She hastily donned a dress and was out of her room, swiftly walking down the corridor to the dining hall. Men all stood as she entered the room. Her eyes darted around the room, taking in Ethan first, then Garner, Roland, Benton, Luke, young Stewart, and even dear old Edmund. Her heart was ready to burst, overflowing with happiness. The room, though the same, looked completely different from yesterday, and felt completely different. These people made all the difference.

Walking first to Edmund, she wrapped her arms around the dear old man that had taught her a great many skills that had kept her alive. He too held her, and she wept in happiness. She didn't want to let him go. This man who in almost every way was a grandfather to her.

Next, she took Garner's forearm and he took hers, and their heads touched.

"Thank you," she responded to him, a lone tear welling in her eye.

"Glad I am to see you healthy and whole, Your Highness," he spoke, moisture sparkling in his gaze.

"And I you," she spoke smiling. She loved him so very much. He whispered in her ear, and she nodded her head in approval and quickly wiped away the stray tear.

She proceeded to Roland, then Benton, each one as special in her heart. When it was Luke's turn, he just picked her up and twirled her around, like he had done hundreds of times before. She laughed aloud, and the other men just smiled, humoring him.

As she came to Stewart, he knelt to the ground his face looking down, the remnants of a black eye still easily visible. She reached out to his forearms which he took as he looked back up at her. "Your Highness?" he asked questioningly. Her gesture made no sense.

"Sir Garner has asked to be your sponsor if you desire to become a knight," she relayed to the young man.

Surprised, followed by resolve and excitement, flashed across his countenance before he managed to nod his head in affirmation.

She saved the best for last, Ethan. he swooped her up into his arms and kissed her in a territorial, get-your-own-lass kind of kiss. It made her feel cherished and loved. The knights hooped and hollered, laughter ringing out. It was a perfect moment.

They all sat down for breakfast, Arabella asking for updates of everyone's families, and breakfast was cleared before they got down to business. Where was Mason, and how were they to bring him down? Search parties had been out all night, but no one had found him. Shortly after breakfast, Benton excused himself to continue the hunt for Mason. Staying around the table, conversation turned to the important matters of crops and their sister countries, but inevitably returned to Mason. Unfortunately, there would be no peace until the man was brought to justice.

Lunch was brought in, and planning continued throughout the day, till Arabella's backside became sore from the contact with the rigid wooden chair.

Dividing up responsibilities, the group finally separated. Arabella watched as each of the men left but Ethan, who yet sat next to her. He took her hand in his and brought it up to his lips to kiss softly. The burning in his eyes and the small kiss made her stomach do a somersault. She was way over her head and didn't care one bit.

"Come," he said, rising from his chair and helping her up. "I have a surprise for you." His face looked giddy with happiness. Out the front door of the castle they walked, and Arabella squealed in delight as she saw Palachio standing outside the door saddled and ready to go, next to Ethan's own mount. She raced to the horse and threw her arms around him.

She looked at Ethan questioningly as he shrugged his shoulders, "I found him on my way here. Smart animal was already headed home."

Arabella hugged Ethan again. "Thank you."

"Anything for you, my love," he whispered into her hair. "Come, let's go for a ride," he said.

"'Tis getting late already, and we haven't even eaten yet," she said dejectedly. She really would have liked to ride, and she had been cooped up in the castle too long.

"I have dinner packed," he said enticingly, indicating the saddlebags.

Without hesitation she jumped onto Palachio's back without touching the stirrup. Ethan threw his head back and laughed at this new trick before mounting his own horse.

He led the way. She wasn't sure if he knew where he was going, but he took the path out to the orchards. Men followed behind them, but not too close to be within hearing, giving them space. He looked all around the orchard before riding to her favorite spot. She looked at him with surprise and asked, "How did you remember?"

"How could I not? You described it perfectly on our first picnic together."

She was amazed that he had listened to her so well, loving this spot in the orchard. Taking a blanket out, he laid it down, then brought the food from the saddlebags.

They sat down and ate. They enjoyed the moment as they spoke of nothing of import, Arabella telling more and more of Anchelle. He listened attentively and asked questions. When they were done eating, they continued to talk, after a while they lay on their backs and watched the clouds pass by, as a few stars started to come out.

"Have you had a good day?" he asked, breaking the silence of the last few minutes, each in their own thoughts.

"'Tis been most wonderful," she replied.

"Do you know I love you," he asked, having leaned up on an elbow, his face inches from her own now.

"Aye, I love you too," she said, her heart full and yet pained at the inevitable departure. He would need to leave now, and she would never see him again. His family, his responsibilities . . . he had been gone a long time as it was. He was going to tell her now.

"I could never thank you enough for coming to our rescue, for championing our cause," she said. "Garner and Luke both said you were pivotal in the defeat of Mason's army. They admire you a great deal."

He smiled before continuing, "You're so beautiful," he said, reaching up and running his hands through the dark locks that had escaped.

"Your family must miss you so much." She needed to distance herself from the pain his leaving would cause, but she would hold fast and treasure every minute till then, she decided.

He smiled at her again, his fingers slowly working their way to her scalp, turning her tummy into jelly. "Did you know I spoke to your grandfather before I left Saldanzia?" he asked.

She shook her head. "He's probably anxious for your return posthaste? Everyone still reeling from the shivers, the war, and Mason fleeing."

Ethan laughed, "Are you trying to get rid of me, love?"

"What?" she sputtered. "No! What?" she sputtered again. "No!"

"I'm in love with you, Arabella!" he declared fervently. She could only stare at him, feeling her heart break a little more. His strong, callused fingers dropped her hair and wrapped around hers.

"I'm. Not. Leaving. You," he said, the message blazing in his eyes, determined for her to understand his words.

Her eyes widened and her heart rate increased rapidly. What? It was what she desperately wanted to hear, but . . .

"Your grandfather gave us his blessing to be married and live in Anchelle," Ethan spoke purposefully, slowly, to articulate each word.

"I also have the blessing of Garner, Luke, Roland, and Benton, which in some cases was hard to earn," he added, rolling his shoulders as though to loosen some tightness.

"He said that?" she asked, referring back to her grandfather. She couldn't believe it.

"Aye. He said that the love for your people was unparalleled, and that it would make you the best of queens."

"He said that?" she repeated. *Wait, he said that, was he asking* . . . Garner, Benton, Roland, and Luke? Her heart beat fast as her mind caught up to what he was really saying.

Ethan pulled her up into a sitting position, and then knelt down in front of her. "Arabella, Queen of Anchelle, of the Ruling Five of Saldanzia, and the keeper of my heart, will you marry me?"

Aye! she said in her head, but doubts plagued her. "What of your family? What about Saldanzia?" she had to ask. Would he hate it here? Would it be worth it for him? Would he hate the responsibilities?

"To be honest, when I left Saldanzia, I realized the only thing holding me there was my family. It was a terrible feeling when I knew my mother's and sister's lives could be in jeopardy, but I felt like at that moment, I still had a responsibility to Saldanzia, to my family, and to you," he said, taking her hand and kissing the inside of her wrist, causing a blaze of heat to erupt along its length. "I had to leave my family's safety to my father. I found some kind of peace. Then, with Mason on his way back here, I felt like it was unfinished. Neither Saldanzia nor anywhere could be safe with him seeking domination. He killed thousands of innocent people. He could not be left to flee, to regroup."

"I left Thomas in charge of the military of Saldanzia. He is most capable," he spoke in all seriousness.

He paused for a moment. "Besides," he said with a smile on his face, "I would rather raise our family in Anchelle."

Arabella couldn't help but smile at that. A family.

"Why is that?" she wondered aloud, aware he hadn't been here very long.

"Because I see what kind of leader you be. I've seen how the men would do anything you asked, and not just because you're

their Queen. This kingdom, it's people truly love you, as do I."
His sincerity touched her.

"We will have to make a few trips to Saldanzia," he continued, "to see our families, and to foster improved political rela-
tionships. But Arabella, I have no doubt this is where we're sup-
posed to be."

Ethan was so earnest in how he spoke of *them* with such ease
that Arabella finally felt the remaining fear, the piece that had
kept her from daring to hope, fall away. Liberated to love him,
and suddenly she couldn't imagine life without him.

"Aye," she said, smiling into his handsome face.

He jumped up and whooped and hollered out. Pulling her to
her feet, he kissed her senseless, and then pulled a ring from his
pocket. "I commissioned this ring made for you after a visit with
Luke one night," he shared. He slipped on the band with beautiful sapphire surrounded by two smaller rubies and several white
diamonds. "I didn't ever want you walking away from me again."

CHAPTER 24

A nightmare had Arabella sitting straight up in bed, as it had for the last two weeks. Mason dragged her from her home, in a violent rage. Arabella held her hand to her chest and slowly lay back down, her heart racing. She had to keep telling herself over and over again that it wasn't real.

The door was thrown open as Ethan came storming in the room with his sword drawn, briskly surveying the room before turning to her.

"Another bad dream?" he asked, concern filling his voice. He had insisted on staying in the room across from her. She hadn't minded in the least. Nodding her head, she let him hold her for a few minutes. He then stood, pulling her up with him. "Come let's go for a ride. The sun will be up soon."

Arabella nodded her head, certain that was exactly what she needed to clear her thoughts. Ethan left her room, and she hastily donned her riding habit and plaited her hair. Since she had stabbed Mason, she had had a nightmare every night, all varying in the details, but always leaving her with the feeling that he was yet alive and was as ever relentless in his pursuit of her. They had made no progress on finding him, though Benton had made every effort. Many believed he had died, there had been so much blood, but she couldn't reconcile it herself.

Leaving her room, she walked out into the dark chilly passageway, where Ethan stood waiting for her. Grabbing her hands, he pulled her toward him and released them only to grab the braid she had just accomplished and unwind the thick strands so that her hair fell around her face. "Leave it down for a little while please, love," he pleaded, running his fingers through her hair. Smiling at him, she grabbed his hand and kissed the back of it before making her way out of her home.

Guards fell in behind her as they exited into the gray morning sky. All of her council had been very insistent on a heavy guard until Mason was found and until any Chiltons remaining were rooted out of the Norlans. Arabella was not complaining, especially recalling her latest nightmare.

Ethan and Arabella slipped into the livery to fetch their horses. Palachio knickered, pleased to see her approach with bridle in hand. Lovingly she stroked the horse's muzzle and whispered endearments, as Ethan retrieved the saddle for her. Ethan began lengthening the stirrups, and Arabella was going to stop him, when he gave her a pointed look, then grinned mischievously. Intrigued, she watched as he mounted her horse, then reached down and grabbed her, sitting her in his lap.

"Much better," he smiled at her.

Blushing, she asked, "What if someone were to see us?"

"They would say, Lord McKenna is surely in love with our queen."

She couldn't argue with that. Ethan headed Palachio toward the mountains, and Arabella sat back against Ethan's firm chest, hard-pressed not to look up at him and stare. Finally she looked up, and he winked at her. He was definitely the most tempting man alive! How was it that she was soon to marry the most handsome, kindest, and strongest man she knew? She was dizzy with joy that he should be hers.

Peaceful in the still mountain air, they rode, enjoying the smell of the crisp morning air and being together to enjoy the beauty. The dew glistened on the grass from the direct sunlight, making it sparkle.

"I'm thinking this wasn't the smartest move after all," he began. "'Tis fortunate we have chaperones with us, because you look absolutely delicious."

"I was thinking the same thing," she replied, blushing, her eyes going wide when she realized what she said.

He laughed hard, then asked, "Just so we're clear, are we talking about the chaperones, or the deliciousness?"

She put her head down and mumbled, "Aye."

Laughing harder, Ethan continued to watch her finally succumb and let out a laugh laden with joy.

She was brought up short as a guard cried out. "Look." He pointed to the southwest. A lone rider ran his horse straight toward them, his arms waving them in the air, like they should go back.

"It's Benton!" Ethan spoke sharply, instantly holding Arabella tighter. "Something isn't right," he said, more to himself. Ethan maneuvered Arabella so she sat astride Palachio and yelled at the men to ride toward the city.

As Ethan reined Palachio around, Arabella eyes continued to follow Benton. Instantaneously Chilton men came through the treeline, in direct pursuit of him. She grabbed Ethan's arm so he could see what she was seeing. With horror she watched as one of the Chilton men stopped his horse and pulled his bow from his horse.

Arabella cried out in horror, as she watched him notch an arrow and take aim at Benton's fleeing body. The arrow hit him in the back, toppling him from his horse.

"No!" Arabella screamed. She watched as Benton slowly got up a sword in his hand, the arrow protruding for his lower back. The invaders didn't slow as they charged toward Benton, and ultimately the queen's party.

"We can't leave him," Arabella begged, her eyes trained on what would surely be a massacre. It was then that she saw Mason in the band. He was no longer interested in Benton but was making a beeline for them. If they didn't go after Benton now, he would be mowed down mercilessly.

She could tell that Ethan was waging an internal battle. That he wanted to keep her safe was obvious, but the chances of making it to the city riding double before Mason could overtake them weren't good. Palachio was fast, but riding double? The two groups seemed evenly matched in number, around three dozen each.

With determination Ethan made the split decision and yelled, "FIGHT!"

Running their horses hard, the queen's guard went before Arabella and Ethan toward Benton. While in motion, with trained precision, Ethan hefted Arabella and smoothly placed her behind his back, then pulled his sword into his right hand, while urging Palachio to move faster.

Arabella drew her own sword, and peered around the left side of Ethan so she didn't hamper his movements.

Mason met her lead guard, striking him down as he plowed forward. The Chilton soldiers met the queens guard just behind him. Mason slowed his horse down and slid off the side, wanting to meet Ethan on the ground.

Ethan pulled Palachio up short, so that Arabella wasn't close to the battle or Mason. "Don't get too close," he commanded. "Watch for Mason's men, and don't get off Palachio," he instructed, never taking his eyes off of Mason. Ethan slowly walked toward Mason.

With his words of warning, Arabella looked momentarily at the battle a few hundred feet away. Each man was engaged in battle. It looked as though Benton had broken off the arrow that pierced his back and continued to fight tooth and nail. With relief she turned back to Ethan and Mason.

"I wouldn't want to hurt what's mine!" Mason looked at Ethan hard before giving an audacious wink at her. Arabella was surprised that Mason held any concern for her, considering she had tried to kill him just a fortnight past. "I didn't know I would be getting her today, but 'tis a most pleasant surprise." He smiled.

Ethan's face hardened. He vibrated with controlled power that spoke of his singular intent and lethalness.

"The lady already proved to the contrary," Ethan said, accepting the challenge. "You have the scar to prove it."

With a bold lunge, Ethan struck out, swords ringing as Mason deflected the blow. Endlessly Ethan struck out over and over again, seeming to gain power and momentum. Mason parried the blows, launching his own offensive in what appeared to be an even match. Arabella had seen more duels than she could count, battles in the lists, and war, but what she was witnessing now she knew was unmatched. Both masters of the sword, each fueled with determination to conquer.

She could hardly breathe but dared not look away. Back and forth they thrusted and parried. Mason seemed surprised to find Ethan a worthy contender. Sweat appeared on his brow, the only sign that he may have met his match.

The conflict behind Ethan and Mason seemed to be abating as Arabella took in quickly a handful of men still fighting and Benton limping toward her.

It was all she could take in as her eyes immediately went back to Ethan.

On they raged, steel against steel, neither showing signs of fatigue. Mason was a few inches taller and had a longer reach, but Ethan was quicker, smooth, and efficient with his strokes, not wasting any energy. The feverish battle was unworldly. Surely their arms had to be aching. A quarter-hour later, sweat poured off both of them, and there were small signs that they both were beginning to tire. They each had small cuts that bled lightly. But as Ethan nicked Mason on the face, it seemed to push Mason over an edge. Like a cornered tiger, he roared brutally, lashing out at Ethan over and over again in a great offensive assault, putting all his mammoth strength into motion. Arabella gasped, her breath ragged, but Ethan parried the blows calmly, his emotions never usurping his control. Like a master he waited, patiently cataloguing Mason's moves, strengths, and weaknesses, waiting with extraordinary patience for the moment there was an opening. Unable to keep up the barrage, and spent, Mason slowly started to ease back. Ethan, seeing the opportunity, stepped in, closing the distance, and unexpectedly shoved him in the chest so that Mason fell down onto one knee. With anger, Mason pulled a knife from his belt and sliced into Ethan's leg. It didn't seem like the pain even registered into Ethan's mind, because he was undeterred, fixed with purpose as he drove his blade into Mason's now unprotected body.

Mason's face held shock as his other knee met the ground. Ethan stepped back, drawing his sword with him as Mason toppled to the side, his eyes empty. Arabella didn't see any more, because Benton stepped into her line of sight. He must have seen the shock on her face. Mason was truly dead.

She had been so mesmerized by the fight that she missed the rest of the battle. Chilton men littered the ground and several Anchellian men surrounded her and Ethan.

Arabella took a deep breath and relaxed her grip on her sword. Exhaustion flooded her as though she had been the one fighting. Her jaw throbbed angrily at the punishing way she'd clenched her teeth together.

Putting her sword away, she looked up and saw Ethan coming toward her, his sword still in his hand. Dropping it on the ground when he got to her, he reached up to her with his hands and pulled her off of Palachio and into his arms. She buried her head into his chest and felt their rapid breaths slow and sync with the steady rhythm of his heart.

EPILOGUE

Fifteen Months Later

A rabella stood atop the parapet and watched the dust clouds from the distance. The day was still and calm. It was unseasonably warm with the harvest already complete. The convoy would arrive by nightfall, and she felt excitement laced with trepidation. It was the first time seeing her grandfather and the McKennas since leaving Saldanzia. The arriving royalty was causing a great stir throughout Anchelle.

Nothing as big had happened since Ethan and Arabella's own wedding. The wedding had lifted the people of Anchelle from the depths of despair and heartache. Festivities and rejoicing had gone throughout the whole kingdom as well into the Norlans, who had been liberated by the army Garner, Luke, Benton, and Roland had gathered on their way back from Saldanzia, as well as the Saldanzian men Ethan had brought with him. The joint army had gone a long way in healing wounds between all the kingdoms and abolishing slavery.

It had been a beautiful wedding only a month from the time Ethan proposed to her in the orchards. People came from all around. Though Arabella would have preferred something more intimate with close friends and loved ones, she knew that the people needed to be present, to believe in their security. The shivers that had ripped through all the land followed so closely with the scourge of war had left the populace broken. The people needed hope, something to rejuvenate their dreams once again.

Dear Edmund had walked her down the aisle, in the church her parents had been married in, as well as her grandparents and great-grandparents.

Marriage had proved heavenly for Arabella. Ethan was loving, attentive, and fully devoted to her and his new country. The people adored him. Not because of his title or his superb skill with a blade, but because of his selfless actions in following after her, leaving all to care of their queen. Having never had someone to share the mantle of leadership, she gratefully let him shoulder many of the responsibilities, including security, allowing her to focus on healing the hearts and homes of her people. They still consulted on things regularly, but it was nice not to have to do everything. The burdens were found to be much easier to bear as they lifted and strengthened one another. Love begat confidence as they grew together in wisdom.

Word had come shortly after their vows that though the Cronan had come close to finding Ethan's family's hiding place, they had not succeeded. Claire McKenna now held the office of the ruling Lady of Saldanzia.

A memorial had been made in honor of George, Charles, Thaddeus, and the many others who had fought so bravely for Anchelle. It wasn't enough, but Arabella tried to find ways to venerate the men and the families of those that had given their lives so freely to secure the future.

Arabella almost jumped out of her skin as Ethan's voice broke her reminiscing.

"I thought I would find you up here," he said, almost beside her.

She swatted his arm, "You must cease startling me so," she stated, her heart starting to beat normal again. "You've been spending too much time with Benton."

"Well, Luke says I spend too much time with you!" he said with a mischievous glint. "I can't seem to go to work when my wife is so beautiful and captivating. I'm ensnared by her."

She smiled at him. "'Tis a problem, to be sure," she commented smugly, and allowed his arms to come around her bulging stomach, sighing in contentment. Ethan and Luke were kindred spirits. They were fast friends. It healed her heart, and she was certain Thaddeus would be pleased as he looked down upon them.

"I'm so nervous," she finally spoke. "Do you really think Grandfather will want to stay here after all?"

Ethan placed a kiss on her neck, sending a delightful shiver to her toes, then turned her around to look up at him. "Aye, love," he spoke, softly running his hand over her swelling stomach. "There is no place on earth I'd rather be. Why would he be any different?" Capturing her lips, all other thoughts fled as she was thoroughly reminded of exactly where his allegiance lay, not to any landmass but to her heart alone.

THE END

ACKNOWLEDGMENTS

FIRST AND FOREMOST, thanks to my Heavenly Father. I owe him everything.

Secondly, to my parents, who gave a love of reading to me and my fabulous sisters.

To Christina Atwood, one the fabulous sisters, who went through edit after edit with me, one of my champions.

To my greatest champion, my husband, who encourages me to write. Thanks Babes!

To Emily Chambers for lining everyone up and giving me opinion after opinion. To the developmental editors Daniel Coleman and Haley Swan; though it was sometimes quite painful, they helped me learn a lot. I hope :) Justin Greer for the copyedit and line edit. Kaitlin Barwick for the interior layout and proofread. Kim Karpowitz and Emily Chambers for being my beta readers. And for the beautiful cover design done by Shawnda Craig.

To Kaylie Hyde, Katie Wells, and all the many people who helped me with the photo shoot. It was so fun and a dream come true!

To Celeste Atwood for the beautiful map.

To my children, who constantly heard, "just let me finish . . ." You're the best kids a mom could wish for.

And to my fruity friends, who keep asking me when it's going to be done. You guys are the best friends a girl could ask for.

ABOUT THE AUTHOR

JODY SCHWENDIMAN was born and raised in Southern Alberta. She went to college in Idaho, where she met her husband in the most dreamy of settings—the tractor. Now married to the most romantic man in the world, and an Idaho spud farmer herself, she enjoys wake-surfing and Jeepin'. She is an avid genealogist, bookworm, cookie monster, and momma of five, and she loves to travel as much as she possibly can.

Made in United States
North Haven, CT
01 July 2022

20866776R00189